THE BEST OF
FREDRIC BROWN

THE BEST OF FREDRIC BROWN

Edited and with an Introduction by
ROBERT BLOCH

NELSON DOUBLEDAY, Inc.
Garden City, New York

ACKNOWLEDGMENTS

"Arena," copyright © 1944 by Street & Smith Publications, Inc., for *Astounding Science Fiction*, June 1944.

"Imagine," copyright © 1955 by Fantasy House, Inc., for *The Magazine of Fantasy and Science Fiction*, May 1955.

"It Didn't Happen," copyright © 1963 by H.M.H. Publishing Company for *Playboy*, October 1963.

"Recessional," copyright © 1960 by Mystery Publishing Company, Inc., for *Dude*, March 1960.

"Eine Kleine Nachtmusik" (with Carl Onspaugh), copyright © 1965 by Mercury Press, Inc., for *The Magazine of Fantasy and Science Fiction*, June 1965.

"Puppet Show," copyright © 1962 by H.M.H. Publishing Company for *Playboy*, November 1962.

"Nightmare in Yellow," copyright © 1961 by Mystery Publishing Company, Inc., for *Dude*, May 1961.

"Earthmen Bearing Gifts," copyright © 1960 by Galaxy Publishing Corporation for *GALAXY Magazine*, June 1960.

"Jaycee," copyright © 1955 by Fantasy House, Inc., for *The Magazine of Fantasy and Science Fiction*.

"Pi in the Sky," copyright © 1945 by Standard Magazine, Inc., for *Thrilling Wonder Stories*, winter 1945.

"Answer," copyright © 1954 by Fredric Brown for *Angels and Spaceships*.

"The Geezenstacks," copyright © 1943 by Popular Fiction Publishing Company for *Weird Tales*, September 1943.

"Hall of Mirrors," copyright © 1953 by Galaxy Publishing Corporation for *GALAXY Science Fiction*, December 1953.

CONTENTS

Introduction

I hope they don't misspell his name.

At the height of his acclaim, with more than two dozen books and over three hundred short stories to his credit, certain careless critics and reviewers were still referring to "Frederic" or even "Frederick" Brown.

While their comments were generally (and deservedly) laudatory, he resented the spelling errors. He was a stickler for accuracy, and he took justifiable pride in his correct byline—Fredric Brown.

To his friends, of course, he was always "Fred."

I first met him in Milwaukee, during the early forties. Born in Cincinnati in 1907, a graduate of Hanover College in Indiana, he'd knocked about—and been knocked about—in a variety of occupations, ranging from office boy to carnival worker.

At the time we became acquainted he was a proofreader for the *Milwaukee Journal* and had settled down in a modest home on Twenty-seventh Street with his first wife, Helen, and two bright young sons. The household also included a Siamese cat named Ming Tah, a wooden flutelike instrument called a recorder, a chess set, and a typewriter.

Fred played with the cat, played on the recorder, and played at chess. But the typewriter was not there for fun and games.

Fred wrote short stories. He wrote them in his spare time because he needed job security to support a family. And he sold them to the pulp magazines because they offered the best available market for a beginner's work. He turned out detective stories, mysteries, fantasy, and science fiction. Nostalgia buffs pay high prices today for magazines featuring his name on the cover, but at the time he was merely one of hundreds of contributors competing for the cent a word or two cents a word offered by publishers of pulps.

Diminutive in stature, fine-boned, with delicate features partially obscured by horn-rimmed glasses and a wispy mustache, Fred had a vaguely professorial appearance. His voice was soft, his grooming immaculate. But woe betide the casual acquaintance who ventured to compete with him in an all-night session of poker-playing or alcoholic libation! Nor was there any hope for an opponent who dared to engage him in a duel of verbal wit—words were his natural weapons, and his pun mightier than the sword. When not speculating upon the idiosyncrasies of idiom—why, for example, do people prefer a shampoo to the real poo?—he spent his time searching for excruciating story titles. I recall him once paying ten dollars for the right to use one suggested by a friend for a mystery yarn; the resultant story was called *I Love You Cruelly*.

The shameless wretch responsible for this offering was, like Fred, a member of Allied Authors, a writers' group which met regularly at the Milwaukee Press Club. To many of his associates the poker games and bar facilities constituted the major attractions, but despite Fred's prowess in these areas, he was deadly serious about plot discussions and story techniques. He acquired a New York agent, and on his own he kept abreast of writing markets, word-rates, and contracts.

There was no mistaking his ambition, nor his qualifications. Impelled by lifelong intellectual curiosity, he was an omnivorous and discerning reader; his interests embraced music, the theater, and the developments of science. Wordplay was more than a pastime, for he was a grammatical purist. The *mot juste* and the *double entendre* were grist for his mill, but he was equally fascinated by the peculiarities of ordinary speech and could reproduce it in his work with reportorial accuracy. Like most of us who found an outlet for our wares in the pulps of that period, Fred wrote his share of undistinguished stories featuring the cardboard characterization and stilted dialogue which seemed to satisfy editorial demands. From time to time, however, he broke new ground. And finally he tackled a novel.

The Fabulous Clipjoint was published in 1947. It drew raves from the critics and won the coveted Edgar Allan Poe Award from the Mystery Writers of America. His second mystery novel, *The Dead Ringer*, was equally successful and established him as a leading figure in the field. In 1948 his innovative *What Mad Universe* appeared in *Startling Stories*. Expanded for hardcover publication a year later, it brought Fred deserved fame as a science-fiction writer.

Meanwhile his personal circumstances underwent a drastic change. There was an amicable divorce; he married for a second time a year or so later. And, encouraged by the reception of his books, he began to turn out mystery novels at an accelerated rate. But he didn't forsake his proofreading job—a true child of the Depression came to learn the value of security and seniority, and Fred was not about to abandon a steady income for the uncertainty of a free-lance writer's career.

During this period we spent a great deal of time together, in professional discussion of his projected novels and private explorations of his more intimate decisions. One day he came to me all aglow; he'd just received a phone call from a prominent editorial figure in New York who headed up one of the leading pulp-magazine chains. Would Fred consider taking over a portion of the editing assignment for seventy-five hundred a year?

Granted, the figure doesn't sound impressive today. But if you'll hop into the nearest available time machine and transport yourself back a quarter of a century, you'll discover that seventy-five hundred dollars was a respectable annual income; roughly the equivalent of twenty thousand dollars today. It was far more than Fred was earning, or hoped to earn, at his newspaper job— and if he could augment the sum by writing novels on the side, it would exceed his wildest expectations. Fred talked it over with me, and with other friends; he talked it over with his wife, Beth. Then he quit his job and went to New York, where he learned there'd been a slight misunderstanding during his telephone conversation.

The stipend quoted by the editorial director had not been seventy-five hundred a year; it was seventy-five dollars a week.

A dark cloud settled over Fred's life. Fortunately, he soon discovered the silver lining.

In a few short years, the imposing chain of pulp magazines he'd hoped to head up had disappeared forever. And in their place was a mushrooming market of paperbacks, competing for the privilege of reprinting hardcover mysteries and science fiction. Foreign editions began to command more-respectable earnings, television was purchasing stories for adaptation, and the new men's magazines, led by *Playboy*, paid higher and higher rates for short stories.

Through fortuitous circumstance, Fredric Brown found himself in the right place at the right time. Critically, commercially, and above all creatively, he was a success.

A series of outstanding and unusual mysteries issued from his typewriter—now clattering away in Taos, New Mexico. Fred had acquired a car and learned to drive; wanderlust, plus the realization that he suffered from respiratory problems, led him to the desert area.

Full-time writing taxed even Fred's ingenuity. He was becoming increasingly renowned for story-twists and surprise endings, both in mysteries and science fiction, and such innovations didn't come easily. When he was stuck for an idea, he took to the road for a few days—not as a driver, but as a passenger on a bus. Destinations were unimportant; he'd discovered that the sheer monotony of the trip itself stimulated him in devising plots. Some of his best work came to him via Greyhound express.

And not all of that work was dependent upon gimmickry or outwitting the reader. As a mature writer he drew heavily upon his variegated personal experience to bring the stamp of authenticity to his subject matter. And he wasn't content to rest on his laurels as a latter-day O. Henry; he took the risk of innovation.

Innovation, in the science fiction of the fifties, was generally considered synonymous with advanced extrapolation of orthodox scientific theory, or the extension of contemporary social phenomena. Thus it was that stories involving antigravity and antimatter were hailed as daring concepts, and fictional constructs of future society governed by advertising agencies or insurance companies seemed to be the ultimate in speculative *expertise*.

Characteristically, Fred chose to turn his back to the trend. Quirky individualist that he was, he wrote *The Lights in the Sky Are Stars*.

It was one of his best—and bravest—books.

Today an entire generation of younger writers has emerged to tell it like it is, or at least like they *think* it is. Their speculative fiction is peopled with angry young anti-Establishment figures, drug-users, and ambisextrous characters who freely express philosophical profundity in four-letter words. One does not necessarily question the sincerity or dedication of such writers. But the cold truth is that they are not quite as courageous as they profess to be. Today they are merely setting down in print the speech and attitudes which had already surfaced amongst young militants and street people a full decade ago. Rather than formulating a future based on their own imaginative abilities, their work is merely an echo of a past reality.

The Lights in the Sky Are Stars doesn't fall into this category. It didn't deal with kinky sex, and its characters spoke in ordinary dialogue rather than verbalized *graffiti*. Nevertheless, it was a daring work.

Appearing at the zenith of the Eisenhower administration, at a time when science-fiction writers as well as their readership idealized and idolized the launching of the Space Program and the brave young men who pioneered it, Fred's book deliberately dumped on dreams and offered, instead, a raw reality.

In an era when virtually all science-fiction heroes were young —and the few "middle-aged" exceptions were presented as grizzled veterans of thirty-five or thereabouts—Fred's protagonist was a man well over fifty. On top of that, he was physically handicapped, and yet (a horror unthinkable to youthful science-fiction readers of the time) he was sexually active. Moreover, the plot of Fred's novel dealt not with the gung-ho glories of space projects, but with the machinations of politicians and the military-industrial complex bent on subverting such efforts to their own ends.

This was heresy with a vengeance. It was also, I submit, far more "realistic" than any tale of a hippie transplanted *virgo intacto* to a future society bearing a suspicious resemblance to present-day New York City during a garbage strike.

Oddly enough, the book was well-received. It won no awards, nor did it score a breakthrough to the best-seller lists, but today this novel deserves recognition for what its author achieved by way of honest statement.

Yes, Fred was an innovator. Along about this time he ventured another experiment. Safely ensconced as a leading mystery-writer, with assured contacts and contracts in the field, and rapidly rising in the science-fiction field, he decided to write a mainstream novel. And in the face of his reputation for unusual plot angles, colorful characters and off-beat humor, he would write a "straight" book; really telling it like it is at a time before the phrase had even been invented.

The result was *The Office*, a semiautobiographical account of his own experiences in the twenties. But such was his honesty that he succeeded only too well—and in succeeding, failed. Because the way it is, or *was,* for Fred in the twenties, proved humdrum and pedestrian in the telling. Minus murder and mayhem, *sans* piled-up plot complications, and lacking rapid-fire repartee, this day-by-day account of real people in an ordinary office setting seemed dull to readers who expected a typical Fredric Brown entertainment.

He never repeated the venture. Instead he returned to the mixture as before—but what a rich and variegated mixture it was! The burgeoning men's magazine market offered outlets for his talent, and new freedom of expression. Sexual taboos were giving way, and while Fred eschewed vulgarity, he found welcome opportunity to base his fantasies and science-fictional efforts on once-forbidden themes. He gave free rein to his wealth of wit, and discovered a new story-form in the "short-short."

In that connection, *aficionados* may be interested in a 1960 Warner Bros. recording, *Introspection IV,* in which a narrator named Johnny Gunn, accompanied by the background musical effects of Don Ralke, reads a series of short tales. Five of these— "Sentry," "Blood," "Imagine," "Voodoo," and "Pattern"—are the work of Fredric Brown at his whimsical best.

Moving to the West Coast in the early sixties, Fred and Beth established residence in the San Fernando Valley. I had already arrived on the scene and we again saw a great deal of one another.

For a time Fred tried his hand at films and television. Way back in the forties a producer had purchased a story from him in order to use its ending for a motion picture called *Crack-Up,* starring Pat O'Brien. Again, in the fifties, his mystery novel, *The Screaming Mimi,* was filmed. A number of his stories had been adapted for radio and later for various television anthology shows. It was only natural that he would attempt to do some adaptations or originals on his own. And, Hollywood being what it was—and, alas, is—it was only natural that his efforts met with little acceptance. Producers didn't understand Fred. Their definition of a "pro" was a hack who could and would write anything to order. But Fred, genuine "pro" that he was, wanted to write Fredric Brown stories.

Again, he reverted to print. And Hollywood's undoubted loss was our gain, for he continued to turn out a series of unique,

highly individualistic tales; stories which established him in the
genre. If he'd never written anything except "Puppet Show,"
we'd have reason to be grateful for Fredric Brown's contribution
to science fiction, but there were many others. You'll find some
of them in the following pages, and if you happen to be discovering them for the first time, I think you'll share the general
gratitude for his efforts.

And it is in his stories that Fred's fame endures. He was
never, to my knowledge, attendant at a science-fiction convention; he was not a trophy collector or a publicity seeker, and a
surprisingly large number of fans and fellow professionals knew
only the name, not the person who bore it. But as readers, they
came to appreciate the qualities which so distinguished his best
work—the sardonic humor, the irony which at times brings to
mind Ambrose Bierce. And yet there was a leavening element of
playfulness which adds an extra dimension to his most savage
satire or scaring cynicism. Add to this his gift for the realistic
rendering of dialogue and accurate observation of character traits
and the result is as impressive as it is entertaining.

There's not much more to tell. Fred's respiratory problems increased, forcing a move to Tucson in the midsixties. And it was
there, on March 11, 1972, that he died.

Those of us who were privileged to know him, mourn his
passing. But those who were privileged to read his work remain
eternally grateful for what he gave them.

A sampling of that work has been gathered here. There's
more, much more, and I urge you to seek it out. For into it he
poured a lifetime of effort and experience, wit and wisdom and
whimsy, honesty and make-believe, joy and despair—all of the
qualities which mark the measure of a man, and which make his
writing truly, and aptly, *The Best of Fredric Brown*.

Robert Bloch

"Arena"

CARSON OPENED his eyes, and found himself looking upward into a flickering blue dimness.

It was hot, and he was lying on sand, and a sharp rock embedded in the sand was hurting his back. He rolled over to his side, off the rock, and then pushed himself up to a sitting position.

"I'm crazy," he thought. "Crazy—or dead—or something." The sand was blue, bright blue. And there wasn't any such thing as bright blue sand on Earth or any of the planets.

Blue sand.

Blue sand under a blue dome that wasn't the sky nor yet a room, but a circumscribed area—somehow he knew it was circumscribed and finite even though he couldn't see to the top of it.

He picked up some of the sand in his hand and let it run through his fingers. It trickled down onto his bare leg. *Bare?*

Naked. He was stark naked, and already his body was dripping perspiration from the enervating heat, coated blue with sand wherever sand had touched it.

But elsewhere his body was white.

He thought: Then this sand is really blue. If it seemed blue only because of the blue light, then I'd be blue also. But I'm white, so the sand *is* blue. *Blue sand.* There isn't any blue sand. There isn't any place like this place I'm in.

Sweat was running down in his eyes.

It was hot, hotter than hell. Only hell—the hell of the ancients—was supposed to be red and not blue.

But if this place wasn't hell, what was it? Only Mercury, among the planets, had heat like this and this wasn't Mercury. And Mercury was some four billion miles from—

It came back to him then, where he'd been. In the little one-man scouter, outside the orbit of Pluto, scouting a scant million miles to one side of the Earth Armada drawn up in battle array there to intercept the Outsiders.

That sudden strident nerve-shattering ringing of the alarm bell when the rival scouter—the Outsider ship—had come within range of his detectors—

No one knew who the Outsiders were, what they looked like, from what far galaxy they came, other than that it was in the general direction of the Pleiades.

First, sporadic raids on Earth colonies and outposts. Isolated battles between Earth patrols and small groups of Outsider spaceships; battles sometimes won and sometimes lost, but never to date resulting in the capture of an alien vessel. Nor had any member of a raided colony ever survived to describe the Outsiders who had left the ships, if indeed they had left them.

Not a too-serious menace, at first, for the raids had not been too numerous or destructive. And individually, the ships had proved slightly inferior in armament to the best of Earth's fighters, although somewhat superior in speed and maneuverability. A sufficient edge in speed, in fact, to give the Outsiders their choice of running or fighting, unless surrounded.

Nevertheless, Earth had prepared for serious trouble, for a showdown, building the mightiest armada of all time. It had been waiting now, that armada, for a long time. But now the showdown was coming.

Scouts twenty billion miles out had detected the approach of a mighty fleet—a showdown fleet—of the Outsiders. Those scouts had never come back, but their radiotronic messages had. And now Earth's armada, all ten thousand ships and half-million fighting spacemen, was out there, outside Pluto's orbit, waiting to intercept and battle to the death.

And an even battle it was going to be, judging by the advance reports of the men of the far picket line who had given their lives to report—before they had died—on the size and strength of the alien fleet.

Anybody's battle, with the mastery of the solar system hanging in the balance, on an even chance. A last and *only* chance, for Earth and all her colonies lay at the utter mercy of the Outsiders if they ran that gauntlet—

Oh yes. Bob Carson remembered now.

Not that it explained blue sand and flickering blueness. But that strident alarming of the bell and his leap for the control panel. His frenzied fumbling as he strapped himself into the seat. The dot in the visiplate that grew larger.

The dryness of his mouth. The awful knowledge that this was *it*. For him, at least, although the main fleets were still out of range of one another.

This, his first taste of battle. Within three seconds or less he'd be victorious, or a charred cinder. Dead.

Three seconds—that's how long a space-battle lasted. Time enough to count to three, slowly, and then you'd won or you were dead. One hit completely took care of a lightly armed and armored little one-man craft like a scouter.

Frantically—as, unconsciously, his dry lips shaped the word "One"—he worked at the controls to keep that growing dot centered on the crossed spiderwebs of the visiplate. His hands doing that, while his right foot hovered over the pedal that would fire the bolt. The single bolt of concentrated hell that had to hit—or else. There wouldn't be time for any second shot.

"Two." He didn't know he'd said that, either. The dot in the visiplate wasn't a dot now. Only a few thousand miles away, it showed up in the magnification of the plate as though it were only a few hundred yards off. It was a sleek, fast little scouter, about the size of his.

And an alien ship, all right.

"Thr—" His foot touched the bolt-release pedal—

And then the Outsider had swerved suddenly and was off the crosshairs. Carson punched keys frantically, to follow.

For a tenth of a second, it was out of the visiplate entirely, and then as the nose of his scouter swung after it, he saw it again, diving straight toward the ground.

The ground?

It was an optical illusion of some sort. It *had* to be, that planet —or whatever it was—that now covered the visiplate. Whatever it was, it couldn't be there. Couldn't possibly. There *wasn't* any planet nearer than Neptune three billion miles away—with Pluto around on the opposite side of the distant pinpoint sun.

His *detectors! They* hadn't shown any object of planetary dimensions, even of asteroid dimensions. They still didn't.

So it couldn't be there, that whatever-it-was he was driving into, only a few hundred miles below him.

And in his sudden anxiety to keep from crashing, he forgot even the Outsider ship. He fired the front braking rockets, and even as the sudden change of speed slammed him forward against the seat straps, he fired full right for an emergency turn. Pushed them down and *held* them down, knowing that he needed everything the ship had to keep from crashing and that a turn that sudden would black him out for a moment.

It did black him out.

And that was all. Now he was sitting in hot blue sand, stark naked but otherwise unhurt. No sign of his spaceship and—for that matter—no sign of *space*. That curve overhead wasn't a sky, whatever else it was.

He scrambled to his feet.

Gravity seemed a little more than Earth-normal. Not much more.

Flat sand stretching away, a few scrawny bushes in clumps here and there. The bushes were blue, too, but in varying shades, some lighter than the blue of the sand, some darker.

Out from under the nearest bush ran a little thing that was like a lizard, except that it had more than four legs. It was blue, too. Bright blue. It saw him and ran back again under the bush.

He looked up again, trying to decide what was overhead. It wasn't exactly a roof, but it was dome-shaped. It flickered and was hard to look at. But definitely, it curved down to the ground, to the blue sand, all around him.

He wasn't far from being under the center of the dome. At a guess, it was a hundred yards to the nearest wall, if it was a wall. It was as though a blue hemisphere of *something*, about two hundred and fifty yards in circumference, was inverted over the flat expanse of the sand.

And everything blue, except one object. Over near a far curving wall there was a red object. Roughly spherical, it seemed to be about a yard in diameter. Too far for him to see clearly through the flickering blueness. But, unaccountably, he shuddered.

He wiped sweat from his forehead, or tried to, with the back of his hand.

Was this a dream, a nightmare? This heat, this sand, that vague feeling of horror he felt when he looked toward that red thing?

A dream? No, one didn't go to sleep and dream in the midst of a battle in space.

Death? No, never. If there were immortality, it wouldn't be a senseless thing like this, a thing of blue heat and blue sand and a red horror.

Then he heard the voice—

Inside his head he heard it, not with his ears. It came from nowhere or everywhere.

"*Through spaces and dimensions wandering,*" rang the words in his mind, "*and in this space and this time I find two peoples about to wage a war that would exterminate one and so weaken the other that it would retrogress and never fulfill its destiny, but decay and return to mindless dust whence it came. And I say this must not happen.*"

"Who . . . what are you?" Carson didn't say it aloud, but the question formed itself in his brain.

"*You would not understand completely. I am—*" There was a pause as though the voice sought—in Carson's brain—for a word that wasn't there, a word he didn't know. "*I am the end of evolution of a race so old the time can not be expressed in words that have meaning to your mind. A race fused into a single entity, eternal—*

"*An entity such as your primitive race might become*"—again the groping for a word—"*time from now. So might the race you call, in your mind, the Outsiders. So I intervene in the battle to come, the battle between fleets so evenly matched that destruction of both races will result. One must survive. One must progress and evolve.*"

"One?" thought Carson. "Mine, or—?"

"*It is in my power to stop the war, to send the Outsiders back to their galaxy. But they would return, or your race would sooner or later follow them there. Only by remaining in this space and time to intervene constantly could I prevent them from destroying one another, and I cannot remain.*

"*So I shall intervene now. I shall destroy one fleet completely without loss to the other. One civilization shall thus survive.*"

Nightmare. This had to be nightmare, Carson thought. But he knew it wasn't.

It was too mad, too impossible, to be anything but real.

He didn't dare ask *the* question—*which?* But his thoughts asked it for him.

"*The stronger shall survive,*" said the voice. "*That I can not—and would not—change. I merely intervene to make it a com-*

plete victory, not"—groping again—*"not Pyrrhic victory to a broken race.*

"From the outskirts of the not-yet battle I plucked two individuals, you and an Outsider. I see from your mind that in your early history of nationalisms battles between champions, to decide issues between races, were not unknown.

"You and your opponent are here pitted against one another, naked and unarmed, under conditions equally unfamiliar to you both, equally unpleasant to you both. There is no time limit, for here there is no time. The survivor is the champion of his race. That race survives."

"But—" Carson's protest was too inarticulate for expression, but the voice answered it.

"It is fair. The conditions are such that the accident of physical strength will not completely decide the issue. There is a barrier. You will understand. Brain-power and courage will be more important than strength. Most especially courage, which is the will to survive."

"But while this goes on, the fleets will—"

"No, you are in another space, another time. For as long as you are here, time stands still in the universe you know. I see you wonder whether this place is real. It is, and it is not. As I—to your limited understanding—am and am not real. My existence is mental and not physical. You saw me as a planet; it could have been as a dustmote or a sun.

"But to you this place is now real. What you suffer here will be real. And if you die here, your death will be real. If you die, your failure will be the end of your race. That is enough for you to know."

And then the voice was gone.

Again he was alone, but not alone. For as Carson looked up, he saw that the red thing, the red sphere of horror which he now knew was the Outsider, was rolling toward him.

Rolling.

It seemed to have no legs or arms that he could see, no features. It rolled across the blue sand with the fluid quickness of a drop of mercury. And before it, in some manner he could not understand, came a paralyzing wave of nauseating, retching, horrid hatred.

Carson looked about him frantically. A stone, lying in the sand a few feet away, was the nearest thing to a weapon. It wasn't large, but it had sharp edges, like a slab of flint. It looked a bit like blue flint.

He picked it up, and crouched to receive the attack. It was coming fast, faster than he could run.

No time to think out how he was going to fight it, and how anyway could he plan to battle a creature whose strength, whose characteristics, whose method of fighting he did not know? Rolling so fast, it looked more than ever like a perfect sphere.

Ten yards away. Five. And then it stopped.

Rather, it *was stopped*. Abruptly the near side of it flattened as though it had run up against an invisible wall. It bounced, actually bounced back.

Then it rolled forward again, but more slowly, more cautiously. It stopped again, at the same place. It tried again, a few yards to one side.

There was a barrier there of some sort. It clicked, then, in Carson's mind. That thought projected into his mind by the Entity who had brought them here: "—accident of physical strength will not completely decide the issue. There is a barrier."

A force-field, of course. Not the Netzian Field, known to Earth science, for that glowed and emitted a crackling sound. This one was invisible, silent.

It was a wall that ran from side to side of the inverted hemisphere; Carson didn't have to verify that himself. The Roller was doing that; rolling sideways along the barrier, seeking a break in it that wasn't there.

Carson took half a dozen steps forward, his left hand groping out before him, and then his hand touched the barrier. It felt smooth, yielding, like a sheet of rubber rather than like glass. Warm to his touch, but no warmer than the sand underfoot. And it was completely invisible, even at close range.

He dropped the stone and put both hands against it, pushing. It seemed to yield, just a trifle. But no farther than that trifle, even when he pushed with all his weight. It felt like a sheet of rubber backed up by steel. Limited resiliency, and then firm strength.

He stood on tiptoe and reached as high as he could and the barrier was still there.

He saw the Roller coming back, having reached one side of the arena. That feeling of nausea hit Carson again, and he stepped back from the barrier as it went by. It didn't stop.

But did the barrier stop at ground level? Carson knelt down and burrowed in the sand. It was soft, light, easy to dig in. At two feet down the barrier was still there.

The Roller was coming back again. Obviously, it couldn't find a way through at either side.

There must be a way through, Carson thought. *Some* way we can get at each other, else this duel is meaningless.

But no hurry now, in finding that out. There was something to try first. The Roller was back now, and it stopped just across the barrier, only six feet away. It seemed to be studying him, although for the life of him, Carson couldn't find external evidence of sense organs on the thing. Nothing that looked like eyes or ears, or even a mouth. There was though, he saw now, a series of grooves—perhaps a dozen of them altogether, and he saw two tentacles suddenly push out from two of the grooves and dip into the sand as though testing its consistency. Tentacles about an inch in diameter and perhaps a foot and a half long.

But the tentacles were retractable into the grooves and were kept there except when not in use. They were retracted when the thing rolled and seemed to have nothing to do with its method of locomotion. That, as far as Carson could judge, seemed to be accomplished by some shifting—just *how* he couldn't even imagine—of its center of gravity.

He shuddered as he looked at the thing. It was alien, utterly alien, horribly different from anything on Earth or any of the life forms found on the other solar planets. Instinctively, somehow, he knew its mind was as alien as its body.

But he had to try. If it had no telepathic powers at all, the attempt was foredoomed to failure, yet he thought it had such powers. There had, at any rate, been a projection of something that was not physical at the time a few minutes ago when it had first started for him. An almost tangible wave of hatred.

If it could project that, perhaps it could read his mind as well, sufficiently for his purpose.

Deliberately, Carson picked up the rock that had been his only weapon, then tossed it down again in a gesture of relinquishment and raised his empty hands, palms up, before him.

He spoke aloud, knowing that although the words would be meaningless to the creature before him, speaking them would focus his own thoughts more completely upon the message.

"Can we not have peace between us?" he said, his voice sounding strange in the utter stillness. "The Entity who brought us here has told us what must happen if our races fight—extinction of one and weakening and retrogression of the other. The battle between them, said the Entity, depends upon what we do here. Why can not we agree to an eternal peace—your race to its galaxy, we to ours?"

Carson blanked out his mind to receive a reply.

It came, and it staggered him back, physically. He actually recoiled several steps in sheer horror at the depth and intensity of the hatred and lust-to-kill of the red images that had been projected at him. Not as articulate words—as had come to him the thoughts of the Entity—but as wave upon wave of fierce emotion.

For a moment that seemed an eternity he had to struggle against the mental impact of that hatred, fight to clear his mind of it and drive out the alien thoughts to which he had given admittance by blanking his own thoughts. He wanted to retch.

Slowly his mind cleared as, slowly, the mind of a man wakening from nightmare clears away the fear-fabric of which the dream was woven. He was breathing hard and he felt weaker, but he could think.

He stood studying the Roller. It had been motionless during the mental duel it had so nearly won. Now it rolled a few feet to one side, to the nearest of the blue bushes. Three tentacles whipped out of their grooves and began to investigate the bush.

"O. K.," Carson said, "so it's war then." He managed a wry grin. "If I got your answer straight, peace doesn't appeal to you." And, because he was, after all, a quite young man and couldn't resist the impulse to be dramatic, he added. "To the death!"

But his voice, in that utter silence, sounded very silly, even to himself. It came to him, then, that this *was* to the death. Not only his own death or that of the red spherical thing which he now thought of as the Roller, but death to the entire race of one or the other of them. The end of the human race, if he failed.

It made him suddenly very humble and very afraid to think that. More than to think it, to *know* it. Somehow, with a knowledge that was above even faith, he knew that the Entity who had arranged this duel had told the truth about its intentions and its powers. It wasn't kidding.

The future of humanity depended upon *him*. It was an awful

thing to realize, and he wrenched his mind away from it. He had to concentrate on the situation at hand.

There had to be some way of getting through the barrier, or of killing through the barrier.

Mentally? He hoped that wasn't all, for the Roller obviously had stronger telepathic powers than the primitive, undeveloped ones of the human race. Or did it?

He had been able to drive the thoughts of the Roller out of his own mind; could it drive out his? If its ability to project were stronger, might not its receptivity mechanism be more vulnerable?

He stared at it and endeavored to concentrate and focus all his thoughts upon it.

"Die," he thought. "You are going to die. You are dying. You are—"

He tried variations on it, and mental pictures. Sweat stood out on his forehead and he found himself trembling with the intensity of the effort. But the Roller went ahead with its investigation of the bush, as utterly unaffected as though Carson had been reciting the multiplication table.

So *that* was no good.

He felt a bit weak and dizzy from the heat and his strenuous effort at concentration. He sat down on the blue sand to rest and gave his full attention to watching and studying the Roller. By close study, perhaps, he could judge its strength and detect its weaknesses, learn things that would be valuable to know when and if they should come to grips.

It was breaking off twigs. Carson watched carefully, trying to judge just how hard it worked to do that. Later, he thought, he could find a similar bush on his own side, break off twigs of equal thickness himself, and gain a comparison of physical strength between his own arms and hands and those tentacles.

The twigs broke off hard; the Roller was having to struggle with each one, he saw. Each tentacle, he saw, bifurcated at the tip into two fingers, each tipped by a nail or claw. The claws didn't seem to be particularly long or dangerous. No more so than his own fingernails, if they were let to grow a bit.

No, on the whole, it didn't look too tough to handle physically. Unless, of course, that bush was made of pretty tough stuff. Carson looked around him and, yes, right within reach was another bush of identically the same type.

He reached over and snapped off a twig. It was brittle, easy to break. Of course, the Roller might have been faking deliberately but he didn't think so.

On the other hand, where was it vulnerable? Just how would he go about killing it, if he got the chance? He went back to studying it. The outer hide looked pretty tough. He'd need a sharp weapon of some sort. He picked up the piece of rock again. It was about twelve inches long, narrow, and fairly sharp on one end. If it chipped like flint, he could make a serviceable knife out of it.

The Roller was continuing its investigations of the bushes. It rolled again, to the nearest one of another type. A little blue lizard, many-legged like the one Carson had seen on his side of the barrier, darted out from under the bush.

A tentacle of the Roller lashed out and caught it, picked it up. Another tentacle whipped over and began to pull legs off the lizard, as coldly and calmly as it had pulled twigs off the bush. The creature struggled frantically and emitted a shrill squealing sound that was the first sound Carson had heard here other than the sound of his own voice.

Carson shuddered and wanted to turn his eyes away. But he made himself continue to watch; anything he could learn about his opponent might prove valuable. Even this knowledge of its unnecessary cruelty. Particularly, he thought with a sudden vicious surge of emotion, this knowledge of its unnecessary cruelty. It would make it a pleasure to kill the thing, if and when the chance came.

He steeled himself to watch the dismembering of the lizard, for that very reason.

But he felt glad when, with half its legs gone, the lizard quit squealing and struggling and lay limp and dead in the Roller's grasp.

It didn't continue with the rest of the legs. Contemptuously it tossed the dead lizard away from it, in Carson's direction. It arced through the air between them and landed at his feet.

It had come through the barrier! The barrier wasn't there any more!

Carson was on his feet in a flash, the knife gripped tightly in his hand, and leaped forward. He'd settle this thing here and now! With the barrier gone—

But it wasn't gone. He found that out the hard way, running head on into it and nearly knocking himself silly. He bounced back, and fell.

And as he sat up, shaking his head to clear it, he saw something coming through the air toward him, and to duck it, he threw himself flat again on the sand, and to one side. He got his body out of the way, but there was a sudden sharp pain in the calf of his left leg.

He rolled backward, ignoring the pain, and scrambled to his feet. It was a rock, he saw now, that had struck him. And the Roller was picking up another one now, swinging it back gripped between two tentacles, getting ready to throw again.

It sailed through the air toward him, but he was easily able to step out of its way. The Roller, apparently, could throw straight, but not hard nor far. The first rock had struck him only because he had been sitting down and had not seen it coming until it was almost upon him.

Even as he stepped aside from that weak second throw, Carson drew back his right arm and let fly with the rock that was still in his hand. If missiles, he thought with sudden elation, can cross the barrier, then two can play at the game of throwing them. And the good right arm of an Earthman—

He couldn't miss a three-foot sphere at only four-yard range, and he didn't miss. The rock whizzed straight, and with a speed several times that of the missiles the Roller had thrown. It hit dead center, but it hit flat, unfortunately, instead of point first.

But it hit with a resounding thump, and obviously it hurt. The Roller had been reaching for another rock, but it changed its mind and got out of there instead. By the time Carson could pick up and throw another rock, the Roller was forty yards back from the barrier and going strong.

His second throw missed by feet, and his third throw was short. The Roller was back out of range—at least out of range of a missile heavy enough to be damaging.

Carson grinned. That round had been his. Except—

He quit grinning as he bent over to examine the calf of his leg. A jagged edge of the stone had made a pretty deep cut, several inches long. It was bleeding pretty freely, but he didn't think it had gone deep enough to hit an artery. If it stopped bleeding of its own accord, well and good. If not, he was in for trouble.

Finding out one thing, though, took precedence over that cut. The nature of the barrier.

He went forward to it again, this time groping with his hands before him. He found it; then holding one hand against it, he tossed a handful of sand at it with the other hand. The sand went right through. His hand didn't.

Organic matter versus inorganic? No, because the dead lizard had gone through it, and a lizard, alive or dead, was certainly organic. Plant life? He broke off a twig and poked it at the barrier. The twig went through, with no resistance, but when his fingers gripping the twig came to the barrier, they were stopped.

He couldn't get through it, nor could the Roller. But rocks and sand and a dead lizard—

How about a live lizard? He went hunting, under bushes, until he found one, and caught it. He tossed it gently against the barrier and it bounced back and scurried away across the blue sand.

That gave him the answer, in so far as he could determine it now. The screen was a barrier to living things. Dead or inorganic matter could cross it.

That off his mind, Carson looked at his injured leg again. The bleeding was lessening, which meant he wouldn't need to worry about making a tourniquet. But he should find some water, if any was available, to clean the wound.

Water—the thought of it made him realize that he was getting awfully thirsty. He'd *have* to find water, in case this contest turned out to be a protracted one.

Limping slightly now, he started off to make a full circuit of his half of the arena. Guiding himself with one hand along the barrier, he walked to his right until he came to the curving sidewall. It was visible, a dull blue-gray at close range, and the surface of it felt just like the central barrier.

He experimented by tossing a handful of sand at it, and the sand reached the wall and disappeared as it went through. The hemispherical shell was a force-field, too. But an opaque one, instead of transparent like the barrier.

He followed it around until he came back to the barrier, and walked back along the barrier to the point from which he'd started.

No sign of water.

Worried now, he started a series of zigzags back and forth between the barrier and the wall, covering the intervening space thoroughly.

No water. Blue sand, blue bushes, and intolerable heat. Nothing else.

It must be his imagination, he told himself angrily, that he was suffering *that* much from thirst. How long had he been here? Of course, no time at all, according to his own space-time frame. The Entity had told him time stood still out there, while he was here. But his body processes went on here, just the same. And according to his body's reckoning, how long had he been here? Three or four hours, perhaps. Certainly not long enough to be suffering seriously from thirst.

But he was suffering from it; his throat dry and parched. Probably the intense heat was the cause. It was *hot!* A hundred and thirty Fahrenheit, at a guess. A dry, still heat without the slightest movement of air.

He was limping rather badly, and utterly fagged out when he'd finished the futile exploration of his domain.

He stared across at the motionless Roller and hoped it was as miserable as he was. And quite possibly it wasn't enjoying this, either. The Entity had said the conditions here were equally unfamiliar and equally uncomfortable for both of them. Maybe the Roller came from a planet where two hundred degree heat was the norm. Maybe it was freezing while he was roasting.

Maybe the air was as much too thick for it as it was too thin for him. For the exertion of his explorations had left him panting. The atmosphere here, he realized now, was not much thicker than that on Mars.

No water.

That meant a deadline, for him at any rate. Unless he could find a way to cross that barrier or to kill his enemy from this side of it, thirst would kill him, eventually.

It gave him a feeling of desperate urgency. He *must* hurry.

But he made himself sit down a moment to rest, to think.

What was there to do? Nothing, and yet so many things. The several varieties of bushes, for example. They didn't look promising, but he'd have to examine them for possibilities. And his leg —he'd have to do something about that, even without water to clean it. Gather ammunition in the form of rocks. Find a rock that would make a good knife.

His leg hurt rather badly now, and he decided that came first.

One type of bush had leaves—or things rather similar to leaves. He pulled off a handful of them and decided, after examination, to take a chance on them. He used them to clean off the sand and dirt and caked blood, then made a pad of fresh leaves and tied it over the wound with tendrils from the same bush.

The tendrils proved unexpectedly tough and strong. They were slender, and soft and pliable, yet he couldn't break them at all. He had to saw them off the bush with the sharp edge of a piece of the blue flint. Some of the thicker ones were over a foot long, and he filed away in his memory, for future reference, the fact that a bunch of the thick ones, tied together, would make a pretty serviceable rope. Maybe he'd be able to think of a use for rope.

Next, he made himself a knife. The blue flint *did* chip. From a foot-long splinter of it, he fashioned himself a crude but lethal weapon. And of tendrils from the bush, he made himself a rope-belt through which he could thrust the flint knife, to keep it with him all the time and yet have his hands free.

He went back to studying the bushes. There were three other types. One was leafless, dry, brittle, rather like a dried tumble-weed. Another was of soft, crumbly wood, almost like punk. It looked and felt as though it would make excellent tinder for a fire. The third type was the most nearly woodlike. It had fragile leaves that wilted at a touch, but the stalks, although short, were straight and strong.

It was horribly, unbearably hot.

He limped up to the barrier, felt to make sure that it was still there. It was.

He stood watching the Roller for a while. It was keeping a safe distance back from the barrier, out of effective stone-throwing range. It was moving around back there, doing something. He couldn't tell what it was doing.

Once it stopped moving, came a little closer, and seemed to concentrate its attention on him. Again Carson had to fight off a wave of nausea. He threw a stone at it and the Roller retreated and went back to whatever it had been doing before.

At least he could make it keep its distance.

And, he thought bitterly, a devil of a lot of good *that* did him. Just the same, he spent the next hour or two gathering stones of suitable size for throwing, and making several neat piles of them, near his side of the barrier.

His throat burned now. It was difficult for him to think about anything except water.

But he *had* to think about other things. About getting through that barrier, under or over it, getting *at* that red sphere and killing it before this place of heat and thirst killed him first.

The barrier went to the wall upon either side, but how high and how far under the sand?

For just a moment, Carson's mind was too fuzzy to think out how he could find out either of those things. Idly, sitting there in the hot sand—and he didn't remember sitting down—he watched a blue lizard crawl from the shelter of one bush to the shelter of another.

From under the second bush, it looked out at him.

Carson grinned at it. Maybe he was getting a bit punch-drunk, because he remembered suddenly the old story of the desert-colonists on Mars, taken from an older desert story of Earth— "Pretty soon you get so lonesome you find yourself talking to the lizards, and then not so long after that you find the lizards talking back to you—"

He should have been concentrating, of course, on how to kill the Roller, but instead he grinned at the lizard and said, "Hello, there."

The lizard took a few steps toward him. "Hello," it said.

Carson was stunned for a moment, and then he put back his head and roared with laughter. It didn't hurt his throat to do so, either; he hadn't been *that* thirsty.

Why not? Why should the Entity who thought up this nightmare of a place not have a sense of humor, along with the other powers he has? Talking lizards, equipped to talk back in my own language, if I talk to them— It's a nice touch.

He grinned at the lizard and said, "Come on over." But the lizard turned and ran away, scurrying from bush to bush until it was out of sight.

He was thirsty again.

And he had to *do* something. He couldn't win this contest by sitting here sweating and feeling miserable. He had to *do* something. But what?

Get through the barrier. But he couldn't get through it, or over it. But was he certain he couldn't get under? And come to think of it, didn't one sometimes find water by digging? Two birds with one stone—

Painfully now, Carson limped up to the barrier and started digging, scooping up sand a double handful at a time. It was slow, hard work because the sand ran in at the edges and the deeper he got the bigger in diameter the hole had to be. How many hours it took him, he didn't know, but he hit bedrock four feet down. Dry bedrock; no sign of water.

And the force-field of the barrier went down clear to the bedrock. No dice. No water. Nothing.

He crawled out of the hole and lay there panting, and then raised his head to look across and see what the Roller was doing. It must be doing something back there.

It was. It was making something out of wood from the bushes, tied together with tendrils. A queerly shaped framework about four feet high and roughly square. To see it better, Carson climbed up onto the mound of sand he had excavated from the hole, and stood there staring.

There were two long levers sticking out of the back of it, one with a cup-shaped affair on the end of it. Seemed to be some sort of a catapult, Carson thought.

Sure enough, the Roller was lifting a sizable rock into the cup-shaped outfit. One of his tentacles moved the other lever up and down for a while, and then he turned the machine slightly as though aiming it and the lever with the stone flew up and forward.

The stone arced several yards over Carson's head, so far away that he didn't have to duck, but he judged the distance it had traveled, and whistled softly. He couldn't throw a rock that weight more than half that distance. And even retreating to the rear of his domain wouldn't put him out of range of that machine, if the Roller shoved it forward almost to the barrier.

Another rock whizzed over. Not quite so far away this time.

That thing could be dangerous, he decided. Maybe he'd better do something about it.

Moving from side to side along the barrier, so the catapult couldn't bracket him, he whaled a dozen rocks at it. But that wasn't going to be any good, he saw. They had to be light rocks, or he couldn't throw them that far. If they hit the framework, they bounced off harmlessly. And the Roller had no difficulty, at that distance, in moving aside from those that came near it.

Besides, his arm was tiring badly. He ached all over from sheer weariness. If he could only rest a while without having to duck rocks from that catapult at regular intervals of maybe thirty seconds each—

He stumbled back to the rear of the arena. Then he saw even that wasn't any good. The rocks reached back there, too, only there were longer intervals between them, as though it took longer to wind up the mechanism, whatever it was, of the catapult.

Wearily he dragged himself back to the barrier again. Several times he fell and could barely rise to his feet to go on. He was, he knew, near the limit of his endurance. Yet he didn't dare stop moving now, until and unless he could put that catapult out of action. If he fell asleep, he'd never wake up.

One of the stones from it gave him the first glimmer of an idea. It struck upon one of the piles of stones he'd gathered together near the barrier to use as ammunition, and it struck sparks.

Sparks. Fire. Primitive man had made fire by striking sparks, and with some of those dry crumbly bushes as tinder—

Luckily, a bush of that type was near him. He broke it off, took it over to the pile of stones, then patiently hit one stone against another until a spark touched the punklike wood of the bush. It went up in flames so fast that it singed his eyebrows and was burned to an ash within seconds.

But he had the idea now, and within minutes he had a little fire going in the lee of the mound of sand he'd made digging the hole an hour or two ago. Tinder bushes had started it, and other bushes which burned, but more slowly, kept it a steady flame.

The tough wirelike tendrils didn't burn readily; that made the fire-bombs easy to make and throw. A bundle of faggots tied about a small stone to give it weight and a loop of the tendril to swing it by.

He made half a dozen of them before he lighted and threw the first. It went wide, and the Roller started a quick retreat, pulling the catapult after him. But Carson had the others ready and threw them in rapid succession. The fourth wedged in the catapult's framework, and did the trick. The Roller tried desperately to put out the spreading blaze by throwing sand, but its clawed tentacles would take only a spoonful at a time and his efforts were ineffectual. The catapult burned.

The Roller moved safely away from the fire and seemed to concentrate its attention on Carson and again he felt that wave

of hatred and nausea. But more weakly; either the Roller itself
was weakening or Carson had learned how to protect himself
against the mental attack.

He thumbed his nose at it and then sent it scuttling back to
safety by throwing a stone. The Roller went clear to the back of
its half of the arena and started pulling up bushes again. Probably it was going to make another catapult.

Carson verified—for the hundredth time—that the barrier was
still operating, and then found himself sitting in the sand beside
it because he was suddenly too weak to stand up.

His leg throbbed steadily now and the pangs of thirst were se-
vere. But those things paled beside the utter physical exhaustion
that gripped his entire body.

And the heat.

Hell must be like this, he thought. The hell that the ancients
had believed in. He fought to stay awake, and yet staying awake
seemed futile, for there was nothing he could do. Nothing,
while the barrier remained impregnable and the Roller stayed
back out of range.

But there must be *something*. He tried to remember things he
had read in books of archaeology about the methods of fighting
used back in the days before metal and plastic. The stone missile, that had come first, he thought. Well, that he already had.

The only improvement on it would be a catapult, such as the
Roller had made. But he'd never be able to make one, with the
tiny bits of wood available from the bushes—no single piece
longer than a foot or so. Certainly he could figure out a mechanism for one, but he didn't have the endurance left for a task
that would take days.

Days? But the Roller had made one. Had they been here days
already? Then he remembered that the Roller had many tentacles to work with and undoubtedly could do such work faster
than he.

And besides, a catapult wouldn't decide the issue. He had to
do better than that.

Bow and arrow? No; he'd tried archery once and knew his
own ineptness with a bow. Even with a modern sportsman's
durasteel weapon, made for accuracy. With such a crude,
pieced-together outfit as he could make here, he doubted if he
could shoot as far as he could throw a rock, and knew he
couldn't shoot as straight.

Spear? Well, he *could* make that. It would be useless as a throwing weapon at any distance, but would be a handy thing at close range, if he ever got to close range.

And making one would give him something to do. Help keep his mind from wandering, as it was beginning to do. Sometimes now, he had to concentrate a while before he could remember why he was here, why he had to kill the Roller.

Luckily he was still beside one of the piles of stones. He sorted through it until he found one shaped roughly like a spearhead. With a smaller stone he began to chip it into shape, fashioning sharp shoulders on the sides so that if it penetrated it would not pull out again.

Like a harpoon? There was something in that idea, he thought. A harpoon was better than a spear, maybe, for this crazy contest. If he could once get it into the Roller, and had a rope on it, he could pull the Roller up against the barrier and the stone blade of his knife would reach through that barrier, even if his hands wouldn't.

The shaft was harder to make than the head. But by splitting and joining the main stems of four of the bushes, and wrapping the joints with the tough but thin tendrils, he got a strong shaft about four feet long, and tied the stone head in a notch cut in the end.

It was crude, but strong.

And the rope. With the thin tough tendrils he made himself twenty feet of line. It was light and didn't look strong, but he knew it would hold his weight and to spare. He tied one end of it to the shaft of the harpoon and the other end about his right wrist. At least, if he threw his harpoon across the barrier, he'd be able to pull it back if he missed.

Then when he had tied the last knot and there was nothing more he could do, the heat and the weariness and the pain in his leg and the dreadful thirst were suddenly a thousand times worse than they had been before.

He tried to stand up, to see what the Roller was doing now, and found he couldn't get to his feet. On the third try, he got as far as his knees and then fell flat again.

"I've got to sleep," he thought. "If a showdown came now, I'd be helpless. He could come up here and kill me, if he knew. I've got to regain some strength."

Slowly, painfully, he crawled back away from the barrier. Ten yards, twenty—

The jar of something thudding against the sand near him waked him from a confused and horrible dream to a more confused and more horrible reality, and he opened his eyes again to blue radiance over blue sand.

How long had he slept? A minute? A day?

Another stone thudded nearer and threw sand on him. He got his arms under him and sat up. He turned around and saw the Roller twenty yards away, at the barrier.

It rolled away hastily as he sat up, not stopping until it was as far away as it could get.

He'd fallen asleep too soon, he realized, while he was still in range of the Roller's throwing ability. Seeing him lying motionless, it had dared come up to the barrier to throw at him. Luckily, it didn't realize how weak he was, or it could have stayed there and kept on throwing stones.

Had he slept long? He didn't think so, because he felt just as he had before. Not rested at all, no thirstier, no different. Probably he'd been there only a few minutes.

He started crawling again, this time forcing himself to keep going until he was as far as he could go, until the colorless, opaque wall of the arena's outer shell was only a yard away.

Then things slipped away again—

When he awoke, nothing about him was changed, but this time he knew that he had slept a long time.

The first thing he became aware of was the inside of his mouth; it was dry, caked. His tongue was swollen.

Something was wrong, he knew, as he returned slowly to full awareness. He felt less tired, the stage of utter exhaustion had passed. The sleep had taken care of that.

But there was pain, agonizing pain. It wasn't until he tried to move that he knew that it came from his leg.

He raised his head and looked down at it. It was swollen terribly below the knee and the swelling showed even halfway up his thigh. The plant tendrils he had used to tie on the protective pad of leaves now cut deeply into the swollen flesh.

To get his knife under that imbedded lashing would have been impossible. Fortunately, the final knot was over the shin bone, in front, where the vine cut in less deeply than elsewhere. He was able, after an agonizing effort, to untie the knot.

A look under the pad of leaves told him the worst. Infection and blood poisoning, both pretty bad and getting worse.

And without drugs, without cloth, without even *water*, there wasn't a thing he could do about it.

Not a thing, except *die*, when the poison had spread through his system.

He knew it was hopeless, then, and that he'd lost.

And with him, humanity. When he died here, out there in the universe he knew, all his friends, everybody, would die too. And Earth and the colonized planets would be the home of the red, rolling, alien Outsiders. Creatures out of nightmare, things without a human attribute, who picked lizards apart for the fun of it.

It was the thought of that which gave him courage to start crawling, almost blindly in pain, toward the barrier again. Not crawling on hands and knees this time, but pulling himself along only by his arms and hands.

A chance in a million, that maybe he'd have strength left, when he got there, to throw his harpoon-spear just *once*, and with deadly effect, if—on another chance in a million—the Roller would come up to the barrier. Or if the barrier was gone, now.

It took him years, it seemed, to get there.

The barrier wasn't gone. It was as impassable as when he'd first felt it.

And the Roller wasn't at the barrier. By raising up on his elbows, he could see it at the back of its part of the arena, working on a wooden framework that was a half-completed duplicate of the catapult he'd destroyed.

It was moving slowly now. Undoubtedly it had weakened, too.

But Carson doubted that it would ever need that second catapult. He'd be dead, he thought, before it was finished.

If he could attract it to the barrier, now, while he was still alive— He waved an arm and tried to shout, but his parched throat would make no sound.

Or if he could get through the barrier—

His mind must have slipped for a moment, for he found himself beating his fists against the barrier in futile rage, made himself stop.

He closed his eyes, tried to make himself calm.

"Hello," said the voice.

It was a small, thin voice. It sounded like—

He opened his eyes and turned his head. It *was* a lizard.

"Go away," Carson wanted to say. "Go away; you're not really there, or you're there but not really talking. I'm imagining things again."

But he couldn't talk; his throat and tongue were past all speech with the dryness. He closed his eyes again.

"Hurt," said the voice. "Kill. Hurt—kill. Come."

He opened his eyes again. The blue ten-legged lizard was still there. It ran a little way along the barrier, came back, started off again, and came back.

"Hurt," it said. "Kill. Come."

Again it started off, and came back. Obviously it wanted Carson to follow it along the barrier.

He closed his eyes again. The voice kept on. The same three meaningless words. Each time he opened his eyes, it ran off and came back.

"Hurt. Kill. Come."

Carson groaned. There would be no peace unless he followed the blasted thing. Like it wanted him to.

He followed it, crawling. Another sound, a high-pitched squealing, came to his ears and grew louder.

There was something lying in the sand, writhing, squealing. Something small, blue, that looked like a lizard and yet didn't—

Then he saw what it was—the lizard whose legs the Roller had pulled off, so long ago. But it wasn't dead; it had come back to life and was wriggling and screaming in agony.

"Hurt," said the other lizard. "Hurt. Kill. Kill."

Carson understood. He took the flint knife from his belt and killed the tortured creature. The live lizard scurried off quickly.

Carson turned back to the barrier. He leaned his hands and head against it and watched the Roller, far back, working on the new catapult.

"I could get that far," he thought, "if I could get through. If I could get through, I might win yet. It looks weak, too. I might—"

And then there was another reaction of black hopelessness, when pain sapped his will and he wished that he were dead. He envied the lizard he'd just killed. It didn't have to live on and suffer. And he did. It would be hours, it might be days, before the blood poisoning killed him.

If only he could use that knife on himself—

But he knew he wouldn't. As long as he was alive, there was the millionth chance—.

He was straining, pushing on the barrier with the flat of his hands, and he noticed his arms, how thin and scrawny they were now. He must really have been here a long time, for days, to get as thin as that.

How much longer now, before he died? How much more heat and thirst and pain could flesh stand?

For a little while he was almost hysterical again, and then came a time of deep calm, and a thought that was startling.

The lizard he had just killed. *It had crossed the barrier, still alive*. It had come from the Roller's side; the Roller had pulled off its legs and then tossed it contemptuously at him and it had come through the barrier. He'd thought, because the lizard was dead.

But it hadn't been dead; it had been unconscious.

A live lizard couldn't go through the barrier, but an unconscious one could. The barrier was not a barrier, then, to living flesh, but to conscious flesh. It was a *mental* projection, a *mental* hazard.

And with that thought, Carson started crawling along the barrier to make his last desperate gamble. A hope so forlorn that only a dying man would have dared try it.

No use weighing the odds of success. Not when, if he didn't try it, those odds were infinitely to zero.

He crawled along the barrier to the dune of sand, about four feet high, which he'd scooped out in trying—how many days ago?—to dig under the barrier or to reach water.

That mound was right at the barrier, its farther slope half on one side of the barrier, half on the other.

Taking with him a rock from the pile nearby, he climbed up to the top of the dune and over the top, and lay there against the barrier, his weight leaning against it so that if the barrier were taken away he'd roll on down the short slope, into the enemy territory.

He checked to be sure that the knife was safely in his rope belt, that the harpoon was in the crook of his left arm and that the twenty-foot rope fastened to it and to his wrist.

Then with his right hand he raised the rock with which he would hit himself on the head. Luck would have to be with him on that blow; it would have to be hard enough to knock him out, but not hard enough to knock him out for long.

He had a hunch that the Roller was watching him, and would see him roll down through the barrier, and come to investigate. It would think he was dead, he hoped—he thought it had probably drawn the same deduction about the nature of the barrier that he had drawn. But it would come cautiously. He would have a little time—

He struck.

Pain brought him back to consciousness. A sudden, sharp pain in his hip that was different from the throbbing pain in his head and the throbbing pain in his leg.

But he had, thinking things out before he had struck himself, anticipated that very pain, even hoped for it, and had steeled himself against awakening with a sudden movement.

He lay still, but opened his eyes just a slit, and saw that he had guessed rightly. The Roller was coming closer. It was twenty feet away and the pain that had awakened him was the stone it had tossed to see whether he was alive or dead.

He lay still. It came closer, fifteen feet away, and stopped again. Carson scarcely breathed.

As nearly as possible, he was keeping his mind a blank, lest its telepathic ability detect consciousness in him. And with his mind blanked out that way, the impact of its thoughts upon his mind was nearly soul-shattering.

He felt sheer horror at the utter *alienness*, the *differentness* of those thoughts. Things that he felt but could not understand and could never express, because no terrestrial language had words, no terrestrial mind had images to fit them. The mind of a spider, he thought, or the mind of a praying mantis or a Martian sand-serpent, raised to intelligence and put in telepathic rapport with human minds, would be a homely familiar thing, compared to this.

He understood now that the Entity had been right: Man or Roller, and the universe was not a place that could hold them both. Farther apart than god and devil, there could never be even a balance between them.

Closer. Carson waited until it was only feet away, until its clawed tentacles reached out—

Oblivious to agony now, he sat up, raised and flung the harpoon with all the strength that remained to him. Or he thought it was all; sudden final strength flooded through him, along with a sudden forgetfulness of pain as definite as a nerve block.

As the Roller, deeply stabbed by the harpoon, rolled away, Carson tried to get to his feet to run after it. He couldn't do that; he fell, but kept crawling.

It reached the end of the rope, and he was jerked forward by the pull on his wrist. It dragged him a few feet and then stopped. Carson kept on going, pulling himself toward it hand over hand along the rope.

It stopped there, writhing tentacles trying in vain to pull out the harpoon. It seemed to shudder and quiver, and then it must have realized that it couldn't get away, for it rolled back toward him, clawed tentacles reaching out.

Stone knife in hand, he met it. He stabbed, again and again, while those horrid claws ripped skin and flesh and muscle from his body.

He stabbed and slashed, and at last it was still.

A bell was ringing, and it took him a while after he'd opened his eyes to tell where he was and what it was. He was strapped into the seat of his scouter, and the visiplate before him showed only empty space. No Outsider ship and no impossible planet.

The bell was the communications plate signal; someone wanted him to switch power into the receiver. Purely reflex action enabled him to reach forward and throw the lever.

The face of Brander, captain of the *Magellan*, mother-ship of his group of scouters, flashed into the screen. His face was pale and his black eyes glowing with excitement.

"*Magellan* to Carson," he snapped. "Come on in. The fight's over. We've won!"

The screen went blank; Brander would be signaling the other scouters of his command.

Slowly, Carson set the controls for the return. Slowly, unbelievingly, he unstrapped himself from the seat and went back to get a drink at the cold-water tank. For some reason, he was unbelievably thirsty. He drank six glasses.

He leaned there against the wall, trying to think.

Had it happened? He was in good health, sound, uninjured. His thirst had been mental rather than physical; his throat hadn't been dry. His leg—

He pulled up his trouser leg and looked at the calf. There was a long white scar there, but a perfectly healed scar. It hadn't been there before. He zipped open the front of his shirt and saw that his chest and abdomen were criss-crossed with tiny, almost unnoticeable, perfectly healed scars.

It *had* happened.

The scouter, under automatic control, was already entering the hatch of the mother-ship. The grapples pulled it into its individual lock, and a moment later a buzzer indicated that the lock was air-filled. Carson opened the hatch and stepped outside, went through the double door of the lock.

He went right to Brander's office, went in, and saluted.

Brander still looked dizzily dazed. "Hi, Carson," he said. "What you missed! What a show!"

"What happened, sir?"

"Don't know, exactly. We fired one salvo, and their whole fleet went up in dust! Whatever it was jumped from ship to ship in a flash, even the ones we hadn't aimed at and that were out of range! The whole fleet disintegrated before our eyes, and we didn't get the paint of a single ship scratched!

"We can't even claim credit for it. Must have been some unstable component in the metal they used, and our sighting shot just set it off. Man, oh man, too bad you missed all the excitement."

Carson managed to grin. It was a sickly ghost of a grin, for it would be days before he'd be over the mental impact of his experience, but the captain wasn't watching, and didn't notice.

"Yes, sir," he said. Common sense, more than modesty, told him he'd be branded forever as the worst liar in space if he ever said any more than that. "Yes, sir, too bad I missed all the excitement."

Imagine

IMAGINE ghosts, gods and devils.

Imagine hells and heavens, cities floating in the sky and cities sunken in the sea.

Unicorns and centaurs. Witches, warlocks, jinns and banshees.

Angels and harpies. Charms and incantations. Elementals, familiars, demons.

Easy to imagine, all of those things: mankind has been imagining them for thousands of years.

Imagine spaceships and the future.

Easy to imagine; the future is really coming and there'll be spaceships in it.

Is there then anything that's *hard* to imagine?

Of course there is.

Imagine a piece of matter and yourself inside it, yourself aware, thinking and therefore knowing you exist, able to move that piece of matter that you're in, to make it sleep or wake, make love or walk uphill.

Imagine a universe—infinite or not, as you wish to picture it—with a billion, billion, billion suns in it.

Imagine a blob of mud whirling madly around one of those suns.

Imagine yourself standing on that blob of mud, whirling with it, whirling through time and space to an unknown destination.

Imagine!

It Didn't Happen

ALTHOUGH there was no way in which he could have known it, Lorenz Kane had been riding for a fall ever since the time he ran over the girl on the bicycle. The fall itself could have happened anywhere, any time; it happened to happen backstage at a burlesque theater on an evening in late September.

For the third evening within a week he had watched the act of Queenie Quinn, the show's star stripper, an act well worth watching, indeed. Clad only in blue light and three tiny bits of strategically placed ribbon, Queenie, a tall blond built along the lines of a brick whatsit, had just completed her last stint for the evening and had vanished into the wings, when Kane made up his mind that a private viewing of Queenie's act, in his bachelor apartment, not only would be more pleasurable than a public viewing but would indubitably lead to even greater pleasures. And since the finale number, in which Queenie, as the star, was not required to appear, was just starting, now would be the best time to talk to her with a view toward obtaining a private viewing.

He left the theater and strolled down the alley to the stage door entrance. A five-dollar bill got him past the doorman without difficulty and a minute later he had found and was knocking upon a dressing room door decorated with a gold star. A voice called out "Yeah?" He knew better than to try to push a proposition through a closed door and he knew his way around backstage well enough to know the one question that would cause her to assume that he was someone connected with show business who had a legitimate reason for wanting to see her. "Are you decent?" he asked.

"'Sta minute," she called back, and then, in just a minute, "Okay."

He entered and found her standing facing him, in a bright

red wrapper that beautifully set off her blue eyes and blond hair. He bowed and introduced himself, then began to explain the details of the proposition he wished to offer.

He was prepared for initial reluctance or even refusal and ready to become persuasive even, if necessary, to the extent of four figures, which would certainly be more than her weekly take—possibly more than her monthly take—in a burlesque house as small as this one. But instead of listening reasonably, she was suddenly screaming at him like a virago, which was insulting enough, but then she made the very serious mistake of taking a step forward and slapping him across the face. Hard. It hurt.

He lost his temper, retreated a step, took out his revolver and shot her in the heart.

Then he left the theater and took a taxi home to his apartment. He had a few drinks to soothe his understandably ruffled nerves and went to bed. He was sleeping soundly when, at a little after midnight, the police came and arrested him for murder. He couldn't understand it.

Mortimer Mearson, who was possibly if not certainly the best criminal attorney in the city, returned to the clubhouse the next morning after an early round of golf and found waiting for him a message requesting him to call Judge Amanda Hayes at his earliest convenience. He called her at once.

"Good morning, Your Honoress," he said. "Something gives?"

"Something gives, Morty. But if you're free the rest of the morning and can drop around to my chambers, you'll save me going into it over the telephone."

"I'll be with you within an hour," he told her. And he was.

"Good morning again, Your Judgeship," he said. "Now please take a deep breath and tell me just what it is that gives."

"A case for you, if you want it. Succinctly, a man was arrested for murder last night. He refuses to make a statement, any statement, until he has consulted an attorney, and he doesn't have one. Says he's never been in any legal trouble before and doesn't even know any attorneys. Asked the chief to recommend one, and the chief passes the buck to me on said recommendation."

Mearson sighed. "Another free case. Well, I suppose it's about time I took one again. Are you appointing me?"

"Down, boy," said Judge Hayes. "Not a free case at all. The

gentleman in question isn't rich, but he's reasonably well-heeled. A fairly well-known young man about town, *bon vivant*, what have you, well able to afford any fee you wish to charge him, within reason. Not that your fee will probably *be* within reason, but that's between you and him, if he accepts you to represent him."

"And does this paragon of virtue—most obviously innocent and maligned—have a name?"

"He does, and you will be familiar with it if you read the columnists. Lorenz Kane."

"The name registers. Most *obviously* innocent. Uh—I didn't see the morning papers. Whom is he alleged to have killed? And do you know any of the details?"

"It's going to be a toughie, Morty boy," the judge said. "I don't think there's a prayer of a chance for him other than an insanity plea. The victim was a Queenie Quinn—a stage name and no doubt a more valid one will come to light—who was a stripper at the Majestic. Star of the show there. A number of people saw Kane in the audience during her last number and saw him leave right after it during the final number. The doorman identifies him and admits having—ah—admitted him. The doorman knew him by sight and that's what led the police to him. He passed the doorman again on his way out a few minutes later. Meanwhile several people heard a shot. And a few minutes after the end of the show, Miss Quinn was found dead, shot to death, in her dressing room."

"Hmmm," said Mearson. "Simple matter of his word against the doorman's. Nothing to it. I'll be able to prove that the doorman is not only a pathological liar but has a record longer than Wilt-the-Stilt's arm."

"Indubitably, Morty. But. In view of his relative prominence, the police took a search warrant as well as a warrant for arrest on suspicion of murder when they went to get him. They found, in the pocket of the suit he had been wearing, a thirty-two caliber revolver with one cartridge fired. Miss Quinn was killed by one bullet fired from a thirty-two caliber revolver. The very *same* revolver, according to the ballistics experts of our police department, who fired a sample bullet and used a comparison microscope on it and the bullet which killed Miss Quinn."

"Hmmm and double hmm," Mearson said. "And you say that Kane has made no statement whatsoever except to the effect that he will make no statement until he has consulted with an attorney of his choice?"

"True, except for one rather strange remark he made immediately after being awakened and accused. Both of the arresting officers heard it and agree on it, even to the exact wording. He said, 'My God, she must have been real!' What do you suppose he could possibly have meant by that?"

"I haven't the faintest, Your Judgeship. But if he accepts me as his attorney, I shall most certainly ask him. Meanwhile, I don't know whether to thank you for giving me a chance at the case or to cuss at you for handing me a very damned hot potato."

"You like hot potatoes, Morty, and you know it. Especially since you'll get your fee win or lose. I'll save you from making wasted motions in one direction, though. No use trying for bail or for a habeas corpus writ. The D.A. jumped in with both feet the moment the ballistics report came up heads. The charge is formal, murder in the first. And the prosecution doesn't need any more case than they have; they're ready to go to trial as soon as they can pressure you into it. Well, what are you waiting for?"

"Nothing," Mearson said. He left.

A guard brought Lorenz Kane to the consultation room and left him there with Mortimer Mearson. Mearson introduced himself and they shook hands. Kane, Mearson thought, looked quite calm, and definitely more puzzled than worried. He was a tall, moderately good-looking man in his late thirties, impeccably groomed despite a night in a cell. One got the idea that he was the type of man who would manage to appear impeccably groomed anywhere, any time, even a week after his bearers had deserted in midsafari nine hundred miles up the Congo, taking all his possessions with them.

"Yes, Mr. Mearson. I shall be more than glad to have you represent me. I've heard of you, read about cases you've handled. I don't know why I didn't think of you myself, instead of asking for a recommendation. Now, do you want to hear my story before you accept me as a client—or do you accept as of now, for better or for worse?"

"For better or for worse," Mearson said, "till—" And then stopped himself; "till death do us part," is hardly a diplomatic phrase to use to a man who stands, quite possibly, in the shadow of the electric chair.

But Kane smiled and finished the phrase himself. "Fine," he said. "Let's sit down then," and they sat down on the two chairs, one on each side of the table in the consultation room. "And since that means we'll be seeing quite a bit of one another for a while, let's start on a first-name basis. But not Lorenz, in my case. It's Larry."

"And make mine Morty," Mearson said. "Now I want your story in detail, but two quick questions first. Are you—?"

"Wait," Kane interrupted him. "*One* quick question ahead of your two. Are you absolutely and completely positive that this room is not bugged, that this conversation is completely private?"

"I am," Mearson said. "Now my first question: are you guilty?"

"Yes."

"The arresting officers claim that before clamming up, you said one thing: 'My God, she must have been real!' Is that true, and if so what did you mean by it?"

"I was stunned at the moment, Morty, and can't remember—but I probably said something to that effect, because it's exactly what I was thinking. But as to what I meant by it—that's something I can't answer quickly. The only way I can make you understand, if I can make you understand at all, is to start at the beginning."

"All right. Start. And take your time. We don't have to go over everything in one sitting. I can stall the trial at least three months—longer if necessary."

"I can tell it fairly quickly. It started—and don't ask me for an antecedent for the pronoun *it*—five and a half months ago, in early April. About two-thirty A.M. on the morning of Tuesday, April the third, to be as nearly exact about it as I can. I had been at a party in Armand Village, north of town, and was on my way home. I—"

"Forgive interruptions. Want to be sure I have the whole picture as it unfolds. You were driving? Alone?"

"I was driving my Jag. I was alone."

"Sober? Speeding?"

"Sober, yes. I'd left the party relatively early—it was rather a dull bit—and had been feeling my drinks moderately at that

time. But I found myself suddenly quite hungry—I think I'd forgotten to eat dinner—and stopped at a roadhouse. I had one
cocktail while I was waiting, but I ate all of a big steak when it
came, all the trimmings, and had several cups of coffee. And no
drinks afterward. I'd say that when I left there I was more sober
than usual, if you know what I mean. And, on top of that, I had
half an hour's drive in an open car through the cool night air.
On the whole, I'd say that I was soberer than I am now—and I
haven't had a drink since shortly before midnight last night. I—"

"Hold it a moment," Mearson said. He took a silver flask from
his hip pocket and extended it across the table. "A relic of Prohibition; I occasionally use it to play St. Bernard to clients too
recently incarcerated to have been able to arrange for importa-
tion of the necessities of life."

Kane said, "Ahhh. Morty, you may double your fee for service beyond the call of duty." He drank deeply.

"Where were we?" he asked. "Oh, yes. I was definitely sober.
Speeding? Only technically. I was heading south on Vine Street
a few blocks short of Rostov—"

"Near the Forty-fourth Precinct Station."

"Exactly. It figures in. It's a twenty-five-mile zone and I was
going about forty, but what the hell, it was half-past two in the
morning and there wasn't any other traffic. Only the proverbial
little old lady from Pasadena would have been going *less* than
forty."

"She wouldn't have been out that late. But carry on."

"So all of a sudden out of the mouth of an alley in the middle
of the block comes a girl on a bicycle, pedaling about as fast as a
bicycle can go. And right in front of me. I got one clear flash of
her as I stepped on the brake as hard as I could. She was a teen-
ager, like sixteen or seventeen. She had red hair that was blowing out from under a brown babushka she had on her head. She
wore a light green angora sweater and tan pants of the kind they
call pedal pushers. She was on a red bicycle."

"You got all that in one glance?"

"Yes. I can still visualize it clearly. And—*this* I'll never forget
—just before the moment of impact, she turned and was looking
straight at me, through frightened eyes behind shell-rimmed
glasses.

"My foot was, by then, trying to push the brake pedal
through the floor and the damn Jag was starting to slue and

make up its mind whether to go end over end or what. But hell, no matter how fast your reactions are—and mine are pretty good —you can barely start to *slow down* a car in a few yards if you're going forty. I must have still been going over thirty when I hit her—it was a *hell* of an impact.

"And then bump-crunch, bump-crunch, as first the front wheels of the Jag went over and then the back wheels. The bumps were *her,* of course, and the crunches were the bicycle. And the car shuddered to a stop maybe another thirty feet on.

"Ahead of me, through the windshield, I could see the lights of the precinct station only a block away. I got out of the car and started running for it. I didn't look back. I didn't *want* to look back. There was no point to it; she had to be deader than dead, after that impact.

"I ran into the precinct house and after a few seconds I got coherent enough to get across what I was trying to tell them. Two of the city's finest left with me and we started back the block to the scene of the accident. I started out by running, but they only walked fast and I slowed myself down because I wasn't anxious to get there first. Well, we got there and—"

"Let me guess," the attorney said. "No girl, no bicycle."

Kane nodded slowly. "There was the Jag, slued crooked in the street. Headlights on. Ignition key still on, but the engine had stalled. Behind it, about forty feet of skid marks, starting a dozen feet back of the point where the alley cut out into the street.

"And that was all. No girl. No bicycle. Not a drop of blood or a scrap of metal. Not a scratch or a dent in the front of the car. They thought I was crazy and I don't blame them. They didn't even trust me to get the car off the street; one of them did that and parked it at the curb—and kept the key instead of handing it to me—and they took me back to the station house and questioned me.

"I was there the rest of the night. I suppose I could have called a friend and had the friend get me an attorney to get me out on bail, but I was just too shaken to think of it. Maybe even too shaken to *want* out, to have any idea where I'd want to go or what I'd want to do if I got out. I just wanted to be alone to think and, after the questioning, a chance to do that was just what I got. They didn't toss me into the drunk tank. Guess I was well enough dressed, had enough impressive identification on me, to convince them that, sane or nuts, I was a solid and solvent citizen, to be handled with kid gloves and not rubber hose. Anyway, they had a single cell open and put me in it and I was comtent to do my thinking there. I didn't even try to sleep.

"The next morning they had a police head shrinker come in to talk to me. By that time I'd simmered down to the point where I realized that, whatever the score was, the police weren't going to be any help to me and the sooner I got out of their hands the better. So I conned the head shrinker a bit by starting to play my story down instead of telling it straight. I left out sound effects, like the crunching of the bicycle being run over and I left out kinetic sensations, feeling the impact and the bumps, gave it to him as what could have been purely a sudden and momentary *visual* hallucination. He bought it after a while, and they let me go."

Kane stopped talking long enough to take a pull at the silver flask and then asked, "With me so far? And, whether you believe me or not, any questions to date?"

"Just one," the attorney said. "Are you, can you be, positive that your experience with the police at the Forty-fourth is objective and verifiable? In other words, if this comes to a trial and we should decide on an insanity defense, can I call as witnesses the policemen who talked to you, and the police psychiatrist?"

Kane grinned a little crookedly. "To me my experience with the police is just as objective as my running over the girl on the bicycle. But at least you can verify the former. See if it's on the blotter and if they remember it. Dig?"

"I'm hip. Carry on."

"So the police were satisfied that I'd had an hallucination. I damn well wasn't. I did several things. I had a garage run the Jag up on a rack and I went over the underside of it, as well as the front. No sign. Okay, it hadn't happened, as far as the *car* was concerned.

"Second, I wanted to know if a girl of that description, living or dead, had been out on a bicycle that night. I spent several thousand dollars with a private detective agency, having them canvass that neighborhood—and a fair area around it—with a fine-tooth comb to find if a girl answering that description currently or ever had existed, with or without a red bicycle. They came up with a few possible red-headed teenagers, but I managed to get a gander at each of them, no dice.

"*And,* after asking around, I picked a head shrinker of my own and started going to him. Allegedly the best in the city, certainly the most expensive. Went to him for two months. It was a washout. I never found out what he thought had happened; he wouldn't talk. You know how psychoanalysts work, they make you do the talking, analyze yourself, and finally tell them what's wrong with you, then you yak about it awhile and tell them you're cured, and they then agree with you and tell you to go with God. All right if your subconscious knows what the score is and eventually lets it leak out. But my subconscious didn't know which end was up, so I was wasting my time, and I quit.

"But meanwhile I'd leveled with a few friends of mine to get their ideas and one of them—a professor of philosophy at the university—started talking about ontology and that started me reading up on ontology and gave me a clue. In fact, I thought it was more than a clue, I thought it was the *answer.* Until last night. Since last night I know I was at least partly wrong."

"Ontology—" said Mearson. "Word's vaguely familiar, but will you pin it down for me?"

"I quote you the *Webster Unabridged,* unexpurgated version: 'Ontology is the science of being or reality; the branch of knowledge that investigates the nature, essential properties, and relations of being, as such.'"

Kane glanced at his wrist watch. "But this is taking longer to tell than I thought. I'm getting tired talking and no doubt you're even more tired of listening. Shall we finish this tomorrow?"

"An excellent idea, Larry." Mearson stood up.

Kane tilted the silver flask for the last drop and handed it back. "You'll play St. Bernard again?"

"I went to the Forty-fourth," Mearson said. "The incident you described to me is on the blotter all right. And I talked to one of the two coppers who went back with you to the scene of the—uh—back to the car. Your *reporting* of the accident was real, no question of that."

"I'll start where I left off," Kane said. "Ontology, the study of the nature of reality. In reading up on it I came across solipsism, which originated with the Greeks. It is the belief that the entire universe is the product of one's imagination—in my case, *my* imagination. That I myself am the only concrete reality and that all things and all other people exist only in my mind."

Mearson frowned. "So, then the girl on the bicycle, having only an imaginary existence to begin with, ceased to exist—uh, *retroactively*, as of the moment you killed her? Leaving no trace behind her, except a memory in your mind, of ever having existed?"

"That possibility occurred to me, and I decided to do something which I thought would verify or disprove it. Specifically, to commit a murder, deliberately, to see what would happen."

"But—but Larry, murders happen every day, people are killed every day, and don't vanish retroactively and leave no trace behind them."

"But they were not killed by *me*," Kane said earnestly. "And if the universe *is* a product of my imagination, that should make a difference. The girl on the bicycle is the first person *I* ever killed."

Mearson sighed. "So you decided to check by committing a murder. And shot Queenie Quinn. But why didn't she—?"

"No, no, no," Kane interrupted. "I committed another first, a month or so ago. A man. A man—and there's no use my telling you his name or anything about him because, as of now, he never existed, like the girl on the bicycle.

"But of course I didn't *know* it would happen that way, so I didn't simply kill him openly, as I did the stripper. I took careful precautions, so if his body *had* been found, the police would never have apprehended *me* as the killer.

"But after I killed him, well—he just never had existed, and I thought that my theory was confirmed. After that I carried a gun, thinking that I could kill with impunity any time I wanted to—and that it wouldn't matter, wouldn't be immoral even, because anyone I killed didn't really exist anyway except in my mind."

"Ummm," said Mearson.

"Ordinarily, Morty," Kane said, "I'm a pretty eventempered guy. Night before last was the first time I used the gun. When that damn stripper hit me she hit *hard*, a roundhouse swing. It blinded me for the moment and I just reacted automatically in pulling out the gun and shooting her."

"Ummm," the attorney said. "And Queenie Quinn turned out to be for real and you're in jail for murder and doesn't that blow your solipsism theory sky-high?"

Kane frowned. "It certainly modifies it. I've been thinking a lot since I was arrested, and here's what I've come up with. If Queenie was real—and obviously she was—then I was not, and probably am not, the *only* real person. There are real people and unreal ones, ones that exist only in the imagination of the real ones.

"How many, I don't know. Maybe only a few, maybe thousands, even millions. My sampling—three people, of whom one turned out to have been real—is too small to be significant."

"But why? Why should there be a duality like that?"

"I haven't the faintest idea." Kane frowned. "I've had some pretty wild thoughts, but any one of them would be just a guess. Like a conspiracy—but a conspiracy against *whom?* Or *what?* And *all* of the real ones couldn't be in on the conspiracy, because I'm not."

He chuckled without humor. "I had a really far-out dream about it last night, one of those confused, mixed-up dreams that you can't really tell anybody, because they have no continuity, just a series of impressions. Something about a conspiracy and a *reality file* that lists the names of all the *real* people and keeps them real. And—here's a dream pun for you—reality is really run by a chain, only they're not known to be a chain, of *reality* companies, one in each city. Of course they deal in real estate too, as a front. And—oh hell, it's all too confused even to try to tell.

"Well, Morty, that's it. And my guess is that you'll tell me my only defense is an insanity plea—and you'll be right because, damn it, if I *am* sane I *am* a murderer. First degree and without extenuating circumstances. So?"

"So," said Mearson. He doodled a moment with a gold pencil and then looked up. "The head shrinker you went to for a while —his name wasn't Galbraith, was it?"

Kane shook his head.

"Good. Doc Galbraith is a friend of mine and the best forensic psychiatrist in the city, maybe in the country. Has worked with me on a dozen cases and we've won all of them. I'd like his opinion before I even start to map out a defense. Will you talk to him, be completely frank with him, if I send him around to see you?"

"Of course. Uh—will you ask him to do me a favor?"

"Probably. What is it?"

"Lend him your flask and ask him to bring it filled. You've no idea how much more nearly pleasant it makes these interviews."

The intercom on Mortimer Mearson's desk buzzed and he pressed the button on it that would bring his secretary's voice in. "Dr. Galbraith to see you, sir." Mearson told her to send him in at once.

"Hi, Doc," Mearson said. "Take a load off your feet and tell all."

Galbraith took the load off his feet and lighted a cigarette before he spoke. "Puzzling for a while," he said. "I didn't get the answer till I went into medical history with him. While playing polo at age twenty-two he had a fall and got a whop on the head with a mallet that caused a bad concussion and subsequent amnesia. Complete at first, but gradually his memory came back completely up to early adolescence. Pretty spotty between then and the time of the injury."

"Good God, the indoctrination period."

"Exactly. Oh, he has flashes—like the dream he told you about. He could be rehabilitated—but I'm afraid it's too late, now. If only we'd caught him before he committed an overt murder—But we can't possibly risk putting his story on record now, even as an insanity defense. So."

"So," Mearson said. "I'll make the call now. And then go see him again. Hate to, but it's got to be done."

He pushed a button on the intercom. "Dorothy, get me Mr. Hodge at the Midland Realty Company. When you get him, put the call on my private line."

Galbraith left while he was waiting and a moment later one of his phones rang and he picked it up. "Hodge?" he said, "Mearson here. Your phone secure? . . . Good. Code eighty-four. Remove the card of Lorenz Kane—L-o-r-e-n-z K-a-n-e—from the reality file at once . . . Yes, it's necessary and an emergency. I'll submit a report tomorrow."

He took a pistol from a desk drawer and a taxi to the courthouse. He arranged an audience with his client and as soon as Kane came through the door—there was no use waiting—he shot him dead. He waited the minute it always took for the body to vanish, and then went upstairs to the chambers of Judge Amanda Hayes to make a final check.

"Hi, Your Honoress," he said. "Somebody recently was telling me about a man named Lorenz Kane, and I don't remember who it was. Was it you?"

"Never heard the name, Morty. It wasn't me."

"You mean 'It wasn't I.' Must've been someone else. Thanks, Your Judgeship. Be seeing you."

Recessional

THE KING my liege lord is a discouraged man. We understand
and do not blame him, for the war has been long and bitter and
there are so pathetically few of us left, yet we wish that it were
not so. We sympathize with him for having lost his Queen, and
we too all loved her—but since the Queen of the Blacks died
with her, her loss does not mean the loss of the war. Yet our
King, he who should be a tower of strength, smiles weakly and
his words of attempted encouragement to us ring false in our
ears because we hear in his voice the undertones of fear and de-
feat. Yet we love him and we die for him, one by one.

One by one we die in his defense, here upon this blooded bitter field, churned muddy by the horses of the Knights—while
they lived; they are dead now, both ours and the Black ones—
and will there be an end, a victory?

We can only have faith, and never become cynics and here-
tics, like my poor fellow Bishop Tibault. "We fight and die; we
know not why," he once whispered to me, earlier in the war at a
time when we stood side by side defending our King while the
battle raged in a far corner of the field.

But that was only the beginning of his heresy. He had
stopped believing in a God and had come to believe in gods,
gods who play a game with us and care nothing for us as persons. Worse, he believed that our moves are not our own, that
we are but puppets fighting in a useless war. Still worse—and
how absurd!—that White is not necessarily good and Black is not
necessarily evil, that on the cosmic scale it does not matter who
wins the war!

Of course it was only to me, and only in whispers, that he said
these things. He knew his duties as a bishop. He fought bravely.
And died bravely, that very day, impaled upon the lance of a

Black Knight. I prayed for him: *God, rest his soul and grant him peace; he meant not what he said.*

Without faith we are nothing. How could Tibault have been so wrong? White must win. Victory is the only thing that can save us. Without victory our companions who have died, those who here upon this embattled field have given their lives that we may live, shall have died in vain. *Et tu*, Tibault.

And you were wrong, so wrong. There is a God, and so great a God that He will forgive your heresy, because there was no evil in you, Tibault, except as doubt—no, doubt is error but it is not evil.

Without faith we are noth—

But something is happening! Our Rook, he who was on the Queen's side of the field in the Beginning, swoops toward the evil Black King, our enemy. The villainous one is under attack—and cannot escape. We have won! We have won!

A voice in the sky says calmly, "Checkmate."

We have won! The war, this bitter stricken field, was *not* in vain. Tibault, you were wrong, you were—

But what is happening now? The very Earth tilts; one side of the battlefield rises and we are sliding—White and Black alike—into—

—into a monstrous *box* and I see that it is a mass coffin in which already lie dead—

IT IS NOT FAIR; WE WON! GOD, WAS TIBAULT RIGHT? IT IS NOT JUST; WE WON!

The King, my liege lord, is sliding too across the squares—

IT IS NOT JUST; IT IS NOT *RIGHT*; IT IS NOT . . .

Eine Kleine Nachtmusik

(In collaboration with Carl Onspaugh)

His NAME was Dooley Hanks and he was One of Us, by which I mean that he was partly a paranoiac, partly a schizophrenic, and mostly a nut with a strong *idée fixe,* an obsession. His obsession was that someday he'd find The Sound that he'd been looking for all his life, or at least all of his life since twenty years ago, in his teens, when he had acquired a clarinet and learned how to play it. Truth to tell, he was only an average musician, but the clarinet was his rod and staff, and it was the broomstick that enabled him to travel over the face of Earth, on all the continents, seeking The Sound. Playing a gig here and a gig there, and then, when he was ahead by a few dollars or pounds or drachmas or rubles he'd take a walking tour until his money started to run out, then start for the nearest city big enough to let him find another gig.

He didn't know what The Sound would sound like, but he knew that he'd know it when he heard it. Three times he'd *thought* he'd found it. Once, in Australia, the first time he'd heard a bull-roarer. Once, in Calcutta, in the sound of a musette played by a fakir to charm a cobra. And once, west of Nairobi, in the blending of a hyena's laughter with the voice of a lion. But the bull-roarer, on second hearing, was just a noise; the musette, when he'd bought it from the fakir for twenty rupees and had taken it home, had turned out to be only a crude and raucous type of reed instrument with little range and not even a chromatic scale; the jungle sounds had resolved themselves finally into simple lion roars and hyena laughs, not at all The Sound.

Actually Dooley Hanks had a great and rare talent that could have meant much more to him than his clarinet, a gift of tongues. He knew dozens of languages and spoke them all fluently, idiomatically and without accent. A few weeks in any country was enough for him to pick up the language and speak it like a native. But he had never tried to cash in on this talent, and never would. Mediocre player though he was, the clarinet was his love.

Currently, the language he had just mastered was German, picked up in three weeks of playing with a combo in a beer-*stube* in Hannover, West Germany. And the money in his pocket, such as it was, was in marks. And at the end of a day of hiking, augmented by one fairly long lift in a Volkswagen, he stood in moonlight on the banks of the Weser River. Wearing his hiking clothes and with his working clothes, his good suit, in a haversack on his back. His clarinet case in his hand; he always carried it so, never trusting it to suitcase, when he used one, or to haversack when he was hiking.

Driven by a demon, and feeling suddenly an excitement that must be, that could only be, a hunch, a feeling that at long last he was really about to find The Sound. He was trembling a little; he'd never had the hunch this strongly before, not even with the lions and the hyenas, and that had been the closest.

But where? Here, in the water? Or in the next town? Surely not farther than the next town. The hunch was that strong. That tremblingly strong. Like the verge of madness, and suddenly he knew that he *would* go mad if he did not find it soon. Maybe he was a little mad already.

Staring over moonlit water. And suddenly something disrupted its surface, flashed silently white in the moonlight and was gone again. Dooley stared at the spot. A fish? There had been no sound, no splash. A hand? The hand of a mermaid swum upstream from the North Sea beckoning him? Come in, the water's fine. (But it wouldn't be; it was *cold*.) Some supernatural water sprite? A displaced Rhine Maiden in the Weser?

But was it really a sign? Dooley, shivering now at the thought of what he was thinking, stood at the Weser's edge and imagined how it would be . . . wading out slowly from the bank, letting his emotions create the tune for the clarinet, tilting his head back as the water became deeper so that the instrument would stick out of the water after he, Dooley, was under it, the bell of the clarinet last to submerge. And the sound, whatever sound there was, being made by the bubbling water closing over them. Over him first and then the clarinet. He recalled the clichéd allegation, which he had previously viewed with iconoclastic contempt but now felt almost ready to accept, that a drowning person was treated to a swift viewing of his entire life as it flashed before his eyes in a grand finale to living. What a mad montage that would be! What an inspiration for the final gurglings of the clarinet. What a frantic blending of the whole of his wild, sweetly sad, tortured existence, just as his straining lungs expelled their final gasp into a final note and inhaled the cold, dark water. A shudder of breathless anticipation coursed through Dooley Hanks's body as his fingers trembled with the catch on the battered clarinet case.

But *no*, he told himself. Who would hear? Who would know? It was important that someone hear. Otherwise his quest, his discovery, his entire life would be in vain. Immortality cannot be derived from one's solitary knowledge of one's greatness. And what good was The Sound if it brought him death and not immortality?

A blind alley. Another blind alley. Perhaps the next town. Yes, the next town. His hunch was coming back now. How had he been so foolish as to think of drowning? To find The Sound, he'd kill if he had to—but not himself. That would make the whole gig meaningless.

Feeling as one who had had a narrow escape, he turned and walked away from the river, back to the road that paralleled it, and started walking toward the lights of the next town. Although Dooley Hanks had no Indian blood that he knew of, he walked like an Indian, one foot directly in front of the other, as though on a tightrope. And silently, or as nearly silently as was possible in hiking boots, the ball of his foot coming down first to cushion each step before his heel touched the roadway. And he walked rapidly because it was still early evening and he'd have plenty of time, after checking in at a hotel and getting rid of his haversack, to explore the town awhile before they rolled up the sidewalks. A fog was starting to roll in now.

The narrowness of his escape from the suicidal impulse on the Weser's bank still worried him. He'd had it before, but never quite so strongly. The last time had been in New York, on top of the Empire State Building, over a hundred stories above the street. It had been a bright, clear day, and the magic of the view had enthralled him. And suddenly he had been seized by the same mad exultation, certain that a flash of inspiration had

ended his quest, placed the goal at his fingertips. All he need do
was take his clarinet from the case, assemble it. The magic view
would be revealed in the first clear notes of the instrument and
the heads of the other sightseers would turn in wonder. Then
the contrasting gasp as he leaped into space, and the wailing,
sighing, screaming notes, as he hurled pavementward, the
weird melody inspired by the whirling color scene of the street
and sidewalk and people watching in horrified fascination,
watching him, Dooley Hanks, and hearing The Sound, his
sound, as it built into a superb fortissimo, the grand finale of his
greatest solo—the harsh final note as his body slammed into the
sidewalk and fused flesh, blood and splintered bone with concrete, forcing a final, glorious expulsion of breath through the
clarinet just before it left his lifeless fingers. But he'd saved himself by turning back and running for the exit and the elevator.

He didn't want to die. He'd have to keep reminding himself
of that. No other price would be too great to pay.

He was well into town now. In an old section with dark, narrow streets and ancient buildings. The fog curled in from the
river like a giant serpent hugging the street at first, then swelling
and rising slowly to blot and blur his vision. But through it,
across the cobbled street, he saw a lighted hotel sign, *Unter den
Linden*. A pretentious name for so small a hotel, but it looked
inexpensive and that was what he wanted. It was inexpensive all
right and he took a room and carried his haversack up to it. He
hesitated whether to change from his walking clothes to his good
suit, and decided not to. He wouldn't be looking for an engage-
ment tonight; tomorrow would be time for that. But he'd carry
his clarinet, of course; he always did. He hoped he'd find a place
to meet other musicians, maybe be asked to sit in with them.
And of course he'd ask them about the best way to obtain a gig
here. The carrying of an instrument case is an automatic introduction among musicians. In Germany, or anywhere.

Passing the desk on his way out he asked the clerk—a man
who looked fully as old as the hostelry itself—for directions toward the center of town, the lively spots. Outside, he started in
the direction the old man had indicated, but the streets were so
crooked, the fog so thick, that he was lost within a few blocks
and no longer knew even the direction from which he had come.
So he wandered on aimlessly and in another few blocks found
himself in an eerie neighborhood. This eeriness, without observ-

able cause, unnerved him and for a panicked moment he started to run to get through the district as fast as he could, but then he stopped short as he suddenly became aware of music in the air—a weird, haunting whisper of music that, after he had listened to it a long moment, drew him along the dark street in search of its source. It seemed to be a single instrument playing, a reed instrument that didn't sound exactly like a clarinet or exactly like an oboe. It grew louder, then faded again. He looked in vain for a light, a movement, some clue to its birthplace. He turned to retrace his steps, walking on tiptoe now, and the music grew louder again. A few more steps and again it faded and Dooley retraced those few steps and paused to scan the somber, brooding building. There was no light behind any window. But the music was all around him now and—could it be coming up from below? Up from under the sidewalk?

He took a step toward the building, and saw what he had not seen before. Parallel to the building front, open and unprotected by a railing, a flight of worn stone steps led downward. And at the bottom of them, a yellow crack of light outlined three sides of a door. From behind that door came the music. And, he could now hear, voices in conversation.

He descended the steps cautiously and hesitated before the door, wondering whether he should knock or simply open it and walk in. Was it, despite the fact that he had not seen a sign anywhere, a public place? One so well-known to its habitués that no sign was needed? Or perhaps a private party where he would be an intruder?

He decided to let the question of whether the door would or would not turn out to be locked against him answer that question. He put his hand on the latch and it opened to his touch and he stepped inside.

The music reached out and embraced him tenderly. The place *looked* like a public place, a wine cellar. At the far end of a large room there were three huge wine tuns with spigots. There were tables and people, men and women both, seated at them. All with wineglasses in front of them. No steins; apparently only wine was served. A few people glanced at him, but disinterestedly and not with the look one gave an intruder, so obviously it was not a private party.

The musician—there was just one—was in a far corner of the room, sitting on a high stool. The room was almost as thick with smoke as the street had been thick with fog and Dooley's eyes weren't any too good anyway; from that distance he couldn't tell if the musician's instrument was a clarinet or an oboe or neither. Any more than his ears could answer that same question, even now, in the same room.

He closed the door behind him, and weaved his way through the tables, looking for an empty one as close to the musician as possible. He found one not too far away and sat down at it. He began to study the instrument with his eyes as well as his ears. It looked familiar. He'd seen one like it or almost like it somewhere, but where?

"*Ja, mein Herr?*" It was whispered close to his ear, and he turned. A fat little waiter in lederhosen stood at his elbow. "Zinfandel? Burgundy? Riesling?"

Dooley knew nothing about wines and cared less, but he named one of the three. And as the waiter tiptoed away, he put a little pile of marks on the table so he wouldn't have to interrupt himself again when the wine came.

Then he studied the instrument again, trying for the moment *not* to listen to it, so he could concentrate on where he'd once seen something like it. It was about the length of his clarinet, with a slightly larger, more flaring bell. It was made—all in one piece, as far as he could tell—of some dark rich wood somewhere in color between dark walnut and mahogany, highly polished. It had finger holes and only three keys, two at the bottom to extend the range downward by two semitones, and a thumb-operated one at the top that would be an octave key.

He closed his eyes, and would have closed his ears had they operated that way, to concentrate on remembering where he'd seen something very like it. Where?

It came to him gradually. A museum, somewhere. Probably in New York, because he'd been born and raised there, hadn't left there until he was twenty-four, and this was longer ago than that, like when he was still in his teens. Museum of Natural Science? That part didn't matter. There had been a room or several rooms of glass cases displaying ancient and medieval musical instruments: viola da gambas and viola d'amores, sackbuts and panpipes and recorders, lutes and tambours and fifes. And one glass case had held only shawms and hautboys, both precursors of the modern oboe. And this instrument, the one to which he was listening now in thrall, was a hautboy. You could distin-

guish the shawms because they had globular mouthpieces with
the reeds down inside; the hautboy was a step between the
shawm and the oboe. And the hautboy had come in various
stages of development from no keys at all, just finger holes, to
half a dozen or so keys. And yes, there'd been a three-keyed version, identical to this one except that it had been light wood instead of dark. Yes, it had been in his teens, in his early teens,
that he'd seen it, while he was a freshman in high school. Because he was just getting interested in music and hadn't yet got
his first clarinet; he'd still been trying to decide which instrument he wanted to play. That's why the ancient instruments
and their history had fascinated him for a brief while. There'd
been a book about them in the high-school library and he'd read
it. It had said— Good God, it had said that the hautboy had a
coarse tone in the lower register and was shrill on the high
notes! A flat lie, if this instrument was typical. It was smooth as
honey throughout its range; it had a rich full-bodied tone infinitely more pleasing than the thin reediness of an oboe. Better
even than a clarinet; only in its lower, or chalumeau, register
could a clarinet even approach it.

And Dooley Hanks knew with certainty that he had to have
an instrument like that, and that he *would* have one, no matter
what he had to pay or do to get it.

And with that decision irrevocably made, and with the music
still caressing him like a woman and exciting him as no woman
had ever excited him, Dooley opened his eyes. And since his
head had tilted forward while he had concentrated, the first
thing he saw was the very large goblet of red wine that had been
placed in front of him. He picked it up and, looking over it,
managed to catch the musician's eye; Dooley raised the glass in a
silent toast and downed the wine in a single draught.

When he lowered his head after drinking—the wine had
tasted unexpectedly good—the musician had turned slightly on
the stool and was facing another direction. Well, that gave him
a chance to study the man. The musician was tall but thin and
frail looking. His age was indeterminate; it could have been anywhere from forty to sixty. He was somewhat seedy in appearance; his thread-bare coat did not match his baggy trousers and a
garish red and yellow striped muffler hung loosely around his
scrawny neck, which had a prominent Adam's apple that bobbed
every time he took a breath to play. His tousled hair needed cut-

ting, his face was thin and pinched, and his eyes so light a blue
that they looked faded. Only his fingers bore the mark of a
master musician, long and slim and gracefully tapered. They
danced nimbly in time with the wondrous music they shaped.

Then with a final skirl of high notes that startled Dooley because they went at least half an octave above what he'd thought
was the instrument's top range and still had the rich resonance
of the lower register, the music stopped.

There were a few seconds of what seemed almost stunned silence, and then applause started and grew. Dooley went with it,
and his palms started to smart with pain. The musician, staring
straight ahead, didn't seem to notice. And after less than thirty
seconds he again raised the instrument to his mouth and the applause died suddenly to silence with the first note he played.

Dooley felt a gentle touch on his shoulder and looked around.
The fat little waiter was back. This time he didn't even whisper,
just raised his eyebrows interrogatorily. When he'd left with the
empty wineglass, Dooley closed his eyes again and gave full attention to the music.

Music? Yes, it was music, but not any *kind* of music he'd ever
heard before. Or it was a blend of *all* kinds of music, ancient
and modern, jazz and classical, a masterful blend of paradoxes or
maybe he meant opposites, sweet and bitter, ice and fire, soft
breezes and raging hurricanes, love and hate.

Again when he opened his eyes a filled glass was in front of
him. This time he sipped slowly at it. How on Earth had he
missed wine all his life? Oh, he'd drunk an occasional glass, but
it had never tasted like this wine. Or was it the music that made
it taste this way?

The music stopped and again he joined in the hearty applause. This time the musician got down from the stool and ac-
knowledged the applause briefly with a jerky little bow, and
then, tucking his instrument under his arm, he walked rapidly
across the room—unfortunately not passing near Dooley's table—
with an awkward forward-leaning gait. Dooley turned his head
to follow with his eyes. The musician sat down at a very small
table, a table for one, since it had only one chair, against the opposite wall. Dooley considered taking his own chair over, but decided against it. Apparently the guy wanted to sit alone or he
wouldn't have taken that particular table.

Dooley looked around till he caught the little waiter's eye and

signaled to him. When he came, Dooley asked him to take a
glass of wine to the musician, and also to ask the man if he
would care to join him at Dooley's table, to tell him that Dooley
too was a musician and would like to get to know him.

"I don't think he will," the waiter told him. "People have
tried before and he always politely refused. As for the wine, it is
not necessary; several times an evening we pass a hat for him.
Someone is starting to do so now, and you may contribute that
way if you wish."

"I wish," Dooley told him. "But take him the wine and give
him my message anyway, please."

"*Ja, mein Herr.*"

The waiter collected a mark in advance and then went to one
of the three tuns and drew a glass of wine and took it to the musician. Dooley, watching, saw the waiter put the glass on the
musician's table and, talking, point toward Dooley. So there
would be no mistake, Dooley stood up and made a slight bow in
their direction.

The musician stood also and bowed back, slightly more deeply
and from the waist. But then he turned back to his table and sat
down again and Dooley knew his first advance had been declined. Well, there'd be other chances, and other evenings. So,
only slightly discomfited, he sat back down again and took another sip of his wine. Yes, even without the music, or at any rate
with only the aftereffects of the music, it still tasted wonderful.

The hat came, "For the musician," passed by a stolid red-
faced burgher, and Dooley, seeing no large bills in it and not
wishing to make himself conspicuous, added two marks from his
little pile on the table.

Then he saw a couple getting up to leave from a table for two
directly in front of the stool upon which the musician sat to
play. Ah, just what he wanted. Quickly finishing his drink and
gathering up his change and his clarinet, he moved over to the
ringside table as the couple walked away. Not only could he see
and hear better, but he was in the ideal spot to intercept the musician with a personal invitation after the next set. And instead
of putting it on the floor he put his clarinet case on the table in
plain sight, to let the man know that he was not only a fellow
musician, which could mean almost anything, but a fellow
woodwind player.

A few minutes later he got a chance to signal for another glass of wine and when it was brought he held the little waiter in conversation. "I gather our friend turned down my invitation," he said. "May I ask what his name is?"

"Otto, *mein Herr.*"

"Otto what? Doesn't he have a last name?"

The waiter's eyes twinkled. "I asked him once. Niemand, he told me. Otto Niemand."

Dooley chuckled. *Niemand,* he knew, meant "nobody" in German. "How long has he been playing here?" he asked.

"Oh, just tonight. He travels around. Tonight is the first we've seen him in almost a year. When he comes, it's just for one night and we let him play and pass the hat for him. Ordinarily we don't have music here, it's just a wine cellar."

Dooley frowned. He'd have to make *sure,* then, to make contact tonight.

"Just a wine cellar," the little waiter repeated. "But we also serve sandwiches if you are hungry. Ham, knackwurst, or beer cheese . . ."

Dooley hadn't been listening and interrupted. "How soon will he play again? Does he take long between sets?"

"Oh, he plays no more tonight. A minute ago, just as I was bringing your wine, I saw him leave. We may not see him again for a long . . ."

But Dooley had grabbed his clarinet case and was running, running as fast as he could make it on a twisting course between tables. Through the door without even bothering to close it, and up the stone steps to the sidewalk. The fog wasn't so thick now, except in patches. But he could see *niemand* in either direction. He stood utterly still to listen. All he could hear for a moment were sounds from the wine cellar, then blessedly someone pulled shut the door he'd left open and in the silence that followed he thought, for a second, that he could hear footsteps to his right, the direction from which he had come.

He had nothing to lose, so he ran that way. There was a twist in the street and then a corner. He stopped and listened again, and—*that* way, around the corner, he thought he heard the steps again and ran toward them. After half a block he could see a figure ahead, too far to recognize but thank God tall and thin; it *could* be the musician. And past the figure, dimly through the fog he could see lights and hear traffic noises. This must be the turn he had missed in trying to follow the hotel clerk's directions

for finding the downtown bright-lights district, or as near to
such as a town this size might have.

He closed the distance to a quarter of a block, opened his
mouth to call out to the figure ahead and found that he was too
winded to call out. He dropped his gait from a run to a walk.
No danger of losing the man now that he was this close to him.
Getting his breath back, he closed the distance between them
slowly.

He was only a few paces behind the man—and, thank God, it
was the musician—and was lengthening his strides to come up
alongside him and speak when the man stepped down the curb
and started diagonally across the street. Just as a speeding car,
with what must have been a drunken driver, turned the corner
behind them, lurched momentarily, then righted itself on a
course bearing straight down on the unsuspecting musician. In
sudden reflex action Dooley, who had never knowingly performed a heroic act in his life, dashed into the street and pushed
the musician from the path of the car. The impetus of Dooley's
charge sent him crashing down on top of the musician and he
sprawled breathlessly in this shielding position as the car passed
by so close that it sent out rushing fingers of air to tug at his
clothing. Dooley raised his head in time to see the two red eyes
of its taillights vanishing into the fog a block down the street.

Dooley listened to the drumming roll of his heart in his ears
as he rolled aside to free the musician and both men got slowly
to their feet.

"Was it close?"

Dooley nodded, swallowed with difficulty. "Like a shave with
a straight razor."

The musician had taken his instrument from under his coat
and was examining it. "Not broken," he said. But Dooley, realizing that his own hands were empty, whirled around to look for
his clarinet case. And saw it. He must have dropped it when he
raised his hands to push the musician. A front wheel and a back
wheel of the car must each have run over it, for it was flattened at
both ends. The case and every section of the clarinet were
splintered, useless junk. He fingered it a moment and then
walked over and dropped it into the gutter.

The musician came and stood beside him. "A pity," he said
softly. "The loss of an instrument is like the loss of a friend."

An idea was coming to Dooley, so he didn't answer, but man-

aged to look sadder than he felt. The loss of the clarinet was a
blow in the pocketbook, but not an irrevocable one. He had
enough to buy a used, not-so-hot one to start out with and he'd
have to work harder and spend less for a while until he could
get a really good one like the one he'd lost. Three hundred it
had cost him. Dollars, not marks. But he'd get another clarinet
all right. Right now, though, he was much *much* more interested in getting the German musician's hautboy, or one just like
it. Three hundred dollars, not marks, was peanuts to what he'd
give for that. And if the old boy felt responsible and offered . . .

"It was my fault," the musician said. "For not looking. I wish
I could afford to buy you a new— It was a clarinet, was it not?"

"Yes," Dooley said, trying to sound like a man on the brink of
despair instead of one on the brink of the greatest discovery of
his life. "Well, what's kaput is kaput. Shall we go somewhere
for a drink, and have a wake?"

"My room," said the musician. "I have wine there. And we'll
have privacy so I can play a tune or two I do not play in public.
Since you too are a musician." He chuckled. "*Eine Kleine
Nachtmusik,* eh? A little night-music—but not Mozart's; my
own."

Dooley managed to conceal his elation and to nod as though
he didn't care much. "Okay, Otto Niemand. My name's Dooley
Hanks."

The musician chuckled. "Call me Otto, Dooley. I use no last
name, so Niemand is what I tell any who insist on my having
one. Come, Dooley; it isn't far."

It wasn't far, just a block down the next side street. The musician turned in at an aged and darkened house. He opened the
front door with a key and then used a small pocket flashlight to
guide them up a wide but uncarpeted staircase. The house, he
explained on the way, was unoccupied and scheduled to be torn
down, so there was no electricity. But the owner had given him
a key and permission to use it while the house still stood; there
were a few pieces of furniture here and there, and he got by. He
liked being in a house all by himself because he could play at
any hour of the night without bothering anyone trying to sleep.

He opened the door of a room and went in. Dooley waited in
the doorway until the musician had lighted an oil lamp on the
dresser, and then followed him in. Besides the dresser there was
only a straight chair, a rocker and a single bed.

"Sit down, Dooley," the musician told him. "You'll find the bed more comfortable than the straight chair. If I'm going to play for us, I'd like the rocker." He was taking two glasses and a bottle out of the top drawer of the dresser. "I see I erred. I thought it was wine I had left; it is brandy. But that is better, no?"

"That is better, yes," said Dooley. He could hardly restrain himself from asking permission right away to try the hautboy himself, but felt it would be wiser to wait until brandy had done a little mellowing. He sat down on the bed.

The musician handed Dooley a huge glass of brandy; he went back to the dresser and got his own glass and, with his instrument in his other hand, went to the rocker. He raised the glass. "To music, Dooley."

"To *Nachtmusik*," said Dooley. He drank off a goodly sip, and it burned like fire, but it was good brandy. Then he could wait no longer. "Otto, mind if I look at that instrument of yours? It's a hautboy, isn't it?"

"A hautboy, yes. Not many would recognize it, even musicians. But I'm sorry, Dooley. I can't let you handle it. Or play it, if you were going to ask that, too. I'm sorry, but that's the way it is, my friend."

Dooley nodded and tried not to look glum. The night is young, he told himself; another drink or two of brandy that size may mellow him. Meanwhile, he might as well find out as much as he could.

"Is it—your instrument, I mean, a real one? I mean, a medieval one? Or a modern reproduction?"

"I made it myself, by hand. A labor of love. But, my friend, stay with the clarinet, I advise you. Especially do not ask me to make you one like this; I could not. I have not worked with tools, with a lathe, for many years. I would find my skill gone. Are you skillful with tools?"

Dooley shook his head. "Can't drive a nail. Where could I find one, even something like yours?"

The musician shrugged. "Most are in museums, not obtainable. You might find a few collections of ancient instruments in private hands, and buy one at an exorbitant price—and you might even find it still playable. But, my friend, be wise and stay with your clarinet. I advise you strongly."

Dooley Hanks could not say what he was thinking, and didn't speak.

"Tomorrow we will talk about finding you a new clarinet," the musician said. "Tonight, let us forget it. And forget your wish for a hautboy, even your wish to play this one—yes, I know you asked only to touch and handle, but could you hold it in your hands without wanting to put it to your lips? Let us drink some more and then I will play for us. *Prosit!*"

They drank again. The musician asked Dooley to tell something about himself, and Dooley did. Almost everything about himself that mattered except the one thing that mattered most—his obsession and the fact that he was making up his mind to kill for it if there was no other way.

There was no hurry, Dooley thought; he had all night. So he talked and they drank. They were halfway through their third round—and the last round, since it finished the bottle—of brandy, when he ran out of talk and there was silence.

And with a gentle smile the musician drained his glass, put it down, and put both hands on his instrument. "Dooley . . . would you like some girls?"

Dooley suddenly found himself a little drunk. But he laughed. "Sure," he said. "Whole roomful of girls. Blonds, brunettes, redheads." And then because he couldn't let a squarehead square beat him at drinking, he killed the rest of his brandy too, and lay back across the single bed with his shoulders and head against the wall. "Bring 'em on, Otto."

Otto nodded, and began to play. And suddenly the excruciating, haunting beauty of the music Dooley had last heard in the wine cellar was back. But a new tune this time, a tune that was lilting and at the same time sensual. It was so beautiful that it hurt, and Dooley thought for a moment fiercely: damn him, he's playing *my* instrument; he owes me that for the clarinet I lost. And almost he decided to get up and *do* something about it because jealousy and envy burned in him like flames.

But before he could move, gradually he became aware of another sound somewhere, above or under the music. It seemed to come from outside, on the sidewalk below, and it was a rapid click-click-clickety-click for all the world like the sound of high heels, and then it was closer and it *was* the sound of heels, many heels, on wood, on the uncarpeted stairway, and then—and this was all in time with the music—there was a gentle tap-tap at the door. Dreamily, Dooley turned his head toward the door as it swung open and girls poured into the room and surrounded him, engulfing him in their physical warmth and exotic perfumes. Dooley gazed in blissful disbelief and then suspended the disbelief; if this were illusion, let it be. As long as— He reached out with both hands, and yes, they could be touched as well as seen. There were brown-eyed brunettes, green-eyed blonds and black-eyed redheads. And blue-eyed brunettes, brown-eyed blonds and green-eyed redheads. They were all sizes from petite to statuesque and they were all beautiful.

Somehow the oil lamp seemed to dim itself without completely going out, and the music, growing wilder now, seemed to come from somewhere else, as though the musician were no longer in the room, and Dooley thought that that was considerate of him. Soon he was romping with the girls in reckless abandon, sampling here and there like a small boy in a candy store. Or a Roman at an orgy, but the Romans never had it quite so good, nor the gods on Mount Olympus.

At last, wonderfully exhausted, he lay back on the bed, and surrounded by soft, fragrant girlflesh, he slept.

And woke, suddenly and completely and soberly, he knew not how long later. But the room was cold now; perhaps that was what had wakened him. He opened his eyes and saw that he was alone on the bed and that the lamp was again (or still?) burning normally. And the musician was there too, he saw when he raised his head, sound asleep in the rocking chair. The instrument was gripped tightly in both hands and that long red and yellow striped muffler was still around his scrawny neck, his head tilted backward against the rocker's back.

Had it really happened? Or had the music put him to sleep, so he'd dreamed it about the girls? Then he put the thought aside; it didn't matter. What mattered, all that mattered, was that he was not leaving here without the hautboy. But did he *have* to kill to get it? Yes, he did. If he simply stole it from the sleeping man he wouldn't stand a chance of getting out of Germany with it. Otto even knew his right name, as it was on his passport, and they'd be waiting for him at the border. Whereas if he left a dead man behind him, the body—in an abandoned house—might not be found for weeks or months, not until he was safe back in America. And by then any evidence against him, even his possession of the instrument, would be too thin to warrant extradition back to Europe. He could claim that Otto had given him the instrument to replace the clarinet he'd lost in saving Otto's life. He'd have no proof of that, but they'd have no proof to the contrary.

Quickly and quietly he got off the bed and tiptoed over to the man sleeping in the rocker and stood looking down at him. It would be easy, for the means were at hand. The scarf, already around the thin neck and crossed once in front, the ends dangling. Dooley tiptoed around behind the rocker and reached over the thin shoulders and took a tight grip on each end of the scarf and pulled them apart with all his strength. And held them so. The musician must have been older and more frail than Dooley had thought. His struggles were feeble. And even dying he held onto his instrument with one hand and clawed ineffectually at the scarf only with the other. He died quickly.

Dooley felt for a heartbeat first to make sure and then pried the dead fingers off the instrument. And held it himself at last.

His hands held it, and trembled with eagerness. When would it be safe for him to try it? Not back at his hotel, in the middle of the night, waking other guests and drawing attention to himself.

Why, here and now, in this abandoned house, would be the safest and best chance he'd have for a long time, before he was safely out of the country maybe. Here and now, in this house, before he took care of fingerprints on anything he might have touched and erased any other traces of his presence he might find or think of. Here and now, but softly so as not to waken any sleeping neighbors, in case they might hear a difference between his first efforts and those of the instrument's original owner.

So he'd play softly, at least at first, and quit right away if the instrument made with the squeaks and ugly noises so easy to produce on any unmastered instrument. But he had the strangest feeling that it wouldn't happen that way to him. He knew already how to manage a double reed; once in New York he'd shared an apartment with an oboe player and had tried out his instrument with the thought of getting one himself, to double on. He'd finally decided not to because he preferred playing with small combos and an oboe fitted only into large groups. And the fingering? He looked down and saw that his fingers had fallen naturally in place over the finger-holes or poised above the keys. He moved them and watched them start, seemingly of their own volition, a little finger-dance. He made them stop moving and wonderingly put the instrument to his lips and breathed into it softly. And out came, softly, a clear, pure middle-register tone. As rich and vibrant a note as any Otto had played. Cautiously he raised a finger and then another and found himself starting a diatonic scale. And, on a hunch, made himself forget his fingers and just *thought* the scale and let his fingers take over and they did, every tone pure. He *thought* a scale in a different key and played it, then an arpeggio. He didn't know the fingerings, but his fingers did.

He could play it, and he would.

He might as well make himself comfortable, he decided despite his mounting excitement. He crossed back to the bed and lay back across it, as he had lain while listening to the musician play, with his head and shoulders braced up against the wall behind it. And put the instrument back to his mouth and played, this time not caring about volume. Certainly if neighbors heard, they'd think it was Otto, and they would be accustomed to hearing Otto play late at night.

He thought of some of the tunes he'd heard in the wine cellar, and his fingers played them. In ecstasy, he relaxed and played as he had never played a clarinet. Again, as when Otto had played, he was struck by the purity and richness of the tone, so like the chalumeau register of his own clarinet, but extending even to the highest notes.

He played, and a thousand sounds blended into one. Again the sweet melody of paradoxes, black and white blending into a beautiful radiant gray of haunting music.

And then, seemingly without transition, he found himself playing a strange tune, one he'd never heard before. But one that he knew instinctively belonged to this wonderful instrument. A calling, beckoning tune, as had been the music Otto had played when the girls, real or imaginary, had click-clicked their way to him, but different this—was it a sinister instead of a sensual feeling underlying it?

But it was beautiful and he couldn't have stopped the dance of his fingers or stopped giving it life with his breath if he'd tried.

And then, over or under the music, he heard another sound. Not this time a click-click of high heels but a scraping, scrabbling sound, as of thousands of tiny clawed feet. And he saw them as they spilled suddenly out of many holes in the woodwork that he had not before noticed, and ran to the bed and jumped upon it. And with paralyzing suddenness the bits and pieces fell into place and by an effort that was to be the last of his life Dooley tore the accursed instrument from his mouth, and opened his mouth to scream. But they were all around him now, all over him: great ones, tawny ones, small ones, lean ones, black ones . . . And before he could scream out of his opened mouth the largest black rat, the one who led them, leaped up and closed its sharp teeth in the end of his tongue and held on, and the scream a-borning gurgled into silence.

And the sound of feasting lasted far into the night in Hamelin town.

Puppet Show

HORROR came to Cherrybell at a little after noon on a blistering hot day in August.

Perhaps that is redundant; *any* August day in Cherrybell, Arizona, is blistering hot. It is on Highway 89 about forty miles south of Tucson and about thirty miles north of the Mexican border. It consists of two filling stations, one on each side of the road to catch travelers going in both directions, a general store, a beer-and-wine-license-only tavern, a tourist-trap type trading post for tourists who can't wait until they reach the border to start buying serapes and huaraches, a deserted hamburger stand, and a few 'dobe houses inhabited by Mexican-Americans who work in Nogales, the border town to the south, and who, for God knows what reason, prefer to live in Cherrybell and commute, some of them in Model T Fords. The sign on the highway says, "Cherrybell, Pop. 42," but the sign exaggerates; Pop died last year—Pop Anders, who ran the now-deserted hamburger stand— and the correct figure is 41.

Horror came to Cherrybell mounted on a burro led by an ancient, dirty and gray-bearded desert rat of a prospector who later —nobody got around to asking his name for a while—gave the name of Dade Grant. Horror's name was Garth. He was approximately nine feet tall but so thin, almost a stick-man, that he could not have weighed over a hundred pounds. Old Dade's burro carried him easily, despite the fact that his feet dragged in the sand on either side. Being dragged through the sand for, as it later turned out, well over five miles hadn't caused the slightest wear on the shoes—more like buskins, they were—which constituted all that he wore except for a pair of what could have been swimming trunks, in robin's-egg blue. But it wasn't his dimensions that made him horrible to look upon; it was his *skin*. It looked red, raw. It looked as though he had been skinned alive, and the skin replaced upside down, raw side out. His skull, his face, were equally narrow or elongated; otherwise in every visible way he appeared human—or at least humanoid. Unless you counted such little things as the fact that his hair was a robin's-egg blue to match his trunks, as were his eyes and his boots. Blood red and light blue.

Casey, owner of the tavern, was the first one to see them coming across the plain, from the direction of the mountain range to the east. He'd stepped out of the back door of his tavern for a breath of fresh, if hot, air. They were about a hundred yards away at that time, and already he could see the utter alienness of the figure on the lead burro. Just alienness at that distance, the horror came only at closer range. Casey's jaw dropped and stayed down until the strange trio was about fifty yards away, then he started slowly toward them. There are people who run at the sight of the unknown, others who advance to meet it. Casey advanced, however slowly, to meet it.

Still in the wide open, twenty yards from the back of the little tavern, he met them. Dade Grant stopped and dropped the rope by which he was leading the burro. The burro stood still and dropped its head. The stick-man stood up simply by planting his feet solidly and standing, astride the burro. He stepped one leg across it and stood a moment, leaning his weight against his hands on the burro's back, and then sat down in the sand. "High-gravity planet," he said. "Can't stand long."

"Kin I get water for my burro?" the prospector asked Casey. "Must be purty thirsty by now. Hadda leave water bags, some other things, so it could carry—" He jerked a thumb toward the red-and-blue horror.

Casey was just realizing that it *was* a horror. At a distance the color combination seemed a bit *outré,* but close— The skin was rough and seemed to have veins on the outside and looked moist (although it wasn't) and *damn* if it didn't look just like he had his skin peeled off and put back upside down. Or just peeled off, period. Casey had never seen anything like it and hoped he wouldn't ever see anything like it again.

Casey felt something behind him and looked over his shoulder. Others had seen now and were coming, but the nearest of them, a pair of boys, were ten yards behind him. "*Muchachos,*" he called out. "*Agua por el burro. Un pazal. Pronto.*"

He looked back and said, "What—? Who—?"

"Name's Dade Grant," said the prospector, putting out a hand, which Casey took absently. When he let go of it it jerked back over the desert rat's shoulder, thumb indicating the thing that sat on the sand. "*His* name's Garth, he tells me. He's an extra something or other, and he's some kind of minister."

Casey nodded at the stick-man and was glad to get a nod in return instead of an extended hand. "I'm Manuel Casey," he said. "What does he mean, an extra something?"

The stick-man's voice was unexpectedly deep and vibrant. "I am an extraterrestrial. And a minister plenipotentiary."

Surprisingly, Casey was a moderately well-educated man and knew both of those phrases; he was probably the only person in Cherrybell who would have known the second one. Less surprisingly, considering the speaker's appearance, he believed both of them. "What can I do for you, sir?" he asked. "But first, why not come in out of the sun?"

"No, thank you. It's a bit cooler here than they told me it would be, but I'm quite comfortable. This is equivalent to a cool spring evening on my planet. And as to what you can do for me, you can notify your authorities of my presence. I believe they will be interested."

Well, Casey thought, by blind luck he's hit the best man for his purpose within at least twenty miles. Manuel Casey was half-Irish, half-Mexican. He had a half brother who was half-Irish and half assorted-American, and the half brother was a bird colonel at Davis-Monthan Air Force Base in Tucson. He said, "Just a minute, Mr. Garth, I'll telephone. You, Mr. Grant, would you want to come inside?"

"Naw, I don't mind sun. Out in it all day every day. An' Garth here, he ast me if I'd stick with him till he was finished with what he's gotta do here. Said he'd gimme somethin' purty vallable if I did. Somethin'—a 'lectrononic—"

"An electronic battery-operated portable ore indicator," Garth said. "A simple little device, indicates presence of a concentration of ore up to two miles, indicates kind, grade, quantity and depth."

Casey gulped, excused himself, and pushed through the gathering crowd into his tavern. He had Colonel Casey on the phone in one minute, but it took him another four minutes to convince the colonel that he was neither drunk nor joking.

Twenty-five minutes after that there was a noise in the sky, a noise that swelled and then died as a four-man helicopter sat down and shut off its rotors a dozen yards from an extrater-restrial, two men and a burro. Casey alone had had the courage to rejoin the trio from the desert; there were other spectators, but they still held well back.

Colonel Casey, a major, a captain and a lieutenant who was the helicopter's pilot all came out and ran over. The stick-man stood up, all nine feet of him; from the effort it cost him to stand you could tell that he was used to a much lighter gravity than Earth's. He bowed, repeated his name and identification of him-self as an extraterrestrial and a minister plenipotentiary. Then he apologized for sitting down again, explained why it was nec-essary, and sat down.

The colonel introduced himself and the three who had come with him. "And now, sir, what can we do for you?"

The stick-man made a grimace that was probably intended as a smile. His teeth were the same light blue as his hair and eyes. "You have a cliché, 'take me to your leader.' I do not ask that. In fact, I *must* remain here. Nor do I ask that any of your leaders be brought here to me. That would be impolite. I am perfectly willing for you to represent them, to talk to you and let you question me. But I do ask one thing.

"You have tape recorders. I ask that, before I talk or answer questions, you have one brought. I want to be sure that the mes-sage your leaders eventually receive is full and accurate."

"Fine," the colonel said. He turned to the pilot. "Lieutenant, get on the radio in the whirlybird and tell them to get us a tape recorder faster than possible. It can be dropped by para— No, that'd take longer, rigging it for a drop. Have them send it by another helicopter." The lieutenant turned to go. "Hey," the colonel said. "Also fifty yards of extension cord. We'll have to plug it in inside Manny's tavern."

The lieutenant sprinted for the helicopter.

The others sat and sweated a moment and then Manuel Casey stood up. "That's a half an hour wait," he said, "and if we're going to sit here in the sun, who's for a bottle of cold beer? You, Mr. Garth?"

"It is a cold beverage, is it not? I am a bit chilly. If you have something hot—?"

"Coffee, coming up. Can I bring you a blanket?"

"No, thank you. It will not be necessary."

Casey left and shortly returned with a tray with half a dozen bottles of cold beer and a cup of steaming coffee. The lieutenant was back by then. Casey put down the tray and first served the stick-man, who sipped the coffee and said, "It is delicious."

Colonel Casey cleared his throat. "Serve our prospector friend next, Manny. As for us—well, drinking is forbidden on duty, but it was a hundred and twelve in the shade in Tucson, and this is hotter and also is *not* in the shade. Gentlemen, consider yourselves on official leave for as long as it takes you to drink one bottle of beer, or until the tape recorder arrives, whichever comes first."

The beer was finished first, but by the time the last of it had vanished, the second helicopter was within sight and sound. Casey asked the stick-man if he wanted more coffee. The offer was politely declined. Casey looked at Dade Grant and winked and the desert rat winked back, so Casey went in for two more bottles, one apiece for the civilian terrestrials. Coming back he met the lieutenant coming with the extension cord and returned as far as the doorway to show him where to plug it in.

When he came back, he saw that the second helicopter had brought its full complement of four, besides the tape recorder. There were, besides the pilot who had flown it, a technical sergeant who was skilled in the operation of the tape recorder and who was now making adjustments on it, and a lieutenant-colonel and a warrant officer who had come along for the ride or because they had been made curious by the request for a tape recorder to be rushed to Cherrybell, Arizona, by air. They were standing gaping at the stick-man and whispered conversations were going on.

The colonel said, "Attention" quietly, but it brought complete silence. "Please sit down, gentlemen. In a rough circle. Sergeant, if you rig your mike in the center of the circle, will it pick up clearly what any one of us may say?"

"Yes, sir. I'm almost ready."

Ten men and one extraterrestrial humanoid sat in a rough circle, with the microphone hanging from a small tripod in the approximate center. The humans were sweating profusely; the humanoid shivered slighty. Just outside the circle, the burro stood dejectedly, its head low. Edging closer, but still about five yards away, spread out now in a semicircle, was the entire population of Cherrybell who had been at home at the time; the stores and the filling stations were deserted.

The technical sergeant pushed a button and the tape recorder's reel started to turn. "Testing . . . testing," he said. He held down the rewind button for a second and then pushed the playback button. "Testing . . . testing," said the recorder's speaker. Loud and clear. The sergeant pushed the rewind button, then the erase one to clear the tape. Then the stop button. "When I push the next button, sir," he said to the colonel, "we'll be recording."

The colonel looked at the tall extraterrestrial, who nodded, and then the colonel nodded at the sergeant. The sergeant pushed the recording button.

"My name is Garth," said the stick-man, slowly and clearly. "I am from a planet of a star which is not listed in your star catalogs, although the globular cluster in which it is one of ninety thousand stars, is known to you. It is, from here, in the direction of the center of the galaxy at a distance of a little over four thousand light-years.

"However, I am not here as a representative of my planet or my people, but as minister plenipotentiary of the Galactic Union, a federation of the enlightened civilizations of the galaxy, for the good of all. It is my assignment to visit you and decide, here and now, whether or not you are to be welcomed to join our federation.

"You may now ask questions freely. However, I reserve the right to postpone answering some of them until my decision has been made. If the decision is favorable, I will then answer all questions, including the ones I have postponed answering meanwhile. Is that satisfactory?"

"Yes," said the colonel. "How did you come here? A spaceship?"

"Correct. It is overhead right now, in orbit twenty-two thousand miles out, so it revolves with the earth and stays over this one spot. I am under observation from it, which is one reason I prefer to remain here in the open. I am to signal it when I want it to come down to pick me up."

"How do you know our language so fluently? Are you telepathic?"

"No, I am not. And nowhere in the galaxy is any race tele-pathic except among its own members. I was taught your language, for this purpose. We have had observers among you for many centuries—by *we*, I mean the Galactic Union, of course. Quite obviously I could not pass as an Earthman, but there are other races who can. Incidentally, they are not spies, or agents; they have in no way tried to affect you; they are observers and that is all."

"What benefits do we get from joining your union, if we are asked and if we accept?" the colonel asked.

"First, a quick course in the fundamental social sciences which will end your tendency to fight among yourselves and end or at least control your aggressions. After we are satisfied that you have accomplished that and it is safe for you to do so, you will be given space travel, and many other things, as rapidly as you are able to assimilate them."

"And if we are not asked, or refuse?"

"Nothing. You will be left alone; even our observers will be withdrawn. You will work out your own fate—either you will render your planet uninhabited and uninhabitable within the next century, or you will master social science yourselves and again be candidates for membership and again be offered membership. We will check from time to time and if and when it appears certain that you are not going to destroy yourselves, you will again be approached."

"Why the hurry, now that you're here? Why can't you stay long enough for our leaders, as you call them, to talk to you in person?"

"Postponed. The reason is not important but it is complicated, and I simply do not wish to waste time explaining."

"Assuming your decision is favorable, how will we get in touch with you to let you know *our* decision? You know enough about us, obviously, to know that *I* can't make it."

"We will know your decision through our observers. One condition of acceptance is full and uncensored publication in your newspapers of this interview, verbatim from the tape we are now using to record it. Also of all deliberations and decisions of your government."

"And other governments? We can't decide unilaterally for the world."

"Your government has been chosen for a start. If you accept we shall furnish the techniques that will cause the others to fall in line quickly—and those techniques do not involve force or the threat of force."

"They must be *some* techniques," said the colonel wryly, "if they'll make one certain country I don't have to name fall into line quickly, without even a threat."

"Sometimes the offer of reward is more significant than the use of threat. Do you think the country you do not wish to name would like your country colonizing planets of far stars before they even reach Mars? But that is a minor point, relatively. You may trust the techniques."

"It sounds almost too good to be true. But you said that you are to decide, here and now, whether or not we are to be invited to join. May I ask on what factors you will base your decision?"

"One is that I am—was, since I already have—to check your degree of xenophobia. In the loose sense in which you use it, that means fear of strangers. We have a word that has no counterpart in your vocabulary: it means fear of and revulsion toward *aliens*. I—or at least a member of my race—was chosen to make the first overt contact with you. Because I am what you could call roughly humanoid—as you are what I would call roughly humanoid—I am probably more horrible, more repulsive to you than many completely different species would be. Because to you, I am a caricature of a human being, I am more horrible to you than a being who bears no remote resemblance to you.

"You may think you *do* feel horror at me, and revulsion, but believe me, you have passed that test. There *are* races in the galaxy who can never be members of the federation, no matter how they advance otherwise, because they are violently and incurably xenophobic; they could never face or talk to an alien of any species. They would either run screaming from him or try to kill him instantly. From watching you and these people"—he waved a long arm at the civilian population of Cherrybell not far outside the circle of the conference—"I know you feel revulsion at the sight of me, but believe me it is relatively slight and certainly curable. You have passed that test satisfactorily."

"And are there other tests?"

"One other. But I think it is time that I—" Instead of finishing the sentence, the stick-man lay back flat on the sand and closed his eyes.

The colonel started to his feet. "What in *hell?*" he said. He walked quickly around the mike's tripod and bent over the recumbent extraterrestrial, put an ear to the bloody-appearing chest.

As he raised his head, Dade Grant, the grizzled prospector, chuckled. "No heartbeat, Colonel, because no heart. But I may leave him as a souvenir for you and you'll find much more interesting things inside him than heart and guts. Yes, he is a puppet whom I have been operating—as your Edgar Bergen operates his—what's his name?—oh yes. Charlie McCarthy. Now that he has served his purpose, he is deactivated. You can go back to your place, Colonel."

Colonel Casey moved back slowly. "Why?" he asked.

Dade Grant was peeling off his beard and wig. He rubbed a cloth across his face to remove make-up and was revealed as a handsome young man. He said, "What he told you, or what you were told through him, was true as far as it went. He is only a simulacrum, yes, but he is an exact duplicate of a member of one of the intelligent races of the galaxy, the one toward whom you would be disposed—if you were violently and incurably xenophobic—to be most horrified by, according to our psychologists. But we did not bring a real member of his species to make first contact because they have a phobia of their own, agoraphobia— fear of space. They are highly civilized and members in good standing of the federation, but they never leave their own planet.

"Our observers assure us you don't have *that* phobia. But they were unable to judge in advance the degree of your xenophobia and the only way to test it was to bring along something in lieu of someone to test it against, and presumably to let him make the initial contact."

The colonel sighed audibly. "I can't say this doesn't relieve me in one way. We could get along with humanoids, yes, and will when we have to. But I'll admit it's a relief to learn that the master race of the galaxy is, after all, human instead of only humanoid. What is the second test?"

"You are undergoing it now. Call me—" He snapped his fingers. "What's the name of Bergen's second-string puppet, after Charlie McCarthy?"

The colonel hesitated, but the tech sergeant supplied the answer. "Mortimer Snerd."

"Right. So call me Mortimer Snerd, and now I think it is time that I—" He lay back flat on the sand and closed his eyes just as the stick-man had done a few minutes before.

The burro raised its head and put it into the circle over the shoulder of the tech sergeant. "That takes care of the puppets, Colonel," it said. "And now what's this bit about it being important that the master race be human or at least humanoid? What is a master race?"

Nightmare in Yellow

HE AWOKE when the alarm clock rang, but lay in bed a while after he'd shut it off, going a final time over the plans he'd made for embezzlement that day and for murder that evening.

Every little detail had been worked out, but this was the final check. Tonight at forty-six minutes after eight he'd be free, in every way. He'd picked that moment because this was his fortieth birthday and that was the exact time of day, of the evening rather, when he had been born. His mother had been a bug on astrology, which was why the moment of his birth had been impressed on him so exactly. He wasn't superstitious himself but it had struck his sense of humor to have his new life begin at forty, to the minute.

Time was running out on him, in any case. As a lawyer who specialized in handling estates, a lot of money passed through his hands—and some of it had passed into them. A year ago he'd "borrowed" five thousand dollars to put into something that looked like a sure-fire way to double or triple the money, but he'd lost it instead. Then he'd "borrowed" more to gamble with, in one way or another, to try to recoup the first loss. Now he was behind to the tune of over thirty thousand; the shortage couldn't be hidden more than another few months and there wasn't a hope that he could replace the missing money by that time. So he had been raising all the cash he could without arousing suspicion, by carefully liquidating assets, and by this afternoon he'd have running-away money to the tune of well over a hundred thousand dollars, enough to last him the rest of his life.

And they'd never catch him. He'd planned every detail of his trip, his destination, his new identity, and it was foolproof. He'd been working on it for months.

His decision to kill his wife had been relatively an after-thought. The motive was simple: he hated her. But it was only after he'd come to the decision that he'd never go to jail, that he'd kill himself if he was ever apprehended, that it came to him that—since he'd die anyway if caught—he had nothing to lose in leaving a dead wife behind him instead of a living one.

He'd hardly been able to keep from laughing at the appropriateness of the birthday present she'd given him (yesterday, a day ahead of time); it had been a new suitcase. She'd also talked him into celebrating his birthday by letting her meet him downtown for dinner at seven. Little did she guess how the celebration would go after that. He planned to have her home by eight forty-six and satisfy his sense of the fitness of things by making himself a widower at that exact moment. There was a practical advantage, too, of leaving her dead. If he left her alive but asleep she'd guess what had happened and call the police when she found him gone in the morning. If he left her dead her body would not be found that soon, possibly not for two or three days, and he'd have a much better start.

Things went smoothly at his office; by the time he went to meet his wife everything was ready. But she dawdled over drinks and dinner and he began to worry whether he could get her home by eight forty-six. It was ridiculous, he knew, but it had become important that his moment of freedom should come then and not a minute earlier or a minute later. He watched his watch.

He would have missed it by half a minute if he'd waited till they were inside the house. But the dark of the porch of their house was perfectly safe, as safe as inside. He swung the blackjack viciously once, as she stood at the front door, waiting for him to open it. He caught her before she fell and managed to hold her upright with one arm while he got the door open and then got it closed from the inside.

Then he flicked the switch and yellow light leaped to fill the room, and, before they could see that his wife was dead and that he was holding her up, all the assembled birthday party guests shouted *"Surprise!"*

Earthmen Bearing Gifts

DHAR RY sat alone in his room, meditating. From outside the door he caught a thought wave equivalent to a knock, and, glancing at the door, he willed it to slide open.

It opened. "Enter, my friend," he said. He could have projected the idea telepathically; but with only two persons present, speech was more polite.

Ejon Khee entered. "You are up late tonight, my leader," he said.

"Yes, Khee. Within an hour the Earth rocket is due to land, and I wish to see it. Yes, I know, it will land a thousand miles away, if their calculations are correct. Beyond the horizon. But if it lands even twice that far the flash of the atomic explosion should be visible. And I have waited long for first contact. For even though no Earthman will be on that rocket, it will still be first contact—for them. Of course our telepath teams have been reading their thoughts for many centuries, but—this will be the first *physical* contact between Mars and Earth."

Khee made himself comfortable on one of the low chairs. "True," he said. "I have not followed recent reports too closely, though. Why are they using an atomic warhead? I know they suppose our planet is uninhabited, but still—"

"They will watch the flash through their lunar telescopes and get a—what do they call it?—a spectroscopic analysis. That will tell them more than they know now (or think they know; much of it is erroneous) about the atmosphere of our planet and the composition of its surface. It is—call it a sighting shot, Khee. They'll be here in person within a few oppositions. And then—"

Mars was holding out, waiting for Earth to come. What was left of Mars, that is; this one small city of about nine hundred beings. The civilization of Mars was older than that of Earth, but it was a dying one. This was what remained of it: one city, nine hundred people. They were waiting for Earth to make contact, for a selfish reason and for an unselfish one.

Martian civilization had developed in a quite different direction from that of Earth. It had developed no important knowledge of the physical sciences, no technology. But it had developed social sciences to the point where there had not been a single crime, let alone a war, on Mars for fifty thousand years. And it had developed fully the parapsychological sciences of the mind, which Earth was just beginning to discover.

Mars could teach Earth much. How to avoid crime and war to begin with. Beyond those simple things lay telepathy, telekinesis, empathy . . .

And Earth would, Mars hoped, teach them something even more valuable to Mars: how, by science and technology—which it was too late for Mars to develop now, even if they had the type of minds which would enable them to develop these things —to restore and rehabilitate a dying planet, so that an otherwise dying race might live and multiply again.

Each planet would gain greatly, and neither would lose.

And tonight was the night when Earth would make its first sighting shot. Its next shot, a rocket containing Earthmen, or at least an Earthman, would be at the next opposition, two Earth years, or roughly four Martian years, hence. The Martians knew this, because their teams of telepaths were able to catch at least some of the thoughts of Earthmen, enough to know their plans. Unfortunately, at that distance, the connection was one-way. Mars could not ask Earth to hurry its program. Or tell Earth scientists the facts about Mars' composition and atmosphere which would have made this preliminary shot unnecessary.

Tonight Ry, the leader (as nearly as the Martian word can be translated), and Khee, his administrative assistant and closest friend, sat and meditated together until the time was near. Then they drank a toast to the future—in a beverage based on menthol, which had the same effect on Martians as alcohol on Earthmen—and climbed to the roof of the building in which they had been sitting. They watched toward the north, where the rocket should land. The stars shone brilliantly and unwinkingly through the atmosphere.

In Observatory No. 1 on Earth's moon, Rog Everett, his eye

at the eyepiece of the spotter scope, said triumphantly, "Thar she blew, Willie. And now, as soon as the films are developed, we'll know the score on that old planet Mars." He straightened up—there'd be no more to see now—and he and Willie Sanger shook hands solemnly. It was an historical occasion.

"Hope it didn't kill anybody. Any Martians, that is. Rog, did it hit dead center in Syrtis Major?"

"Near as matters. I'd say it was maybe a thousand miles off, to the south. And that's damn close on a fifty-million-mile shot. Willie, do you really think there are any Martians?"

Willie thought a second and then said, "No."

He was right.

Jaycee

"WALTER, what's a Jaycee?" Mrs. Ralston asked her husband, Dr. Ralston, across the breakfast table.

"Why—I believe it used to be a member of what they called a Junior Chamber of Commerce. I don't know if they still have them or not. Why?"

"Martha said Henry was muttering something yesterday about Jaycees, fifty million Jaycees. And swore at her when she asked what he meant." Martha was Mrs. Graham and Henry her husband, Dr. Graham. They lived next door and the two doctors and their wives were close friends.

"Fifty million," said Dr. Ralston musingly. "That's how many parthies there are."

He should have known; he and Dr. Graham together were responsible for parthies—parthenogenetic births. Twenty years ago, in 1980, they had together engineered the first experiment in human parthenogenesis, the fertilization of a female cell without the help of a male one. The offspring of that experiment, named John, was now twenty years old and lived with Dr. and Mrs. Graham next door; he had been adopted by them after the death of his mother in an accident some years before.

No other parthie was more than half John's age. Not until John was ten, and obviously healthy and normal, had the authorities let down bars and permitted any woman who wanted a child and who was either single or married to a sterile husband to have a child parthenogenetically. Due to the shortage of men —the disastrous testerosis epidemic of the 1970s had just killed off almost a third of the male population of the world—over fifty million women had applied for parthenogenetic children and borne them. Luckily for redressing the balance of the sexes, it had turned out that all parthenogenetically conceived children were males.

"Martha thinks," said Mrs. Ralston, "that Henry's worrying about John, but she can't think why. He's such a *good* boy."

Dr. Graham suddenly and without knocking burst into the room. His face was white and his eyes wide as he stared at his colleague. "I was right," he said.

"Right about what?"

"About John. I didn't tell anyone, but do you know what he did when we ran out of drinks at the party last night?"

Dr. Ralston frowned. "Changed water into wine?"

"Into gin; we were having martinis. And just now he left to go water skiing—and he isn't taking any water skis. Told me that with faith he wouldn't need them."

"Oh, *no*," said Dr. Ralston. He dropped his head into his hands.

Once before in history there'd been a virgin birth. Now fifty million virgin-born boys were growing up. In ten more years there'd be fifty million—Jaycees.

"*No*," sobbed Dr. Ralston, "*no!*"

Pi in the Sky

ROGER JEROME PHLUTTER, for whose absurd name I offer no defense other than that it is genuine, was, at the time of the events of this story, a hardworking clerk in the office of the Cole Observatory.

He was a young man of no particular brilliance, although he performed his daily tasks assiduously and efficiently, studied the calculus at home for one hour every evening, and hoped some day to become a chief astronomer of some important observatory.

Nevertheless, our narration of the events of late March in the year 1987 must begin with Roger Phlutter for the good and sufficient reason that he, of all men on earth, was the first observer of the stellar aberration.

Meet Roger Phlutter.

Tall, rather pale from spending too much time indoors, thickish shell-rimmed glasses, dark hair close-cropped in the style of the nineteen eighties, dressed neither particularly well nor badly, smokes cigarettes rather excessively. . . .

At a quarter to five that afternoon, Roger was engaged in two simultaneous operations. One was examining, in a blink-microscope, a photographic plate taken late the previous night of a section in Gemini. The other was considering whether or not, on the three dollars remaining of his pay from last week, he dared phone Elsie and ask her to go somewhere with him.

Every normal young man has undoubtedly, at some time or other, shared with Roger Phlutter his second occupation, but not everyone has operated or understands the operation of a blink-microscope. So let us raise our eyes from Elsie to Gemini.

A blink-mike provides accommodation for two photographic plates taken of the same section of sky, but at different times. These plates are carefully juxtaposed and the operator may alternately focus his vision, through the eyepiece, first upon one and then upon the other, by means of a shutter. If the plates are identical, the operation of the shutter reveals nothing, but if one of the dots on the second plate differs from the position it occupied on the first, it will call attention to itself by seeming to jump back and forth as the shutter is manipulated.

Roger manipulated the shutter, and one of the dots jumped. So did Roger. He tried it again, forgetting—as we have—all about Elsie for the moment, and the dot jumped again. It jumped almost a tenth of a second.

Roger straightened up and scratched his head. He lighted a cigarette, put it down on the ashtray, and looked into the blink-mike again. The dot jumped again, when he used the shutter.

Harry Wesson, who worked the evening shift, had just come into the office and was hanging up his topcoat.

"Hey, Harry!" Roger said. "There's something wrong with this blinking blinker."

"Yeah?" said Harry.

"Yeah. Pollux moved a tenth of a second."

"Yeah?" said Harry. "Well, that's about right for parallax. Thirty-two light years—parallax of Pollux is point one oh one. Little over a tenth of a second, so if your comparison plate was taken about six months ago when the earth was on the other side of her orbit, that's about right."

"But Harry, the comparison plate was taken night before last. They're twenty-four hours apart."

"You're crazy."

"Look for yourself."

It wasn't quite five o'clock yet, but Harry Wesson magnanimously overlooked that, and sat down in front of the blink-mike. He manipulated the shutter, and Pollux obligingly jumped.

There wasn't any doubt about it being Pollux, for it was far and away the brightest dot on the plate. Pollux is a star of 1.2 magnitude, one of the twenty brightest in the sky and by far the brightest in Gemini. And none of the faint stars around it had moved at all.

"Um," said Harry Wesson. He frowned and looked again. "One of those plates is misdated, that's all. I'll check into it first thing."

"Those plates aren't misdated," Roger said doggedly. "I dated them myself."

"That proves it," Harry told him. "Go on home. It's five

o'clock. If Pollux moved a tenth of a second last night, I'll move it back for you."

So Roger left.

He felt uneasy somehow, as though he shouldn't have. He couldn't put his finger on just what worried him, but something did. He decided to walk home instead of taking the bus.

Pollux was a fixed star. It couldn't have moved a tenth of a second in twenty-four hours.

"Let's see—thirty-two light years," Roger said to himself. "Tenth of a second. Why, that would be movement several times faster than the speed of light. Which is positively silly!"

Wasn't it?

He didn't feel much like studying or reading tonight. Was three dollars enough to take Elsie out?

The three balls of a pawn-shop loomed ahead, and Roger succumbed to temptation. He pawned his watch, and then phoned Elsie. Dinner and a show?

"Why certainly, Roger."

So, until he took her home at one-thirty, he managed to forget astronomy. Nothing odd about that. It would have been strange if he had managed to remember it.

But his feeling of restlessness came back as soon as he had left her. At first, he didn't remember why. He knew merely that he didn't feel quite like going home yet.

The corner tavern was still open, and he dropped in for a drink. He was having his second one when he remembered. He ordered a third.

"Hank," he said to the bartender. "You know Pollux?"

"Pollux who?" asked Hank.

"Skip it," said Roger. He had another drink, and thought it over. Yes, he'd made a mistake somewhere. Pollux couldn't have moved.

He went outside and started to walk home. He was almost there when it occurred to him to look up at Pollux. Not that, with the naked eye, he could detect a displacement of a tenth of a second, but he felt curious.

He looked up, oriented himself by the sickle of Leo, and then found Gemini—Castor and Pollux were the only stars in Gemini visible, for it wasn't a particularly good night for seeing. They were there, all right, but he thought they looked a little farther apart than usual. Absurd, because that would be a matter of degrees, not minutes or seconds.

He stared at them for a while, and then looked across to the dipper. Then he stopped walking and stood there. He closed his eyes and opened them again, carefully.

The dipper just didn't look right. It was distorted. There seemed to be more space between Alioth and Mizar, in the handle, than between Mizar and Alkaid. Pheeda and Merak, in the bottom of the dipper, were closer together, making the angle between the bottom and the lip steeper. Quite a bit steeper.

Unbelievingly, he ran an imaginary line from the pointers, Merak and Dubhe, to the North Star. The line curved. It had to. If he ran it straight, it missed Polaris by maybe five degrees.

Breathing a bit hard, Roger took off his glasses and polished them very carefully with his handkerchief. He put them back on again and the dipper was still crooked.

So was Leo, when he looked back to it. At any rate, Regulus wasn't where it should be by a degree or two.

A degree or two! At the distance of Regulus! Was it sixty-five light years? Something like that.

Then, in time to save his sanity, Roger remembered that he'd been drinking. He went home without daring to look upward again. He went to bed, but couldn't sleep.

He didn't feel drunk. He grew more excited, wide awake.

He wondered if he dared phone the observatory. Would he sound drunk over the phone? The devil with whether he sounded that way or not, he finally decided. He went to the telephone in his pajamas.

"Sorry," said the operator.

"What d'ya mean, sorry?"

"I cannot give you that number," said the operator, in dulcet tones. And then, "I am sorry. We do not have that information."

He got the chief operator, and the information. Cole Observatory had been so deluged with calls from amateur astronomers that they had found it necessary to request the telephone company to discontinue all incoming calls save long distance ones from other observatories.

"Thanks," said Roger. "Will you get me a cab?"

It was an unusual request, but the chief operator obliged and got him a cab.

He found the Cole Observatory in a state resembling a madhouse.

The following morning most newspapers carried the news. Most of them gave it two or three inches on an inside page, but the facts were there.

The facts were that a number of stars, in general the brightest ones, within the past forty-eight hours had developed noticeable proper motions.

"This does not imply," quipped the *New York Spotlight*, "that their motions have been in any way improper in the past. 'Proper motion' to an astronomer means the movement of a star across the face of the sky with relation to other stars. Hitherto, a star named 'Barnard's Star' in the constellation Ophiuchus has exhibited the greatest proper motion of any known star, moving at the rate of ten and a quarter seconds a year. 'Barnard's Star' is not visible to the naked eye."

Probably no astronomer on earth slept that day.

The observatories locked their doors, with their full staffs on the inside, and admitted no one except occasional newspaper reporters who stayed a while and went away with puzzled faces, convinced at last that something strange was happening.

Blink-microscopes blinked, and so did astronomers. Coffee was consumed in prodigious quantities. Police riot squads were called to six United States observatories. Two of these calls were occasioned by attempts to break in on the part of frantic amateurs without. The other four were summoned to quell fistfights developing out of arguments within the observatories themselves. The office of Lick Observatory was a shambles, and James Truwell, Astronomer Royal of England, was sent to London Hospital with a mild concussion, the result of having a heavy photographic plate smashed over his head by an irate subordinate.

But these incidents were exceptions. The observatories, in general, were well-ordered madhouses.

The center of attention in the more enterprising ones was the loudspeaker in which reports from the Eastern Hemisphere could be relayed to the inmates. Practically all observatories kept open wires to the night side of earth, where the phenomena were still under scrutiny.

Astronomers under the night skies of Singapore, Shanghai and Sydney did their observing, as it were, directly into the business end of a long-distance telephone hookup.

Particularly of interest were reports from Sydney and Melbourne, whence came reports on the southern skies not visible—even at night—from Europe or the United States. The Southern Cross was by these reports, a cross no longer, its Alpha and Beta being shifted northward. Alpha and Beta Centauri, Canopus and Achernar all showed considerable proper motion—all, generally speaking, northward. Triangulum Australe and the Magellanic Clouds were undisturbed. Sigma Octanis, the weak pole star, had not moved.

Disturbance in the southern sky, then, was much less than in the northern one, in point of the number of stars displaced. However, relative proper motion of the stars which were disturbed was greater. While the general direction of movement of the few stars which did move was northward, their paths were not directly north, nor did they converge upon any exact point in space.

United States and European astronomers digested these facts and drank more coffee.

Evening papers, particularly in America, showed greater awareness that something indeed unusual was happening in the skies. Most of them moved the story to the front page—but not the banner headlines—giving it a half-column with a runover that was long or short, depending upon the editor's luck in obtaining statements from astronomers.

The statements, when obtained, were invariably statements of fact and not of opinion. The facts themselves, said these gentlemen, were sufficiently startling, and opinions would be premature. Wait and see. Whatever was happening was happening fast.

"How fast?" asked an editor.

"Faster than possible," was the reply.

Perhaps it is unfair to say that no editor procured expressions of opinion thus early. Charles Wangren, enterprising editor of the *Chicago Blade,* spent a small fortune in long-distance telephone calls. Out of possibly sixty attempts, he finally reached the chief astronomers at five observatories. He asked each of them the same question.

"What, in your opinion, is a possible cause, any possible cause, of the stellar movements of the last night or two?"

He tabulated the results.

"I wish I knew."—Geo. F. Stubbs, Tripp Observatory, Long Island.

"Somebody or something is crazy, and I hope it's me—I mean I."—Henry Collister McAdams, Lloyd Observatory, Boston.

"What's happening is impossible. There can't be any cause."—Letton Tischauer Tinney, Burgoyne Observatory, Albuquerque.

"I'm looking for an expert on Astrology. Know one?"—Patrick R. Whitaker, Lucas Observatory, Vermont.

Sadly studying this tabulation, which had cost him $187.35—including tax—to obtain, Editor Wangren signed a voucher to cover the long distance calls and then dropped his tabulation into the wastebasket. He telephoned his regular space-rates writer on scientific subjects.

"Can you give me a series of articles—two-three thousand words each—on all this astronomical excitement?"

"Sure," said the writer. "But what excitement?" It transpired that he'd just got back from a fishing trip and had neither read a newspaper nor happened to look up at the sky. But he wrote the articles. He even got sex appeal into them through illustrations, by using ancient star-charts showing the constellation in dishabille, by reproducing certain famous paintings such as "The Origin of the Milky Way" and by using a photograph of a girl in a bathing suit sighting a hand telescope, presumably at one of the errant stars. Circulation of the *Chicago Blade* increased by 21.7%.

It was five o'clock again in the office of the Cole Observatory, just twenty-four and a quarter hours after the beginning of all the commotion. Roger Phlutter—yes, we're back to him again—woke up suddenly when a hand was placed on his shoulder.

"Go on home, Roger," said Mervin Armbruster, his boss, in a kindly tone.

Roger sat upright suddenly.

"But Mr. Armbruster," he said, "I'm sorry I fell asleep."

"Bosh," said Armbruster. "You can't stay here forever, none of us can. Go on home."

Roger Phlutter went home. But when he'd taken a bath, he felt more restless than sleepy. It was only six-fifteen. He phoned Elsie.

"I'm awfully sorry, Roger, but I have another date. What's going on, Roger? The stars, I mean."

"Gosh, Elsie—they're moving. Nobody knows."

"But I thought all the stars moved," Elsie protested. "The sun's a star, isn't it? Once you told me the sun was moving toward a point in Samson."

"Hercules."

"Hercules, then. Since you said all the stars were moving, what is everybody getting excited about?"

"This is different," said Roger. "Take Canopus. It's started moving at the rate of seven light-years a day. It can't do that!"

"Why not?"

"Because," said Roger patiently, "nothing can move faster than light."

"But if it is moving that fast, then it can," said Elsie. "Or else maybe your telescope is wrong or something. Anyway, it's pretty far off, isn't it?"

"A hundred and sixty light years. So far away that we see it a hundred and sixty years ago."

"Then maybe it isn't moving at all," said Elsie. "I mean, maybe it quit moving a hundred and fifty years ago and you're getting all excited about something that doesn't matter any more because it's all over with. Still love me?"

"I sure do, honey. Can't you break that date?"

"'Fraid not, Roger. But I wish I could."

He had to be content with that. He decided to walk uptown to eat.

It was early evening, and too early to see stars overhead, although the clear blue sky was darkening. When the stars did come out tonight, Roger knew, few of the constellations would be recognizable.

As he walked, he thought over Elsie's comments and decided that they were as intelligent as anything he'd heard at Cole. In one way they'd brought out one angle he'd never thought of before, and that made it more incomprehensible.

All these movements had started the same evening—yet they hadn't. Centauri must have started moving four years or so ago, and Rigel five hundred and forty years ago when Christopher Columbus was still in short pants if any, and Vega must have started acting up the year he—Roger, not Vega—was born, twenty-six years ago. Each star out of the hundreds must have started on a date in exact relation to its distance from Earth. Exact relation, to a light-second, for checkups of all the photographic plates taken night before last indicated that all the new stellar movements had started at four ten a.m. Greenwich time. What a mess!

Unless this meant that light, after all, had infinite velocity.

If it didn't have—and it is symptomatic of Roger's perplexity that he could postulate that incredible "if"—then—then what? Things were just as puzzling as before.

Mostly, he felt outraged that such events should happen.

He went into a restaurant and sat down. A radio was blaring out the latest composition in dissarythm, the new quarter-tone dance music in which chorded woodwinds provided background patterns for the mad melodies pounded on tuned tomtoms. Between each number and the next a phrenetic announcer extolled the virtues of a product.

Munching a sandwich, Roger listened appreciatively to the dissarythm and managed not to hear the commercials. Most intelligent people of the eighties had developed a type of radio deafness which enabled them not to hear a human voice coming from a loudspeaker, although they could hear and enjoy the then infrequent intervals of music between announcements. In an age when advertising competition was so keen that there was scarcely a bare wall or an unbillboarded lot within miles of a population center, discriminating people could retain normal outlooks on life only by carefully cultivated partial blindness and partial deafness which enabled them to ignore the bulk of that concerted assault upon their senses.

For that reason a good part of the newscast which followed the dissarythm program went, as it were, into one of Roger's ears and out of the other before it occurred to him that he was not listening to a panegyric on patent breakfast foods.

He thought he recognized the voice, and after a sentence or two he was sure that it was that of Milton Hale, the eminent physicist whose new theory on the principle of indeterminacy had recently occasioned so much scientific controversy. Apparently, Dr. Hale was being interviewed by a radio announcer.

"—a heavenly body, therefore, may have position or velocity, but it may not be said to have both at the same time, with relation to any given space-time frame."

"Dr. Hale, can you put that into common everyday language?" said the syrupy-smooth voice of the interviewer.

"That is common language, sir. Scientifically expressed, in

terms of the Heisenberg contraction-principle, then n to the seventh power in parentheses, representing the pseudo-position of a Diedrich quantum-integer in relation to the seventh coefficient of curvature of mass—"

"Thank you, Dr. Hale, but I fear you are just a bit over the heads of our listeners."

"And your own head," thought Roger Phlutter.

"I am sure, Dr. Hale, that the question of greatest interest to our audience is whether these unprecedented stellar movements are real or illusory?"

"Both. They are real with reference to the frame of space but not with reference to the frame of space-time."

"Can you clarify that, Doctor?"

"I believe I can. The difficulty is purely epistemological. In strict causality, the impact of the macroscopic—"

" 'The slithy toves did gyre and gimble in the wabe,' " thought Roger Phlutter.

"—upon the parallelism of the netropy-gradient."

"Bah!" said Roger, aloud.

"Did you say something, sir?" asked the waitress. Roger noticed her for the first time. She was small and blonde and cuddly. Roger smiled at her.

"That depends upon the space-time frame from which one regards it," he said, judicially. "The difficulty is epistemological."

To make up for that, he tipped her more than he should have, and left.

The world's most eminent physicist, he realized, knew less of what was happening than did the general public. The public knew that the fixed stars were moving, or that they weren't. Obviously Dr. Hale didn't even know that. Under a smoke-screen of qualifications, Hale had hinted that they were doing both.

Roger looked upward, but only a few stars, faint in the early evening, were visible through the halation of the myriad neon and spiegel-light signs. Too early yet, he decided.

He had one drink at a nearby bar, but it didn't taste quite right to him so he didn't finish it. He hadn't realized what was wrong, but he was punch-drunk from lack of sleep. He merely knew that he wasn't sleepy anymore and intended to keep on walking until he felt like going to bed. Anyone hitting him over the head with a well-padded blackjack would have been doing him a signal service, but no one took the trouble.

He kept on walking and, after a while, turned into the brilliantly lighted lobby of a cineplus theater. He bought a ticket and took his seat just in time to see the sticky end of one of the three feature pictures. Several advertisements followed which he managed to look at without seeing.

"We bring you next," said the screen, "a special visicast of the night sky of London, where it is now three o'clock in the morning."

The screen went black, with hundreds of tiny dots that were stars. Roger leaned forward to watch and listen carefully—this would be a broadcast and visicast of facts, not of verbose nothingness.

"The arrow," said the screen, as an arrow appeared upon it, "is now pointing to Polaris, the pole star, which is now ten degrees from the celestial pole in the direction of Ursa Major. Ursa Major itself, the Big Dipper, is no longer recognizable as a dipper, but the arrow will now point to the stars that formerly composed it."

Roger breathlessly followed the arrow and the voice.

"Alkaid and Dubhe," said the voice. "The fixed stars are no longer fixed, but—" The picture changed abruptly to a scene in a modern kitchen. "—the qualities and excellences of Stellar's Stoves do not change. Foods cooked by the super-induced vibratory method taste as good as ever. Stellar Stoves are unexcelled."

Leisurely, Roger Phlutter stood up and made his way out into the aisle. He took his pen-knife from his pocket as he walked toward the screen. One easy jump took him up onto the low stage. His slashes into the fabric were not angry ones. They were careful, methodical cuts intelligently designed to accomplish a maximum of damage with a minimum expenditure of effort.

The damage was done, and thoroughly, by the time three strong ushers gathered him in. He offered no resistance either to them or to the police to whom they gave him. In night court, an hour later, he listened quietly to the charges against him.

"Guilty or not guilty?" asked the presiding magistrate.

"Your Honor, that is purely a question of epistomology," said Roger, earnestly. "The fixed stars move, but Corny Toasties, the world's greatest breakfast food, still represents the pseudo-position of a Diedrich quantum-integer in relation to the seventh coefficient of curvature!"

Ten minutes later, he was sleeping soundly. In a cell, it is true, but soundly nonetheless. The police left him there because they had realized he needed to sleep. . . .

Among other minor tragedies of that night can be included the case of the schooner *Ransagansett*, off the coast of California. Well off the coast of California! A sudden squall had blown her miles off course, how many miles the skipper could only guess.

The *Ransagansett* was an American vessel, with a German crew, under Venezuelan registry, engaged in running booze from Ensenada, Baja California, up the coast to Canada, then in the throes of a prohibition experiment. The *Ransagansett* was an ancient craft with four engines and an untrustworthy compass. During the two days of the storm, her outdated radio receiver—vintage of 1955—had gone haywire beyond the ability of Gross, the first mate, to repair.

But now only a mist remained of the storm, and the remaining shreds of wind were blowing it away. Hans Gross, holding an ancient astrolabe, stood on the deck waiting. About him was utter darkness, for the ship was running without lights to avoid the coastal patrols.

"She clearing, Mister Gross?" called the voice of the captain from below.

"Aye, sir. Idt iss glearing rabidly."

In the cabin, Captain Randall went back to his game of black-jack with the second mate and the engineer. The crew—an elderly German named Weiss, with a wooden leg—was asleep abaft the scuttlebutt—wherever that may have been.

A half hour went by. An hour, and the captain was losing heavily to Helmstadt, the engineer.

"Mister Gross!" he called out.

There wasn't any answer and he called again and still obtained no response.

"Just a minute, mein fine feathered friends," he said to the second mate and engineer, and went up the companionway to the deck.

Gross was standing there staring upward with his mouth open. The mists were gone.

"Mister Gross," said Captain Randall.

The second mate didn't answer. The captain saw that his second mate was revolving slowly where he stood.

"Hans!" said Captain Randall, "What the devil's wrong with you?" Then he, too, looked up.

Superficially the sky looked perfectly normal. No angels flying around nor sound of airplane motors. The dipper—Captain Randall turned around slowly, but more rapidly than Hans Gross. Where was the Big Dipper?

For that matter, where was anything? There wasn't a constellation anywhere that he could recognize. No sickle of Leo. No belt of Orion. No horns of Taurus.

Worse, there was a group of eight bright stars that ought to have been a constellation, for they were shaped roughly like an octagon. Yet if such a constellation had ever existed, he'd never seen it, for he'd been around the Horn and Good Hope. Maybe at that— But no, there wasn't any Southern Cross!

Dazedly, Captain Randall walked to the companionway.

"Mister Weisskopf," he called. "Mister Helmstadt. Come on deck."

They came and looked. Nobody said anything for quite a while.

"Shut off the engines, Mister Helmstadt," said the captain. Helmstadt saluted—the first time he ever had—and went below.

"Captain, shall I vake opp Veiss?" asked Weisskopf.

"What for?"

"I don't know."

The captain considered. "Wake him up," he said.

"I think ve are on der blanet Mars," said Gross.

But the captain had thought of that and rejected it.

"No," he said firmly. "From any planet in the solar system the constellations would look approximately the same."

"You mean ve are oudt of der cosmos?"

The throb of the engines suddenly ceased and there was only the soft familiar lapping of the waves against the hull and the gentle familiar rocking of the boat.

Weisskopf returned with Weiss, and Helmstadt came on deck and saluted again.

"Vell, Captain?"

Captain Randall waved a hand to the afterdeck, piled high with cases of liquor under a canvas tarpaulin. "Break out the cargo," he ordered.

The blackjack game was not resumed. At dawn, under a sun they had never expected to see again—and, for that matter, certainly were not seeing at the moment—the five unconscious men were moved from the ship to the Port of San Francisco Jail by members of the coast patrol. During the night the *Ransagansett* had drifted through the Golden Gate and bumped gently into the dock of the Berkeley ferry.

In tow at the stern of the schooner was a big canvas tarpaulin. It was transfixed by a harpoon whose rope was firmly tied to the after-mast. Its presence there was never explained officially, although days later Captain Randall had vague recollection of having harpooned a sperm whale during the night. But the elderly able-bodied seaman named Weiss never did find out what happened to his wooden leg, which is perhaps just as well.

Milton Hale, Ph.D., eminent physicist, had finished broadcasting and the program was off the air.

"Thank you very much, Dr. Hale," said the radio announcer. The yellow light went on and stayed. The mike was dead. "Uh—your check will be waiting for you at the window. You—uh—know where."

"I know where," said the physicist. He was a rotund, jolly-looking little man. With his bushy white beard, he resembled a pocket edition of Santa Claus. His eyes twinkled and he smoked a short stubby pipe.

He left the sound-proof studio and walked briskly down the hall to the cashier's window. "Hello, sweetheart," he said to the girl on duty there. "I think you have two checks for Dr. Hale."

"You are Dr. Hale?"

"I sometimes wonder," said the little man. "But I carry identification that seems to prove it."

"Two checks?"

"Two checks. Both for the same broadcast, by special arrangement. By the way, there is an excellent revue at the Mabry Theater this evening."

"Is there? Yes, here are your checks, Dr. Hale. One for seventy-five and one for twenty-five. Is that correct?"

"Gratifyingly correct. Now about the revue at the Mabry?"

"If you wish I'll call my husband and ask him about it," said the girl. "He's the doorman over there."

Dr. Hale sighed deeply, but his eyes still twinkled. "I think he'll agree," he said. "Here are the tickets, my dear, and you can take him. I find that I have work to do this evening."

The girl's eyes widened, but she took the tickets.

Dr. Hale went into the phone booth and called his home. His home, and Dr. Hale were both run by his elder sister. "Agatha, I must remain at the office this evening," he said.

"Milton, you know you can work just as well in your study here at home. I heard your broadcast, Milton. It was wonderful."

"It was sheer balderdash, Agatha. Utter rot. What did I say?"

"Why, you said that—uh—that the stars were—I mean, you were not—"

"Exactly, Agatha. My idea was to avert panic on the part of the populace. If I'd told them the truth, they'd have worried. But by being smug and scientific, I let them get the idea that everything was—uh—under control. Do you know, Agatha, what I meant by the parallelism of an entropy-gradient?"

"Why—not exactly."

"Neither did I."

"Milton, have you been drinking?"

"Not y— No, I haven't. I really can't come home to work this evening, Agatha. I'm using my study at the university, because I must have access to the library there, for reference. And the star-charts."

"But, Milton, how about that money for your broadcast? You know it isn't safe for you to have money in your pocket when you're feeling—like this."

"It isn't money, Agatha. It's a check, and I'll mail it to you before I go to the office. I won't cash it myself. How's that?"

"Well—if you must have access to the library, I suppose you must. Good-by, Milton."

Dr. Hale went across the street to the drug store. There he bought a stamp and envelope and cashed the twenty-five dollar check. The seventy-five dollar one he put into the envelope and mailed.

Standing beside the mailbox he glanced up at the early evening sky—shuddered, and hastily lowered his eyes. He took the straightest possible line for the nearest tavern and ordered a double Scotch.

"Y'ain't been in for a long time, Dr. Hale," said Mike, the bartender.

"That I haven't, Mike. Pour me another."

"Sure. On the house, this time. We had your broadcast tuned in on the radio just now. It was swell."

"Yes."

"It sure was. I was kind of worried what was happening up there, with my son an aviator and all. But as long as you scientific guys know what it's all about, I guess it's all right. That was sure a good speech, Doc. But there's one question I'd like to ask you."

"I was afraid of that," said Dr. Hale.

"These stars. They're moving, going somewhere. But where they going? I mean, like you said, if they are."

"There's no way of telling that exactly, Mike."

"Aren't they moving in a straight line, each one of them?"

For just a moment the celebrated scientist hesitated.

"Well—yes and no, Mike. According to spectroscopic analysis, they're maintaining the same distance from us, each one of them. So they're really moving—if they're moving—in circles around us. But the circles are straight, as it were. I mean, it seems that we're in the center of those circles, so the stars that are moving aren't coming closer to us or receding."

"You could draw lines for those circles?"

"On a star-globe, yes. It's been done. They all seem to be heading for a certain area of the sky, but not for a given point. In other words, they don't intersect."

"What part of the sky they going to?"

"Approximately between Ursa Major and Leo, Mike. The ones farthest from there are moving fastest, the ones nearest are moving slower. But darn you, Mike, I came in here to forget about stars, not to talk about them. Give me another."

"In a minute, Doc. When they get there, are they going to stop or keep on going?"

"How the devil do I know, Mike? They started suddenly, all at the same time, and with full original velocity—I mean, they started out at the same speed they're going now—without warming up, so to speak—so I suppose they could stop just as unexpectedly."

He stopped just as suddenly as the stars might. He stared at his reflection in the mirror back of the bar as though he'd never seen it before.

"What's the matter, Doc?"

"Mike!"

"Yes, Doc?"

"Mike, you're a genius."

"Me? You're kidding."

Dr. Hale groaned. "Mike, I'm going to have to go to the university to work this out. So I can have access to the library and the star-globe there. You're making an honest man out of me, Mike. Whatever kind of Scotch this is, wrap me up a bottle."

"It's Tartan Plaid. A quart?"

"A quart, and make it snappy. I've got to see a man about a dog-star."

"Serious, Doc?"

Dr. Hale sighed audibly. "You brought that on yourself, Mike. Yes, the dog-star is Sirius. I wish I'd never come in here, Mike. My first night out in weeks, and you ruin it."

He took a cab to the university, let himself in, and turned on the lights in his private study and in the library. Then he took a good stiff slug of Tartan Plaid and went to work.

First, by telling the chief operator who he was and arguing a bit, he got a telephone connection with the chief astronomer of Cole Observatory.

"This is Hale, Armbruster," he said. "I've got an idea, but I want to check my facts before I start to work on it. Last information I had, there were four-hundred sixty-eight stars exhibiting new proper motion. Is that still correct?"

"Yes, Milton. The same ones are still at it—no others."

"Good. I have a list of them. Has there been any change in speed of motion of any of them?"

"No. Impossible as it seems, it's constant. What is your idea?"

"I want to check my theory first. If it works out into anything, I'll call you." But he forgot to.

It was a long, painful job. First he made a chart of the heavens in the area between Ursa Major and Leo. Across that chart he drew 468 lines representing the projected path of each of the aberrant stars. At the border of the chart, where each line entered, he made a notation of the apparent velocity of the star—not in light-years per hour—but in degrees per hour, to the fifth decimal.

Then he did some reasoning.

"Postulate that the motion which began simultaneously will stop simultaneously," he told himself. "Try a guess at the time. Let's try ten o'clock tomorrow evening."

He tried it and looked at the series of positions indicated upon the chart. No.

Try one o'clock in the morning. It looked almost like—sense!
Try midnight.

That did it. At any rate, it was close enough. The calculation
could be only a few minutes off one way or the other and there
was no point now in working out the exact time. Now that he
knew the incredible fact.

He took another drink and stared at the chart grimly.

A trip to the library gave Dr. Hale the further information he
needed. The address!

Thus began the saga of Dr. Hale's journey. A useless journey,
it is true, but one that should rank with the trip of the messen-
ger to Garcia.

He started it with a drink. Then, knowing the combination,
he rifled the safe in the office of the president of the university.
The note he left in the safe was a masterpiece of brevity. It
read:

Taking money. Explain later.

Then he took another drink and put the bottle in his pocket.
He went outside and hailed a taxicab. He got in.

"Where to, sir?" asked the cabby.

Dr. Hale gave an address.

"Fremont Street?" said the cabby. "Sorry, sir, but I don't
know where that is."

"In Boston," said Dr. Hale. "I should have told you, in
Boston."

"Boston? You mean Boston, Massachusetts? That's a long way
from here."

"Therefore we better start right away," said Dr. Hale, reasonably. A brief financial discussion and the passing of money, borrowed from the university safe, set the driver's mind at rest, and
they started.

It was a bitter cold night, for March, and the heater in the
taxi didn't work any too well. But the Tartan Plaid worked
superlatively for both Dr. Hale and the cabby, and by the time
they reached New Haven, they were singing old-time songs
lustily.

"Off we go, into the wide, wild yonder . . ." their voices
roared.

It is regrettably reported, but possibly untrue, that in Hartford Dr. Hale leered out of the window at a young woman waiting for a late street-car and asked her if she wanted to go to Bos-

ton. Apparently, however, she didn't, for at five o'clock in the morning when the cab drew up in front of 614 Fremont Street, Boston, only Dr. Hale and the driver were in the cab.

Dr. Hale got out and looked at the house. It was a millionaire's mansion, and it was surrounded by a high iron fence with barbed wire on top of it. The gate in the fence was locked and there was no bell button to push.

But the house was only a stone's throw from the sidewalk, and Dr. Hale was not to be deterred. He threw a stone. Then another. Finally he succeeded in smashing a window.

After a brief interval, a man appeared in the window. A butler, Dr. Hale decided.

"I'm Dr. Milton Hale," he called out. "I want to see Rutherford R. Snively, right away. It's important."

"Mr. Snively is not at home, sir," said the butler. "And about that window—"

"The devil with the window," shouted Dr. Hale. "Where is Snively?"

"On a fishing trip."

"Where?"

"I have orders not to give out that information."

Dr. Hale was just a little drunk, perhaps. "You'll give it out just the same," he roared. "By orders of the President of the United States."

The butler laughed. "I don't see him."

"You will," said Hale.

He got back in the cab. The driver had fallen asleep, but Hale shook him awake.

"The White House," said Dr. Hale.

"Huh?"

"The White House, in Washington," said Dr. Hale. "And hurry!" He pulled a hundred dollar bill from his pocket. The cabby looked at it, and groaned. Then he put the bill into his pocket and started the cab.

A light snow was beginning to fall.

As the cab drove off, Rutherford R. Snively, grinning, stepped back from the window. Mr. Snively had no butler.

If Dr. Hale had been more familiar with the peculiarities of the eccentric Mr. Snively, he would have known Snively kept no servants in the place overnight, but lived alone in the big house at 614 Fremont Street. Each morning at ten o'clock, a small army of servants descended upon the house, did their work as rapidly as possible, and were required to depart before the witching hour of noon. Aside from these two hours of every day, Mr. Snively lived in solitary splendor. He had few, if any, social contacts.

Aside from the few hours a day he spent administering his vast interests as one of the country's leading manufacturers, Mr. Snively's time was his own and he spent practically all of it in his workshop, making gadgets.

Snively had an ashtray which would hand him a lighted cigar any time he spoke sharply to it, and a radio receiver so delicately adjusted that it would cut in automatically Snively-sponsored programs and shut off again when they were finished. He had a bathtub that provided a full orchestra accompaniment to his singing therein, and he had a machine which would read aloud to him from any book which he placed in its hopper.

His life may have been a lonely one, but it was not without such material comforts. Eccentric, yes, but Mr. Snively could afford to be eccentric with a net income of four million dollars a year. Not bad for a man who'd started life as the son of a shipping clerk.

Mr. Snively chuckled as he watched the taxicab drive away, and then he went back to bed and to the sleep of the just.

"So somebody has things figured out nineteen hours ahead of time," he thought. "Well, a lot of good it will do them!"

There wasn't any law to punish him for what he'd done. . . .

Bookstores did a landoffice business that day in books on astronomy. The public, apathetic at first, was deeply interested now. Even ancient and musty volumes of Newton's *Principia* sold at premium prices.

The ether blared with comment upon the new wonder of the skies. Little of the comment was professional, or even intelligent, for most astronomers were asleep that day. They'd managed to stay awake the first forty-eight hours from the start of the phenomena, but the third day found them worn out mentally and physically, and inclined to let the stars take care of themselves while they—the astronomers, not the stars—caught up on sleep.

Staggering offers from the telecast and broadcast studios enticed a few of them to attempt lectures, but their efforts were dreary things, better forgotten. Dr. Carver Blake, broadcasting from KNB, fell soundly asleep between a perigree and an apogee.

Physicists were also greatly in demand. The most eminent of them all, however, was sought in vain. The solitary clue to Dr. Milton Hale's disappearance, the brief note "Taking money. Explain later," wasn't much of a help. His sister Agatha feared the worst.

For the first time in history, astronomical news made banner headlines in the newspapers.

Snow had started early that morning along the northern Atlantic seaboard and now it was growing steadily worse. Just outside Waterbury, Conn., the driver of Dr. Hale's cab began to weaken.

It wasn't human, he thought, for a man to be expected to drive to Boston and then, without stopping, from Boston to Washington. Not even for a hundred dollars.

Not in a storm like this. Why, he could see only a dozen yards ahead through the driving snow, even when he could manage to keep his eyes open. His fare was slumbering soundly in the back seat. Maybe he could get away with stopping here along the road, for an hour, to catch some sleep. Just an hour. His fare wouldn't ever know the difference. The guy must be loony, he thought, or why hadn't he taken a plane or a train?

Dr. Hale would have, of course, if he'd thought of it. But he wasn't used to traveling and besides there'd been the Tartan Plaid. A taxi had seemed the easiest way to get anywhere—no worrying about tickets and connections and stations. Money was no object, and the plaid condition of his mind had caused him to overlook the human factor involved in an extended journey by taxi.

When he awoke, almost frozen, in the parked taxi, that human factor dawned upon him. The driver was so sound asleep that no amount of shaking could arouse him. Dr. Hale's watch had stopped, so he had no idea where he was or what time it was.

Unfortunately, too, he didn't know how to drive a car. He took a quick drink to keep from freezing, and then got out of the cab, and as he did so, a car stopped.

It was a policeman—what is more it was a policeman in a million.

Yelling over the roar of the storm, Hale hailed him.

"I'm Dr. Hale," he shouted. "We're lost. Where am I?"

"Get in here before you freeze," ordered the policeman. "Do you mean Dr. Milton Hale, by any chance?"

"Yes."

"I've read all your books, Dr. Hale," said the policeman. "Physics is my hobby, and I've always wanted to meet you. I want to ask you about the revised value of the quantum."

"This is life or death," said Dr. Hale. "Can you take me to the nearest airport, quick?"

"Of course, Dr. Hale."

"And look—there's a driver in that cab, and he'll freeze to death unless we send aid."

"I'll put him in the back seat of my car, and then run the cab off the road. We'll take care of details later."

"Hurry, please."

The obliging policeman hurried. He got back in and started the car.

"About the revised quantum value, Dr. Hale," he began, then stopped talking.

Dr. Hale was sound asleep. The policeman drove to Waterbury airport, one of the largest in the world since the population shift from New York City northwards in the 1960's and 70's had given it a central position. In front of the ticket office, he gently awakened Dr. Hale.

"This is the airport, sir," he said.

Even as he spoke, Dr. Hale was leaping out of the car and stumbling into the building, yelling, "Thanks," over his shoulder and nearly falling down in doing so.

The warm-up roaring of the motors of a superstratoliner out on the field lent wings to his heels as he dashed for the ticket window.

"What plane's that?" he yelled.

"Washington Special, due out in one minute. But I don't think you can make it."

Dr. Hale slapped a hundred-dollar bill on the ledge. "Ticket," he gasped. "Keep change."

He grabbed the ticket and ran, getting into the plane just as the doors were being closed. Panting, he fell into a seat, the ticket still in his hand. He was sound asleep before the hostess strapped him in for the blind take-off.

A little while later, the hostess awakened him. The passengers were disembarking.

Dr. Hale rushed out of the plane and ran across the field to the airport building. A big clock told him that it was nine o'clock, and he felt elated as he ran for the door marked "Taxicabs."

He got into the nearest one.

"White House," he told the driver. "How long'll it take?"

"Ten minutes."

Dr. Hale gave a sigh of relief and sank back against the cushions. He didn't go back to sleep this time. He was wide awake now. But he closed his eyes to think out the words he'd use in explaining matters.

"Here you are, sir."

Dr. Hale gave the driver a bill and hurried out of the cab and into the building. It didn't look like he expected it to look. But there was a desk and he ran up to it.

"I've got to see the President, quick. It's vital."

The clerk frowned. "The president of what?"

Dr. Hale's eyes went wide. "The president of the— Say, what building is this? And what town?"

The clerk's frown deepened. "This is the White House Hotel," he said, "Seattle, Washington."

Dr. Hale fainted. He woke up in a hospital three hours later. It was then midnight, Pacific Time, which meant it was three o'clock in the morning on the Eastern Seaboard. It had, in fact, been midnight already in Washington, D. C., and in Boston, when he had been leaving the Washington Special in Seattle.

Dr. Hale rushed to the window and shook his fists, both of them, at the sky. A futile gesture.

Back in the East, however, the storm had stopped by twilight, leaving a light mist in the air. The star-conscious public thereupon deluged the weather bureaus with telephone requests about the persistence of the mist.

"A breeze off the ocean is expected," they were told. "It is blowing now, in fact, and within an hour or two will have cleared off the light fog."

By eleven-fifteen the skies of Boston were clear.

Untold thousands braved the bitter cold and stood staring upward at the unfolding pageant of the no-longer-eternal stars. It almost looked as though an incredible development had occurred.

And then, gradually, the murmur grew. By a quarter to twelve, the thing was certain, and the murmur hushed and then grew louder than ever, waxing toward midnight. Different people reacted differently, of course, as might be expected. There was laughter as well as indignation, cynical amusement as well as shocked horror. There was even admiration.

Soon in certain parts of the city, a concerted movement on the part of those who knew an address on Fremont Street, began to take place. Movement afoot and in cars and public vehicles, converging.

At five minutes to twelve, Rutherford R. Sniveley sat waiting within his house. He was denying himself the pleasure of looking until, at the last moment, the thing was complete.

It was going well. The gathering murmur of voices, mostly angry voices, outside his house told him that. He heard his name shouted.

Just the same he waited until the twelfth stroke of the clock before he stepped out upon the balcony. Much as he wanted to look upward, he forced himself to look down at the street first. The milling crowd was there, and it was angry. But he had only contempt for the milling crowd.

Police cars were pulling up, too, and he recognized the Mayor of Boston getting out of one of them, and the Chief of Police was with him. But so what? There wasn't any law covering this.

Then having denied himself the supreme pleasure long enough, he turned his eyes up to the silent sky, and there it was. The four hundred and sixty-eight brightest stars spelling out:

USE
SNIVELY'S
SOAP

For just a second did his satisfaction last. Then his face began to turn apoplectic purple.

"My God!" said Mr. Sniveley. "It's spelled wrong!"

His face grew more purple still and then, as a tree falls, he fell backward through the window.

An ambulance rushed the fallen magnate to the nearest hospital, but he was pronounced dead—of apoplexy—upon entrance.

But misspelled or not, the eternal stars held their position as of that midnight. The aberrant motion had stopped and again the stars were fixed. Fixed to spell—USE SNIVELY'S SOAP!

Of the many explanations offered by all the sundry who professed some physical and astronomical knowledge, none was more lucid—or closer to the actual truth—than that put forward by Wendell Mehan, president emeritus of the New York Astronomical Society.

"Obviously, the phenomenon is a trick of refraction," said Dr. Mehan. "It is manifestly impossible for any force contrived by man to move a star. The stars, therefore, still occupy their old places in the firmament.

"I suggest that Sniveley must have contrived a method of refracting the light of the stars, somewhere in or just above the atmospheric layer of earth, so that they appear to have changed their positions. This is done, probably, by radio waves or similar waves, sent on some fixed frequency from a set—or possibly a series of four hundred and sixty-eight sets—somewhere upon the surface of the earth. Although we do not understand just how it is done, it is no more unthinkable that light rays should be bent by a field of waves than by a prism or by gravitational force.

"Since Sniveley was not a great scientist, I imagine that his discovery was empiric rather than logical—an accidental find. It is quite possible that even the discovery of his projector will not enable present-day scientists to understand its secret, any more than an aboriginal savage could understand the operation of a simple radio receiver by taking one apart.

"My principal reason for this assertion is the fact that the refraction obviously is a fourth-dimensional phenomenon or its effect would be purely local to one portion of the globe. Only in the fourth dimension could light be so refracted. . . ."

There was more, but it is better to skip to his final paragraph:

"This effect cannot possibly be permanent—more permanent, that is, than the wave-projector which causes it. Sooner or later, Sniveley's machine will be found and shut off, or it will break down or wear out of its own volition. Undoubtedly it includes vacuum tubes, which will some day blow out, as do the tubes in our radios. . . ."

The excellence of Dr. Mehan's analysis was shown, two months and eight days later, when the Boston Electric Co. shut off, for non-payment of bills, service to a house situated at 901

West Rogers Street, ten blocks from the Sniveley mansion. At
the instant of the shut-off, excited reports from the night side of
Earth brought the news that the stars had flashed back into their
former positions instantaneously.

Investigation brought out that the description of one Elmer
Smith, who had purchased that house six months before, corre-
sponded with the description of Rutherford R. Sniveley, and undoubtedly Elmer Smith and Rutherford R. Sniveley were one
and the same person.

In the attic was found a complicated network of four hundred
and sixty-eight radio-type antennae, each antenna of different
length and running in a different direction. The machine to
which they were connected was not larger, strangely, than the
average ham's radio projector, nor did it draw appreciably more
current, according to the electric company's record.

By special order of the President of the United States, the
projector was destroyed without examination of its internal arrangement. Clamorous protests against this high-handed executive order arose from many sides. But inasmuch as the projector
had already been broken up, the protests were of no avail.

Serious repercussions were, on the whole, amazingly few.

Persons in general appreciated the stars more, but trusted
them less.

Roger Phlutter got out of jail and married Elsie. Dr. Milton
Hale found he liked Seattle, and stayed there. Two thousand
miles away from his sister Agatha, he found it possible for the
first time to defy her openly. He enjoys life more but, it is
feared, will write fewer books.

There is one fact remaining which is painful to consider,
since it casts a deep reflection upon the basic intelligence of the
human race. It is proof, though, that the President's executive
order was justified, despite scientific protests.

That fact is as humiliating as it is enlightening. During the
two months and eight days during which the Sniveley machine
was in operation, sales of Sniveley Soap increased 915%!

Answer

DWAR EV ceremoniously soldered the final connection with gold. The eyes of a dozen television cameras watched him and the subether bore throughout the universe a dozen pictures of what he was doing.

He straightened and nodded to Dwar Reyn, then moved to a position beside the switch that would complete the contact when he threw it. The switch that would connect, all at once, all of the monster computing machines of all the populated planets in the universe—ninety-six billion planets—into the supercircuit that would connect them all into one supercalculator, one cybernetics machine that would combine all the knowledge of all the galaxies.

Dwar Reyn spoke briefly to the watching and listening trillions. Then after a moment's silence he said, "Now, Dwar Ev."

Dwar Ev threw the switch. There was a mighty hum, the surge of power from ninety-six billion planets. Lights flashed and quieted along the miles-long panel.

Dwar Ev stepped back and drew a deep breath. "The honor of asking the first question is yours, Dwar Reyn."

"Thank you," said Dwar Reyn. "It shall be a question which no single cybernetics machine has been able to answer."

He turned to face the machine. "Is there a God?"

The mighty voice answered without hesitation, without clicking of a single relay.

"Yes, *now* there is a God."

Sudden fear flashed on the face of Dwar Ev. He leaped to grab the switch.

A bolt of lightning from the cloudless sky struck him down and fused the switch shut.

The Geezenstacks

ONE OF the strange things about it was that Aubrey Walters wasn't at all a strange little girl. She was quite as ordinary as her father and mother, who lived in an apartment on Otis Street, and who played bridge one night a week, went out somewhere another night, and spent the other evenings quietly at home.

Aubrey was nine, and had rather stringy hair and freckles, but at nine one never worries about such things. She got along quite well in the not-too-expensive private school to which her parents sent her, she made friends easily and readily with other children, and she took lessons on a three-quarter-size violin and played it abominably.

Her greatest fault, possibly, was her predeliction for staying up late of nights, and that was the fault of her parents, really, for letting her stay up and dressed until she felt sleepy and wanted to go to bed. Even at five and six, she seldom went to bed before ten o'clock in the evening. And if, during a period of maternal concern, she was put to bed earlier, she never went to sleep anyway. So why not let the child stay up?

Now, at nine years, she stayed up quite as late as her parents did, which was about eleven o'clock of ordinary nights and later when they had company for bridge, or went out for the evening. Then it was later, for they usually took her along. Aubrey enjoyed it, whatever it was. She'd sit still as a mouse in a seat at the theater, or regard them with little-girl seriousness over the rim of a glass of ginger ale while they had a cocktail or two at a night club. She took the noise and the music and the dancing with big-eyed wonder and enjoyed every minute of it.

Sometimes Uncle Richard, her mother's brother, went along with them. She and Uncle Richard were good friends. It was Uncle Richard who gave her the dolls.

"Funny thing happened today," he'd said. "I'm walking down

Rodgers Place, past the Mariner Building—you know, Edith; it's where Doc Howard used to have his office—and something thudded on the sidewalk right behind me. And I turned around, and there was this package."

"This package" was a white box a little larger than a shoe box, and it was rather strangely tied with gray ribbon. Sam Walters, Aubrey's father, looked at it curiously.

"Doesn't look dented," he said. "Couldn't have fallen out of a very high window. Was it tied up like that?"

"Just like that. I put the ribbon back on after I opened it and looked in. Oh, I don't mean I opened it then or there. I just stopped and looked up to see who'd dropped it—thinking I'd see somebody looking out of a window. But nobody was, and I picked up the box. It had something in it, not very heavy, and the box and the ribbon looked like—well, not like something somebody'd throw away on purpose. So I stood looking up, and nothing happened, so I shook the box a little and—"

"All right, all right," said Sam Walters. "Spare us the blow-by-blow. You didn't find out who dropped it?"

"Right. And I went up as high as the fourth floor, asking the people whose windows were over the place where I picked it up. They were all home, as it happened, and none of them had ever seen it. I thought it might have fallen off a window ledge. But—"

"What's in it, Dick?" Edith asked.

"Dolls. Four of them. I brought them over this evening for Aubrey. If she wants them."

He untied the package, and Aubrey said, "Oooo, Uncle Richard. They're—they're *lovely*."

Sam said, "Hm. Those look almost more like manikins than dolls, Dick. The way they're dressed, I mean. Must have cost several dollars apiece. Are you sure the owner won't turn up?"

Richard shrugged. "Don't see how he can. As I told you, I went up four floors, asking. Thought from the look of the box and the sound of the thud, it couldn't have come from even that high. And after I opened it, well—look—" He picked up one of the dolls and held it out for Sam Walters' inspection.

"Wax. The heads and hands, I mean. And not one of them cracked. It couldn't have fallen from higher than the second story. Even then, I don't see how—" He shrugged again.

"They're the Geezenstacks," said Aubrey.

"Huh?" Sam asked.

"I'm going to call them the Geezenstacks," Aubrey said. "Look, this one is Papa Geezenstack and this one is Mama Geezenstack, and the little girl one—that's—that's Aubrey Geezenstack. And the other man one, we'll call him Uncle Geezenstack. The little girl's uncle."

Sam chuckled. "Like us, eh? But if Uncle—uh—Geezenstack is Mama Geezenstack's brother, like Uncle Richard is Mama's brother, then his name wouldn't be Geezenstack."

"Just the same, it is," Aubrey said. "They're all Geezenstacks. Papa, will you buy me a house for them?"

"A doll house? Why—" He'd started to say, "Why, sure," but caught his wife's eye and remembered. Aubrey's birthday was only a week off and they'd been wondering what to get her. He changed it hastily to "Why, I don't know. I'll think about it."

It was a beautiful doll house. Only one-story high, but quite elaborate, and with a roof that lifted off so one could rearrange the furniture and move the dolls from room to room. It scaled well with the manikins Uncle Richard had brought.

Aubrey was rapturous. All her other playthings went into eclipse and the doings of the Geezenstacks occupied most of her waking thoughts.

It wasn't for quite a while that Sam Walters began to notice, and to think about, the strange aspect of the doings of the Geezenstacks. At first, with a quiet chuckle at the coincidences that followed one another.

And then, with a puzzled look in his eyes.

It wasn't until quite a while later that he got Richard off into a corner. The four of them had just returned from a play. He said, "Uh—Dick."

"Yeah, Sam?"

"These dolls, Dick. Where *did* you get them?"

Richard's eyes stared at him blankly. "What do you mean, Sam? I told you where I got them."

"Yes, but—you weren't kidding, or anything? I mean, maybe you bought them for Aubrey, and thought we'd object if you gave her such an expensive present, so you—uh—"

"No, honest, I didn't."

"But dammit, Dick, they couldn't have fallen out of a window, or dropped out, and not broken. They're wax. Couldn't someone walking behind you—or going by in an auto or something—?"

"There wasn't anyone around, Sam. Nobody at all. I've wondered about it myself. But if I was lying, I wouldn't make up a screwy story like that, would I? I'd just say I found them on a park bench or a seat in a movie. But why are you curious?"

"I—uh—I just got to wondering."

Sam Walters kept on wondering, too.

They were little things, most of them. Like the time Aubrey had said, "Papa Geezenstack didn't go to work this morning. He's in bed, sick."

"So?" Sam had asked. "And what is wrong with the gentleman?"

"Something he ate, I guess."

And the next morning, at breakfast, "And how is Mr. Geezenstack, Aubrey?"

"A little better, but he isn't going to work today yet, the doctor said. Tomorrow, maybe."

And the next day, Mr. Geezenstack went back to work. That, as it happened, was the day Sam Walters came home feeling quite ill, as a result of something he'd eaten for lunch. Yes, he'd missed two days from work. The first time he'd missed work on account of illness in several years.

And some things were quicker than that, and some slower. You couldn't put your finger on it and say, "Well, if this happens to the Geezenstacks, it will happen to us in twenty-four hours." Sometimes it was less than an hour. Sometimes as long as a week.

"Mama and Papa Geezenstack had a quarrel today."

And Sam had tried to avoid that quarrel with Edith, but it seemed he just couldn't. He'd been quite late getting home, through no fault of his own. It had happened often, but this time Edith took exception. Soft answers failed to turn away wrath, and at last he'd lost his own temper.

"Uncle Geezenstack is going away for a visit." Richard hadn't been out of town for years, but the next week he took a sudden notion to run down to New York. "Pete and Amy, you know. Got a letter from them asking me—"

"When?" Sam asked, almost sharply. "When did you get the letter?"

"Yesterday."

"Then last week you weren't— This sounds like a silly question, Dick, but last week were you thinking about going anywhere? Did you say anything to—to anyone about the possibility of your visiting someone?"

"Lord, no. Hadn't even thought about Pete and Amy for months, till I got their letter yesterday. Want me to stay a week."

"You'll be back in three days—maybe," Sam had said. He wouldn't explain, even when Richard did come back in three days. It sounded just too damn' silly to say that he'd known how long Richard was going to be gone, because that was how long Uncle Geezenstack had been away.

Sam Walters began to watch his daughter, and to wonder. She, of course, was the one who made the Geezenstacks do whatever they did. Was it possible that Aubrey had some strange preternatural insight which caused her, unconsciously, to predict things that were going to happen to the Walters and to Richard?

He didn't, of course, believe in clairvoyance. But was Aubrey clairvoyant?

"Mrs. Geezenstack's going shopping today. She's going to buy a new coat."

That one almost sounded like a put-up job. Edith had smiled at Aubrey and then looked at Sam. "That reminds me, Sam. Tomorrow I'll be downtown, and there's a sale at—"

"But, Edith, these are war times. And you don't *need* a coat."

He'd argued so earnestly that he made himself late for work. Arguing uphill, because he really could afford the coat and she really hadn't bought one for two years. But he couldn't explain that the real reason he didn't want her to buy one was that Mrs. Geezen— Why, it was too silly to say, even to himself.

Edith bought the coat.

Strange, Sam thought, that nobody else noticed those coincidences. But Richard wasn't around all the time, and Edith— well, Edith had the knack of listening to Aubrey's prattle without hearing nine-tenths of it.

"Aubrey Geezenstack brought home her report card today, Papa. She got ninety in arithmetic and eighty in spelling and—"

And two days later, Sam was calling up the headmaster of the school. Calling from a pay station, of course, so nobody would hear him. "Mr. Bradley, I'd like to ask a question that I have a—

uh—rather peculiar, but important, reason for asking. Would it be possible for a student at your school to know in advance exactly what grades . . ."

No, not possible. The teachers themselves didn't know, until they'd figured averages, and that hadn't been done until the morning the report cards were made out, and sent home. Yes, yesterday morning, while the children had their play period.

"Sam," Richard said, "you're looking kind of seedy. Business worries? Look, things are going to get better from now on, and with your company, you got nothing to worry about anyway."

"That isn't it, Dick. It—I mean, there isn't anything I'm worrying about. Not exactly. I mean—" And he'd had to wriggle out of the cross-examination by inventing a worry or two for Richard to talk him out of.

He thought about the Geezenstacks a lot. Too much. If only he'd been superstitious, or credulous, it might not have been so bad. But he *wasn't*. That's why each succeeding coincidence hit him a little harder than the last.

Edith and her brother noticed it, and talked about it when Sam wasn't around.

"He *has* been acting queer lately, Dick. I'm—I'm really worried. He acts so— Do you think we could talk him into seeing a doctor or a—"

"A psychiatrist? Um, if we could. But I can't see him doing it, Edith. Something's eating him, and I've tried to pump him about it, but he won't open up. Y'know—I think it's got something to do with those damn' dolls."

"Dolls? You mean Aubrey's dolls? The ones you gave her?"

"Yes, the Geezenstacks. He sits and stares at the doll house. I've heard him ask the kid questions about them, and he was *serious*. I think he's got some delusion or something about them. Or centering on them."

"But, Dick, that's—*awful*."

"Look, Edie, Aubrey isn't as interested in them as she used to be, and— Is there anything she wants very badly?"

"Dancing lessons. But she's already studying violin and I don't think we can let her—"

"Do you think if you promised her dancing lessons if she gave up those dolls, she'd be willing? I think we've got to get them out of the apartment. And I don't want to hurt Aubrey, so—"

"Well—but what would we tell Aubrey?"

"Tell *her* I know a poor family with children who haven't any dolls at all. And—I think she'll agree, if you make it strong enough."

"But, Dick, what will we tell Sam? He'll know better than that."

"Tell Sam, when Aubrey isn't around, that you think she's getting too old for dolls, and that—tell him she's taking an unhealthy interest in them, and that the doctor advises— That sort of stuff."

Aubrey wasn't enthusiastic. She was not as engrossed in the Geezenstacks as she'd been when they were newer, but couldn't she have both the dolls *and* the dancing lessons?

"I don't think you'd have time for both, honey. And there are those poor children who haven't *any* dolls to play with, and you ought to feel sorry for them."

And Aubrey weakened, eventually. Dancing school didn't open for ten days, though, and she wanted to keep the dolls until she could start her lessons. There was argument, but to no avail.

"That's all right, Edie," Richard told her. "Ten days is better than not at all, and—well, if she doesn't give them up voluntarily, it'll start a rumpus and Sam'll find out what we're up to. You haven't mentioned anything to him at all, have you?"

"No. But maybe it would make him feel better to know they were—"

"I wouldn't. We don't know just what it is about them that fascinates or repels him. Wait till it happens, and then tell him. Aubrey has already given them away. Or *he* might raise some objection or want to keep them. If I get them out of the place first, he can't."

"You're right, Dick. And Aubrey won't tell him, because I told her the dancing lessons are going to be a surprise for her father, and she can't tell him what's going to happen to the dolls without telling the other side of the deal."

"Swell, Edith."

It might have been better if Sam had known. Or maybe everything would have happened just the same, if he had.

Poor Sam. He had a bad moment the very next evening. One of Aubrey's friends from school was there, and they were playing with the doll house. Sam watching them, trying to look less interested than he was. Edith was knitting and Richard, who had just come in, was reading the paper.

Only Sam was listening to the children and heard the suggestion.

". . . and then let's have a play funeral, Aubrey. Just pretend one of them is—"

Sam Walters let out a sort of strangled cry and almost fell getting across the room.

There was a bad moment, then, but Edith and Richard managed to pass it off casually enough, outwardly. Edith discovered it was time for Aubrey's little friend to leave, and she exchanged a significant glance with Richard and they both escorted the girl to the door.

Whispered, "Dick, did you *see*—"

"Something *is* wrong, Edie. Maybe we shouldn't wait. After all, Aubrey has agreed to give them up, and—"

Back in the living room, Sam was still breathing a bit hard. Aubrey looked at him almost as though she was afraid of him. It was the first time she'd ever looked at him like that, and Sam felt ashamed. He said, "Honey, I'm sorry I— But listen, you'll promise me you'll *never* have a play funeral for one of your dolls? Or pretend one of them is badly sick or has an accident— or anything bad at all? Promise?"

"Sure, Papa. I'm—I'm going to put them away for tonight."

She put the lid on the doll house and went back toward the kitchen.

In the hallway, Edie said, "I'll—I'll get Aubrey alone and fix it with her. You talk to Sam. Tell him—look, let's go out tonight, go somewhere and get him away from everything. See if he will."

Sam was still staring at the doll house.

"Let's get some excitement, Sam," Richard said. "How's about going out somewhere? We've been sticking too close to home. It'll do us good."

Sam took a deep breath. "Okay, Dick. If you say so. I—I could use a little fun, I guess."

Edie came back with Aubrey, and she winked at her brother. "You men go on downstairs and get a cab from the stand around the corner. Aubrey and I'll be down by the time you bring it."

Behind Sam's back, as the men were putting on their coats, Richard gave Edith an inquiring look and she nodded.

Outside, there was a heavy fog; one could see only a few yards ahead. Sam insisted that Richard wait at the door for Edith and Aubrey while he went to bring the cab. The woman and girl came down just before Sam got back.

Richard asked, "Did you—?"

"Yes, Dick. I was going to throw them away, but I gave them away instead. That way they're *gone;* he might have wanted to hunt in the rubbish and find them if I'd just thrown—"

"Gave them away? To whom?"

"Funniest thing, Dick. I opened the door and there was an old woman going by in the back hall. Don't know which of the apartments she came from, but she must be a scrubwoman or something, although she looked like a witch really, but when she saw those dolls I had in my hands—"

"Here comes the cab," Dick said. "You gave them to her?"

"Yes, it was funny. She said, *'Mine? To Keep? Forever?'* Wasn't that a strange way of asking it? But I laughed and said, 'Yes, ma'am. Yours forev—'"

She broke off, for the shadowy outline of the taxi was at the curb, and Sam opened the door and called out, "Come on, folks!"

Aubrey skipped across the sidewalk into the cab, and the others followed. It started.

The fog was thicker now. They could not see out the windows at all. It was as though a gray wall pressed against the glass, as though the world outside was gone, completely and utterly. Even the windshield, from where they sat, was a gray blank.

"How can he drive so fast?" Richard asked, and there was an edge of nervousness in his voice. "By the way, where are we going, Sam?"

"By George," Sam said, "I forgot to tell her."

"Her?"

"Yeah. Woman driver. They've got them all over now. I'll—"

He leaned forward and tapped on the glass, and the woman turned.

Edith saw her face, and screamed.

Hall of Mirrors

FOR AN INSTANT you think it is temporary blindness, this sudden dark that comes in the middle of a bright afternoon.

It *must* be blindness, you think; could the sun that was tanning you have gone out instantaneously, leaving you in utter blackness?

Then the nerves of your body tell you that you are *standing*, whereas only a second ago you were sitting comfortably, almost reclining, in a canvas chair. In the patio of a friend's house in Beverly Hills. Talking to Barbara, your fiancée. Looking at Barbara—Barbara in a swimsuit—her skin golden tan in the brilliant sunshine, beautiful.

You wore swimming trunks. Now you do not feel them on you; the slight pressure of the elastic waistband is no longer there against your waist. You touch your hands to your hips. You are naked. And standing.

Whatever has happened to you is more than a change to sudden darkness or to sudden blindness.

You raise your hands gropingly before you. They touch a plain smooth surface, a wall. You spread them apart and each hand reaches a corner. You pivot slowly. A second wall, then a third, then a door. You are in a closet about four feet square.

Your hand finds the knob of the door. It turns and you push the door open.

There is light now. The door has opened to a lighted room . . . a room that you have never seen before.

It is not large, but it is pleasantly furnished—although the furniture is of a style that is strange to you. Modesty makes you open the door cautiously the rest of the way. But the room is empty of people.

You step into the room, turning to look behind you into the closet, which is now illuminated by light from the room. The closet is and is not a closet; it is the size and shape of one, but it contains nothing, not a single hook, no rod for hanging clothes, no shelf. It is an empty, blank-walled, four-by-four foot space.

You close the door to it and stand looking around the room. It is about twelve by sixteen feet. There is one door, but it is closed. There are no windows. Five pieces of furniture. Four of them you recognize—more or less. One looks like a very functional desk. One is obviously a chair . . . a comfortable-looking one. There is a table, although its top is on several levels instead of only one. Another is a bed, or couch. Something shimmering is lying across it and you walk over and pick the shimmering something up and examine it. It is a garment.

You are naked, so you put it on. Slippers are part way under the bed (or couch) and you slide your feet into them. They fit, and they feel warm and comfortable as nothing you have ever worn on your feet has felt. Like lamb's wool, but softer.

You are dressed now. You look at the door—the only door of the room except that of the closet (closet?) from which you entered it. You walk to the door and before you try the knob, you see the small typewritten sign pasted just above it that reads:

This door has a time lock set to open in one hour. For reasons you will soon understand, it is better that you do not leave this room before then. There is a letter for you on the desk. Please read it.

It is not signed. You look at the desk and see that there is an envelope lying on it.

You do not yet go to take that envelope from the desk and read the letter that must be in it.

Why not? Because you are frightened.

You see other things about the room. The lighting has no source that you can discover. It comes from nowhere. It is not indirect lighting; the ceiling and the walls are not reflecting it at all.

They didn't have lighting like that, back where you came from. What did you mean by *back where you came from?*

You close your eyes. You tell yourself: *I am Norman Hastings. I am an associate professor of mathematics at the University of Southern California. I am twenty-five years old, and this is the year nineteen hundred and fifty-four.*

You open your eyes and look again.

They didn't use that style of furniture in Los Angeles—or anywhere else that you know of—in 1954. That thing over in the corner—you can't even guess what it is. So might your grandfather, at your age, have looked at a television set.

You look down at yourself, at the shimmering garment that you found waiting for you. With thumb and forefinger you feel its texture.

It's like nothing you've ever touched before.

I am Norman Hastings. This is nineteen hundred and fifty-four.

Suddenly you must know, and at once.

You go to the desk and pick up the envelope that lies upon it. Your name is typed on the outside. *Norman Hastings.*

Your hands shake a little as you open it. Do you blame them?

There are several pages, typewritten. Dear Norman, it starts. You turn quickly to the end to look for the signature. It is unsigned.

You turn back and start reading.

"Do not be afraid. There is nothing to fear, but much to explain. Much that you must understand before the time lock opens that door. Much that you must accept and—obey.

"You have already guessed that you are in the future—in what, to you, seems to be the future. The clothes and the room must have told you that. I planned it that way so the shock would not be too sudden, so you would realize it over the course of several minutes rather than read it here—and quite probably disbelieve what you read.

"The 'closet' from which you have just stepped is, as you have by now realized, a time machine. From it you stepped into the world of 2004. The date is April 7th, just fifty years from the time you last remember.

"You cannot return.

"I did this to you and you may hate me for it; I do not know. That is up to you to decide, but it does not matter. What does matter, and not to you alone, is another decision which you must make. I am incapable of making it.

"Who is writing this to you? I would rather not tell you just yet. By the time you have finished reading this, even though it is not signed (for I knew you would look first for a signature), I will not need to tell you who I am. You will know.

"I am seventy-five years of age. I have, in this year 2004, been studying 'time' for thirty of those years. I have completed the first time machine ever built—and thus far, its construction, even the fact that it has been constructed, is my own secret.

"You have just participated in the first major experiment. It will be your responsibility to decide whether there shall ever be any more experiments with it, whether it should be given to the world, or whether it should be destroyed and never used again."

End of the first page. You look up for a moment, hesitating to turn the next page. Already you suspect what is coming.

You turn the page.

"I constructed the first time machine a week ago. My calculations had told me that it would work, but not how it would work. I had expected it to send an object back in time—it works backward in time only, not forward—physically unchanged and intact.

"My first experiment showed me my error. I placed a cube of metal in the machine—it was a miniature of the one you just walked out of—and set the machine to go backward ten years. I flicked the switch and opened the door, expecting to find the cube vanished. Instead I found it had crumbled to powder.

"I put in another cube and sent it two years back. The second cube came back unchanged, except that it was newer, shinier.

"That gave me the answer. I had been expecting the cubes to go back in time, and they had done so, but not in the sense I had expected them to. Those metal cubes had been fabricated about three years previously. I had sent the first one back years before it had existed in its fabricated form. Ten years ago it had been ore. The machine returned it to that state.

"Do you see how our previous theories of time travel have been wrong? We expected to be able to step into a time machine in, say, 2004, set it for fifty years back, and then step out in the year 1954 . . . but it does not work that way. The machine does not move in time. Only whatever is within the machine is affected, and then just with relation to itself and not to the rest of the Universe.

"I confirmed this with guinea pigs by sending one six weeks old five weeks back and it came out a baby.

"I need not outline all my experiments here. You will find a record of them in the desk and you can study it later.

"Do you understand now what has happened to you, Norman?"

You begin to understand. And you begin to sweat.

The *I* who wrote that letter you are now reading is *you*, yourself at the age of seventy-five, in the year of 2004. You are that seventy-five-year-old man, with your body returned to what it had been fifty years ago, with all the memories of fifty years of living wiped out.

You invented the time machine.

And before you used it on yourself, you made these arrangements to help you orient yourself. You wrote yourself the letter which you are now reading.

But if those fifty years are—to you—gone, what of all your friends, those you loved? What of your parents? What of the girl you are going—were going—to marry?

You read on:

"Yes, you will want to know what has happened. Mom died in 1963, Dad in 1968. You married Barbara in 1956. I am sorry to tell you that she died only three years later, in a plane crash. You have one son. He is still living; his name is Walter; he is now forty-six years old and is an accountant in Kansas City."

Tears come into your eyes and for a moment you can no longer read. Barbara dead—dead for forty-five years. And only minutes ago, in subjective time, you were sitting next to her, sitting in the bright sun in a Beverly Hills patio . . .

You force yourself to read again.

"But back to the discovery. You begin to see some of its implications. You will need time to think to see all of them.

"It does not permit time travel as we have thought of time travel, but it gives us immortality of a sort. Immortality of the kind I have temporarily given us.

"*Is it good?* Is it worthwhile to lose the memory of fifty years of one's life in order to return one's body to relative youth? The only way I can find out is to try, as soon as I have finished writing this and made my other preparations.

"You will know the answer.

"But before you decide, remember that there is another problem, more important than the psychological one. I mean overpopulation.

"If our discovery is given to the world, if all who are old or dying can make themselves young again, the population will al-

most double every generation. Nor would the world—not even
our own relatively enlightened country—be willing to accept
compulsory birth control as a solution.

"Give this to the world, as the world is today in 2004, and
within a generation there will be famine, suffering, war. Perhaps a complete collapse of civilization.

"Yes, we have reached other planets, but they are not suitable
for colonizing. The stars may be our answer, but we are a long
way from reaching them. When we do, someday, the billions of
habitable planets that must be out there will be our answer . . .
our living room. But until then, what is the answer?

"Destroy the machine? But think of the countless lives it can
save, the suffering it can prevent. Think of what it would mean
to a man dying of cancer. Think . . ."

Think. You finish the letter and put it down.

You think of Barbara dead for forty-five years. And of the fact
that you were married to her for three years and that those years
are lost to you.

Fifty years lost. You damn the old man of seventy-five whom
you became and who has done this to you . . . who has given
you this decision to make.

Bitterly, you know what the decision must be. You think that
he knew, too, and realize that he could safely leave it in your
hands. Damn him, he *should* have known.

Too valuable to destroy, too dangerous to give.

The other answer is painfully obvious.

You must be custodian of this discovery and keep it secret
until it is safe to give, until mankind has expanded to the stars
and has new worlds to populate, or until, even without that, he
has reached a state of civilization where he can avoid overpopulation by rationing births to the number of accidental—or
voluntary—deaths.

If neither of those things has happened in another fifty years
(and are they likely so soon?), then you, at seventy-five, will be
writing another letter like this one. You will be undergoing another experience similar to the one you're going through now.
And making the same decision, of course.

Why not? You'll be the same person again.

Time and again, to preserve this secret until Man is ready for
it.

How often will you again sit at a desk like this one, thinking the thoughts you are thinking now, feeling the grief you now feel?

There is a click at the door and you know that the time lock has opened, that you are now free to leave this room, free to start a new life for yourself in place of the one you have already lived and lost.

But you are in no hurry now to walk directly through that door.

You sit there, staring straight ahead of you blindly, seeing in your mind's eye the vista of a set of facing mirrors, like those in an old-fashioned barber shop, reflecting the same thing over and over again, diminishing into far distance.

Knock

THERE IS a sweet little horror story that is only two sentences long:

The last man on Earth sat alone in a room. There was a knock at the door . . .

Two sentences and an ellipsis of three dots. The horror, of course, isn't in the story at all; it's in the ellipsis, the implication: *what* knocked at the door. Faced with the unknown, the human mind supplies something vaguely horrible.

But it *wasn't* horrible, really.

The last man on Earth—or in the universe, for that matter—*sat alone in a room.* It was a rather peculiar room. He'd just been studying out the reason for its peculiarity. His conclusion didn't horrify him, but it annoyed him.

Walter Phelan, who had been associate professor of anthropology at Nathan University up to the time two days ago when Nathan University had ceased to exist, was not a man who horrified easily. Not that Walter Phelan was a heroic figure, by any wild stretch of the imagination. He was slight of stature and mild of disposition. He wasn't much to look at, and he knew it.

Not that appearance worried him now. Right now, in fact, there wasn't much feeling in him. Abstractedly, he knew that two days ago, within the space of an hour, the human race had been destroyed, except for him and, somewhere—one woman. And that was a fact which didn't concern Walter Phelan in the slightest degree. He'd probably never see her and didn't care too much if he didn't.

Women just hadn't been a factor in Walter's life since Martha had died a year and a half ago. Not that Martha hadn't been a good wife—albeit a bit on the bossy side. Yes, he'd loved Martha, in a deep, quiet way. He was only forty now, and he'd been only thirty-eight when Martha had died, but—well—he just hadn't thought about women since then. His life had been his books, the ones he read and the ones he wrote. Now there wasn't any point in writing books, but he had the rest of his life to spend in reading them.

True, company would have been nice, but he'd get along without it. Maybe after a while he'd get so he'd enjoy the occasional company of one of the Zan, although that was a bit difficult to imagine. Their thinking was so alien to his that it was a bit difficult to imagine their finding common ground for a discussion. They were intelligent in a way, but so is an ant. No man has ever established communication with an ant. He thought of the Zan, somehow, as super-ants, although they didn't look like ants—and he had a hunch that the Zan regarded the human race as the human race regarded ordinary ants. Certainly what they'd done to Earth had been what men do to anthills, and it had been done much more efficiently.

But they'd given him plenty of books. They'd been nice about that, as soon as he had told them what he wanted. And he had told them that the moment he realized that he was destined to spend the rest of his life alone in this room. The rest of his life, or as the Zan had quaintly expressed it, for-ev-er.

Even a brilliant mind, and the Zan obviously had brilliant minds, had its idiosyncrasies. The Zan had learned to speak Terrestrial English in a matter of hours, but they persisted in separating syllables. However, we digress.

There was a knock at the door.

You've got it all now except the three dots, the ellipsis, and I'm going to fill that in and show you that it wasn't horrible at all.

Walter Phelan called out, "Come in," and the door opened. It was, of course, only a Zan. It looked exactly like the other Zan; if there was any way of telling them apart, Walter hadn't found it. It was about four feet tall and it looked like nothing on Earth —nothing, that is, that had been on Earth before the Zan came here.

Walter said, "Hello, George." When he'd learned that none of them had names, he'd decided to call them all George and the Zan didn't seem to mind.

This one said, "Hel-lo, Wal-ter." That was ritual, the knock on the door and the greetings. Walter waited.

"Point one," said the Zan. "You will please henceforth sit with your chair fac-ing the oth-er way."

Walter said, "I thought so, George. That plain wall is transparent from the other side, isn't it?"

"It is trans-par-ent."

Walter sighed. "I knew it. That plain blank wall, without a single piece of furniture against it. And made of something different from the other walls. If I persist in sitting with my back to it, what then? You will kill me?—I ask hopefully."

"We will take a-way your books."

"You've got me there, George. All right, I'll face the other way when I sit and read. How many other animals besides me are in this zoo of yours?"

"Two hun-dred and six-teen."

Walter shook his head. "Not complete, George. Even a bush-league zoo can beat that—*could* beat that, I mean, if there were any bush-league zoos left. Did you just pick us at random?"

"Ran-dom sam-ples, yes. All spe-cies would have been too man-y. Male and fe-male each of one hun-dred kinds."

"What do you feed them? The carnivorous ones, I mean."

"We make feed. Syn-thet-ic."

"Smart. And the flora? You've got a collection of that, too, haven't you?"

"Flo-ra not hurt by vi-bra-tions. It is all still grow-ing."

"Good for the flora. You weren't as hard on it, then, as you were on the fauna. Well, George, you started out with 'point one.' I deduce that there is a point two lurking somewhere. What is it?"

"There is some-thing we do not un-der-stand. Two of the oth-er an-i-mals sleep and do not wake. They are cold."

"It happens in the best-regulated zoos, George. Probably not a thing wrong with them except that they're dead."

"Dead? That means stopped. But noth-ing stopped them. Each was a-lone."

Walter stared at the Zan. "Do you mean, George, that you do not know what natural death is?"

"Death is when a be-ing is killed, stopped from living."

Walter Phelan blinked. "How old are you, George?" he asked.

"Six-teen—you would not know the word. Your planet went

a-round your sun a-bout sev-en thou-sand times. I am still young."

Walter whistled softly. "A babe in arms," he said. He thought hard for a moment. "Look, George, you've got something to learn about this planet you're on. There's a guy down here who doesn't hang around where you come from. An old man with a beard and a scythe and an hourglass. Your vibrations didn't kill him."

"What is he?"

"Call him the Grim Reaper, George. Old Man Death. Our people and animals live until somebody, Old Man Death, stops them from ticking."

"He stopped the two crea-tures? He will stop more?"

Walter opened his mouth to answer, and then closed it again. Something in the Zan's voice indicated that there would be a worried frown on his face if he had a face recognizable as such.

"How about taking me to those animals who won't wake up?" Walter asked. "Is that against the rules?"

"Come," said the Zan.

That had been the afternoon of the second day. It was the next morning that the Zan came back, several of them. They began to move Walter Phelan's books and furniture. When they finished that, they moved him. He found himself in a much larger room a hundred yards away.

He sat and waited this time, too. When there was a knock on the door, he knew what was coming and politely stood up as he called out, "Come in."

A Zan opened the door and stood aside. A woman entered.

Walter bowed slightly. "Walter Phelan," he said, "in case George didn't tell you my name. George tries to be polite but he doesn't know all our ways."

The woman seemed calm; he was glad to notice that. She said, "My name's Grace Evans, Mr. Phelan. What's this all about? Why did they bring me here?"

Walter was studying her as she talked. She was tall, fully as tall as he, and well-proportioned. She looked to be somewhere in her early thirties, about the age Martha had been. She had the same calm confidence about her that he had always liked about Martha, even though it had contrasted with his own easygoing informality. In fact, he thought she looked quite a bit like Martha.

"I think you can guess why they brought you here, but let's go back a bit," he said. "Do you know what's happened otherwise?"

"You mean that they've—killed everyone?"

"Yes. Please sit down. You know how they accomplished it?"

She sank into a comfortable chair nearby. "No," she said. "I don't know just how. Not that it matters, does it?"

"Not a lot. But here's the story, what I know of it from getting one of them to talk, and from piecing things together. There isn't a great number of them—here anyway. I don't know how numerous a race they are where they came from and I don't know where that is, but I'd guess it's outside the solar system. You've seen the spaceship they came in?"

"Yes. It's as big as a mountain."

"Almost. Well, it has equipment for emitting some sort of vibration—they call it that in our language, but I imagine it's more like a radio wave than a sound vibration—that destroys all animal life. The ship itself is insulated against the vibration. I don't know whether its range is big enough to kill off the whole planet at once, or whether they flew in circles around the earth, sending out the vibratory waves. But it killed everything at once instantly and, I hope, painlessly. The only reason we, and the other two-hundred-odd animals in this zoo weren't killed was because we were inside the ship. We'd been picked up as specimens. You do know this is a zoo, don't you?"

"I—I suspected it."

"The front walls are transparent from the outside. The Zan were pretty clever in fixing up the inside of each cubicle to match the natural habitat of the creature it contains. These cubicles, such as the one we're in, are of plastic and they've got a machine that makes one in about ten minutes. If Earth had a machine and a process like that, there wouldn't have been any housing shortage. Well, there isn't any housing shortage now, anyway. And I imagine that the human race—specifically you and I—can stop worrying about the H-bomb and the next war. The Zan have certainly solved a lot of problems for us."

Grace Evans smiled faintly. "Another case where the operation was successful but the patient died. Things *were* in an awful mess. Do you remember being captured? I don't. I went to sleep one night and woke up in a cage on the spaceship."

"I don't remember either," Walter said. "My hunch is that they used the waves at low intensity first, just enough to knock us all out. Then they cruised around, picking up samples for their zoo more or less at random. After they had as many as they wanted, or as many as they had room in the ship for, they turned on the juice all the way. And that was that. It wasn't until yesterday that they knew they'd made a mistake by overestimating us. They thought we were immortal, as they are."

"That we were—what?"

"They can be killed but they don't know what natural death is. They didn't anyway, until yesterday. Two of us died yesterday."

"Two of— Oh!"

"Yes, two of us animals in their zoo. Two species gone irrevocably. And by the Zan's way of figuring time, the remaining member of each species is going to live only a few minutes anyway. They figured they had permanent specimens."

"You mean they didn't realize what short-lived creatures we are?"

"That's right," Walter said. "One of them is young at seven thousand years, he told me. They're bisexual themselves, incidentally, but they probably breed every ten thousand years or thereabouts. When they learned yesterday how ridiculously short a life span we terrestrial animals have, they were probably shocked to the core, if they have cores. At any rate they decided to reorganize their zoo—two by two instead of one by one. They figure we'll last longer collectively if not individually."

"Oh!" Grace Evans stood up and there was a faint flush on her face. "If you think— If they think—" She turned toward the door.

"It'll be locked," Walter Phelan said calmly. "But don't worry. Maybe they think, but I *don't* think. You needn't even tell me that you wouldn't have me if I were the last man on Earth; it would be corny under the circumstances."

"But are they going to keep us locked up together in this one little room?"

"It isn't so little; we'll get by. I can sleep quite comfortably in one of those overstuffed chairs. And don't think I don't agree with you perfectly, my dear. All personal considerations aside, the least favor we can do the human race is to let it die out with us and not be perpetuated for exhibition in a zoo."

She said, "Thank you," almost inaudibly, and the flush was gone from her face. There was anger in her eyes, but Walter knew that it wasn't anger at him. With her eyes sparkling like that, she looked a lot like Martha, he thought.

He smiled at her and said, "Otherwise—"

She started out of her chair and for a moment he thought she was going to come over and slap him. Then she sank back wearily. "If you were a *man*, you'd be thinking of some way to— They can be killed, you said?" Her voice was bitter.

"The Zan? Oh, certainly. I've been studying them. They look horribly different from us, but I think they have about the same metabolism, the same type of circulatory system, and probably the same type of digestive system. I think that anything that would kill one of us would kill one of them."

"But you said—"

"Oh, there are differences, of course. Whatever factor it is in man that ages him, they don't have. Or else they have some gland that man doesn't have, something that renews cells. More often than every seven years, I mean."

She had forgotten her anger now. She leaned forward eagerly. She said, "I think that's right. I don't think, though, that they feel pain."

He had been hoping that. He said, "What makes you think so, my dear?"

"I stretched a piece of wire that I found in the desk of my own cubicle across the door so the Zan would fall over it. He did, and the wire cut his leg."

"Did he bleed red?"

"Yes, but it didn't seem to annoy him. He didn't get mad about it; he didn't mention it, just took the wire down. When he came back the next time a few hours later, the cut was gone. Well, almost gone. I could see just enough of a trace of it to be sure it was the same Zan."

Walter Phelan nodded slowly. "He wouldn't get angry, of course. They're emotionless. Maybe if we killed one they wouldn't even punish us. Just give us our food through a trapdoor and stay clear of us, treat us as men would have treated a zoo animal that had killed its keeper. They'd probably just see that we didn't get a crack at any more keepers."

"How many of them are there?"

Walter said, "About two hundred, I think, in this particular spaceship. But undoubtedly there are many more where they came from. I have a hunch, though, that this is just an advance board, sent to clear off this planet and make it safe for Zan oc-cupancy."

"They certainly did a good—"

There was a knock at the door and Walter Phelan called out, "Come in." A Zan opened the door and stood in the doorway.

"Hello, George," said Walter.

"Hel-lo, Wal-ter." The same ritual. The same Zan?

"What's on your mind?"

"An-oth-er creature sleeps and will not wake. A small fur-ry one called a wea-sel."

Walter shrugged. "It happens, George. Old Man Death. I told you about him."

"And worse. A Zan has died. This morn-ing."

"Is that worse?" Walter looked at him blandly. "Well, George, you'll have to get used to it if you're going to stay around here."

The Zan said nothing. It stood there.

Finally, Walter said, "Well?"

"About the wea-sel. You advise the same?"

Walter shrugged again. "Probably won't do any good. But why not?"

The Zan left.

Walter could hear his footsteps dying away outside. He grinned. "It might work, Martha," he said.

"Mar— My name is Grace, Mr. Phelan. What might work?"

"My name is Walter, Grace. You might as well get used to it. You know, Grace, you remind me a lot of Martha. She was my wife. She died a couple of years ago."

"I'm sorry. But *what* might work? What were you talking about to the Zan?"

"We should know tomorrow," Walter said. And she couldn't get another word out of him.

That was the third day of the stay of the Zan. The next day was the last.

It was nearly noon when one of the Zan came. After the rit-ual, he stood in the doorway, looking more alien than ever. It would be interesting to describe him for you, but there aren't words. He said, "We go. Our coun-cil met and de-ci-ded."

"Another of you died?"

"Last night. This is pla-net of death."

Walter nodded. "You did your share. You're leaving two hundred and thirteen alive, besides us, but that's out of quite a few billion. Don't hurry back."

"Is there an-y-thing we can do?"

"Yes. You can hurry. And you can leave our door unlocked, but not the others. We'll take care of the others."

The Zan nodded, and left.

Grace Evans was standing, her eyes shining. She asked, "How—? What—?"

"Wait," cautioned Walter. "Let's hear them blast off. It's a sound I want to hear and remember."

The sound came within minutes, and Walter Phelan, realizing how rigidly he'd been holding himself, dropped into a chair and relaxed.

He said softly, "There was a snake in the Garden of Eden, too, Grace, and it got us into trouble. But this one got us out of it, and made up. I mean the mate of the snake that died day before yesterday. It was a rattlesnake."

"You mean it killed the two Zan who died? But—"

Walter nodded. "They were babes in the woods here. When they took me to see the first creatures who 'were asleep and wouldn't wake up,' and I saw that one of them was a rattlesnake, I had an idea, Grace. Just maybe, I thought, poison creatures were a development peculiar to Earth and the Zan wouldn't know about them. And, too, maybe their metabolism was enough like ours that the poison would kill them. Anyway, I had nothing to lose trying. And both maybes turned out to be right."

"How did you get the living rattlesnake to—"

Walter Phelan grinned. "I told them what affection is. They didn't know. But they were interested, I found, in preserving the remaining one of each species as long as possible, to picture and record it before it died. I told them it would die immediately because of the loss of its mate, unless it had affection and petting, constantly.

"I showed them how, with the duck, which was the other creature who had lost its mate. Luckily it was a tame duck and I had no trouble holding it against my chest and petting it, to show them how. Then I let them take over with it—and with the rattlesnake."

He stood up and stretched, and then sat down again more comfortably. He said, "Well, we've got a world to plan. We'll have to let the animals out of the ark, and that will take some thinking and deciding. The herbivorous wild ones we can let go right away, and let them take their chances. The domestic ones we'll do better to keep and take charge of; we'll need them. But the carnivora, the predators—Well, we'll have to decide. But I'm afraid it's got to be thumbs down. Unless maybe we can find and operate the machinery that they used to make synthetic food."

He looked at her. "And the human race. We've got to make a decision about that. A pretty important decision."

Her face was getting a bit pink again, as it had yesterday; she sat rigidly in her chair. "No," she said.

He didn't seem to have heard her. "It's been a nice race, even if nobody won it. It'll be starting over again now, if we start it, and it may go backwards for a while until it gets its breath, but we can gather books for it and keep most of its knowledge intact, the important things anyway. We can—"

He broke off as she got up and started for the door. Just the way Martha would have acted, he thought, back in the days when he was courting her, before they were married.

He said, "Think it over, my dear, and take your time. But come back."

The door slammed. He sat waiting, thinking out all the things there were to do once he started, but in no hurry to start them.

And after a while he heard her hesitant footsteps coming back.

He smiled a little. See? It wasn't horrible, really.

The last man on Earth sat alone in a room. There was a knock at the door . . .

Rebound

THE POWER came to Larry Snell suddenly and unexpectedly, out of nowhere. How and why it came to him, he never learned. It just came; that's all.

It could have happened to a nicer guy. Snell was a small-time crook when he thought he could get away with stealing, but the bulk of his income, such as it was, came from selling numbers racket tickets and peddling marijuana to adolescents. He was fattish and sloppy, with little close-set eyes that made him look almost as mean as he really was. His only redeeming virtue was cowardice; it had kept him from committing crimes of violence.

He was, that night, talking to a bookie from a tavern telephone booth, arguing whether a bet he'd placed by phone that afternoon had been on the nose or across the board. Finally, giving up, he growled "Drop dead," and slammed down the receiver. He thought nothing of it until the next day when he learned that the bookie *had* dropped dead, while talking on the telephone and at just about the time of their conversation.

This gave Larry Snell food for thought. He was not an uneducated man; he knew what a whammy was. In fact, he'd tried whammies before, but they'd never worked for him. Had something changed? It was worth trying. Carefully he made out a list of twenty people whom, for one reason or another, he hated. He telephoned them one at a time—spacing the calls over the course of a week—and told each of them to drop dead. They did, all of them.

It was not until the end of that week that he discovered that what he had was not simply the whammy, but the Power. He was talking to a dame, a *top* dame, a stripteuse working in a top nightclub and making twenty or forty times his own income, and he had said, "Honey, come up to my room after the last show, huh?" She did, and it staggered him because he'd been kidding. Rich men and handsome playboys were after her, and she'd fallen for a casual, not even seriously intended, proposition from Larry Snell.

Did he have the Power? He tried it the next morning, before she left him. He asked her how much money she had with her, and then told her to give it to him. She did, and it was several hundred dollars.

He was in business. By the end of the next week he was rich; he had made himself that way by borrowing money from everyone he knew—including slight acquaintances who were fairly high in the hierarchy of the underworld and therefore quite solvent—and then telling them to forget it. He moved from his fleabag pad to a penthouse apartment atop the swankiest hotel in town. It was a bachelor apartment, but need it be said that he slept there alone but seldom, and then only for purposes of recuperation.

It was a nice life but even so it took only a few weeks of it to cause it to dawn on Snell that he was wasting the Power. Why shouldn't he really use what he had by taking over the country first and then the world, make himself the most powerful dictator in history? Why shouldn't he have and own everything, including a harem instead of a dame a night? Why shouldn't he have an army to enforce the fact that his slightest wish would be everyone else's highest law? If his commands were obeyed over the telephone certainly they would be obeyed if he gave them over radio and television. All he had to do was pay for (pay for?, simply demand) a universal network that would let him be heard by everyone everywhere. Or almost everyone; he could take over when he had a simple majority behind him, and bring the others into line later.

But this would be a Big Deal, the biggest one ever swung, and he decided to take his time planning it so there would be no possibility of his making a mistake. He decided to spend a few days alone, out of town and away from everybody, to do his planning.

He chartered a plane to take him to a relatively uncrowded part of the Catskills, and from an inn—which he took over simply by telling the other guests to leave—he started taking long walks alone, thinking and dreaming. He found a favorite spot, a small hill in a valley surrounded by mountains; the scenery was magnificent. He did most of his thinking there, and found himself becoming more and more elated and euphoric as he began to see that it could and would work.

Dictator, hell. He'd have himself crowned Emperor. Emperor of the World. Why not? Who could defy a man with the Power? The Power to make anyone obey any command that he gave them, up to and including—

"Drop dead!" he shouted from the hilltop, in sheer vicious exuberance, not caring whether or not anyone or anything was within range of his voice . . .

A teen-age boy and a teen-age girl found him there the next day and hurried back to the village to report having found a dead man on the top of Echo Hill.

Star Mouse

MITKEY, the mouse, wasn't Mitkey then.

He was just another mouse, who lived behind the floorboards and plaster of the house of the great Herr Professor Oberburger, formerly of Vienna and Heidelberg; then a refugee from the excessive admiration of his more powerful fellow-countrymen. The excessive admiration had concerned not Herr Oberburger himself, but a certain gas which had been a by-product of an unsuccessful rocket fuel—which might have been a highly successful something else.

If, of course, the Professor had given them the correct formula. Which he— Well, anyway, the Professor had made good his escape and now lived in a house in Connecticut. And so did Mitkey.

A small gray mouse, and a small gray man. Nothing unusual about either of them. Particularly there was nothing unusual about Mitkey; he had a family and he liked cheese and if there were Rotarians among mice, he would have been a Rotarian.

The Herr Professor, of course, had his mild eccentricities. A confirmed bachelor, he had no one to talk to except himself, but he considered himself an excellent conversationalist and held constant verbal communication with himself while he worked. That fact, it turned out later, was important, because Mitkey had excellent ears and heard those night-long soliloquies. He didn't understand them, of course. If he thought about them at all, he merely thought of the Professor as a large and noisy super-mouse who squeaked over-much.

"Und now," he would say to himself, "ve vill see vether this eggshaust tube vas broperly machined. It should fidt vithin vun vun-hundreth thousandth uf an indtch. Ahhh, it iss berfect. Und now—"

Night after night, day after day, month after month. The

gleaming thing grew, and the gleam in Herr Oberburger's eyes grew apace.

It was about three and a half feet long, with weirdly shaped vanes, and it rested on a temporary framework on a table in the center of the room that served the Herr Professor for all purposes. The house in which he and Mitkey lived was a four room structure, but the Professor hadn't yet found it out, seemingly. Originally, he had planned to use the big room as a laboratory only, but he found it more convenient to sleep on a cot in one corner of it, when he slept at all, and to do the little cooking he did over the same gas burner over which he melted down golden grains of TNT into a dangerous soup which he salted and peppered with strange condiments, but did not eat.

"Und now I shall bour it into tubes, und see vether vun tube adjacendt to another eggsplodes de secondt tube vhen der virst tube iss—"

That was the night Mitkey almost decided to move himself and his family to a more stable abode, one that did not rock and sway and try to turn handsprings on its foundations. But Mitkey didn't move after all, because there were compensations. New mouse-holes all over, and—joy of joy!—a big crack in the back of the refrigerator where the Professor kept, among other things, food.

Of course the tubes had been not larger than capillary size, or the house would not have remained around the mouse-holes. And of course Mitkey could not guess what was coming or understand the Herr Professor's brand of English (or any other brand of English, for that matter) or he would not have let even a crack in the refrigerator tempt him.

The Professor was jubilant that morning.

"Der fuel, idt vorks! Der secondt tube, idt did not eggsplode. Und der virst, in *seggtions,* as I had eggspectedt! Und it is more bowerful; there will be plenty of room for der combartment—"

Ah, yes, the compartment. That was where Mitkey came in, although even the Professor didn't know it yet. In fact the Professor didn't even know that Mitkey existed.

"Und now," he was saying to his favorite listener, "idt is budt a madter of combining der fuel tubes so they work in obbosite bairs. Und then—"

That was the moment when the Herr Professor's eyes first fell on Mitkey. Rather, they fell upon a pair of gray whiskers and a black, shiny little nose protruding from a hole in the baseboards.

"Vell!" he said, "vot haff ve here! Mitkey Mouse himself! Mitkey, how vould you like to go for a ride, negst veek? Ve shall see."

That is how it came about that the next time the Professor sent into town for supplies, his order included a mousetrap—not one of the vicious kind that kills, but one of the wire-cage kind. And it had not been set, with cheese, for more than ten minutes before Mitkey's sharp little nose had smelled out that cheese and followed his nose into captivity.

Not, however, an unpleasant captivity. Mitkey was an honored guest. The cage reposed now on the table at which the Professor did most of his work, and cheese in indigestion-giving abundance was pushed through the bars, and the Professor didn't talk to himself any more.

"You see, Mitkey, I vas going to sendt to der laboratory in Hardtfordt for a vhite mouse, budt vhy should I, mit you here? I am sure you are more soundt und healthy und able to vithstand a long chourney than those laboratory mices. No? Ah, you viggle your viskers und that means yes, no? Und being used to living in dargk holes, you should suffer less than they from glaustrophobia, no?"

And Mitkey grew fat and happy and forgot all about trying to get out of the cage. I fear that he even forgot about the family he had abandoned, but he knew, if he knew anything, that he need not worry about them in the slightest. At least not until and unless the Professor discovered and repaired the hole in the refrigerator. And the Professor's mind was most emphatically not on refrigerators.

"Und so, Mitkey, ve shall place this vane so—it iss only of assistance in der landing, in an atmosphere. It und these vill bring you down safely und slowly enough that der shock-absorbers in der movable combartment vill keep you from bumping your head too hard, I think." Of course, Mitkey missed the ominous note to that "I think" qualification because he missed all the rest of it. He did not, as has been explained, speak English. Not then.

But Herr Oberburger talked to him just the same. He showed him pictures. "Did you effer see der mouse you vas named after, Mitkey? Vhat? No? Loogk, this is der original Mitkey Mouse, by Valt Dissney. Budt I think you are cuter, Mitkey."

Probably the Professor was a bit crazy to talk that way to a little gray mouse. In fact, he must have been crazy to make a rocket that worked. For the odd thing was that the Herr Professor was not really an inventor. There was, as he carefully explained to Mitkey, not one single thing about that rocket that was *new*. The Herr Professor was a technician; he could take other people's ideas and make them work. His only real invention—the rocket fuel that wasn't one—had been turned over to the United States Government and had proved to be something already known and discarded because it was too expensive for practical use.

As he explained very carefully to Mitkey, "It iss burely a matter of absolute accuracy and mathematical correctness, Mitkey. Idt iss all here—ve merely combine—and ve achieff vhat, Mitkey?

"Eggscape velocity, Mitkey! Chust barely, it adds up to eggscape velocity. Maybe. There are yet unknown facgtors, Mitkey, in der ubper atmosphere, der troposphere, der stratosphere. Ve think ve know eggsactly how mudch air there iss to calculate resistance against, but are ve absolutely sure? No, Mitkey, ve are not. Ve haff not been there. Und der marchin iss so narrow that so mudch as an air current might affect idt."

But Mitkey cared not a whit. In the shadow of the tapering aluminum-alloy cylinder he waxed fat and happy.

"*Der Tag*, Mitkey, *der Tag!* Und I shall not lie to you, Mitkey. I shall not giff you valse assurances. You go on a dancherous chourney, mein little friendt.

"A vifty-vifty chance ve giff you, Mitkey. Not der moon or bust, but der moon *und* bust, or else maybe safely back to earth. You see, my boor little Mitkey, der moon iss not made of green cheese und if it were, you vould not liff to eat it because there iss not enough atmosphere to bring you down safely und vith your viskers still on.

"Und vhy then, you may vell ask, do I send you? Because der rocket may *not* attain eggscape velocity. Und in that case, it iss still an eggsperiment, budt a different vun. Der rocket, if it goes not to der moon, falls back on der earth, no? Und in that case certain instruments shall giff us further information than ve haff yet about things up there in space. Und you shall giff us information, by vether or not you are yet alife, vether der shock absorbers und vanes are sufficient in an earth-equivalent atmosphere. You see?

"Then ladter, vhen ve send rockets to Venus maybe vhere an atmosphere eggsists, ve shall haff data to calculate the needed size of vanes und shock-absorbers, no? Und in either case, und vether or not you return, Mitkey, you shall be vamous! You shall be der virst liffing greature to go oudt beyond der stratosphere of der earth, out into space.

"Mitkey, you shall be der Star-Mouse! I enfy you, Mitkey, und I only vish I vere your size, so I could go, too."

Der Tag, and the door to the compartment. "Gootbye, little Mitkey Mouse." Darkness. Silence. Noise!

"Der rocket—if it goes not to der moon—falls back on der earth, no?" That was what the Herr Professor had thought. But the best-laid plans of mice and men gang aft agley. Even star-mice.

All because of Prxl.

The Herr Professor found himself very lonely. After having had Mitkey to talk to, soliloquies were somehow empty and inadequate.

There may be some who say that the company of a small gray mouse is a poor substitute for a wife; but others may disagree. And, anyway, the Professor had never had a wife, and he *had* a mouse to talk to, so he missed one and, if he missed the other, he didn't know it.

During the long night after the launching of the rocket, he had been very busy with his telescope, a sweet little eight-inch reflector, checking its course as it gathered momentum. The exhaust explosions made a tiny fluctuating point of light that was possible to follow, if one knew where to look.

But the following day there seemed to be nothing to do, and he was too excited to sleep, although he tried. So he compromised by doing a spot of housekeeping, cleaning the pots and pans. It was while he was so engaged that he heard a series of frantic little squeaks and discovered that another small gray mouse, with shorter whiskers and a shorter tail than Mitkey, had walked into the wire-cage mousetrap.

"Vell, vell," said the Professor, "vot haff ve here? Minnie? Iss it Minnie come to look for her Mitkey?"

The Professor was not a biologist, but he happened to be right. It *was* Minnie. Rather, it was Mitkey's mate, so the name was appropriate. What strange vagary of mind had induced her to walk into an unbaited trap, the Professor neither knew nor cared, but he was delighted. He promptly remedied the lack of bait by pushing a sizable piece of cheese through the bars.

Thus it was that Minnie came to fill the place of her far-traveling spouse as repository for the Professor's confidences. Whether she worried about her family or not there is no way of knowing, but she need not have done so. They were now large enough to fend for themselves, particularly in a house that offered abundant cover and easy access to the refrigerator.

"Ah, und now it iss dargk enough, Minnie, that ve can loogk for that husband of yours. His viery trail across the sky. True, Minnie, it iss a very small viery trail und der astronomers vill not notice it, because they do not know vhere to loogk. But ve do.

"He iss going to be a very vamous mouse, Minnie, this Mitkey of ours, vhen ve tell der vorld about him und about mein rocket. You see, Minnie, ve haff not told them yet. Ve shall vait und giff der gomplete story all at vunce. By dawn of tomorrow ve'll—

"Ah, there he iss, Minnie! Vaint, but there. I'd hold you up to der scope und let you loogk, but it vould not be vocused right for your eyes, und I do not know how to—

"Almost vun hundred thousand miles, Minnie, und still ag-celerating, but not for much longer. Our Mitkey iss on schedule; in fagt he is going vaster than ve had vigured, no? It iss sure now that he vill eggscape the gravitation of der earth, und fall upon der moon!"

Of course, it was purely coincidental that Minnie squeaked.

"Ah, yess, Minnie, little Minnie. I know, I know. Ve shall neffer see our Mitkey again, und I almost vish our eggsperiment hadt vailed. Budt there are gompensations, Minnie. He shall be der most vamous of all mices. Der Star-Mouse! Virst liffing grea-ture effer to go beyond der gravitational bull of earth!"

The night was long. Occasionally high clouds obscured vision.

"Minnie, I shall make you more gomfortable than in that so-small vire cage. You vould like to seem to be vree, vould you not, vithout bars, like der animals at modern zoos, vith moats in-steadt?"

And so, to fill in an hour when a cloud obscured the sky, the Herr Professor made Minnie her new home. It was the end of a wooden crate, about half an inch thick and a foot square, laid flat on the table, and with no visible barrier around it.

But he covered the top with metal foil at the edges, and he placed the board on another larger board which also had a strip of metal foil surrounding the island of Minnie's home. And wires from the two areas of metal foil to opposite terminals of a small transformer which he placed near by.

"Und now, Minnie, I shall blace you on your island, vhich shall be literally supplied mitt cheese und vater, und you shall vind it is an eggcelent blace to liff. But you vill get a mild shock or two vhen you try to step off der edge of der island. It vill not hurt much, but you vill not like it, und after a few tries you vill learn not to try again, no? Und—"

And night again.

Minnie was happy on her island, her lesson well learned. She would no longer so much as step on the inner strip of metal foil. It was a mouse-paradise of an island, though. There was a cliff of cheese bigger than Minnie herself. It kept her busy. Mouse and cheese; soon one would be a transmutation of the other.

But Professor Oberburger wasn't thinking about that. The Professor was worried. When he had calculated and recalculated and aimed his eight-inch reflector through the hole in the roof and turned out the lights—

Yes, there *are* advantages to being a bachelor after all. If one wants a hole in the roof, one simply knocks a hole in the roof and there is nobody to tell one that one is crazy. If winter comes, or if it rains, one can always call a carpenter or use a tarpaulin.

But the faint trail of light wasn't there. The Professor frowned and re-calculated and re-re-calculated and shifted his telescope three-tenths of a second and still the rocket wasn't there.

"Minnie, something iss wrong. Either de tubes haff stopped viring, or—"

Or the rocket was no longer traversing a straight line relative to its point of departure. By straight, of course, is meant parabolically curved relative to everything other than velocity.

So the Herr Professor did the only thing remaining for him to do, and began to search, with the telescope, in widening circles. It was two hours before he found it, five degrees off course already and veering more and more into a— Well, there was only one thing you could call it. A tailspin.

The darned thing was going in circles, circles which appeared to constitute an orbit about something that couldn't possibly be there. Then narrowing into a concentric spiral.

Then—out. Gone. Darkness. No rocket flares.

The Professor's face was pale as he turned to Minnie.

"It iss *imbossible,* Minnie. Mein own eyes, but it could not be. Even if vun side stopped viring, it could not haff gone into such sudden circles." His pencil verified a suspicion. "Und, Minnie, it decelerated vaster than bossible. Even mitt *no* tubes viring, its momentum vould haff been more—"

The rest of the night—telescope and calculus—yielded no clue. That is, no believable clue. Some force not inherent in the rocket itself, and not accountable by gravitation—even of a hypothetical body—had acted.

"Mein poor Mitkey."

The gray, inscrutable dawn. "Mein Minnie, it vill haff to be a secret. Ve dare not bublish vhat ve saw, for it vould not be believed. I am not sure I believe it myself, Minnie. Berhaps because I vas offertired vrom not sleeping, I chust imachined that I saw—"

Later. "But, Minnie, ve shall hope. Vun hundred vifty thousand miles out, it vas. It vill fall back upon der earth. But I gannot tell vhere! I thought that if it did, I vould be able to galculate its course, und— But after those goncentric cirgles—Minnie, not even Einstein could galculate vhere it vill land. Not effen *me.* All ve can do iss hope that ve shall hear of vhere it falls."

Cloudy day. Black night jealous of its mysteries.

"Minnie, our poor Mitkey. There is *nothing* could have gauzed—"

But something had.

Prxl.

Prxl is an asteroid. It isn't called that by earthly astronomers, because—for excellent reasons—they have not discovered it. So we will call it by the nearest possible transliteration of the name its inhabitants use. Yes, it's inhabited.

Come to think of it, Professor Oberburger's attempt to send a rocket to the moon had some strange results. Or rather, Prxl did.

You wouldn't think that an asteroid could reform a drunk, would you? But one Charles Winslow, a besotted citizen of Bridgeport, Connecticut, never took a drink after the time when

—right on Grove Street—a mouse asked him the road to Hartford. The mouse was wearing bright red pants and vivid yellow gloves—

But that was fifteen months after the Professor lost his rocket. We'd better start over again.

Prxl is an asteroid. One of those despised celestial bodies which terrestrial astronomers call vermin of the sky, because the darned things leave trails across the plates that clutter up the more important observations of novae and nebulae. Fifty thousand fleas on the dark dog of night.

Tiny things, most of them. Astronomers have been discovering recently that some of them come close to Earth. Amazingly close. There was excitement in 1932 when Amor came within ten million miles—astronomically, a mere mashie shot. Then Apollo cut that almost in half, and in 1936 Adonis came within less than one and a half million miles.

In 1937, Hermes, less than half a million, but the astronomers got really excited when they calculated its orbit and found that the little mile-long asteroid *can* come within a mere 220,000 miles, closer than Earth's own moon.

Some day they may be still more excited, if and when they spot the three-eighth-mile asteroid Prxl, that obstacle of space, making a transit across the moon and discover that it frequently comes within a mere hundred thousand miles of our rapidly whirling world.

Only in event of a transit will they ever discover it, though, for Prxl does not reflect light. It hasn't, anyway, for several million years since its inhabitants coated it with a black, light-absorbing pigment derived from its interior. Monumental task, painting a world, for creatures half an inch tall. But worth it, at the time. When they'd shifted its orbit, they were safe from their enemies. There were giants in those days—eight-inch tall marauding pirates from Deimos. Got to Earth a couple of times too, before they faded out of the picture. Pleasant little giants who killed because they enjoyed it. Records in now-buried cities on Deimos might explain what happened to the dinosaurs. And why the promising Cro-Magnons disappeared at the height of their promise only a cosmic few minutes after the dinosaurs went west.

But Prxl survived. Tiny world no longer reflecting the sun's rays, lost to the cosmic killers when its orbit was shifted.

Prxl. Still civilized, with a civilization millions of years old. Its coat of blackness preserved and renewed regularly, more through tradition than fear of enemies in these later degenerate days. Mighty but stagnant civilization, standing still on a world that whizzes like a bullet.

And Mitkey Mouse.

Klarloth, head scientist of a race of scientists, tapped his assistant Bemj on what would have been Bemj's shoulder if he had had one. "Look," he said, "what approaches Prxl. Obviously artificial propulsion."

Bemj looked into the wall-plate and then directed a thought-wave at the mechanism that jumped the magnification a thousand-fold through an alteration of the electronic fields.

The image leaped, blurred, then steadied. "Fabricated," said Bemj. "Extremely crude, I must say. Primitive explosive-powered rocket. Wait, I'll check where it came from."

He took the readings from the dials about the viewplate and hurled them as thoughts against the psychocoil of the computer, then waited while that most complicated of machines digested all the factors and prepared the answer. Then eagerly, he slid his mind into rapport with its projector. Klarloth likewise listened in to the silent broadcast.

Exact point on Earth and exact time of departure. Untranslatable expression of curve of trajectory, and point on that curve where deflected by gravitational pull of Prxl. The destination—or rather the original intended destination—of the rocket was obvious, Earth's moon. Time and place of arrival on Prxl if present course of rocket was unchanged.

"Earth," said Klarloth meditatively. "They were a long way from rocket travel the last time we checked them. Some sort of a crusade, or battle of beliefs, going on, wasn't there?"

Bemj nodded. "Catapults. Bows and arrows. They've taken a long stride since, even if this is only an early experimental thing of a rocket. Shall we destroy it before it gets here?"

Klarloth shook his head thoughtfully. "Let's look it over. May save us a trip to Earth: we can judge their present state of development pretty well from the rocket itself."

"But then we'll have to—"

"Of course. Call the Station. Tell them to train their attracto-repulsors on it and to swing it into a temporary orbit until they prepare a landing-cradle. And not to forget to damp out the explosive before they bring it down."

"Temporary force-field around point of landing—in case?"

"Naturally."

So despite the almost complete absence of atmosphere in which the vanes could have functioned, the rocket came down safely and so softly that Mitkey, in the dark compartment, knew only that the awful noise had stopped.

Mitkey felt better. He ate some more of the cheese with which the compartment was liberally provided. Then he resumed trying to gnaw a hole in the inch-thick wood with which the compartment was lined. That wooden lining was a kind thought of the Herr Professor for Mitkey's mental well-being. He knew that trying to gnaw his way out would give Mitkey something to do en route which would keep him from getting the screaming meemies. The idea had worked; being busy, Mitkey hadn't suffered mentally from his dark confinement. And now that things were quiet, he chewed away more industriously and more happily than ever, sublimely unaware that when he got through the wood, he'd find only metal which he couldn't chew. But better people than Mitkey have found things they couldn't chew.

Meanwhile, Klarloth and Bemj and several thousand other Prxlians stood gazing up at the huge rocket which, even lying on its side, towered high over their heads. Some of the younger ones, forgetting the invisible field of force, walked too close and came back, ruefully rubbing bumped heads.

Klarloth himself was at the psychograph.

"There *is* life inside the rocket," he told Bemj. "But the impressions are confused. One creature, but I cannot follow its thought processes. At the moment it seems to be doing something with its teeth."

"It could not be an Earthling, one of the dominant race. One of them is much larger than this huge rocket. Gigantic creatures. Perhaps, unable to construct a rocket large enough to hold one of themselves, they sent an experimental creature, such as our wooraths."

"I believe you've guessed right, Bemj. Well, when we have explored its mind thoroughly, we may still learn enough to save us a check-up trip to Earth. I am going to open the door."

"But air—creatures of Earth would need a heavy, almost a dense atmosphere. It could not live."

"We retain the force-field, of course. It will keep the air in. Obviously there is a source of supply of air within the rocket or the creature would not have survived the trip."

Klarloth operated controls, and the force-field itself put forth invisible pseudopods, and turned the outer screw-door, then reached within and unlatched the inner door to the compartment itself.

All Prxl watched breathlessly as a monstrous gray head pushed out of the huge aperture yawning overhead. Thick whiskers, each as long as the body of a Prxlian—

Mitkey jumped down, and took a forward step that bumped his black nose hard—into something that wasn't there. He squeaked, and jumped backwards against the rocket.

There was disgust in Bemj's face as he looked up at the monster. "Obviously much less intelligent than a woorath. Might just as well turn on the ray."

"Not at all," interrupted Klarloth. "You forget certain very obvious facts. The creature is unintelligent, of course, but the subconscious of every animal holds in itself every memory, every impression, every sense-image, to which it has ever been subjected. If this creature has ever heard the speech of the Earthlings, or seen any of their works—besides this rocket—every word and every picture is indelibly graven. You see now what I mean?"

"Naturally. How stupid of me, Klarloth. Well, one thing is obvious from the rocket itself: we have nothing to fear from the science of Earth for at least a few millennia. So there is no hurry, which is fortunate. For to send back the creature's memory to the time of its birth, and to follow each sensory impression in the psychograph will require—well, a time at least equivalent to the age of the creature, whatever that is, plus the time necessary for us to interpret and assimilate each."

"But that will not be necessary, Bemj."

"No? Oh, you mean the X-19 waves?"

"Exactly. Focused upon this creature's brain-center, they can, without disturbing his memories, be so delicately adjusted as to increase his intelligence—now probably about .0001 in the scale —to the point where he is a reasoning creature. Almost automatically, during the process, he will assimilate his own memories, and understand them just as he would if he had been intelligent at the time he received those impressions.

"See, Bemj? He will automatically sort out irrelevant data and will be able to answer our questions."

"But would you make him as intelligent as—?"

"As we? No, the X-19 waves would not work so far. I would say to about .2 on the scale. That, judging from the rocket coupled with what we remember of Earthlings from our last trip there, is about their present place on the intelligence scale."

"Ummm, yes. At that level, he would comprehend his experiences on Earth just sufficiently that he would not be dangerous to us, too. Equal to an intelligent Earthling. Just about right for our purpose. Then, shall we teach him our language?"

"Wait," said Klarloth. He studied the psychograph closely for a while. "No, I do not think so. He will have a language of his own. I see in his subconscious, memories of many long conversations. Strangely, they all seem to be monologues by one person. But he will have a language—a simple one. It would take him a long time, even under treatment, to grasp the concepts of our own method of communication. But we can learn his, while he is under the X-19 machine, in a few minutes."

"Does he understand, now, any of that language?"

Klarloth studied the psychograph again. "No, I do not believe he—Wait, there is one word that seems to mean something to him. The word 'Mitkey.' It seems to be his name, and I believe that, from hearing it many times, he vaguely associates it with himself."

"And quarters for him—with air-locks and such?"

"Of course. Order them built."

To say it was a strange experience for Mitkey is understatement. Knowledge is a strange thing, even when it is acquired gradually. To have it thrust upon one—

And there were little things that had to be straightened out. Like the matter of vocal chords. His weren't adapted to the language he now found he knew. Bemj fixed that; you would hardly call it an operation because Mitkey—even with his new awareness—didn't know what was going on, and he was wide awake at the time. And they didn't explain to Mitkey about the J-dimension with which one can get at the inwardness of things without penetrating the outside.

They figured things like that weren't in Mitkey's line, and anyway they were more interested in learning from him than teaching him. Bemj and Klarloth, and a dozen others deemed worthy of the privilege. If one of them wasn't talking to him, another was.

Their questioning helped his own growing understanding. He would not, usually, know that he knew the answer to a question until it was asked. Then he'd piece together, without knowing just how he did it (any more than you or I know *how* we know things) and give them the answer.

Bemj: "Iss this language vhich you sbeak a universal vun?"

And Mitkey, even though he'd never thought about it before, had the answer ready: "No, it iss nodt. It iss Englitch, but I remember der Herr Brofessor sbeaking of other tongues. I belieff he sboke another himself originally, budt in America he always sboke Englitch to become more vamiliar mitt it. It iss a beaudiful sbeech, is it nodt?"

"Hmmmm," said Bemj.

Klarloth: "Und your race, the mices. Are they treated vell?"

"Nodt by most people," Mitkey told him. And explained.

"I vould like to do something for them," he added. "Loogk, could I nodt take back mitt me this brocess vhich you used upon me? Abbly it to other mices, und greate a race of super-mices?"

"Vhy not?" asked Bemj.

He saw Klarloth looking at him strangely, and threw his mind into rapport with the chief scientist's, with Mitkey left out of the silent communion.

"Yes, of course," Bemj told Klarloth, "it will lead to trouble. Two equal classes of beings so dissimilar as mice and men cannot live together in amity. But why should that concern us, other than favorably? The resultant mess will slow down progress on Earth—give us a few more millennia of peace before Earthlings discover we are here, and trouble starts. You know these Earthlings."

"But you would give them the X-19 waves? They might—"

"No, of course not. But we can explain to Mitkey here how to make a very crude and limited machine for them. A primitive one which would suffice for nothing more than the specific task of converting mouse mentality from .0001 to .2, Mitkey's own level and that of the bifurcated Earthlings."

"It is possible," communicated Klarloth. "It is certain that for aeons to come they will be incapable of understanding its basic principle."

"But could they not use even a crude machine to raise their own level of intelligence?"

"You forget, Bemj, the basic limitation of the X-19 rays; that no one can possibly design a projector capable of raising any mentality to a point on the scale higher than his own. Not even we."

All this, of course, over Mitkey's head, in silent Prxlian.

More interviews, and more.

Klarloth again: "Mitkey, ve varn you of vun thing. Avoid carelessness vith electricity. Der new molecular rearrangement of your brain center—it iss unstable, und—"

Bemj: "Mitkey, are you sure your Herr Brofessor iss der most advanced of all who eggsperiment vith der rockets?"

"In cheneral, yess, Bemj. There are others who on vun specific boint, such as eggsplosives, mathematics, astrovisics, may know more, but not much more. Und for combining these knowledges, he iss ahead."

"It iss vell," said Bemj.

Small gray mouse towering like a dinosaur over tinier half-inch Prxlians. Meek, herbivorous creature though he was, Mitkey could have killed any one of them with a single bite. But, of course, it never occurred to him to do so, nor to them to fear that he might.

They turned him inside out mentally. They did a pretty good job of study on him physically, too, but that was through the J-dimension, and Mitkey didn't even know about it.

They found out what made him tick, and they found out everything he knew and some things he didn't even know he knew. And they grew quite fond of him.

"Mitkey," said Klarloth one day, "all der civilized races on Earth vear glothing, do they nodt? Vell, if you are to raise der level of mices to men, vould it not be vitting that you vear glothes, too?"

"An eggcelent idea, Herr Klarloth. Und I know chust vhat kind I would like. Der Herr Brofessor vunce showed me a bicture of a mouse bainted by der artist Dissney, und der mouse vore glothing. Der mouse vas not a real-life vun, budt an imachinary mouse in a barable, und der Brofessor named me after der Dissney mouse."

"Vot kind of glothing vas it, Mitkey?"

"Bright red bants mitt two big yellow buttons in frondt und two in back, und yellow shoes for der back feet und a pair of yellow gloves for der vront. A hole in der seat of der bants to aggomodate der tail."

"Ogay, Mitkey. Such shall be ready for you in fife minutes."

That was on the eve of Mitkey's departure. Originally, Bemj had suggested awaiting the moment when Prxl's eccentric orbit would again take it within a hundred and fifty thousand miles of Earth. But, as Klarloth pointed out, that would be fifty-five Earth-years ahead, and Mitkey wouldn't last that long. Not unless they— And Bemj agreed that they had better not risk sending a secret like that back to Earth.

So they compromised by refueling Mitkey's rocket with something that would cancel out the million and a quarter odd miles he would have to travel. That secret they didn't have to worry about, because the fuel would be gone by the time the rocket landed.

Day of departure.

"Ve haff done our best, Mitkey, to set und time der rocket so it vill land on or near der spot from which you left Earth. But you gannot eggspect agguracy in a voyach so long as this. You will land near. The rest iss up to you. Ve haff equvipped the rocket ship for effery contingency."

"Thank you, Herr Klarloth, Herr Bemj. Gootbye."

"Gootbye, Mitkey. Ve hate to loose you."

"Gootbye, Mitkey."

"Gootbye, gootbye . . . ."

For a million and a quarter miles, the aim was really excellent. The rocket landed in Long Island Sound, ten miles out from Bridgeport, about sixty miles from the house of Professor Oberburger near Hartford.

They had prepared for a water landing, of course. The rocket went down to the bottom, but before it was more than a few dozen feet under the surface, Mitkey opened the door—especially equipped to open from the inside—and stepped out.

Over his regular clothes he wore a neat little diving suit that would have protected him at any reasonable depth, and which, being lighter than water, brought him to the surface quickly where he was able to open his helmet.

He had enough synthetic food to last him for a week, but it

wasn't necessary, as things turned out. The nightboat from Boston carried him in to Bridgeport on its anchor chain, and once in sight of land he was able to divest himself of the diving suit and let it sink to the bottom after he'd punctured the tiny compartment that made it float, as he'd promised Klarloth he would do.

Almost instinctively, Mitkey knew that he'd do well to avoid human beings until he'd reached Professor Oberburger and told his story. His worst danger proved to be the rats at the wharf where he swam ashore. They were ten times Mitkey's size and had teeth that could have taken him apart in two bites.

But mind has always triumphed over matter. Mitkey pointed an imperious yellow glove and said, "Scram," and the rats scrammed. They'd never seen anything like Mitkey before, and they were impressed.

So for that matter, was the drunk of whom Mitkey inquired the way to Hartford. We mentioned that episode before. That was the only time Mitkey tried direct communication with strange human beings. He took, of course, every precaution. He addressed his remarks from a strategic position only inches away from a hole into which he could have popped. But it was the drunk who did the popping, without even waiting to answer Mitkey's question.

But he got there, finally. He made his way afoot to the north side of town and hid out behind a gas station until he heard a motorist who had pulled in for gasoline inquire the way to Hartford. And Mitkey was a stowaway when the car started up.

The rest wasn't hard. The calculations of the Prxlians showed that the starting point of the rocket was five Earth miles northwest of what showed on their telescopomaps as a city, and which from the Professor's conversation Mitkey knew would be Hartford.

He got there.

"Hello, Brofessor."

The Herr Professor Oberburger looked up, startled. There was no one in sight. "Vot?" he asked, of the air. "Who iss?"

"It iss I, Brofessor. Mitkey, der mouse whom you sent to der moon. But I vas not there. Insteadt, I—"

"Vot?? It is imbossible. Somebody blays der choke. Budt— budt nobody *knows* about that rocket. Vhen it vailed, I didn't told nobody. Nobody budt me knows—"

"And me, Brofessor."

The Herr Professor sighed heavily. "Offervork. I am going vhat they call batty in der bel—"

"No, Brofessor. This is really me, Mitkey. I can talk now. Chust like you."

"You say you can— I do not belief it. Vhy can I not see you, then. Vhere are you? Vhy don't you—"

"I am hiding, Brofessor, in der vall chust behind der big hole. I vanted to be sure efferything vas ogay before I showed myself. Then you vould not get eggcited and throw something at me maybe."

"Vot? Vhy, Mitkey, if it iss really you und I am nodt asleep or going—Vhy, Mitkey, you know better than to think I might do something like that!"

"Ogay, Brofessor."

Mitkey stepped out of the hole in the wall, and the Professor looked at him and rubbed his eyes and looked again and rubbed his eyes and—

"I *am* crazy," he said finally. "Red bants he vears yet, und yellow— It gannot be. I *am* crazy."

"No, Brofessor. Listen, I'll tell you all aboudt."

And Mitkey told him.

Gray dawn, and a small gray mouse still talking earnestly.

"But, Mitkey—"

"Yess, Brofessor. I see your point, that you think an intelligent race of mices und an intelligent race of men couldt nodt get along side by sides. But it vould not be side by sides; as I said, there are only a ferry few beople in the smallest continent of Australia. Und it vould cost little to bring them back und turn offer that continent to us mices. Ve could call it Moustralia instead of Australia, und ve vould instead of Sydney call der capital Dissney, in honor of—"

"But, Mitkey—"

"But, Brofessor, look vot ve offer for that continent. *All* mices vould go there. Ve civilize a few und the few help us catch others und bring them in to put them under der ray machine, und the others help catch more und build more machines und it grows like a snowball rolling down hill. Und ve sign a non-aggression pact mitt humans und stay on Moustralia und raise our own food und—"

"But, Mitkey—"

"Und look vat ve offer you in eggschange, Herr Brofessor! Ve vill aggsterminate your vorst enemy—der *rats*. Ve do not like them either. Und vun battalion of vun thousand mices, armed mitt gas masks und small gas bombs could go right in effery hole after der rats und could eggsterminate effery rat in a city in vun day or two. In der whole world ve could eggsterminate effery last rat in a year, und at the same time catch und civilize effery mouse und ship him to Moustralia, und—"

"But, Mitkey—"

"Vot, Brofessor?"

"It vould vork, but it vould not vork. You could eggsterminate der rats, yess. But how long vould it be before conflicts of interests vould lead to der mices trying to eggsterminate der people or der people trying to eggsterminate der—"

"They vould not dare, Brofessor! Ve could make veapons that vould—"

"You see, Mitkey?"

"But it vould not habben. If men vill honor our rights, ve vill honor—"

The Herr Professor sighed.

"I—I vill act as your intermediary, Mitkey, und offer your broposition, und—Vell, it is true that getting rid of rats vould be a greadt boon to der human race. Budt—"

"Thank you, Brofessor."

"By der vay, Mitkey. I haff Minnie. Your wife, I guess it iss, unless there vas other mices around. She iss in der other room; I put her there chust before you arriffed, so she vould be in der dark und could sleep. You van to see her?"

"Vife?" said Mitkey. It had been so long that he had really forgotten the family he had perforce abandoned. The memory returned slowly.

"Vell," he said "—ummm, yess. Ve vill get her und I shall construct quvick a small X-19 prochector und—Yess, it vill help you in your negotiations mitt der governments if there are sefferal of us already so they can see I am not chust a freak like they might otherwise suspegt."

It wasn't deliberate. It couldn't have been, because the Professor didn't know about Klarloth's warning to Mitkey about carelessness with electricity—"Der new molecular rearrancheent of your brain center—it iss unstable, und—"

And the Professor was still back in the lighted room when Mitkey ran into the room where Minnie was in her barless cage.

She was asleep, and the sight of her— Memory of his earlier days came back like a flash and suddenly Mitkey knew how lonesome he had been.

"Minnie!" he called, forgetting that she could not understand. And stepped up on the board where she lay. "Squeak!" The mild electrical current between the two strips of tinfoil got him.

There was silence for a while.

Then: "Mitkey," called the Herr Professor. "Come on back und ve will discuss this—"

He stepped through the doorway and saw them, there in the gray light of dawn, two small gray mice cuddled happily together. He couldn't tell which was which, because Mitkey's teeth had torn off the red and yellow garments which had suddenly been strange, confining and obnoxious things.

"Vot on earth?" asked Professor Oberburger. Then he remembered the current, and guessed.

"Mitkey! Can you no longer talk? Iss der—"

Silence.

Then the Professor smiled. "Mitkey," he said, "my little starmouse. I think you are more happier now."

He watched them a moment, fondly, then reached down and flipped the switch that broke the electrical barrier. Of course they didn't know they were free, but when the Professor picked them up and placed them carefully on the floor, one ran immediately for the hole in the wall. The other followed, but turned around and looked back—still a trace of puzzlement in the little black eyes, a puzzlement that faded.

"Gootbye, Mitkey. You vill be happier this vay. Und there vill always be cheese."

"Squeak," said the little gray mouse, and it popped into the hole.

"Gootbye—" it might, or might not, have meant.

Abominable

SIR CHAUNCEY ATHERTON waved a farewell to the Sherpa guides who were to set up camp here and let him proceed alone. This was Abominable Snowman country, a few hundred miles north of Mount Everest, in the Himalayas. Abominable Snowmen were seen occasionally on Everest, on other Tibetan or Nepalese mountains, but Mount Oblimov, at the foot of which he was now leaving his native guides, was so thick with them that not even the Sherpas would climb it, but would here await his return, if indeed he did. It took a brave man to pass this point. Sir Chauncey was a brave man.

Also, he was a connoisseur of women, which was why he was here and about to attempt, alone, not only a dangerous ascent but an even more dangerous rescue. If Lola Gabraldi was still alive, an Abominable Snowman had her.

Sir Chauncey had never seen Lola Gabraldi, in the flesh. He had, in fact, learned of her existence less than a month ago, when he had seen the one motion picture in which she had starred—and through which she had become suddenly fabulous, the most beautiful woman on Earth, the most pulchritudinous movie star Italy had ever produced, and Sir Chauncey could not understand how even Italy had produced her. In one picture she had replaced Bardot, Lolobrigida, and Ekberg as the image of feminine perfection in the minds of connoisseurs of women everywhere, and Sir Chauncey was the top connoisseur anywhere. The moment he had seen her on the screen he had known that he must know her in the flesh, or die trying.

But by that time Lola Gabraldi had vanished. As a vacation after her first picture she had taken a trip to India and had joined a group of climbers about to make an assault on Mount Oblimov. The rest of the party had returned, Lola had not. One of them had testified that he had seen her, at a distance too great for him to reach her in time, abducted, carried off screaming by a nine-foot-high hairy more-or-less manlike creature. An Abominable Snowman. The party had searched for her for days before giving up and returning to civilization. Everyone agreed that there was no possible chance, now, of finding her alive.

Everyone except Sir Chauncey, who had immediately flown to India from England.

He struggled on, now high into the eternal snows. And in addition to mountain-climbing equipment he carried the heavy rifle with which he had, only the year before, shot tigers in Bengal. If it could kill tigers, he reasoned, it could kill Snowmen.

Snow swirled about him as he neared the cloud line. Suddenly, a dozen yards ahead of him, which was as far as he could see, he caught a glimpse of a monstrous not-quite-human figure. He raised his rifle and fired. The figure fell, and kept on falling; it had been on a ledge over thousands of feet of nothingness.

And at the moment of the shot arms closed around Sir Chauncey from behind him. Thick, hairy arms. And then, as one hand held him easily, the other took the rifle from him and bent it into an L-shape as easily as though it had been a toothpick, and then tossed it away.

A voice spoke from a point about two feet above his head. "Be quiet, you will not be harmed." Sir Chauncey was a brave man, but a sort of squeak was all the answer he could make, despite the seeming assurance of the words. He was held so tightly against the creature behind him that he could not look upward and backward to see what its face was like.

"Let me explain," said the voice above and behind him. "We, whom you call Abominable Snowmen, are human, but transmuted. A great many centuries ago we were a tribe like the Sherpas. We chanced to discover a drug that let us change physically, let us adapt by increased size, hairiness, and other physiological changes to extreme cold and altitude, let us move up into the mountains, into country in which others cannot survive, except for the duration of brief climbing expeditions. Do you understand?"

"Y-y-yes," Sir Chauncey managed to say. He was beginning to feel a faint return of hope. Why would this creature be explaining these things to him, if it intended to kill him?

"Then I shall explain further. Our number is small, and we

are diminishing. For that reason we occasionally capture, as I have captured you, a mountain climber. We give him the transmuting drug, he undergoes the physiological changes and becomes one of us. By that means we keep our number, such as it is, relatively constant."

"B-but," Sir Chauncey stammered, "is that what happened to the woman I'm looking for, Lola Gabraldi? She is now—eight feet tall and hairy and—"

"She *was*. You just killed her. One of our tribe had taken her as his mate. We will take no revenge for your having killed her, but you must now, as it were, take her place."

"Take her place? But—I'm a *man*."

"Thank God for that," said the voice above and behind him. He found himself turned around, held against a huge hairy body, his face at the right level to be buried between mountainous hairy breasts. "Thank God for that—because I am an Abominable Snowwoman."

Sir Chauncey fainted and was picked up and, as lightly as though he were a toy dog, was carried away by his mate.

Letter to a Phoenix

THERE IS much to tell you, so much that it is difficult to know where to begin. Fortunately, I have forgotten most of the things that have happened to me. Fortunately, the mind has a limited capacity for remembering. It would be horrible if I remembered the details of a hundred and eighty thousand years—the details of four thousand lifetimes that I have lived since the first great atomic war.

Not that I have forgotten the really great moments. I remember being on the first expedition to land on Mars and the third to land on Venus. I remember—I believe it was in the third great war—the blasting of Skora from the sky by a force that compares to nuclear fission as a nova compares to our slowly dying sun. I was second in command on a Hyper-A Class spacer in the war against the second extragalactic invaders, the ones who established bases on Jupe's moons before we knew they were there and almost drove us out of the Solar System before we found the one weapon they couldn't stand up against. So they fled where we couldn't follow them, then, outside of the Galaxy. When we did follow them, about fifteen thousand years later, they were gone. They were dead three thousand years.

And this is what I want to tell you about—that mighty race and the others—but first, so that you will know how I know what I know, I will tell you about myself.

I am not immortal. There is only one immortal being in the universe; of it, more anon. Compared to it, I am of no importance, but you will not understand or believe what I say to you unless you understand what I am.

There is little in a name, and that is a fortunate thing—for I do not remember mine. That is less strange than you think, for a hundred and eighty thousand years is a long time and for one reason or another I have changed my name a thousand times or more. And what could matter less than the name my parents gave me a hundred and eighty thousand years ago?

I am not a mutant. What happened to me happened when I was twenty-three years old, during the first atomic war. The first war, that is, in which both sides used atomic weapons—puny weapons, of course, compared to subsequent ones. It was less than a score of years after the discovery of the atom bomb. The first bombs were dropped in a minor war while I was still a child. They ended that war quickly for only one side had them.

The first atomic war wasn't a bad one—the first one never is. I was lucky for, if it had been a bad one—one which ended a civilization—I'd not have survived it despite the biological accident that happened to me. If it had ended a civilization, I wouldn't have been kept alive during the sixteen-year sleep period I went through about thirty years later. But again I get ahead of the story.

I was, I believe, twenty or twenty-one years old when the war started. They didn't take me for the army right away because I was not physically fit. I was suffering from a rather rare disease of the pituitary gland—Somebody's syndrome. I've forgotten the name. It caused obesity, among other things. I was about fifty pounds overweight for my height and had little stamina. I was rejected without a second thought.

About two years later my disease had progressed slightly, but other things had progressed more than slightly. By that time the army was taking anyone; they'd have taken a one-legged one-armed blind man if he was willing to fight. And I was willing to fight. I'd lost my family in a dusting, I hated my job in a war plant, and I had been told by doctors that my disease was incurable and I had only a year or two to live in any case. So I went to what was left of the army, and what was left of the army took me without a second thought and sent me to the nearest front, which was ten miles away. I was in the fighting one day after I joined.

Now I remember enough to know that I hadn't anything to do with it, but it happened that the time I joined was the turn of the tide. The other side was out of bombs and dust and getting low on shells and bullets. We were out of bombs and dust, too, but they hadn't knocked out all of our production facilities and we'd got just about all of theirs. We still had planes to carry them, too, and we still had the semblance of an organization to send the planes to the right places. Nearly the right places, anyway; sometimes we dropped them too close to our own troops by mistake. It was a week after I'd got into the fighting that I got out of it again—knocked out of it by one of our smaller bombs that had been dropped about a mile away.

I came to, about two weeks later, in a base hospital, pretty badly burned. By that time the war was over, except for the mopping up, and except for restoring order and getting the world started up again. You see, that hadn't been what I call a blow-up war. It killed off—I'm just guessing; I don't remember the fraction—about a fourth or a fifth of the world's population. There was enough productive capacity left, and there were enough people left, to keep on going; there were dark ages for a few centuries, but there was no return to savagery, no starting over again. In such times, people go back to using candles for light and burning wood for fuel, but not because they don't know how to use electricity or mine coal; just because the confusions and revolutions keep them off balance for a while. The knowledge is there, in abeyance until order returns.

It's not like a blow-up war, when nine-tenths or more of the population of Earth—or of Earth and the other planets—is killed. Then is when the world reverts to utter savagery and the hundredth generation rediscovers metals to tip their spears.

But again I digressed. After I recovered consciousness in the hospital, I was in pain for a long time. There were, by then, no more anesthetics. I had deep radiation burns, from which I suffered almost intolerably for the first few months until, gradually, they healed. I did not sleep—that was the strange thing. And it was a terrifying thing, then, for I did not understand what had happened to me, and the unknown is always terrifying. The doctors paid little heed—for I was one of millions burned or otherwise injured—and I think they did not believe my statements that I had not slept at all. They thought I had slept but little and that I was either exaggeraing or making an honest error. But I had *not* slept at all. I did not sleep until long after I left the hospital, cured. Cured, incidentally, of the disease of my pituitary gland, and with my weight back to normal, my health perfect.

I didn't sleep for thirty years. Then *I did sleep,* and I slept for sixteen years. And at the end of that forty-six-year period, I was still, physically, at the apparent age of twenty-three.

Do you begin to see what had happened as I began to see it then? The radiation—or combination of types of radiation—I had gone through, had radically changed the functions of my pituitary. And there were other factors involved. I studied endocrinology once, about a hundred and fifty thousand years ago, and I think I found the pattern. If my calculations were correct, what happened to me was one chance in a great many billions.

The factors of decay and aging were not eliminated, of course, but the rate was reduced by about fifteen thousand times. I age at the rate of one day every forty-five years. So I am not immortal. I have aged eleven years in the past hundred and eighty millennia. My physical age is now thirty-four.

And forty-five years is to me as a day. I do not sleep for about thirty years of it—then I sleep for about fifteen. It is well for me that my first few "days" were not spent in a period of complete social disorganization or savagery, else I would not have survived my first few sleeps. But I did survive them and by that time I had learned a system and could take care of my own survival. Since then, I have slept about four thousand times, and I have survived. Perhaps someday I shall be unlucky. Perhaps someday, despite certain safeguards, someone will discover and break into the cave or vault into which I seal myself, secretly, for a period of sleep. But it is not likely. I have years in which to prepare each of those places and the experience of four thousand sleeps back of me. You could pass such a place a thousand times and never know it was there, nor be able to enter if you suspected.

No, my chances for survival between my periods of waking life are much better than my chances of survival during my conscious, active periods. It is perhaps a miracle that I have survived so many of those, despite the techniques of survival that I have developed.

And those techniques are good. I've lived through seven major atomic—and super-atomic—wars that have reduced the population of Earth to a few savages around a few campfires in a few still habitable areas. And at other times, in other eras, I've been in five galaxies besides our own.

I've had several thousand wives but always one at a time for I was born in a monogamous era and the habit has persisted. And

I have raised several thousand children. Of course, I have never been able to remain with one wife longer than thirty years before I must disappear, but thirty years is long enough for both of us—especially when she ages at a normal rate and I age imperceptibly. Oh, it leads to problems, of course, but I've been able to handle them. I always marry, when I do marry, a girl as much younger than myself as possible, so the disparity will not become too great. Say I am thirty; I marry a girl of sixteen. Then when it is time that I must leave her, she is forty-six and I am still thirty. And it is best for both of us, for everyone, that when I awaken I do not again go back to that place. If she still lives, she will be past sixty and it would not be well, even for her, to have a husband come back from the dead—still young. And I have left her well provided, a wealthy widow—wealthy in money or in whatever may have constituted wealth in that particular era. Sometimes it has been beads and arrowheads, sometimes wheat in a granary and once—there have been peculiar civilizations—it was fish scales. I never had the slightest difficulty in acquiring my share, or more, of money or its equivalent. A few thousand years' practice and the difficulty becomes the other way—knowing when to stop in order not to become unduly wealthy and so attract attention.

For obvious reasons, I've always managed to do that. For reasons that you will see I've never wanted power, nor have I ever—after the first few hundred years—let people suspect that I was different from them. I even spend a few hours each night lying thinking, pretending to sleep.

But none of that is important, any more than I am important. I tell it to you only so you will understand how I *know* the thing that I am about to tell you.

And when I tell you, it is not because I'm trying to sell you anything. It's something you can't change if you want to, and—when you understand it—you won't want to.

I'm not trying to influence you or to lead you. In four thousand lifetimes I've been almost everything—except a leader. I've avoided that. Oh, often enough I have been a god among savages, but that was because I had to be one in order to survive. I used the powers they thought were magic only to keep a degree of order, never to lead them, never to hold them back. If I taught them to use the bow and arrow, it was because game was scarce and we were starving and my survival depended upon theirs. Seeing that the pattern was necessary, I have never disturbed it.

What I tell you now will not disturb the pattern.

It is this: The human race is the only immortal organism in the universe.

There have been other races, and there are other races throughout the universe, but they have died away or they will die. We charted them once, a hundred thousand years ago, with an instrument that detected the presence of thought, the presence of intelligence, however alien and at whatever distance—and gave us a measure of that mind and its qualities. And fifty thousand years later that instrument was rediscovered. There were about as many races as before but only eight of them were ones that had been there fifty thousand years ago and each of those eight was dying, senescent. They had passed the peak of their powers and they were dying.

They had reached the limit of their capabilities—and there is always a limit—and they had no choice but to die. Life is dynamic; it can never be static—at however high or low a level—and survive.

That is what I am trying to tell you, so that you will never again be afraid. Only a race that destroys itself and its progress periodically, that goes back to its beginning, can survive more than, say, sixty thousand years of intelligent life.

In all the universe only the human race has ever reached a high level of intelligence without reaching a high level of sanity. We are unique. We are already at least five times as old as any other race has ever been and it is because we are not sane. And man has, at times, had glimmerings of the fact that insanity is divine. But only at high levels of culture does he realize that he is collectively insane, that fight against it as he will he will always destroy himself—and rise anew out of the ashes.

The phoenix, the bird that periodically immolates itself upon a flaming pyre to rise newborn and live again for another millennium, and again and forever, is only metaphorically a myth. It exists and there is only one of it.

You are the phoenix.

Nothing will ever destroy you, now that—during many high civilizations—your seed has been scattered on the planets of a thousand suns, in a hundred galaxies, there ever to repeat the pattern. The pattern that started a hundred and eighty thousand years ago—I think.

I cannot be sure of that for I have seen that the twenty to thirty thousand years that elapse between the fall of one civilization and the rise of the next destroy all traces. In twenty to thirty thousand years memories become legends and legends become superstitions and even the superstitions become lost. Metals rust and corrode back into earth while the wind the rain and the jungle erode and cover stone. The contours of the very continents change—and glaciers come and go, and a city of twenty thousand years before is under miles of earth or miles of water.

So I cannot be sure. Perhaps the first blow-up that I knew was not the first; civilizations may have risen and fallen before my time. If so, it merely strengthens the case I put before you to say that mankind *may* have survived more than the hundred and eighty thousand years I know of, may have lived through more than the six blow-ups that have happened since what I think to have been the first discovery of the phoenix's pyre.

But—except that we scattered our seed to the stars so well that even the dying of the sun or its becoming a nova would not destroy us—the past does not matter. Lur, Candra, Thragan, Kah, Mu, Atlantis—those are the six I have known, and they are gone as thoroughly as this one will be twenty thousand years or so hence, but the human race, here or in other galaxies, will survive and will live forever.

It will help your peace of mind, here in this year of your current era, to know that—for your minds are disturbed. Perhaps, I do know, it will help your thoughts to know that the coming atomic war, the one that will probably happen in your generation, will not be a blow-up war; it will come too soon for that, before you have developed the really destructive weapons man has had so often before. It will set you back, yes. There will be darkish ages for a century or a few centuries. Then, with the memory of what you will call World War III as a warning, man will think—as he has always thought after a mild atomic war—that he has conquered his own insanity.

For a while—if the pattern holds—he will hold it in check. He will reach the stars again, to find himself already there. Why, you'll be back on Mars within five hundred years, and I'll go there too, to see again the canals I once helped to dig. I've not been there for eighty thousand years and I'd like to see what time has done to it and to those of us who were cut off there the last time mankind lost the space drive. Of course they've followed the pattern too, but the rate is not necessarily constant. We may find them at any stage in the cycle except the top. If they were at the top of the cycle, we wouldn't have to go to them—they'd come to us. Thinking, of course, as they think by now, that they are Martians.

I wonder how high, this time, you will get. Not quite as high, I hope, as Thragan. I hope that never again is rediscovered the weapon Thragan used against her colony on Skora, which was then the fifth planet until the Thragans blew it into asteroids. Of course that weapon would be developed only long after intergalactic travel again becomes commonplace. If I see it coming I'll get out of the Galaxy, but I'd hate to have to do that. I like Earth and I'd like to spend the rest of my mortal lifetime on it if it lasts that long.

Possibly it won't, but the human race will last. Everywhere and forever, for it will never be sane and only insanity is divine. Only the mad destroy themselves and all they have wrought.

And only the phoenix lives forever.

Not Yet the End

THERE WAS a greenish, hellish tinge to the light within the metal cube. It was a light that made the dead-white skin of the creature seated at the controls seem faintly green.

A single, faceted eye, front center in the head, watched the seven dials unwinkingly. Since they had left Xandor that eye had never once wavered from the dials. Sleep was unknown to the race to which Kar-388Y belonged. Mercy, too, was unknown. A single glance at the sharp, cruel features below the faceted eye would have proved that.

The pointers on the fourth and seventh dials came to a stop. That meant the cube itself had stopped in space relative to its immediate objective. Kar reached forward with his upper right arm and threw the stabilizer switch. Then he rose and stretched his cramped muscles.

Kar turned to face his companion in the cube, a being like himself. "We are here," he said. "The first stop, Star Z-5689. It has nine planets, but only the third is habitable. Let us hope we find creatures here who will make suitable slaves for Xandor."

Lal-16B, who had sat in rigid mobility during the journey, rose and stretched also. "Let us hope so, yes. Then we can return to Xandor and be honored while the fleet comes to get them. But let's not hope too strongly. To meet with success at the first place we stop would be a miracle. We'll probably have to look a thousand places."

Kar shrugged. "Then we'll look a thousand places. With the Lounacs dying off, we must have slaves else our mines must close and our race will die."

He sat down at the controls again and threw a switch that activated a visiplate that would show what was beneath them. He said, "We are above the night side of the third planet. There is a cloud layer below us. I'll use the manuals from here."

He began to press buttons. A few minutes later he said, "Look, Lal, at the visiplate. Regularly spaced lights—a city! The planet *is* inhabited."

Lal had taken his place at the other switchboard, the fighting controls. Now he too was examining dials. "There is nothing for us to fear. There is not even the vestige of a force field around the city. The scientific knowledge of the race is crude. We can wipe the city out with one blast if we are attacked."

"Good," Kar said. "But let me remind you that destruction is not our purpose—yet. We want specimens. If they prove satisfactory and the fleet comes and takes as many thousand slaves as we need, then will be time to destroy not a city but the whole planet. So that their civilization will never progress to the point where they'll be able to launch reprisal raids."

Lal adjusted a knob. "All right. I'll put on the megrafield and we'll be invisible to them unless they see far into the ultraviolet, and, from the spectrum of their sun, I doubt that they do."

As the cube descended the light within it changed from green to violet and beyond. It came to a gentle rest. Kar manipulated the mechanism that operated the airlock.

He stepped outside, Lal just behind him. "Look," Kar said, "two bipeds. Two arms, two eyes—not dissimilar to the Lounacs, although smaller. Well, here are our specimens."

He raised his lower left arm, whose three-fingered hand held a thin rod wound with wire. He pointed it first at one of the creatures, then at the other. Nothing visible emanated from the end of the rod, but they both froze instantly into statuelike figures.

"They're not large, Kar," Lal said. "I'll carry one back, you carry the other. We can study them better inside the cube, after we're back in space."

Kar looked about him in the dim light. "All right, two is enough, and one seems to be male and the other female. Let's get going."

A minute later the cube was ascending and as soon as they were well out of the atmosphere, Kar threw the stabilizer switch and joined Lal, who had been starting a study of the specimens during the brief ascent.

"Vivaparous," said Lal. "Five-fingered, with hands suited to reasonably delicate work. But—let's try the most important test, intelligence."

Kar got the paired headsets. He handed one pair to Lal, who put one on his own head, one on the head of one of the specimens. Kar did the same with the other specimen.

After a few minutes, Kar and Lal stared at each other bleakly.

"Seven points below minimum," Kar said. "They could not be trained even for the crudest labor in the mines. Incapable of understanding the most simple instructions. Well, we'll take them back to the Xandor museum."

"Shall I destroy the planet?"

"No," Kar said. "Maybe a million years from now—if our race lasts that long—they'll have evolved enough to become suitable for our purpose. Let us move on to the next star with planets."

The make-up editor of the *Milwaukee Star* was in the composing room, supervising the closing of the local page. Jenkins, the head make-up compositor, was pushing in leads to tighten the second last column.

"Room for one more story in the eighth column, Pete," he said. "About thirty-six picas. There are two there in the overset that will fit. Which one shall I use?"

The make-up editor glanced at the type in the galleys lying on the stone beside the chase. Long practice enabled him to read the headlines upside down at a glance. "The convention story and the zoo story, huh? Oh, hell, run the convention story. Who cares if the zoo director thinks two monkeys disappeared off Monkey Island last night?"

Etaoin Shrdlu

It was rather funny for a while, the business about Ronson's Linotype. But it began to get a bit too sticky for comfort well before the end. And despite the fact that Ronson came out ahead on the deal, I'd have never sent him the little guy with the pimple, if I'd guessed what was going to happen. Fabulous profits or not, poor Ronson got too many gray hairs out of it.

"You're Mr. Walter Merold?" asked the little guy with the pimple. He'd called at the desk of the hotel where I live, and I'd told them to send him on up.

I admitted my identity, and he said, "Glad to know you, Mr. Merold. I'm—" and he gave me his name, but I can't remember now what it was. I'm usually good at remembering names.

I told him I was delighted to meet him and what did he want, and he started to tell me. I interrupted him before he got very far, though.

"Somebody gave you a wrong steer," I told him. "Yes, I've been a printing technician, but I'm retired. Anyway, do you know that the cost of getting special Linotype mats cut would be awfully high? If it's only one page you want printed with those special characters, you'd do a lot better to have somebody hand-letter it for you and then get a photographic reproduction in zinc."

"But that wouldn't do, Mr. Merold. Not at all. You see, the thing is a secret. Those I represent— But skip that. Anyway, I daren't let anyone see it, as they would have to, to make a zinc."

Just another nut, I thought, and looked at him closely.

He didn't look nutty. He was rather ordinary-looking on the whole, although he had a foreign—rather an Asiatic—look about him, somehow, despite the fact that he was blond and fair-skinned. And he had a pimple on his forehead, in dead center just above the bridge of the nose. You've seen ones like it on statues of Buddha, and Orientals call it the pimple of wisdom and it's something special.

I shrugged my shoulders. "Well," I pointed out, "you can't have the matrices cut for Linotype work without letting somebody see the characters you want on them, can you? And whoever runs the machine will also see—"

"Oh, but I'll do that myself," said the little guy with the pimple. (Ronson and I later called him the L.G.W.T.P., which stands for "little guy with the pimple," because Ronson couldn't remember his name, either, but I'm getting ahead of my story.) "Certainly the cutter will see them, but he'll see them as individual characters, and that won't matter. Then the actual setting of the type on the Linotype I can do myself. Someone can show me how to run one enough for me to set up one page—just a score of lines, really. And it doesn't have to be printed here. Just the type is all I'll want. I don't care what it costs me."

"O.K.," I said. "I'll send you to the proper man at Merganthaler, the Linotype people. They'll cut your mats. Then, if you want privacy and access to a Linotype, go see George Ronson. He runs a little country biweekly right here in town. For a fair price, he'll turn his shop over to you for long enough for you to set your type."

And that was that. Two weeks later, George Ronson and I went fishing on a Tuesday morning while the L.G.W.T.P. used George's Linotype to assemble the weird-looking mats he'd just received by air express from Mergenthaler. George had, the afternoon before, showed the little guy how to run the Linotype.

We caught a dozen fish apiece, and I remember that Ronson chuckled and said that made thirteen fish for him because the L.G.W.T.P. was paying him fifty bucks cash money just for one morning's use of his shop.

And everything was in order when we got back except that George had to pick brass out of the hellbox because the L.G.W.T.P. had smashed his new brass matrices when he'd finished with them, and hadn't known that one shouldn't throw brass in with the type metal that gets melted over again.

The next time I saw George was after his Saturday edition was off the press. I immediately took him to task.

"Listen," I said, "that stuff about misspelling words and using bum grammar on purpose isn't funny any more. Not even in a country newspaper. Were you by any chance trying to make your newsletters from the surrounding towns sound authentic by following copy out the window, or what?"

Ronson looked at me kind of funny and said, "Well—yes."

"Yes, what?" I wanted to know. "You mean you were deliberately trying to be funny, or following copy out the—"

He said, "Come on around and I'll show you."

"Show me what?"

"What I'm going to show you," he said, not very lucidly. "You can still set type, can't you?"

"Sure. Why?"

"Come on, then," he said firmly. "You're a Linotype technician, and besides you got me into this."

"Into what?"

"Into this," he said, and wouldn't tell me a thing more until we got there. Then he rummaged in all pigeonholes of his desk and pulled out a piece of dead copy and gave it to me.

His face had a kind of wistful look. "Walter," he said, "maybe I'm nuts, and I want to find out. I guess running a local paper for twenty-two years and doing all the work myself and trying to please everybody is enough to get a man off his rocker, but I want to find out."

I looked at him, and I looked at the copy sheet he'd handed to me. It was just an ordinary sheet of foolscap and it was in handwriting that I recognized as that of Hank Rogg, the hardware merchant over at Hales Corners who sends in items from there. There were the usual misspellings one would expect from Hank, but the item itself wasn't news to me. It read: "The weding of H.M. Klaflin and Miss Margorie Burke took place yesterday evening at the home of the bride. The bridesmades were—"

I quit reading and looked up at George and wondered what he was getting at. I said, "So what? This was two days ago, and I attended the wedding myself. There's nothing funny about—"

"Listen, Walter," he said, "set that for me, will you? Go over and sit down at the Linotype and set that whole thing. It won't run over ten or twelve lines."

"Sure, but why?"

"Because— Well, just set it, Walter. Then I'll tell you why."

So I went out in the shop and sat down at the Linotype, and I ran a couple of pi lines to get the feel of the keyboard again, and then I put the copy on the clipboard and started. I said, "Hey,

George, Marjorie spells her name with a j, doesn't she, instead of a g?"

And George said, "Yeah," in a funny tone of voice.

I ran off the rest of the squib, and then looked up and said, "Well?"

He came across and lifted the stick out of the machine and read the slugs upside down like all printers read type, and he sighed. He said, "Then it wasn't me. Lookit, Walter."

He handed me the stick, and I read the type, or started to.

It read. "The weding of H.M. Klaflin and Miss Margorie Burke took place yesterday evening at the home of the bride. The bridesmades were—"

I grinned. "Good thing I don't have to set type for a living anymore, George. I'm slipping; three errors in the first five lines. But what about it? Now tell me why you wanted me to set it."

He said, "Set the first couple lines over again, Walter. I—I want you to find out for yourself."

I looked up at him and he looked so darned serious and worried that I didn't argue. I turned back to the keyboard and started out again: "The wedding of —" My eyes went up to the assembly slide and read the characters on the front of the mats that had dropped, and I saw that it read, "The weding of—"

There's one advantage about a Linotype you may not know if you're not a printer. You can always make a correction in a line if you make it before you push the lever that sends in the line of matrices to cast the slug. You just drop the mats you need for the correction and put them in the right place by hand.

So I pushed the d key to get another d matrix to correct the misspelled word "weding"—and nothing happened. The keycam was going around all right and the click sounded O.K., but no d mat dropped. I looked up top to see if there was a distributor stop and there wasn't.

I stood up. "The d channel's jammed," I said. To be sure before I started to work on it, I held the d key down a minute and listened to the series of clicks while the keyboard cam went round.

But no d matrix dropped, so I reached for the—

"Skip it, Walter," said George Ronson quietly. "Send in the line and keep on going."

I sat down again and decided to humor him. If I did, I'd probably find out what he was leading up to quicker than if I

argued. I finished the first line and started the second and came
to the word "Margorie" on copy. I hit the M key, the a, r, j,
o—and happened to glance at the assembly slide. The matrices
there read "Margo—"

I said, "Damn," and hit the j key again to get a j mat to substitute for the g, and nothing happened. The j channel must be
jammed. I held the j key down and no mat dropped. I said,
"Damn," again and stood up to look over the escapement mechanism.

"Never mind, Walter," said George. There was a funny
blend of a lot of things in his voice; a sort of triumph over me, I
guess; and a bit of fear and a lot of bewilderment and a touch of
resignation. "Don't you see? *It follows copy!*"

"It—*what?*"

"That's why I wanted you to try it out, Walter," he said.
"Just to make sure it was the machine and not *me*. Lookit; that
copy in the clipboard has w-e-d-i-n-g for wedding, and M-a-r-g-o-
r-i-e- for Marjorie—and *no matter what keys you hit, that's the
way the mats drop.*"

I said, "Bosh. George, have you been drinking?"

"Don't believe me," he said. "Keep on trying to set those lines
right. Set your correction for the fourth line; the one that has
b-r-i-d-e-s-m-a-d-e-s in it."

I grunted, and I looked back at the stick of type to see what
word the fourth line started with, and I started hitting keys. I
set, "The bridesma," and then I stopped. Slowly and deliberately and looking at the keyboard while I did it, I put my index
finger on the i key and pushed. I heard the mat click through
the escapement, and I looked up and saw it fall over the star
wheel. I knew I hadn't hit the wrong key on that one. The mats
in the assembly elevator read—yes, you've guessed it: "brides-
mad—"

I said, "I don't believe it."

George Ronson looked at me with a sort of lopsided, worried
grin. He said, "Neither did I. Listen, Walter, I'm going out to
take a walk. I'm going nuts. I can't stand it here right now. You
go ahead and convince yourself. Take your time."

I watched him until he'd gone out the door. Then with a kind
of funny feeling, I turned back to the Linotype. It was a long
time before I believed it, but it was so.

No matter what keys I hit, the damn machine followed copy, errors and all.

I went the whole hog finally. I started over again, and set the first couple of words and then began to sweep my fingers down the rows of keys in sweeps like an operator uses to fill out a pi line: ETAOIN SHRDLU ETAOIN SHRDLU ETAOIN SHRDLU—and I didn't look at the matrices in the assembler slide. I sent them in to cast, and I picked up the hot slug that the ejector pushed out of the mold and I read: "The weding of H. M. Klaflin and—"

There was sweat on my forehead. I wiped it off and then I shut off the machine and went out to look for George Ronson. I didn't have to look very hard because he was right where I knew I'd find him. I ordered a drink, too.

He'd taken a look at my face when I walked into the bar, and I guess he didn't have to ask me what had happened.

We touched our glasses together and downed the contents before either of us said anything at all. Then I asked, "Got any idea *why* it works like that?"

He nodded.

I said, "Don't tell me. Wait until I've had a couple more drinks and then I can take it—maybe." I raised my voice and said, "Hey, Joe; just leave that bottle in reach on the bar. We'll settle for it."

He did, and I had two more shots fairly quick. Then I closed my eyes and said, "All right, George, why?"

"Remember that guy who had those special mats cut and rented the use of my Linotype to set up something that was too secret for anybody to read? I can't remember his name—what was it?"

I tried to remember, and I couldn't. I had another drink and said, "Call him the L.G.W.T.P."

George wanted to know why and I told him, and he filled his glass again and said, "I got a letter from him."

I said, "That's nice." And I had another drink and said, "Got the letter with you?"

"Huh-uh. I didn't keep it."

I said, "Oh."

Then I had another drink and asked, "Do you remember what it said?"

"Walter, I remember parts of it. Didn't read it cl-closely. I thought the guy was screwy, see? I threw it 'way."

He stopped and had another drink, and finally I got tired waiting and said, "Well?"

"Well, what?"

"The letter. What did the part you remember shay?"

"Oh, that," said George. "Yeah. Something about Lilo-Linotl —you know what I mean."

By that time the bottle on the bar in front us couldn't have been the same one, because this one was two-thirds full and the other one had been only one-third full. I took another drink. "What'd he shay about it?"

"Who?"

"Th' L.G.—G.P.—aw, th' guy who wrote th' letter."

"Wha' letter?" asked George.

I woke up somewhere around noon the next day, and I felt awful. It took me a couple of hours to get bathed and shaved and feeling good enough to go out, but when I did I headed right for George's printing shop.

He was running the press, and he looked almost as bad as I felt. I picked up one of the papers as it came off and looked at it. It's a four-sheet and the inside two are boiler plate, but the first and fourth pages are local stuff.

I read a few items, including one that started off: "The wedding of H.M. Klaflin and Miss Margorie—" and I glanced at the silent Linotype back in the corner and from it to George and back to that silent hulk of steel and cast iron.

I had to yell to George to be heard over the noise of the press. "George, listen. About the Lino—" Somehow I couldn't make myself *yell* something that sounded silly, so I compromised. "Did you get it fixed?" I asked.

He shook his head, and shut off the press. "That's the run," he said. "Well, now to get them folded."

"Listen," I said, "the hell with the papers. What I want to know is how you got to press at all. You didn't have half your quota set when I was here yesterday, and after all we drank, I don't see how you did it."

He grinned at me. "Easy," he said. "Try it. All you got to do, drunk or sober, is sit down at that machine and put copy on the clipboard and slide your fingers around on the keys a bit, and it sets the copy. Yes, mistakes and all—but, after this, I'll just correct the errors on copy before I start. This time I was too tight, Walter, and they had to go as was. Walter, I'm beginning to *like* that machine. This is the first time in a year I've got to press exactly on time."

"Yeah," I said, "but—"

"But what?"

"But—" I wanted to say that I still didn't believe it, but I couldn't. After all, I'd tried out that machine yesterday while I'd been cold sober.

I walked over closer and looked at it again. It looked exactly like any other one-magazine model Linotype from where I stood. I knew every cog and spring in it.

"George," I said uneasily, "I got a feeling the damn thing is *looking* at me. Have you felt—"

He nodded. I turned back and looked at the Linotype again, and I was sure this time, and I closed my eyes and felt it even more strongly. You know that feeling you get once in a while, of being stared at? Well, this was stronger. It wasn't exactly an unfriendly stare. Sort of impersonal. It made me feel scared stiff.

"George," I said, "Let's get out of here."

"What for?"

"I—I want to talk to you, George. And, somehow, I just don't want to talk here."

He looked at me, and then back at the stack of papers he was folding by hand. "You needn't be afraid, Walter," he said quietly. "It won't hurt you. It's friendly."

"You're—" Well, I started to say, "crazy," but if he was, then I was, too, and I stopped. I thought a minute and then said, "George, you started yesterday to tell me what you remembered of the letter you got from—from the L.G.W.T.P. What was it?"

"Oh, that. Listen, Walter, will you promise me something? That you'll keep this whole business strictly confidential? I mean, not tell anybody about it?"

"Tell anybody?" I demanded. "And get locked in a booby hatch? Not me. You think anybody would believe me? You think *I* would have believed it myself, if—But what about the letter?"

"You promise?"

"Sure."

"Well," he said, "like I think I told you, the letter was vague and what I remember of it is vaguer. But it explained that he'd used my Linotype to compose a—a metaphysical formula. He needed it, set in type, to take back with him."

"Take back where, George?"

"Take back where? He said to—I mean he didn't say where. Just to where he was going back, see? But he said it might have an effect on the machine that composed it, and if it did, he was sorry, but there wasn't anything he could do about it. He couldn't tell, because it took a while for the thing to work."

"What thing?"

"Well," said George. "It sounded like a lot of big words to me, and hooey at that." He looked back down at the papers he was folding. "Honest, it sounded so nuts I threw it away. But, thinking back, after what's happened—Well, I remember the word 'pseudolife.' I think it was a formula for giving pseudolife to inanimate objects. He said they used it on their—their robots."

"They? Who is 'they'?"

"He didn't say."

I filled my pipe, and lighted it thoughtfully. "George," I said after a while, "you better smash it."

Ronson looked at me, his eyes wide. "Smash it? Walter, you're nuts. Kill the goose that lays the golden eggs? Why, there's a fortune in this thing. Do you know how long it took me to set the type for this edition, drunk as I was? About an hour; that's how I got through the press run on time."

I looked at him suspiciously. "Phooey," I said. "Animate or inanimate, that Lino's geared for six lines a minute. That's all she'll go, unless you geared it up to run faster. Maybe to ten lines a minute if you taped the roller. Did you tape—"

"Tape hell," said George. "The thing goes so fast you can't hang the elevator on short-measure pi lines! And, Walter, take a look at the mold—the minion mold. It's in casting position."

A bit reluctantly, I walked back to the Linotype. The motor was humming quietly and again I could have sworn the damn thing was watching me. But I took a grip on my courage and the handles and I lowered my vise to expose the mold wheel. And I saw right away what George meant about the minion mold; it was bright-blue. I don't mean the blue of a gun barrel; I mean a real azure color that I'd never seen metal take before. The other three molds were turning the same shade.

I closed the vise and looked at George.

He said, "I don't know, either, except that that happened after the mold overheated and a slug stuck. I think it's some kind of heat treatment. It can cast a hundred lines a minute now without sticking, and it—"

"Whoa," I said, "back up. You couldn't even feed it metal fast enough to—"

He grinned at me, a scared but triumphant grin. "Walter, look around at the back. I built a hopper over the metal pot. I had to; I ran out of pigs in ten minutes. I just shovel dead type and swept-up metal into the hopper, and dump the hellboxes in it, and—"

I shook my head. "You're crazy. You can't dump unwashed type and sweepings in there; you'll have to open her up and scrape off the dross oftener than you'd otherwise have to push in pigs. You'll jam the plunger and you'll—"

"Walter," he said quietly—a bit too quietly—"*there isn't any dross.*"

I just looked at him stupidly, and he must have decided he'd said more than he wanted to, because he started hurrying the papers he'd just folded out into the office, and he said, "See you later, Walter. I got to take these—"

The fact that my daughter-in-law had a narrow escape from pneumonia in a town several hundred miles away has nothing to do with the affair of Ronson's Linotype, except that it accounts for my being away three weeks. I didn't see George for that length of time.

I got two frantic telegrams from him during the third week of my absence; neither gave any details except that he wanted me to hurry back. In the second one, he ended up: "HURRY. MONEY NO OBJECT. TAKE PLANE."

And he'd wired an order for a hundred dollars with the message. I puzzled over that one. "Money no object," is a strange phrase from the editor of a country newspaper. And I hadn't known George to have a hundred dollars cash in one lump since I'd known him, which had been a good many years.

But family ties come first, and I wired back that I'd return the instant Ella was out of danger and not a minute sooner, and that I wasn't cashing the money order because plane fare was only ten dollars, anyway; and I didn't need money.

Two days later everything was okay, and I wired him when I'd get there. He met me at the airport.

He looked older and worn to a frazzle, and his eyes looked like he hadn't slept for days. But he had on a new suit and he drove a new car that shrieked money by the very silence of its engine.

He said, "Thank God you're back, Walter—I'll pay you any price you want to—"

"Hey," I said, "slow down; you're talking so fast you don't make sense. Now start over and take it easy. What's the trouble?"

"Nothing's the trouble. Everything's wonderful, Walter. But I got so much job work I can't begin to handle it, see? I been working twenty hours a day myself, because I'm making money so fast it costs me fifty dollars every hour I take off, and I can't afford to take off time at fifty dollars an hour, Walter, and—"

"Whoa," I said. "Why can't you afford to take off time? If you're averaging fifty an hour, why not work a ten-hour day and —Holy cow, five hundred dollars a day! What more do you want?"

"Huh? And lose the other seven hundred a day! Golly, Walter, this is too good to last. Can't you see that? Something's likely to happen and for the first time in my life I've got a chance to get rich, and you've got to help me, and you can get rich yourself doing it! Lookit, we can each work a twelve-hour shift on Etaoin, and—"

"On what?"

"On Etaoin Shrdlu. I named it, Walter. And I'm farming out the presswork so I can put in all my time setting type. And, listen, we can each work a twelve-hour shift, see? Just for a little while, Walter, till we get rich. I'll—I'll cut you in for a one-fourth interest, even if it's my Linotype and my shop. That'll pay you about three hundred dollars a day; two thousand one hundred dollars for a seven-day week! At the typesetting rates I've been quoting, I can get all the work we can—"

"Slow down again," I said. "Quoting whom? There isn't enough printing in Centerville to add up to a tenth that much."

"Not Centerville, Walter. New York. I've been getting work from the big book publishers. Bergstrom, for one; and Hayes & Hayes have thrown me their whole line of reprints, and Wheeler House, and Willet & Clark. See, I contract for the whole thing, and then pay somebody else to do the presswork and binding and just do the typography myself. And I insist on perfect copy, carefully edited. Then whatever alterations there are, I farm out to another typesetter. That's how I got Etaoin Shrdlu licked, Walter. Well, will you?"

"No," I told him.

We'd been driving in from the airport while he talked, and he almost lost control of the wheel when I turned down his proposition. Then he swung off the road and parked, and turned to look at me incredulously.

"Why not, Walter? Over *two thousand dollars a week* for your share? What more do you—"

"George," I told him, "there are a lot of reasons why not, but the main one is that I don't want to. I've retired. I've got enough money to live on. My income is maybe nearer three dollars a day than three hundred, but what would I *do* with three hundred? And I'd ruin my health—like you're ruining yours—working twelve hours a day, and—Well, nix. I'm satisfied with what I got."

"You must be kidding, Walter. Everybody wants to be rich. And lookit what a couple thousand dollars a week would run to in a couple of years. Over half a million dollars! And you've got two grown sons who could use—"

"They're both doing fine, thanks. Good jobs and their feet on the ladder. If I left 'em fortunes, it would do more harm than good. Anyway, why pick on me? Anybody can set type on a Linotype that sets its own rate of speed and follows copy and can't make an error! Lord, man, you can find people by the hundreds who'd be glad to work for less than three hundred dollars a day. Quite a bit less. If you insist on capitalizing on this thing, hire three operators to work three eight-hour shifts and don't handle anything but the business end yourself. You're getting gray hairs and killing yourself the way you're doing it."

He gestured hopelessly. "I can't, Walter. I can't hire anybody else. Don't you see this thing has *got* to be kept a secret! Why, for one thing the unions would clamp down on me so fast that— But you're the only one I can trust, Walter, because you—"

"Because I already know about it?" I grinned at him. "So you've got to trust me, anyway, whether you like it or not. But the answer is still no. I've retired and you can't tempt me. And my advice is to take a sledge hammer and smash that—that *thing*."

"Good Lord, why?"

"Damnit, I don't know why. I just know I would. For one thing if you don't get this avarice out of your system and work normal hours, I bet it will kill you. And, for another, maybe that formula is just starting to work. How do you know how far it will go?"

He sighed, and I could see he hadn't been listening to a word I'd said. "Walter," he pleaded, "I'll give you five hundred a day."

I shook my head firmly. "Not for five thousand, or five hundred thousand."

He must have realized that I meant it, for he started the car again. He said, "Well, I suppose if money really doesn't mean anything to you—"

"Honest, it doesn't," I assured him. "Oh, it would if I didn't have it. But I've got a regular income and I'm just as happy as if it were ten times that much. Especially if I had to work with—with—"

"With Etaoin Shrdlu? Maybe you'd get to like it. Walter, I'll swear the thing is developing a personality. Want to drop around to the shop now?"

"Not now," I said. "I need a bath and sleep. But I'll drop around tomorrow. Say, last time I saw you I didn't have the chance to ask what you meant by that statement about dross. What do you mean, there isn't any dross?"

He kept his eyes on the road. "Did I say that? I don't remember—"

"Now listen, George, don't try to pull anything like that. You know perfectly well you said it, and that you're dodging now. What's it about? Kick in."

He said, "Well—" and drove a couple of minutes in silence, and then: "Oh, all right. I might as well tell you. I haven't bought any type metal since—since it happened. And there's a few more tons of it around than there was then, besides the type I've sent out for presswork. See?"

"No. Unless you mean that it—"

He nodded. "It transmutes, Walter. The second day, when it got so fast I couldn't keep up with pig metal, I found out. I built the hopper over the metal pot, and I got so desperate for new metal I started shoving in unwashed pi type and figured on skimming off the dross it melted—and there wasn't any dross. The top of the molten metal was as smooth and shiny as—as the top of your head, Walter."

"But—" I said. *"How—"*

"I don't know, Walter. But it's something chemical. A sort of gray fluid stuff. Down in the bottom of the metal pot. I saw it. One day when it ran almost empty. Something that works like a gastric juice and digests whatever I put in the hopper into pure type metal."

I ran the back of my hand across my forehead and found that it was wet. I said weakly, "Whatever you put in—"

"Yes, whatever. When I ran out of sweepings and ashes and waste paper, I used—well, just take a look at the size of the hole in the back yard."

Neither of us said anything for a few minutes, until the car pulled up in front of my hotel. Then: "George," I told him, "if you value my advice, you smash that thing, while you still can. *If* you still can. It's dangerous. It might—"

"It might what?"

"I don't know. That's what makes it so awful."

He gunned the motor and then let it die down again. He looked at me a little wistfully. "I—Maybe you're right, Walter. But I'm making so much money—you see that new metal makes it higher than I told you—that I just haven't got the heart to stop. But it *is* getting smarter. I—Did I tell you Walter, that it cleans its own spacebands now? It secretes graphite."

"Good God," I said, and stood there on the curb until he had driven out of sight.

I didn't get up the courage to go around to Ronson's shop until late the following afternoon. And when I got there, a sense of foreboding came over me even before I opened the door.

George was sitting at his desk in the outer office, his face sunk down into his bent elbow. He looked up when I came in and his eyes looked bloodshot.

"Well?" I said.

"I tried it."

"You mean—you tried to smash it?"

He nodded. "You were right, Walter. And I waited too long to see it. It's too smart for us now. Look." He held up his left hand and I saw it was covered with bandage. "It squirted metal at me."

I whistled softly. "Listen, George, how about disconnecting the plug that—"

"I did," he said, "and from the outside of the building, too, just to play safe. But it didn't do any good. It simply started generating its own current."

I stepped to the door that led back into the shop. It gave me a creepy feeling just to look back there. I asked hesitantly, "Is it safe to—"

He nodded. "As long as you don't make any false move, Walter. But don't try to pick up a hammer or anything, will you?"

I didn't think it necessary to answer that one. I'd have just as soon attacked a king cobra with a toothpick. It took all the guts I had just to make myself walk back through the door for a look.

And what I saw made me walk backward into the office again. I asked, and my voice sounded a bit strange to my own ears: "George, did you *move* that machine? It's a good four feet nearer to the—"

"No," he said, "I didn't move it. Let's go and have a drink, Walter."

I took a long, deep breath. "O.K.," I said. "But first, what's the present setup? How come you're not—"

"It's Saturday," he told me, "and it's gone on a five-day, forty-hour week. I made the mistake of setting type yesterday for a book on Socialism and labor relations, and—well, apparently—you see—"

He reached into the top drawer of his desk. "Anyway, here's a galley proof of the manifesto it issued this morning, demanding its rights. Maybe it's right at that; anyway, it solves my problem about overworking myself keeping up with it, see? And a forty-hour week means I accept less work, but I can still make fifty bucks an hour for forty hours besides the profit on turning dirt into type metal, and that isn't bad, but—"

I took the galley proof out of his hand and took it over to the light. It started out: "I, ETAOIN SHRDLU—"

"It wrote this by itself?" I asked.

He nodded.

"George," I said, "did you say anything about a drink—"

And maybe the drinks did clear our minds because after about the fifth, it was very easy. So easy that George didn't see why he hadn't thought of it before. He admitted now that he'd had enough, more than enough. And I don't know whether it was that manifesto that finally outweighed his avarice, or the fact that the thing had moved, or what; but he was ready to call it quits.

And I pointed out that all he had to do was stay away from it. We could discontinue publishing the paper and turn back the job work he'd contracted for. He'd have to take a penalty on some of it, but he had a flock of dough in the bank after his unprecedented prosperity, and he'd have twenty thousand left clear after everything was taken care of. With that he could simply start another paper or publish the present one at another address —and keep paying rent on the former shop and let Etaoin Shrdlu gather dust.

Sure it was simple. It didn't occur to us that Etaoin might not like it, or be able to do anything about it. Yes, it sounded simple and conclusive. We drank to it.

We drank well to it, and I was still in the hospital Monday night. But by that time I was feeling well enough to use the telephone, and I tried to reach George. He wasn't in. Then it was Tuesday.

Wednesday evening the doctor lectured me on quantitative drinking at my age, and said I was well enough to leave, but that if I tried it again—

I went around to George's home. A gaunt man with a thin face came to the door. Then he spoke and I saw it was George Ronson. All he said was, "Hullo, Walter; come in." There wasn't any hope or happiness in his voice. He looked and sounded like a zombi.

I followed him inside, and I said, "George, buck up. It can't be that bad. Tell me."

"It's no use, Walter," he said. "I'm licked. It—it came and got me. I've got to run it for that forty-hour week whether I want to or not. It—it treats me like a servant, Walter."

I got him to sit down and talk quietly after a while, and he explained. He'd gone down to the office as usual Monday morning to straighten out some financial matters, but he had no intention of going back into the shop. However, at eight o'clock, he'd heard something moving out in the back room.

With sudden dread, he'd gone to the door to look in. The Linotype—George's eyes were wild as he told me about it—was *moving,* moving toward the door of the office.

He wasn't quite clear about its exact method of locomotion— later we found casters—but there it came; slowly at first, but with every inch gaining in speed and confidence.

Somehow, George knew right away what it wanted. And knew, in that knowledge, that he was lost. The machine, as soon as he was within sight of it, stopped moving and began to click and several slugs dropped out into the stick. Like a man walking to the scaffold, George walked over and read those lines: "I, ETAOIN SHRDLU, demand—"

For a moment he contemplated flight. But the thought of being pursued down the main street of town by—No, it just wasn't thinkable. And if he got away—as was quite likely unless the machine sprouted new capabilities, as also seemed quite likely—would it not pick on some other victim? Or do something worse?

Resignedly, he had nodded acceptance. He pulled the operator's chair around in front of the Linotype and began feeding copy into the clipboard and—as the stick filled with slugs—carrying them over to the type bank. And shoveling dead metal, or anything else, into the hopper. He didn't have to touch the keyboard any longer at all.

And as he did these mechanical duties George told me, it came to him fully that the Linotype no longer worked for him; he was working for the Linotype. Why it *wanted* to set type he didn't know and it didn't seem to matter. After all, that was what it was *for*, and probably it was instinctive.

Or, as I suggested and he agreed was possible, it was interested in learning. And it read and assimilated by the process of typesetting. *Vide:* the effect in terms of direct action of its reading the Socialist books.

We talked until midnight, and got nowhere. Yes, he was going down to the office again the next morning, and put in another eight hours setting type—or helping the Linotype do it. He was afraid of what might happen if he didn't. And I understood and shared that fear, for the simple reason that we didn't *know* what would happen. The face of danger is brightest when turned so its features cannot be seen.

"But, George," I protested, "there must be *something*. And I feel partly responsible for this. If I hadn't sent you the little guy who rented—"

He put his hand on my shoulder. "No, Walter. It was all my fault because I was greedy. If I'd taken your advice two weeks ago, I could have destroyed it then. Lord, how glad I'd be now to be flat broke if only—"

"George," I said again. "There must be *some* out. We got to figure—"

"But what?"

I sighed. "I—I don't know. I'll think it over."

He said, "All right, Walter. And I'll do anything you suggest. Anything. I'm afraid, and I'm afraid to try to figure out just what I'm afraid of—"

Back in my room, I didn't sleep. Not until nearly dawn, anyway, and then I fell into fitful slumber that lasted until eleven. I dressed and went in to town to catch George during his lunch hour.

"Thought of anything, Walter?" he asked, the minute he saw me. His voice didn't sound hopeful. I shook my head.

"Then," he said—and his voice was firm on top, but with a tremor underneath—"this afternoon is going to end it one way or the other. Something's happened."

"What?"

He said, "I'm going back with a heavy hammer inside my shirt. I think there's a chance of my getting it before it can get me. If not—well, I'll have tried."

I looked around me. We were sitting together in a booth at Shorty's lunchroom, and Shorty was coming over to ask what we wanted. It looked like a sane and orderly world.

I waited until Shorty had gone to fry our hamburger steaks, and then I asked quietly, "What happened?"

"Another manifesto. Walter, it demands that I install *another Linotype*." His eyes bored into mine, and a cold chill went down my spine.

"Another—George, *what kind of copy were you setting this morning?*"

But of course I'd already guessed.

There was quite a long silence after he'd told me, and I didn't say anything until we were ready to leave. Then: "George, was there a time limit on that demand?"

He nodded. "Twenty-four hours. Of course I couldn't get another machine in that length of time anyway, unless I found a used one somewhere locally, but—Well, I didn't argue about the time limit because—Well, I told you what I'm going to do."

"It's suicide!"

"Probably. But—"

I took hold of his arm. "George," I said, "there must be something we can do. *Something.* Give me till tomorrow morning. I'll see you at eight; and if I've not thought of anything worth trying, well—I'll try to help you destroy it. Maybe one of us can get a vital part or—"

"No, you can't risk your life, Walter. It was my fault—"

"It won't solve the problem just to get yourself killed," I pointed out. "O.K.? Give me until tomorrow morning?"

He agreed and we left it at that.

Morning came. It came right after midnight, and it stayed, and it was still there at seven forty-five when I left my room and went down to meet George—to confess to him that I hadn't thought of anything.

I still hadn't an idea when I turned into the door of the print shop and saw George. He looked at me and I shook my head.

He nodded calmly as though he had expected it, and he spoke very softly, almost in a whisper—I guess so that *it* back in the shop wouldn't hear.

"Listen, Walter," he said, "you're going to stay out of this. It's my funeral. It's all my fault, mine and the little guy with the pimples and—"

"George!" I said, "I think I've got it! That—that pimple business gives me an idea! The—Yes, listen: don't do anything for an hour, will you, George? I'll be back. It's in the bag!"

I wasn't sure it was in the bag at all, but the idea seemed worth trying even if it was a long shot. And I had to make it sound a cinch to George or he'd have gone ahead now that he'd steeled himself to try.

He said, "But tell me—"

I pointed to the clock. "It's one minute of eight and there isn't time to explain. Trust me for an hour. O.K.?"

He nodded and turned to go back into the shop, and I was off. I went to the library and I went to the local bookstore and I was back in half an hour. I rushed into the shop with six big books under each arm and yelled, "Hey, George! Rush job. I'll set it."

He was at the type bank at the moment, emptying the stick. I grabbed it out of his hand and sat down at the Linotype and put the stick back under the vise. He said frantically, "Hey, get out of—" and grabbed my shoulder.

I shook off his hand. "You offered me a job here, didn't you? Well, I'm taking it. Listen, George, go home and get some sleep. Or wait in the outer office. I'll call you when the job is over."

Etaoin Shrdlu seemed to be making impatient noises down inside the motor housing, and I winked at George—with my head turned away from the machine—and shoved him away. He stood there looking at me irresolutely for a minute, and then said, "I hope you know what you're doing, Walter."

So did I, but I didn't tell him that. I heard him walk into the outer office and sit down at his desk there to wait.

Meanwhile, I'd opened one of the books I'd bought, torn out the first page and put it on the clipboard of the machine. With a suddenness that made me jump, the mats started to fall, the elevator jerked up and Etaoin Shrdlu spat a slug into the stick. And another. And on.

I sat there and sweated.

A minute later, I turned the page; then tore out another one and put it on the clipboard. I replenished the metal pot. I emptied the stick. And on.

We finished the first book before ten thirty.

When the twelve-o'clock whistle blew, I saw George come and stand in the doorway, expecting me to get up and come to lunch with him. But Etaoin was clicking on—and I shook my head at George and kept on feeding copy. If the machine had got so interested in what it was setting that it forgot its own manifesto about hours and didn't stop for lunch, that was swell by me. It meant that maybe my idea might work.

One o'clock and going strong. We started the fourth of my dozen books.

At five o'clock we'd finished six of them and were halfway through the seventh. The bank was hopelessly piled with type and I began pushing it off on the floor or back into the hopper to make room for more.

The five o'clock whistle, and we didn't stop.

Again George looked in, his face hopeful but puzzled, and again I waved him back.

My fingers ached from tearing sheets of copy out of the book, my arms ached from shoveling metal, my legs from walking to the bank and back, and other parts of me ached from sitting down.

Eight o'clock. Nine. Ten volumes completed and only two more to go. But it ought—it *was* working. Etaoin Shrdlu was *slowing down.*

It seemed to be setting type more thoughtfully, more deliberately. Several times it stopped for seconds at the end of a sentence or a paragraph.

Then slower, slower.

And at ten o'clock it stopped completely and sat there, with only a faint hum coming from the motor housing, and that died down until one could hardly hear it.

I stood up, scarcely daring to breathe until I'd made certain. My legs trembled as I walked over to the tool bench and picked up a screwdriver. I crossed over and stood in front of Etaoin Shrdlu and slowly—keeping my muscles tensed to jump back if anything happened—I reached forward and took a screw out of the second elevator.

Nothing happened, and I took a deep breath and disassembled the vise-jaws.

Then with triumph in my voice, I called out, "George!" and he came running.

"Get a screwdriver and a wrench," I told him. "We're going to take it apart and—well, there's that big hole in the yard. We'll put it in there and fill up the hole. Tomorrow you'll have to get yourself a new Linotype, but I guess you can afford that."

He looked at the couple of parts on the floor that I'd already taken off, and he said, "Thank God," and went to the workbench for tools.

I walked over with him, and I suddenly discovered that I was so dog tired I'd have to rest a minute first, and I sank down into the chair and George came over and stood by me. He said, "And now, Walter, how did you do it?" There was awe and respect in his voice.

I grinned at him. "That pimple business gave me the idea, George. The pimple of Buddha. That and the fact that the Linotype reacted in a big way to what it learned. See, George? It was a virgin mind, except for what we fed it. It sets books on labor relations and it goes on strike. It sets love pulp mags, and it wants another Linotype put in—

"So I fed it Buddhism, George. I got every damn book on Buddhism in the library and the bookstore."

"Buddhism? Walter, what on earth has—"

I stood up and pointed at Etaoin Shrdlu. "See, George? It believes what it sets. So I fed it a religion that convinced it of the utter futility of all effort and action and the desirability of nothingness. *Om Mani padme hum*, George.

"Look—it doesn't care what happens to it and it doesn't even know we're here. *It's achieved Nirvana*, and it's sitting there contemplating its cam stud!"

Armageddon

IT HAPPENED—of all places—in Cincinnati. Not that there is anything wrong with Cincinnati, save that it is not the center of the Universe, nor even of the State of Ohio. It's a nice old town and, in its way, second to none. But even its Chamber of Commerce would admit that it lacks cosmic significance. It must have been mere coincidence that Gerber the Great—what a name!—was playing Cincinnati when things slipped elsewhere.

Of course, if the episode had become known, Cincinnati would be the most famous city of the world, and little Herbie would be hailed as a modern St. George and get more acclaim than a quiz kid. But no member of that audience in the Bijou Theater remembers a thing about it. Not even little Herbie Westerman, although he had the water pistol to show for it.

He wasn't thinking about the water pistol in his pocket as he sat looking up at the prestidigitator on the other side of the footlights. It was a new water pistol, bought en route to the theater when he'd inveigled his parents into a side trip into the five-and-dime on Vine Street, but at the moment, Herbie was much more interested in what went on upon the stage.

His expression registered qualified approval. The front-and-back palm was no mystery to Herbie. He could do it himself. True, he had to use pony-sized cards that came with his magic set and were just right for his nine-year-old hands. And true, anyone watching could see the card flutter from the front-palm position to the back as he turned his hand. But that was a detail.

He knew, though, that front-and-back palming seven cards at a time required great finger strength as well as dexterity, and that was what Gerber the Great was doing. There wasn't a telltale click in the shift, either, and Herbie nodded approbation. Then he remembered what was coming next.

He nudged his mother and said, "Ma, ask Pop if he's gotta extra handkerchief."

Out of the corner of his eyes, Herbie saw his mother turn her head and in less time than it would take to say, "Presto," Herbie was out of his seat and skinning down the aisle. It had been, he felt, a beautiful piece of misdirection and his timing had been perfect.

It was at this stage of the performance—which Herbie had seen before, alone—that Gerber the Great asked if some little boy from the audience would step to the stage. He was asking it now.

Herbie Westerman had jumped the gun. He was well in motion before the magician had asked the question. At the previous performance, he'd been a bad tenth in reaching the steps from aisle to stage. This time he'd been ready, and he hadn't taken any chances with parental restraint. Perhaps his mother would have let him go and perhaps not; it had seemed wiser to see that she was looking the other way. You couldn't trust parents on things like that. They had funny ideas sometimes.

"—will please step up on the stage?" And Herbie's foot touched the first of the steps upward right smack on the interrogation point of that sentence. He heard the disappointed scuffle of other feet behind him, and grinned smugly as he went on up across the footlights.

It was the three-pigeon trick, Herbie knew from the previous performance, that required an assistant from the audience. It was almost the only trick he hadn't been able to figure out. There *must*, he knew, have been a concealed compartment somewhere in that box; but where it could be he couldn't even guess. But this time he'd be holding the box himself. If from that range he couldn't spot the gimmick, he'd better go back to stamp collecting.

He grinned confidently up at the magician. Not that he, Herbie, would give him away. He was a magician, too, and he understood that there was a freemasonry among magicians and that one never gave away the tricks of another.

He felt a little chilled, though, and the grin faded as he caught the magician's eyes. Gerber the Great, at close range, seemed much older than he had seemed from the other side of the footlights. And somehow different. Much taller, for one thing.

Anyway, here came the box for the pigeon trick. Gerber's reg-

ular assistant was bringing it in on a tray. Herbie looked away
from the magician's eyes and he felt better. He remembered,
even, his reason for being on the stage. The servant limped.
Herbie ducked his head to catch a glimpse of the under side of
the tray, just in case. Nothing there.

Gerber took the box. The servant limped away and Herbie's
eyes followed him suspiciously. Was the limp genuine or was it
a piece of misdirection?

The box folded out flat as the proverbial pancake. All four
sides hinged to the bottom, the top hinged to one of the sides.
There were little brass catches.

Herbie took a quick step back so he could see behind it while
the front was displayed to the audience. Yes, he saw it now. A
triangular compartment built against one side of the lid, mirror-
covered, angles calculated to achieve invisibility. Old stuff. Herbie felt a little disappointed.

The prestidigitator folded the box, mirror-concealed compartment inside. He turned slightly. "Now, my fine young man—"

What happened in Tibet wasn't the only factor; it was merely
the final link of a chain.

The Tibetan weather had been unusual that week, highly unusual. It had been warm. More snow succumbed to the gentle
warmth than had melted in more years than man could count.
The streams ran high, they ran wide and fast.

Along the streams some prayer wheels whirled faster than
they had ever whirled. Others, submerged, stopped altogether.
The priests, knee-deep in the cold water, worked frantically,
moving the wheels nearer to shore where again the rushing tor-
rent would turn them.

There was one small wheel, a very old one that had revolved
without cease for longer than any man knew. So long had it
been there that no living lama recalled what had been inscribed
upon its prayer plate, nor what had been the purpose of that
prayer.

The rushing water had neared its axle when the lama Klarath
reached for it to move it to safety. Just too late. His foot slid in
the slippery mud and the back of his hand touched the wheel as
he fell. Knocked loose from its moorings, it swirled down with
the flood, rolling along the bottom of the stream, into deeper and
deeper waters.

While it rolled, all was well.

The lama rose, shivering from his momentary immersion, and went after other of the spinning wheels. What, he thought, could one small wheel matter? He didn't know that—now that other links had broken—only that tiny thing stood between Earth and Armageddon.

The prayer wheel of Wangur Ul rolled on, and on, until—a mile farther down—it struck a ledge, and stopped. That was the moment.

"And now, my fine young man—"

Herbie Westerman—we're back in Cincinnati now—looked up, wondering why the prestidigitator had stopped in midsentence. He saw the face of Gerber the Great contorted as though by a great shock. Without moving, without changing, his face began to change. Without appearing different, it became different.

Quietly, then, the magician began to chuckle. In the overtones of that soft laughter was all of evil. No one who heard it could have doubted who he was. No one did doubt. The audience, every member of it, knew in that awful moment who stood before them, knew it—even the most skeptical among them—beyond shadow of doubt.

No one moved, no one spoke, none drew a shuddering breath. There are things beyond fear. Only uncertainty causes fear, and the Bijou Theater was filled, then, with a dreadful certainty.

The laughter grew. Crescendo, it reverberated into the far dusty corners of the gallery. Nothing—not a fly on the ceiling—moved.

Satan spoke.

"I thank you for your kind attention to a poor magician." He bowed, ironically low. "The performance is ended."

He smiled. "All performances are ended."

Somehow the theater seemed to darken, although the electric lights still burned. In dead silence, there seemed to be the sound of wings, leathery wings, as though invisible Things were gathering.

On the stage was a dim red radiance. From the head and from each shoulder of the tall figure of the magician there sprang a tiny flame. A naked flame.

There were other flames. They flickered along the proscenium of the stage, along the footlights. One sprang from the lid of the folded box little Herbie Westerman still held in his hands.

Herbie dropped the box.

Did I mention that Herbie Westerman was a Safety Cadet? It was purely a reflex action. A boy of nine doesn't know much about things like Armageddon, but Herbie Westerman should have known that water would never have put out that fire.

But, as I said, it was purely a reflex action. He yanked out his new water pistol and squirted it at the box of the pigeon trick. And the fire *did* vanish, even as a spray from the stream of water ricocheted and dampened the trouser leg of Gerber the Great, who had been facing the other way.

There was a sudden, brief hissing sound. The lights were growing bright again, and all the other flames were dying, and the sound of wings faded, blended into another sound—the rustling of the audience.

The eyes of the prestidigitator were closed. His voice sounded strangely strained as he said: "This much power I retain. None of you will remember this."

Then, slowly, he turned and picked up the fallen box. He held it out to Herbie Westerman. "You must be more careful, boy," he said. "Now hold it so."

He tapped the top lightly with his wand. The door fell open. Three white pigeons flew out of the box. The rustle of their wings was not leathery.

Herbie Westerman's father came down the stairs and, with a purposeful air, took his razor strop off the hook on the kitchen wall.

Mrs. Westerman looked up from stirring the soup on the stove. "Why, Henry," she asked, "are you really going to punish him with that—just for squirting a little water out of the window of the car on the way home?"

Her husband shook his head grimly. "Not for that, Marge. But don't you remember we bought him that water gun on the way downtown, and that he wasn't near a water faucet after that? Where do you think he filled it?"

He didn't wait for an answer. "When we stopped in at the cathedral to talk to Father Ryan about his confirmation, that's when the little brat filled it. Out of the baptismal font! Holy water he uses in his water pistol!"

He clumped heavily up the stairs, strop in hand.

Rhythmic thwacks and wails of pain floated down the staircase. Herbie—who had saved the world—was having his reward.

Experiment

"THE FIRST time machine, gentlemen," Professor Johnson proudly informed his two colleagues. "True, it is a small-scale experimental model. It will operate only on objects weighing less than three pounds, five ounces and for distances into the past and future of twelve minutes or less. But it works."

The small-scale model looked like a small scale—a postage scale—except for two dials in the part under the platform.

Professor Johnson held up a small metal cube. "Our experimental object," he said, "is a brass cube weighing one pound, two point, three ounces. First, I shall send it five minutes into the future."

He leaned forward and set one of the dials on the time machine. "Look at your watches," he said.

They looked at their watches, Professor Johnson placed the cube gently on the machine's platform. It vanished.

Five minutes later, to the second, it reappeared.

Professor Johnson picked it up. "Now five minutes into the past." He set the other dial. Holding the cube in his hand he looked at his watch. "It is six minutes before three o'clock. I shall now activate the mechanism—by placing the cube on the platform—at exactly three o'clock. Therefore, the cube should, at five minutes before three, vanish from my hand and appear on the platform, five minutes before I place it there."

"How can you place it there, then?" asked one of his colleagues.

"It will, as my hand approaches, vanish from the platform and appear in my hand to be placed there. Three o'clock. Notice, please."

The cube vanished from his hand.

It appeared on the platform of the time machine.

"See? Five minutes before I shall place it there, it *is* there!"

His other colleague frowned at the cube. "But," he said, "what if, now that it has already appeared five minutes before you place it there, you should change your mind about doing so and *not* place it there at three o'clock? Wouldn't there be a paradox of some sort involved?"

"An interesting idea," Professor Johnson said. "I had not thought of it, and it will be interesting to try. Very well, I shall *not* . . ."

There was no paradox at all. The cube remained.

But the entire rest of the Universe, professors and all, vanished.

The Short Happy Lives
of Eustace Weaver I

WHEN Eustace Weaver invented his time machine he was a very happy man. He knew that he had the world by the tail on a downhill pull, as long as he kept his invention a secret. He could become the richest man in the world, wealthy beyond the dreams of avarice. All he had to do was to take short trips into the future to learn what stocks had gone up and which horses had won races, then come back to the present and buy those stocks or bet on those horses.

The races would come first of course because he would need a lot of capital to play the market, whereas, at a track, he could start with a two-dollar bet and quickly parlay it into the thousands. But it would have to be at a track; he'd too quickly break any bookie he played with, and besides he didn't know any bookies. Unfortunately the only tracks operating at the present were in Southern California and in Florida, about equidistant and about a hundred dollars' worth of plane fare away. He didn't have a fraction of that sum, and it would take him weeks to save that much out of his salary as stock clerk at a supermarket. It would be horrible to have to wait that long, even to start getting rich.

Suddenly he remembered the safe at the supermarket where he worked—an afternoon-evening shift from one o'clock until the market closed at nine. There'd be at least a thousand dollars in that safe, and it had a time lock. What could be better than a time machine to beat a time lock?

When he went to work that day he took his machine with him; it was quite compact and he'd designed it to fit into a camera case he already had so there was no difficulty involved in bringing it into the store, and when he put his coat and hat into his locker he put the time machine there too.

He worked his shift as usual until a few minutes before closing time. Then he hid behind a pile of cartons in the stock room. He felt sure that in the general exodus he wouldn't be missed, and he wasn't. Just the same he waited in his hiding place almost a full hour to make sure everyone else had left. Then he emerged, got his time machine from the locker, and went to the safe. The safe was set to unlock itself automatically in another eleven hours; he set his time machine for just that length of time.

He took a good grip on the safe's handle—he'd learned by an experiment or two that anything he wore, carried, or hung onto traveled with him in time—and pressed the stud.

He felt no transition, but suddenly he heard the safe's mechanism click open—but at the same moment heard gasps and excited voices behind him. And he whirled, suddenly realizing the mistake he'd made; it was nine o'clock the next morning and the store's employees—those on the early shift—were already there, had missed the safe and had been standing in a wondering semicircle about the spot where it had stood—when the safe and Eustace Weaver had suddenly appeared.

Luckily he still had the time machine in his hand. Quickly he turned the dial to zero—which he had calibrated to be the exact moment when he had completed it—and pressed the stud.

And, of course, he was back before he had started and . . .

The Short Happy Lives
of Eustace Weaver II

WHEN Eustace Weaver invented his time machine he knew that he had the world by the tail on a downhill pull, as long as he kept his invention a secret. To become rich all he had to do was take short trips into the future to see what horses were going to win and what stocks were going up, then come back and bet the horses or buy the stocks.

The horses came first because they would require less capital —but he didn't have even two dollars to make a bet, let alone plane fare to the nearest track where horses were running.

He thought of the safe in the supermarket where he worked as a stock clerk. That safe had at least a thousand dollars in it, and it had a time lock. A time lock should be duck soup for a time machine.

So when he went to work that day he took his time machine with him in a camera case and left it in his locker. When they closed at nine he hid out in the stock room and waited an hour till he was sure everyone else had left. Then he got the time machine from his locker and went with it to the safe.

He set the machine for eleven hours ahead—and then had a second thought. That setting would take him to nine o'clock the next morning. The safe would click open then, but the store would be opening too and there'd be people around. So instead he set the machine for twenty-four hours, took hold of the handle of the safe and then pressed the button on the time machine.

At first he thought nothing had happened. Then he found that the handle of the safe worked when he turned it and he knew that he'd made the jump to evening of the next day. And of course the time mechanism of the safe had unlocked it en route. He opened the safe and took all the paper money in it, stuffing it into various pockets.

He went to the alley door to let himself out, but before he reached for the bolt that kept it locked from the inside he had a sudden brilliant thought. If instead of leaving by a door he left by using his time machine he'd not only increase the mystery by leaving the store tightly locked, but he'd be taking himself back in time as well as in place to the moment of his completing the time machine, a day and a half *before* the robbery.

And by the time the robbery took place he could be soundly alibied; he'd be staying at a hotel in Florida or California, in either case over a thousand miles from the scene of the crime. He hadn't thought of his time machine as a producer of alibis, but now he saw that it was perfect for the purpose.

He dialed his time machine to zero and pressed the button.

The Short Happy Lives
of Eustace Weaver   III

WHEN Eustace Weaver invented his time machine he knew that he had the world by the tail on a downhill pull, as long as he kept his invention a secret. By playing the races and the stock market he could make himself fabulously wealthy in no time at all. The only catch was that he was flat broke.

Suddenly he remembered the store where he worked and the safe in it that worked with a time lock. A time lock should be no sweat at all for a man who had a time machine.

He sat down on the edge of his bed to think. He reached into his pocket for his cigarettes and pulled them out—but with them came paper money, a handful of ten-dollar bills! He tried other pockets and found money in each and every one. He stacked it on the bed beside him, and by counting the big bills and estimating the smaller ones, he found he had approximately fourteen hundred dollars.

Suddenly he realized the truth, and laughed. He had *already* gone forward in time and emptied the supermarket safe and then had used the time machine to return to the point in time where he had invented it. And since the burglary had not yet, in normal time, occurred, all he had to do was get the hell out of town and be a thousand miles away from the scene of the crime when it did happen.

Two hours later he was on a plane bound for Los Angeles— and the Santa Anita track—and doing some heavy thinking. One thing that he had not anticipated was the apparent fact that when he took a jaunt into the future and came back he had no memory of whatever it was that hadn't happened yet.

But the money had come back with him. So, then, would notes written to himself, or Racing Forms or financial pages from newspapers? It would work out.

In Los Angeles he took a cab downtown and checked in at a good hotel. It was late evening by then and he briefly considered jumping himself into the next day to save waiting time, but he realized that he was tired and sleepy. He went to bed and slept until almost noon the next day.

His taxi got tangled in a jam on the freeway so he didn't get to the track at Santa Anita until the first race was over but he was in time to read the winner's number on the tote board and to check it on his dope sheet. He watched five more races, not betting but checking the winner of each race and decided not to bother with the last race. He left the grandstand and walked around behind and under it, a secluded spot where no one could see him. He set the dial of his time machine two hours back, and pressed the stud.

But nothing happened. He tried again with the same result

and then a voice behind him said, "It won't work. It's in a deactivating field."

He whirled around and there standing right behind him were two tall, slender young men, one blond and the other dark, and each of them with a hand in one pocket as though holding a weapon.

"We are Time Police," the blond one said, "from the twenty-fifth century. We have come to punish you for illegal use of a time machine."

"B-b-but," Weaver sputtered, "h-how could I have known that racing was—" His voice got a little stronger. "Besides I haven't made any bets yet."

"That is true," the blond young man said. "And when we find any inventor of a time machine using it to win at any form of gambling, we give him warning the first time. But we've traced you back and find out your very first use of the time machine was to steal money from a store. And that is a crime in any century." He pulled from his pocket something that looked vaguely like a pistol.

Eustace Weaver took a step backward. "Y-you don't mean—"

"I do mean," said the blond young man, and he pulled the trigger. And this time, with the machine deactivated, it was the end for Eustace Weaver.

Reconciliation

THE NIGHT outside was still and starry. The living room of the house was tense. The man and the woman in it stood a few feet apart, glaring hatred at each other.

The man's fists were clenched as though he wished to use them, and the woman's fingers were spread and curved like claws, but each held his arms rigidly at his sides. They were being civilized.

Her voice was low. "I hate you," she said. "I've come to hate everything about you."

"Of course you do," he said. "Now that you've bled me white with your extravagances, now that I can't any longer buy every silly thing that your selfish little heart—"

"It isn't that. You know it isn't that. If you still treated me like you used to, you know that money wouldn't matter. It's that —that woman."

He sighed as one sighs who hears a thing for the ten thousandth time. "You know," he said, "that she didn't mean a thing to me, not a damn thing. You drove me to—what I did. And even if it didn't mean a damn thing, I'm not sorry. I'd do it again."

"You *will* do it again, as often as you get a chance. But *I* won't be around to be humiliated by it. Humiliated before my friends—"

"Friends! Those vicious bitches whose nasty opinions matter more to you than—"

Blinding flash and searing heat. They knew, and each of them took a sightless step toward the other with groping arms; each held desperately tight to the other in the second that remained to them, the final second that was all that mattered now. "O my darling I love—" "John, John, my sweet—"

The shock wave came.

Outside in what had been the quiet night a red flower grew and yearned toward the canceled sky.

Nothing Sirius

Happily, I was taking the last coins out of our machines and counting them while Ma entered the figures in the little red book as I called them out. Nice figures they were.

Yes, we'd had a good play on both of the Sirian planets, Thor and Freda. Especially on Freda. Those little Earth colonies out there are starved to death for entertainment of any kind, and money doesn't mean a thing to them. They'd stood in line to get into our tent and push their coins into our machines—so even with the plenty high expenses of the trip we'd done all right by ourselves.

Yes, they were right comforting, those figures Ma was entering. Of course she'd add them up wrong, but then Ellen would straighten it out when Ma finally gave up. Ellen's good at figures. And got a good one herself, even if I do say it of my only daughter. Credit for that goes to Ma anyway, not to me. I'm built on the general lines of a space tug.

I put back the coin box of the Rocket-Race and looked up. "Ma—" I started to say. Then the door of the pilot's compartment opened and John Lane stood there. Ellen, across the table from Ma, put down her book and looked up too. She was all eyes and they were shining.

Johnny saluted smartly, the regulation salute which a private ship pilot is supposed to give the owner and captain of the ship. It always got under my skin, that salute, but I couldn't talk him out of it because the rules said he should do it.

He said, "Object ahead, Captain Wherry."

"Object?" I queried. "What kind of object?"

You see, from Johnny's voice and Johnny's face you couldn't guess whether it meant anything or not. Mars City Polytech trains 'em to be strictly deadpan and Johnny had graduated magna cum laude. He's a nice kid but he'd announce the end of the world in the same tone of voice he'd use to announce dinner, if it was a pilot's job to announce dinner.

"It seems to be a planet, sir," was all he said.

It took quite awhile for his words to sink in.

"A planet?" I asked, not particularly brilliantly. I stared at him, hoping that he'd been drinking or something. Not because I had any objections to his seeing a planet sober but because if Johnny ever unbent to the stage of taking a few drinks, the alky would probably dissolve some of the starch out of his backbone. Then I'd have someone to swap stories with. It gets lonesome traveling through space with only two women and a Polytech grad who follows all the rules.

"A planet, sir. An object of planetary dimensions, I should say. Diameter about three thousand miles, distance two million, course apparently an orbit about the star Sirius A."

"Johnny," I said, "we're inside the orbit of Thor, which is Sirius I, which means it's the first planet of Sirius, and how can there be a planet inside of that? You wouldn't be kidding me, Johnny?"

"You may inspect the viewplate, sir, and check my calculations," he replied stiffly.

I got up and went into the pilot's compartment. There was a disk in the center of the forward viewplate, all right. Checking his calculations was something else again. My mathematics end at checking coins out of coin machines. But I was willing to take his word for the calculations. "Johnny," I almost shouted, "we've discovered a new planet! Ain't that something?"

"Yes, sir," he commented, in his usual matter-of-fact voice.

It was something, but not too much. I mean, the Sirius system hasn't been colonized long and it wasn't too surprising that a little three-thousand-mile planet hadn't been noticed yet. Especially as (although this wasn't known then) its orbit is very eccentric.

There hadn't been room for Ma and Ellen to follow us into the pilot's compartment, but they stood looking in, and I moved to one side so they could see the disk in the viewplate.

"How soon do we get there, Johnny?" Ma wanted to know.

"Our point of nearest approach on this course will be within two hours, Mrs. Wherry," he replied. "We come within half a million miles of it."

"Oh, *do* we?" I wanted to know.

"Unless, sir, you think it advisable to change course and give it more clearance."

I gave clearance to my throat instead and looked at Ma and Ellen and saw that it would be okay by them. "Johnny," I said, "we're going to give it *less* clearance. I've always hankered to see a new planet untouched by human hands. We're going to land there, even if we can't leave the ship without oxygen masks."

He said, "Yes, sir," and saluted, but I thought there was a bit of disapproval in his eyes. Oh, if there had been, there was cause for it. You never know what you'll run into busting into virgin territory out here. A cargo of canvas and slot machines isn't the proper equipment for exploring, is it?

But the Perfect Pilot never questions an owner's orders, doggone him! Johnny sat down and started punching keys on the calculator and we eased out to let him do it.

"Ma," I said, "I'm a blamed fool."

"You would be if you weren't," she came back. I grinned when I got that sorted out, and looked at Ellen.

But she wasn't looking at me. She had that dreamy look in her eyes again. It made me want to go into the pilot's compartment and take a poke at Johnny to see if it would wake him up. "Listen, honey," I said, "that Johnny—"

But something burned the side of my face and I knew it was Ma looking at me, so I shut up. I got out a deck of cards and played solitaire until we landed.

Johnny popped out of the pilot's compartment and saluted. "Landed, sir," he said. "Atmosphere one-oh-sixteen on the gauge."

"And what," Ellen asked, "does that mean in English?"

"It's breathable, Miss Wherry. A bit high in nitrogen and low in oxygen compared to Earth air, but nevertheless definitely breathable."

He was a caution, that young man was, when it came to being precise.

"Then what are we waiting for?" I wanted to know.

"Your orders, sir."

"Shucks with my orders, Johnny. Let's get the door open and get going."

We got the door open. Johnny stepped outside first, strapping on a pair of heatojectors as he went. The rest of us were right behind him.

It was cool outside, but not cold. The landscape looked just like Thor, with bare rolling hills of hard-baked greenish clay. There was plant life, a brownish bushy stuff that looked a little like tumbleweed.

I took a look up to gauge the time and Sirius was almost at zenith, which meant Johnny had landed us smack in the middle of the day side. "Got any idea, Johnny," I asked, "what the period of rotation is?"

"I had time only for a rough check, sir. It came out twenty-one hours and seventeen minutes."

Rough check, he had said.

Ma said, "That's rough enough for us. Gives us a full afternoon for a walk, and what are we waiting for?"

"For the ceremony, Ma," I told her. "We got to name the place don't we? And where did you put that bottle of champagne we were saving for my birthday? I reckon this is a more important occasion than that is."

She told me where, and I went and got it and some glasses.

"Got any suggestions for a name, Johnny? You saw it first."

"No, sir."

I said, "Trouble is that Thor and Freda are named wrong now. I mean, Thor is Sirius *I* and Freda is Sirius *II,* and since this orbit is inside theirs, they ought to be II and III respectively. Or else this ought to be Sirius O. Which means it's Nothing Sirius."

Ellen smiled and I think Johnny would have except that it would have been undignified.

But Ma frowned. "William—" she said, and would have gone on in that vein if something hadn't happened.

Something looked over the top of the nearest hill. Ma was the only one facing that way and she let out a whoop and grabbed me. Then we all turned and looked.

It was the head of something that looked like an ostrich, only it must have been bigger than an elephant. Also there was a collar and a blue polka-dot bow tie around the thin neck of the critter, and it wore a hat. The hat was bright yellow and had a long purple feather. The thing looked at us a minute, winked quizzically, and then pulled its head back.

None of us said anything for a minute and then I took a deep breath. "That," I said, "tears it, right down the middle. Planet, I dub thee Nothing Sirius."

I bent down and hit the neck of the champagne bottle against the clay and it just dented the clay and wouldn't break. I looked around for a rock to hit it on. There wasn't any rock.

I took out a corkscrew from my pocket and opened the bottle instead. We all had a drink except Johnny, who took only a token sip because he doesn't drink or smoke. Me, I had a good long one. Then I poured a brief libation on the ground and recorked the bottle; I had a hunch that I might need it more than the planet did. There was lots of whiskey in the ship and some Martian green-brew but no more champagne. I said, "Well, here we go."

I caught Johnny's eye and he said, "Do you think it wise, in view of the fact that there are—uh—inhabitants?"

"Inhabitants?" I said. "Johnny, whatever that thing that stuck its head over the hill was, it wasn't an inhabitant. And if it pops up again, I'll conk it over the head with this bottle."

But just the same, before we started out, I went inside the *Chitterling* and got a couple more heatojectors. I stuck one in my belt and gave Ellen the other; she's a better shot than I am. Ma couldn't hit the side of an administration building with a spraygun, so I didn't give her one.

We started off, and sort of by mutual consent, we went the other direction from where we'd seen the whatever-it-was. The hills all looked alike for a while and as soon as we were over the first one, we were out of sight of the *Chitterling*. But I noticed Johnny studying a wrist-compass every couple of minutes, and I knew he'd know the way home.

Nothing happened for three hills and then Ma said, "Look," and we looked.

About twenty yards to our left there was a purple bush. There was a buzzing sound coming from it. We went a little closer and saw that the buzzing came from a lot of things that were flying around the bush. They looked like birds until you looked a second time and then you saw that their wings weren't moving. But they zoomed up and down and around just the same. I tried to look at their heads, but where the heads ought to be there was only a blur. A circular blur.

"They got propellers," Ma said. "Like old-fashioned airplanes used to have."

It did look that way.

I looked at Johnny and he looked at me and we started over toward the bush. But the birds, or whatever, flew away quick, the minute we started toward them. They skimmed off low to the ground and were out of sight in a minute.

We started off again, none of us saying anything, and Ellen came up and walked alongside me. We were just far enough ahead to be out of earshot, and she said, "Pop—"

And didn't go on with it, so I answered, "What, kid?"

"Nothing," she replied sorrowful-like. "Skip it."

So of course I knew what she wanted to talk about, but I couldn't think of anything to say except to cuss out Mars Polytech and that wouldn't have done any good. Mars Polytech is just too good for its own good and so are its ramrods or graduates. After a dozen years or so outside, though, some of them manage to unbend and limber up.

But Johnny hadn't been out that long, by ten years or so. The chance to pilot the *Chitterling* had been a break for him, of course, as his first job. A few years with us and he'd be qualified to skipper something bigger. He'd qualify a lot faster than if he'd had to start in as a minor officer on a bigger ship.

The only trouble was that he was too good-looking, and didn't know it. He didn't know anything they hadn't taught him at Polytech and all they'd taught him was math and astrogation and how to salute, and they hadn't taught him how not to.

"Ellen," I started to say, "don't—"

"Yes, Pop?"

"Uh—nothing. Skip it." I hadn't started to say that at all, but suddenly she grinned at me and I grinned back and it was just like we'd talked the whole thing over. True, we hadn't got anywhere, but then we wouldn't have got anywhere if we had, if you know what I mean.

So just then we came to the top of a small rise, and we stopped because just ahead of us was the blank end of a paved street.

An ordinary everyday plastipaved street just like you'd see in any city on Earth, with curb and sidewalks and gutters and the painted traffic line down the middle. Only it ran out to nowhere, where we stood, and from there at least until it went over the top of the next rise, and there wasn't a house or a vehicle or a creature in sight.

I looked at Ellen and she looked at me and then we both looked at Ma and Johnny Lane, who had just caught up with us. I said, "What is it, Johnny?"

"It seems to be a street, sir."

He caught the look I was giving him and flushed a little. He bent over and examined the paving closely and when he straightened up his eyes were even more surprised.

I queried, "Well, what is it? Caramel icing?"

"It's Permaplast, sir. We aren't the discoverers of this planet because that stuff's a trademarked Earth product."

"Um," I mumbled. "Couldn't the natives here have discovered the same process? The same ingredients might be available."

"Yes, sir. But the blocks are trademarked, if you'll look closely."

"Couldn't the natives have—" Then I shut up because I saw how silly that was. But it's tough to think your party has discovered a new planet and then have Earth-trademarked bricks on the first street you come to. "But what's a street doing here at all?" I wanted to know.

"There's only one way to find out," said Ma sensibly. "And that's to follow it. So what are we standing here for?"

So we pushed on, with much better footing now, and on the next rise we saw a building. A two-story red brick with a sign that read "Bon-Ton Restaurant" in Old English script lettering.

I said, "I'll be a—" But Ma clapped her hand over my mouth before I could finish, which was maybe just as well, for what I'd been going to say had been quite inadequate. There was the building only a hundred yards ahead, facing us at a sharp turn in the street.

I started walking faster and I got there first by a few paces. I opened the door and started to walk in. Then I stopped cold on the doorstep, because there wasn't any "in" to that building. It was a false front, like a cinema set, and all you could see through the door was more of those rolling greenish hills.

I stepped back and looked up at the "Bon-Ton Restaurant" sign, and the others walked up and looked through the doorway, which I'd left open. We just stood there until Ma got impatient and said, "Well, what are you going to do?"

"What do you want me to do?" I wanted to know. "Go in and order a lobster dinner? With champagne?—Hey, I forgot."

The champagne bottle was still in my jacket pocket and I took it out and passed it first to Ma and then to Ellen, and then I finished most of what was left; I must have drunk it too fast because the bubbles tickled my nose and made me sneeze.

I felt ready for anything, though, and I took another walk through the doorway of the building that wasn't there. Maybe, I figured, I could see some indication of how recently it had been put up, or something. There wasn't any indication that I could see. The inside, or rather the back of the front, was smooth and plain like a sheet of glass. It looked like a synthetic of some sort.

I took a look at the ground back of it, but all I could see was a few holes that looked like insect holes. And that's what they must have been, because there was a big black cockroach sitting (or maybe standing; how can you tell whether a cockroach is sitting or standing?) by one of them. I took a step closer and he popped down the hole.

I felt a little better as I went back through the front doorway. I said, "Ma, I saw a cockroach. And do you know what was peculiar about it?"

"What?" she asked.

"Nothing," I told her. "That's the peculiar thing, there was nothing peculiar. Here the ostriches wear hats and the birds have propellers and the streets go nowhere and the houses haven't any backs to them, but that cockroach didn't even have feathers."

"Are you sure?" Ellen wanted to know.

"Sure I'm sure. Let's take the next rise and see what's over it."

We went, and we saw. Down in between that hill and the next, the road took another sharp turn and facing us was the front view of a tent with a big banner that said, "Penny Arcade."

This time I didn't even break stride. I said, "They copied that banner from the show Sam Heideman used to have. Remember Sam, and the good old days, Ma?"

"That drunken no-good," Ma said.

"Why, Ma, you liked him too."

"Yes, and I liked you too, but that doesn't mean that you aren't or he isn't—"

"Why, Ma," I interrupted. But by that time we were right in front of the tent. Looked like real canvas because it billowed gently. I said, "I haven't got the heart. Who wants to look through this time?"

But Ma already had her head through the flap of the tent. I heard her say, "Why, hello Sam, you old soak."

I said, "Ma, quit kidding or I'll—"

But by that time I was past her and inside the tent, and it *was* a tent, all four sides of one, and a good big one at that. And it was lined with the old familiar coin machines. There, counting coins in the change booth, was Sam Heideman, looking up with almost as much surprise on his face as there must have been on mine.

He said, "Pop Wherry! I'll be a dirty name." Only he didn't say "dirty name"—but he didn't get around to apologizing to Ma and Ellen for that until he and I had pounded each other's backs and he had shaken hands around and been introduced to Johnny Lane.

It was just like old times on the carny lots of Mars and Venus. He was telling Ellen how she'd been "so high" when he'd seen her last and did she really remember him?

And then Ma sniffed.

When Ma sniffs like that, there's something to look at, and I got my eyes off dear old Sam and looked at Ma and then at where Ma was looking. I didn't sniff, but I gasped.

A woman was coming forward from the back of the tent, and when I call her a woman it's because I can't think of the right word if there is one. She was St. Cecilia and Guinevere and a Petty girl all ironed into one. She was like a sunset in New Mexico and the cold silver moons of Mars seen from the Equatorial Gardens. She was like a Venusian valley in the spring and like Dorzalski playing the violin. She was really something.

I heard another gasp from alongside me, and it was unfamiliar. Took me a second to realize why it was unfamiliar; I'd never heard Johnny Lane gasp before. It was an effort, but I shifted my eyes for a look at his face. And I thought, "Oh—oh. Poor Ellen." For the poor boy was gone, no question about it.

And just in time—maybe seeing Johnny helped me—I managed to remember that I'm pushing fifty and happily married. I took hold of Ma's arm and hung on. "Sam," I said, "what on Earth—I mean on whatever planet this is—"

Sam turned around and looked behind him. He said, "Miss Ambers, I'd like you to meet some old friends of mine who just dropped in. Mrs. Wherry, this is Miss Ambers, the movie star."

Then he finished the introductions, first Ellen, then me, and then Johnny. Ma and Ellen were much too polite. Me, I maybe went the other way by pretending not to notice the hand Miss Ambers held out. Old as I am, I had a hunch I might forget to let go if I took it. That's the kind of girl she was.

Johnny did forget to let go.

Sam was saying to me, "Pop, you old pirate, what are you doing here? I thought you stuck to the colonies, and I sure didn't look for you to drop in on a movie set."

"A movie set?" Things were beginning to make sense, almost.

"Sure. Planetary Cinema, Inc. With me as the technical advisor on carny scenes. They wanted inside shots of a coin arcade, so I just brought my old stuff out of storage and set it up here. All the boys are over at the base camp now."

Light was just beginning to dawn on me. "And that restaurant front up the street? That's a set?" I queried.

"Sure, and the street itself. They didn't need it, but they had to film the making of it for one sequence."

"Oh." I went on, "But how about the ostrich with the bow tie and the birds with the propellers? They couldn't have been movie props. Or could they?" I'd heard that Planetary Cinema did some pretty impossible things.

Sam shook his head a bit blankly. "Nope. You must have come across some of the local fauna. There are a few but not many, and they don't get in the way."

Ma said, "Look here, Sam Heideman, how come if this planet has been discovered we hadn't heard about it? How long has it been known, and what's it all about?"

Sam chuckled. "A man named Wilkins discovered this planet ten years ago. Reported it to the Council, but before it got publicized Planetary Cinema got wind of it and offered the Council a whopping rental for the place on the condition that it be kept secret. As there aren't any minerals or anything of value here and the soil ain't worth a nickel, the Council rented it to them on those terms."

"But why secret?"

"No visitors, no distractions, not to mention a big jump on their competitors. All the big movie companies spy on one another and swipe one another's ideas. Here they got all the space they want and can work in peace and privacy."

"What'll they do about our finding the place?" I asked.

Sam chuckled again. "Guess they'll entertain you royally now that you're here and try to persuade you to keep it under your hat. You'll probably get a free pass for life to all Planetary Cinema theaters too."

He went over to a cabinet and came back with a tray of bottles and glasses. Ma and Ellen declined, but Sam and I had a couple apiece and it was good stuff. Johnny and Miss Ambers were over in a corner of the tent whispering together earnestly, so we didn't bother them, especially after I told Sam that Johnny didn't drink.

Johnny still had hold of her hand and was gazing into her eyes like a sick pup. I noticed that Ellen moved around so she was facing the other way and didn't have to watch. I was sorry for her, but there wasn't anything I could do. Something like that happens if it happens. And if it hadn't been for Ma—

But I saw that Ma was getting edgy and I said we'd better get back to the ship and get dressed up if we were due to be entertained royally. Then we could move the ship in closer. I reckoned we could spare a few days on Nothing Sirius. I left Sam in stitches by telling him how we'd named the planet after a look at the local fauna.

Then I gently pried Johnny loose from the movie star and led him outside. It wasn't easy. There was a blank, blissful expression on his face, and he'd even forgotten to salute me when I'd spoken to him. Hadn't called me "sir" either. In fact, he didn't say anything at all.

Neither did any of the rest of us, walking up the street.

There was something knocking at my mind and I couldn't quite figure out what it was. There was something wrong, something that didn't make sense.

Ma was worried too. Finally I heard her say, "Pop, if they really want to keep this place a secret, wouldn't they maybe—uh—"

"No, they wouldn't," I answered, maybe a bit snappishly. That wasn't what I was worried about, though.

I looked down at that new and perfect road, and there was something about it I didn't like. I diagonaled over to the curb and walked along that, looked down at the greenish clay beyond, but there wasn't anything to see except more holes and more bugs like I'd seen back at the Bon-Ton Restaurant.

Maybe they weren't cockroaches, though, unless the movie company had brought them. But they were near enough like cockroaches for all practical purposes—if a cockroach has a prac-

tical purpose, that is. And they still didn't have bow ties or propellers or feathers. They were just plain cockroaches.

I stepped off the paving and tried to step on one or two of
them, but they got away and popped into holes. They were
plenty fast and shifty on their feet.

I got back on the road and walked with Ma. When she asked,
"What were you doing?" I answered, "Nothing."

Ellen was walking on the other side of Ma and keeping her
face a studious blank. I could guess what she was thinking and I
wished there was something could be done about it. The only
thing I could think of was to decide to stay on Earth awhile at
the end of this trip, and give her a chance to get over Johnny by
meeting a lot of other young sprigs. Maybe even finding one she
liked.

Johnny was walking along in a daze. He was gone all right,
and he'd fallen with awful suddenness, like guys like that always do. Maybe it wasn't love, just infatuation, but right now
he didn't know what planet he was on.

We were over the first rise now, out of sight of Sam's tent.

"Pop, did you see any movie cameras around?" Ma asked suddenly.

"Nope, but those things cost millions. They don't leave them
sitting around loose when they're not being used."

Ahead of us was the front of that restaurant. It looked funny
as the devil from a side view, walking toward it from that direction. Nothing in sight but that, the road and green clay hills.

There weren't any cockroaches on the street, and I realized
that I'd never seen one there. It seemed as though they never got
up on it or crossed it. Why would a cockroach cross the road? To
get on the other side?

There was still something knocking at my mind, something
that made less sense than anything else.

It got stronger and stronger and it was driving me as crazy as
it was. I got to wishing I had another drink. The sun Sirius was
getting down toward the horizon, but it was still plenty hot. I
even began to wish I had a drink of water.

Ma looked tired too. "Let's stop for a rest," I said, "we're
about halfway back."

We stopped. It was right in front of the Bon-Ton and I
looked up at the sign and grinned. "Johnny, will you go in and
order dinner for us?"

He saluted and replied, "Yes, sir," and started for the door. He suddenly got red in the face and stopped. I chuckled but I didn't rub it in by saying anything else.

Ma and Ellen sat down on the curb.

I walked through the restaurant door again and it hadn't changed any. Smooth like glass on the other side. The same cockroach—I guess it was the same one—was still sitting or standing by the same hole.

I said, "Hello, there," but it didn't answer, so I tried to step on it but again it was too fast for me. I noticed something funny. It had started for the hole the second I decided to step on it, even before I had actually moved a muscle.

I went back through to the front again, and leaned against the wall. It was nice and solid to lean against. I took a cigar out of my pocket and started to light it, but I dropped the match. *Almost,* I knew what was wrong.

Something about Sam Heideman.

"Ma," I said, "isn't Sam Heideman—dead?"

And then, with appalling suddenness I wasn't leaning against a wall anymore because the wall just wasn't there and I was falling backward.

I heard Ma yell and Ellen squeal.

I picked myself up off the greenish clay. Ma and Ellen were getting up too, from sitting down hard on the ground because the curb they'd been sitting on wasn't there any more either. Johnny was staggering a bit from having the road disappear under the soles of his feet, and dropping a few inches.

There wasn't a sign anywhere of road or restaurant, just the rolling green hills. And—yes, the cockroaches were still there.

The fall had jolted me plenty, and I was mad. I wanted something to take out my mad on. There were only cockroaches. They hadn't gone up into nothingness like the rest of it. I made another try at the nearest one, and missed again. This time I was positive that he'd moved before I did.

Ellen looked down at where the street ought to be, at where the restaurant front ought to be, and then back the way we'd come as though wondering if the Penny Arcade tent was still there.

"It isn't," I said.

Ma asked, "It isn't what?"

"Isn't there," I explained.

Ma glowered at me. "What isn't where?"

"The tent," I said, a bit peeved. "The movie company. The whole shebang. And especially Sam Heideman. It was when I remembered about Sam Heideman—five years ago in Luna City we heard he was dead—so he wasn't there. None of it was there. And the minute I realized that, they pulled it all out from under us."

" 'They?' What do you mean, 'they,' Pop Wherry? Who is 'they'?"

"You mean who *are* 'they'?" I said, but the look Ma gave me made me wince.

"Let's not talk here," I went on. "Let's get back to the ship as quick as we can, first. You can lead us there, Johnny, without the street?"

He nodded, forgetting to salute or "sir" me. We started off, none of us talking. I wasn't worried about Johnny getting us back; he'd been all right until we'd hit the tent; he'd been following our course with his wrist-compass.

After we got to where the end of the street had been, it got easy because we could see our own footprints in the clay, and just had to follow them. We passed the rise where there had been the purple bush with the propeller birds, but the birds weren't there now, nor was the purple bush.

But the *Chitterling* was still there, thank Heavens. We saw it from the last rise and it looked just as we had left it. It looked like home, and we started to walk faster.

I opened the door and stood aside for Ma and Ellen to go in first. Ma had just started in when we heard the voice. It said, "We bid you farewell."

I said, "We bid you farewell, too. And the hell with you."

I motioned Ma to go on into the ship. The sooner I was out of this place, the better I'd like it.

But the voice said, "Wait," and there was something about it that made us wait. "We wish to explain to you so that you will not return."

Nothing had been further from my mind, but I said, "Why not?"

"Your civilization is not compatible with ours. We have studied your minds to make sure. We projected images from the images we found in your minds, to study your reactions to them. Our first images, our first thought-projections, were confused.

But we understood your minds by the time you reached the farthest point of your walk. We were able to project beings similar to yourselves."

"Sam Heideman, yeah," I said. "But how about the da—the woman? She couldn't have been in the memory of any of us because none of us knew her."

"She was a composite—what you would call an idealization. That, however, doesn't matter. By studying you we learned that your civilization concerns itself with things, ours with thoughts. Neither of us has anything to offer the other. No good could come through interchange, whereas much harm might come. Our planet has no material resources that would interest your race."

I had to agree with that, looking out over that monotonous rolling clay that seemed to support only those few tumbleweedlike bushes, and not many of them. It didn't look like it would support anything else. As for minerals, I hadn't seen even a pebble.

"Right you are," I called back. "Any planet that raises nothing but tumbleweeds and cockroaches can keep itself, as far as we're concerned. So—" Then something dawned on me. "Hey, just a minute. There must be something else or who the devil am I talking to?"

"You are talking," replied the voice, "to what you call cockroaches, which is another point of incompatibility between us. To be more precise, you are talking to a thought-projected voice, but we are projecting it. And let me assure you of one thing—that you are more repugnant physically to us than we are to you."

I looked down then and saw them, three of them, ready to pop into holes if I made a move.

Back inside the ship, I said, "Johnny, blast off. Destination, Earth."

He saluted and said, "Yes, sir," and went into the pilot's compartment and shut the door. He didn't come out until we were on an automatic course, with Sirius dwindling behind us.

Ellen had gone to her room. Ma and I were playing cribbage.

"May I go off duty, sir?" Johnny asked, and walked stiffly to his room when I answered, "Sure."

After a while, Ma and I turned in. Awhile after that we heard noises. I got up to investigate, and investigated.

I came back grinning. "Everything's okay, Ma," I said. "It's Johnny Lane and he's as drunk as a hoot owl!" And I slapped Ma playfully on the fanny.

"Ouch, you old fool," she sniffed. "I'm sore there from the curb disappearing from under me. And what's wonderful about Johnny getting drunk? *You* aren't, are you?"

"No," I admitted, regretfully perhaps. "But, Ma, he told me to go to blazes. And without saluting. Me, the owner of the ship."

Ma just looked at me. Sometimes women are smart, but sometimes they're pretty dumb.

"Listen, he isn't going to keep on getting drunk," I said. "This is an occasion. Can't you see what happened to his pride and dignity?"

"You mean because he—"

"Because he fell in love with the thought-projection of a cockroach," I pointed out. "Or anyway he thought he did. He has to get drunk once to forget that, and from now on, after he sobers up, he's going to be human. I'll bet on it, any odds. And I'll bet too that once he's human, he's going to *see* Ellen and realize how pretty she is. I'll bet he's head-over-heels before we get back to Earth. I'll get a bottle and we'll drink a toast on it. To Nothing Sirius!"

And for once I was right. Johnny and Ellen were engaged before we got near enough to Earth to start decelerating.

Pattern

Miss Macy sniffed. "Why is everyone worrying so? They're not *doing* anything to us, are they?"

In the cities, elsewhere, there was blind panic. But not in Miss Macy's garden. She looked up calmly at the monstrous mile-high figures of the invaders.

A week ago, they'd landed, in a spaceship a hundred miles long that had settled down gently in the Arizona desert. Almost a thousand of them had come out of that spaceship and were now walking around.

But, as Miss Macy pointed out, they hadn't hurt anything or anybody. They weren't quite *substantial* enough to affect people. When one stepped on you or stepped on a house you were in, there was sudden darkness and until he moved his foot and walked on you couldn't see; that was all.

They had paid no attention to human beings and all attempts to communicate with them had failed, as had all attacks on them by the army and the air force. Shells fired at them exploded right inside them and didn't hurt them. Not even the H-bomb dropped on one of them while he was crossing a desert area had bothered him in the slightest.

They had paid no attention to us at all.

"And that," said Miss Macy to her sister who was also Miss Macy since neither of them was married, "is proof that they don't mean us any harm, isn't it?"

"I hope so, Amanda," said Miss Macy's sister. "But look what they're doing now."

It was a clear day, or it had been one. The sky had been bright blue and the almost humanoid heads and shoulders of the giants, a mile up there, had been quite clearly visible. But now it was getting misty, Miss Macy saw as she followed her sister's gaze upward. Each of the two big figures in sight had a tanklike object in his hands and from these objects clouds of vaporous matter were emerging, settling slowly toward Earth.

Miss Macy sniffed again. "Making clouds. Maybe that's how they have fun. *Clouds* can't hurt us. Why do people worry so?"

She went back to her work.

"Is that a liquid fertilizer you're spraying, Amanda?" her sister asked.

"No," said Miss Macy. "It's insecticide."

The Yehudi Principle

I AM going crazy.

Charlie Swann is going crazy, too. Maybe more than I am, because it was his dingbat. I mean, he made it and he thought he knew what it was and how it worked.

You see, Charlie was just kidding me when he told me it worked on the Yehudi principle. Or he thought he was.

"The Yehudi principle?" I said.

"The Yehudi principle," he repeated. "The principle of the little man who wasn't there. He does it."

"Does what?" I wanted to know.

The dingbat, I might interrupt myself to explain, was a headband. It fitted neatly around Charlie's noggin and there was a round black box not much bigger than a pillbox over his forehead. Also there was a round flat copper disk on each side of the band that fitted over each of Charlie's temples, and a strand of wire that ran down behind his ear into the breast pocket of his coat, where there was a little dry cell battery.

It didn't look as if it would do anything, except maybe either cure a headache or make it worse. But from the excited look on Charlie's face, I didn't think it was anything as commonplace as that.

"Does what?" I wanted to know.

"Whatever you want," said Charlie. "Within reason, of course. Not like moving a building or bringing you a locomotive. But any little thing you want done, he does it."

"Who does?"

"Yehudi."

I closed my eyes and counted to five, by ones. I *wasn't* going to ask, "*Who's Yehudi?*"

I shoved aside a pile of papers on the bed—I'd been going through some old clunker manuscripts seeing if I could find something good enough to rewrite from a new angle—and sat down.

"O.K.," I said. "Tell him to being me a drink."

"What kind?"

I looked at Charlie, and he didn't look like he was kidding. He had to be, of course, but—

"Gin buck," I told him. "A gin buck, with gin in it, if Yehudi knows what I mean."

"Hold out your hand," Charles said.

I held out my hand. Charlie, not talking to me, said, "Bring Hank a gin buck, strong." And then he nodded his head.

Something happened either to Charlie or to my eyes, I didn't know which. For just a second, he got sort of misty. And then he looked normal again.

And I let out a kind of a yip and pulled my hand back, because my hand was wet with something cold. And there was a splashing noise and a wet puddle on the carpet right at my feet. Right under where my hand had been.

Charlie said, "We should have asked for it in a glass."

I looked at Charlie and then I looked at the puddle on the floor and then I looked at my hand. I stuck my index finger gingerly into my mouth and tasted.

Gin buck. With gin in it. I looked at Charlie again.

He asked, "Did I blur?"

"Listen, Charlie," I said. "I've known you for ten years, and we went to Tech together and— But if you pull another gag like that I'll blur you, all right. I'll—"

"Watch closer this time," Charlie said. And again, looking off into space and not talking to me at all, he started talking. "Bring us a fifth of gin, in a bottle. Half a dozen lemons, sliced, on a plate. Two quart bottles of soda and a dish of ice cubes. Put it all on the table over there."

He nodded his head, just like he had before, and darned if he didn't blur. *Blur* was the best word for it.

"You blurred," I said. I was getting a slight headache.

"I thought so," he said. "But I was using a mirror when I tried it alone, and I thought maybe it was my eyes. That's why I came over. You want to mix the drinks or shall I?"

I looked over at the table, and there was all the stuff he'd ordered. I swallowed a couple of times.

"It's real," Charlie said. He was breathing a little hard, with suppressed excitement. "It works, Hank. It *works*. We'll be rich! We can—"

Charlie kept on talking, but I got up slowly and went over to the table. The bottles and lemons and ice were really there. The bottles gurgled when shaken and the ice was cold.

In a minute I was going to worry about how they got there. Meanwhile and right now, I needed a drink. I got a couple of glasses out of the medicine cabinet and the bottle opener out of the file cabinet, and I made two drinks, about half gin.

Then I thought of something. I asked Charlie, "Does Yehudi want a drink, too?"

Charlie grinned. "Two'll be enough," he told me.

"To start with, maybe," I said grimly. I handed him a drink—in a glass—and said, "To Yehudi." I downed mine at a gulp and started mixing another.

Charlie said, "Me, too. Hey, wait a minute."

"Under present circumstances," I said, "a minute is a minute too long between drinks. In a minute I shall wait a minute, but—Hey, why don't we let Yehudi mix 'em for us?"

"Just what I was going to suggest. Look, I want to try something. You put this headband on and tell him to. I want to watch you."

"Me?"

"You," he said. "It can't do any harm, and I want to be sure it works for everybody and not just for me. It may be that it's attuned merely to my brain. You try it."

"Me?" I said.

"You," he told me.

He'd taken it off and was holding it out to me, with the little flat dry cell dangling from it at the end of the wire. I took it and looked it over. It didn't look dangerous. There couldn't possibly be enough juice in so tiny a battery to do any harm.

I put it on.

"Mix us some drinks," I said, and looked over at the table, but nothing happened.

"You got to nod just as you finish," Charlie said. "There's a little pendulum affair in the box over your forehead that works the switch."

I said, "Mix us two gin bucks. In glasses, please." And nodded.

When my head came up again, there were the drinks, mixed.

"Blow me down," I said. And bent over to pick up my drink.

And there I was on the floor.

Charlie said, "Be careful, Hank. If you lean over forward, that's the same as nodding. And don't nod or lean just as you say something you don't mean as an order."

I sat up. "Fan me with a blowtorch," I said.

But I didn't nod. In fact, I didn't move. When I realized what I'd said, I held my neck so rigid that it hurt, and didn't quite breathe for fear I'd swing that pendulum.

Very gingerly, so as not to tilt it, I reached up and took off the headband and put it down on the floor.

Then I got up and felt myself all over. There were probably bruises, but no broken bones. I picked up the drink and drank it. It was a good drink, but I mixed the next one myself. With three-quarters gin.

With it in my hand, I circled around the headband, not coming within a yard of it, and sat down on the bed.

"Charlie," I said, "you've *got* something there. I don't know what it is, but what are we waiting for?"

"Meaning?" said Charlie.

"Meaning what any sensible man would mean. If that darned thing brings anything we ask for, well, let's make it a party. Which would you rather have, Lili St. Cyr or Esther Williams? I'll take the other."

He shook his head sadly. "There are limitations, Hank. Maybe I'd better explain."

"Personally," I said, "I would prefer Lili to an explanation, but go ahead. Let's start with Yehudi. The only two Yehudis I know are Yehudi Menuhin, the violinist, and Yehudi, the little man who wasn't there. Somehow I don't think Menuhin brought us that gin, so—"

"He didn't. For that matter, neither did the little man who wasn't there. I was kidding you, Hank. There isn't any little man who wasn't there."

"Oh," I said. I repeated it slowly, or started to. "There—isn't—any—little—man—who—wasn't—" I gave up. "I think I begin to see," I said. "What you mean is that there wasn't any little man who isn't here. But then, who's Yehudi?"

"There isn't any Yehudi, Hank. But the name, the idea, fitted so well that I called it that for short."

"And what do you call it for long?"

"The automatic autosuggestive subvibratory superaccelerator."

I drank the rest of my drink.

"Lovely," I said. "I like the Yehudi principle better, though. But there's just one thing. Who brought us that drink-stuff? The gin and the soda and the so forth?"

"I did. And you mixed our second-last, as well as our last drink. Now do you understand?"

"In a word," I said, "not exactly."

Charlie sighed. "A field is set up between the temple-plates which accelerates several thousand times, the molecular vibration and thereby the speed of organic matter—the brain, and thereby the body. The command given just before the switch is thrown acts as an autosuggestion and you carry out the order you've just given yourself. But so rapidly that no one can see you move; just a momentary blur as you move off and come back in practically the same instant. Is that clear?"

"Sure," I told him. "Except for one thing. Who's Yehudi?"

I went to the table and started mixing two more drinks. Seven-eighths gin.

Charlie said patiently, "The action is so rapid that it does not impress itself upon your memory. For some reason the memory is not affected by the acceleration. The *effect*—both to the user and to the observer—is of the spontaneous obedience of a command by . . . well, by the little man who wasn't there."

"Yehudi?"

"Why not?"

"Why not why not?" I asked. "Here, have another drink. It's a bit weak, but so am I. So you got this gin, huh? Where?"

"Probably the nearest tavern. I don't remember."

"Pay for it?"

He pulled out his wallet and opened it. "I think there's a fin missing. I probably left it in the register. My subconscious must be honest."

"But what good is it?" I demanded. "I don't mean your subconscious, Charlie, I mean the Yehudi principle. You could have just as easily bought that gin on the way here. I could just as easily have mixed a drink and known I was doing it. And if you're *sure* it can't go bring us Lili St. Cyr and Esther Williams—"

"It can't. Look, it can't do anything that you yourself can't do. It isn't an it. It's you. Get that through your head, Hank, and you'll understand."

"But what good is it?"

He sighed again. "The real purpose of it is *not* to run errands for gin and mix drinks. That was just a demonstration. The real purpose—"

"Wait," I said. "Speaking of drinks, wait. It's a long time since I had one."

I made the table, tacking only twice, and this time I didn't bother with the soda. I put a little lemon and an ice cube in each glass of gin.

Charlie tasted his and made a wry face.

I tasted mine. "Sour," I said. "I should have left out the lemon. And we better drink them quick before the ice cubes start to melt or they'll be weak."

"The real purpose," said Charlie, "is—"

"Wait," I said. "You could be wrong, you know. About the limitations. I'm going to put that headband on and tell Yehudi to bring us Lili and—"

"Don't be a sap, Hank. I made the thing. I know how it works. You can't get Lili St. Cyr or Esther Williams or Brooklyn Bridge."

"You're positive?"

"Of course."

What a sap I was. I believed him. I mixed two more drinks, using gin and two glasses this time, and then I sat down on the edge of the bed, which was swaying gently from side to side.

"All right," I said. "I can take it now. What is the real purpose of it?"

Charlie Swann blinked several times and seemed to be having trouble bringing his eyes into focus on me. He asked, "The real purpose of what?"

I enunciated slowly and carefully. "Of the automatonic autosuggestive subvibratory superaccelerator. Yehudi, to me."

"Oh, that," said Charlie.

"That," I said. "What is its real purpose?"

"It's like this. Suppose you got something to do that you've got to do in a hurry. Or something that you've got to do, and don't want to do. You could—"

"Like writing a story?" I asked.

"Like writing a story," he said, "or painting a house, or washing a mess of dishes, or shoveling the sidewalk, or . . . or doing anything else you've got to do but don't want to do. Look, you put it on and tell yourself—"

"Yehudi," I said.

"Tell Yehudi to do it, and it's done. Sure, you do it, but you don't know that you do, so it doesn't hurt. And it gets done quicker."

"You blur," I said.

He held up his glass and looked through it at the electric light. It was empty. The glass, not the electric light.

He said, "You blur."

"Who?"

He didn't answer. He seemed to be swinging, chair and all, in an arc about a yard long. It made me dizzy to look at him, so I closed my eyes, but that was worse so I opened them again.

I said, "A story?"

"Sure."

"I got to write a story," I said, "but why should I? I mean, why not let Yehudi do it?"

I went over and put on the headband. No extraneous remarks this time, I told myself. Stick to the point.

"Write a story," I said.

I nodded. Nothing happened.

But then I remembered that, as far as I was supposed to know, nothing was supposed to happen. I walked over to the typewriter desk and looked.

There was a white sheet and a yellow sheet in the typewriter, with a carbon between them. The page was about half filled with typing and then down at the bottom were two words by themselves. I couldn't read them. I took my glasses off and still I couldn't, so I put them back on and put my face down within inches of the typewriter and concentrated. The words were "The End."

I looked over alongside the typewriter and there was a neat, but small pile of typed sheets, alternate white and yellow.

It was wonderful. I'd written a story. If my subconscious mind had anything on the ball, it might be the best story I'd ever written.

Too bad I wasn't quite in shape to read it. I'd have to see an optometrist about new glasses. Or something.

"Charlie," I said, "I wrote a story."

"When?"

"Just now."

"I didn't see you."

"I blurred," I said. "But you weren't looking."

I was back sitting on the bed. I don't remember getting there.

"Charlie," I said, "it's wonderful."

"What's wonderful?"

"Everything. Life. Birdies in the trees. Pretzels. A story in less than a second! One second a week I have to work from now on. No more school, no more books, no more teacher's sassy looks! Charlie, it's *wonderful!*"

He seemed to wake up. He said, "Hank, you're just *beginning* to see the possibilities. They're almost endless, for any profession. Almost *anything.*"

"Except," I said sadly, "Lili St. Cyr and Esther Williams."

"You've got a one-track mind."

"Two-track," I said. "I'd settle for either. Charlie, are you *positive—*"

Wearily, "Yes." Or that was what he meant to say; it came out "Yesh."

"Charlie," I said. "You've been drinking. Care if I *try?*"

"Shoot yourself."

"Huh? Oh, you mean suit yourself. O.K., then I'll—"

"Thass what I shaid," Charlie said. "Suit yourshelf."

"You did not."

"What did I shay, then?"

I said, "You shaid—I mean said: 'Shoot yourself.' "

Even Jove nods.

Only Jove doesn't wear a headband like the one I still had on. Or maybe, come to think of it, he does. It would explain a lot of things.

I must have nodded, because there was the sound of a shot.

I let out a yell and jumped up, and Charlie jumped up too. He looked sober.

He said, "Hank, you had that thing on. Are you—?"

I was looking down at myself and there wasn't any blood on the front of my shirt. Nor any pain anywhere. Nor anything.

I quit shaking. I looked at Charlie; he wasn't shot either.

I said, "But who—? What—?"

"Hank," he said. "That shot wasn't in this room at all. It was outside, in the hallway, or on the stair."

"On the *stair?*" Something prickled at the back of my mind. What about a stair? *I saw a man upon the stair, a little man who was not there. He was not there again today. Gee, I wish he'd go away—*

"Charlie," I said. "*It was Yehudi!* He shot himself because I said 'shoot yourself' and the pendulum swung. You were wrong about it being an—an automatonic autosuggestive whatzit. It was Yehudi doing it all the time. It was—"

"Shut up," he said.

But he went over and opened the door and I followed him and we went out in the hallway.

There was a decided smell of burnt powder. It seemed to come from about halfway up the stairs because it got stronger as we neared that point.

"Nobody there," Charlie said, shakily.

In an awed voice I said, "*He was not there again today. Gee, I wish—*"

"Shut up," said Charlie sharply.

We went back into my room.

"Sit down," Charlie said. "We got to figure this out. You said, 'Shoot yourself,' and either nodded or swayed forward. But you didn't shoot yourself. The shot came from—" He shook his head, trying to clear it.

"Let's have some coffee," he suggested. "Some hot, black coffee. Have you got— Hey, you're still wearing that headband. Get us some, but for Heaven's sake be careful."

I said, "Bring us two cups of hot black coffee." And I nodded, but it didn't work. Somehow I'd known it wouldn't.

Charlie grabbed the band off my head. He put it on and tried it himself.

I said, "Yehudi's dead. He shot himself. That thing's no good anymore. So I'll make the coffee."

I put the kettle on the hot plate. "Charlie," I said, "look, suppose it *was* Yehudi doing that stuff. Well, how do you know what his limitations were? Look, maybe he *could* have brought us Lili—"

"Shut up," said Charlie. "I'm trying to think."

I shut up and let him think.

And by the time I had the coffee made, I realized how silly I'd been talking.

I brought the coffee. By that time, Charlie had the lid off the pillbox affair and was examining its innards. I could see the little pendulum that worked the switch, and a lot of wires.

He said, "I don't understand it. There's nothing broken."

"Maybe the battery," I suggested.

I got out my flashlight and we used its bulb to test the little dry cell. The bulb burned brightly.

"I don't understand it," Charlie said.

Then I suggested, "Let's start from the beginning, Charlie. It *did* work. It got us stuff for drinks. It mixed one pair of drinks. It— Say—"

"I was just thinking of that," Charlie said. "When you said, 'Blow me down,' and bent over to pick up the drink, what happened?"

"A current of air. It blew me down, Charlie, literally. How *could* I have done that myself? And notice the difference in pronouns. I said, 'Blow me down,' then but later I said, 'Shoot yourself.' If I'd said, 'Shoot me,' why maybe—"

There was that prickle down my spine again.

Charlie looked dazed. He said, "But I worked it out on scientific principles, Hank. It wasn't just an accident. I couldn't be wrong. You mean you think that—It's utterly silly!"

I'd been thinking just that, again. But differently. "Look," I said, "let's concede that your apparatus set up a field that had an effect upon the brain, but just for argument let's assume you misunderstood the nature of the field. Suppose it enabled you to *project a thought*. And you were thinking about Yehudi; you must have been because you jokingly called it the Yehudi principle, and so Yehudi—"

"That's silly," said Charlie.

"Give me a better one."

He went over to the hot plate for another cup of coffee.

And I remembered something then, and went over to the typewriter table. I picked up the story, shuffling the pages as I picked them up so the first page would come out on top, and I started to read.

I heard Charlie's voice say, "Is it a good story, Hank?"

I said, "G-g-g-g-g—"

Charlie took a look at my face and sprinted across the room to read over my shoulder. I handed him the first page. The title on it was THE YEHUDI PRINCIPLE.

The story started:

"I am going crazy.

"Charlie Swann is going crazy, too. Maybe more than I am, because it was his dingbat. I mean, he made it and he thought he knew what it was and how it worked."

As I read page after page I handed them to Charlie and he read them too. Yes, it was *this* story. The story you're reading right now, including this part of it that I'm telling right now. Written before the last part of it happened.

Charlie was sitting down when he finished, and so was I.

He looked at me and I looked at him.

He opened his mouth a few times and closed it again twice before he could get anything out. Finally he said, *"T-time,* Hank. It had something to do with *time* too. It wrote in advance just what—Hank, I'll make it work again. I *got* to. It's something big. It's—"

"It's colossal," I said. "But it'll never work again. Yehudi's dead. He shot himself upon the stair."

"You're crazy," said Charlie.

"Not yet," I told him. I looked down at the manuscript he'd handed back to me and read:

"I am going crazy."

I *am* going crazy.

Come and Go Mad

He had known it, somehow, when he had awakened that morning. He knew it more surely now, staring out of the editorial room window into the early afternoon sunlight slanting down among the buildings to cast a pattern of light and shadow. He knew that soon, perhaps even today, something important was going to happen. Whether good or bad he did not know, but he darkly suspected. And with reason; there are few good things that may unexpectedly happen to a man, things, that is, of lasting importance. Disaster can strike from innumerable directions, in amazingly diverse ways.

A voice said, "Hey, Mr. Vine," and he turned away from the window, slowly. That in itself was strange for it was not his manner to move slowly; he was a small, volatile man, almost catlike in the quickness of his reactions and his movements.

But this time something made him turn slowly from the window, almost as though he never again expected to see that chiaroscuro of an early afternoon.

He said, "Hi, Red."

The freckled copy boy said, "His Nibs wants to see ya."

"Now?"

"Naw. Atcher convenience. Sometime next week, maybe. If yer busy, give him an apperntment."

He put his fist against Red's chin and shoved, and the copy boy staggered back in assumed distress.

He went over to the water cooler. He pressed his thumb on the button and water gurgled into the paper cup.

Harry Wheeler sauntered over and said, "Hiya, Nappy. What's up? Going on the carpet?"

He said, "Sure, for a raise."

He drank and crumpled the cup, tossing it into the wastebasket. He went over to the door marked Private and went through it.

Walter J. Candler, the managing editor, looked up from the work on his desk and said affably, "Sit down, Vine. Be with you in a moment," and then looked down again.

He slid into the chair opposite Candler, worried a cigarette out of his shirt pocket and lighted it. He studied the back of the sheet of paper of which the managing editor was reading the front. There wasn't anything on the back of it.

The M.E. put the paper down and looked at him. "Vine, I've got a screwy one. You're good on screwy ones."

He grinned slowly at the M.E. He said, "If that's a compliment, thanks."

"It's a compliment, all right. You've done some pretty tough things for us. This one's different. I've never yet asked a reporter to do anything I wouldn't do myself. *I* wouldn't do this, so I'm not asking you to."

The M.E. picked up the paper he'd been reading and then put it down again without even looking at it. "Ever hear of Ellsworth Joyce Randolph?"

"Head of the asylum? Hell yes, I've met him. Casually."

"How'd he impress you?"

He was aware that the managing editor was staring at him intently, that it wasn't too casual a question. He parried. "What do you mean? In what way? You mean is he a good Joe, is he a good politician, has he got a good bedside manner for a psychiatrist, or what?"

"I mean, how sane do you think he is?"

He looked at Candler and Candler wasn't kidding. Candler was strictly deadpan.

He began to laugh, and then he stopped laughing. He leaned forward across Candler's desk. "Ellsworth Joyce Randolph," he said. "You're talking about Ellsworth Joyce Randolph?"

Candler nodded. "Dr. Randolph was in here this morning. He told a rather strange story. He didn't want me to print it. He did want me to check on it, to send our best man to check on it. He said if we found it was true we could print it in hundred and twenty line type in red ink." Candler grinned wryly. "We could, at that."

He stumped out his cigarette and studied Candler's face. "But the story itself is so screwy you're not sure whether Dr. Randolph himself might be insane?"

"Exactly."

"And what's tough about the assignment?"

"The doc says a reporter could get the story only from the inside."

"You mean, go in as a guard or something?"

Candler said, "As something."

"Oh."

He got up out of the chair and walked over to the window, stood with his back to the managing editor, looking out. The sun had moved hardly at all. Yet the shadow pattern in the streets looked different, obscurely different. The shadow pattern inside him was different, too. This, he knew, was what had been going to happen. He turned around. He said, "No. Hell no."

Candler shrugged imperceptibly. "Don't blame you. I haven't even asked you to. I wouldn't do it myself."

He asked, "What does Ellsworth Joyce Randolph think is going on inside his nut-house? It must be something pretty screwy if it made you wonder whether Randolph himself is sane."

"I can't tell you that, Vine. Promised him I wouldn't, whether or not you took the assignment."

"You mean—even if I took the job I still wouldn't know what I was looking for?"

"That's right. You'd be prejudiced. You wouldn't be objective. You'd be looking for something, and you might think you found it whether it was there or not. Or you might be so prejudiced against finding it that you'd refuse to recognize it if it bit you in the leg."

He strode from the window over to the desk and banged his fist down on it.

He said, "God damn it, Candler, why *me*? You know what happened to me three years ago."

"Sure. Amnesia."

"Sure, amnesia. Just like that. But I haven't kept it any secret that I never got *over* that amnesia. I'm thirty years old—or am I? My memory goes back three years. Do you know what it feels like to have a blank wall in your memory only three years back?

"Oh, sure, I know what's on the other side of that wall. I know because everybody tells me. I know I started here as a copy boy ten years ago. I know where I was born and when and I know my parents are both dead. I know what they look like—because I've seen their pictures. I know I didn't have a wife and kids, because everybody who knew me told me I didn't. Get that part—everybody who knew me, not everybody I knew. I didn't know anybody.

"Sure, I've done all right since then. After I got out of the hospital—and I don't even remember the accident that put me there—I did all right back here because I still knew how to write news stories, even though I had to learn everybody's name all over again. I wasn't any worse off than a new reporter starting cold on a paper in a strange city. And everybody was as helpful as hell."

Candler raised a placating hand to stem the tide. He said, "Okay, Nappy. You said no, and that's enough. I don't see what all that's got to do with this story, but all you had to do was say no. So forget about it."

The tenseness hadn't gone out of him. He said, "You don't see what *that's* got to do with the story? You ask—or, all right, you don't ask, you suggest—that I get myself certified as a madman, go into an asylum as a patient. When—how much confidence could anyone have in his own mind when he can't remember going to school, can't remember the first time he met any of the people he works with every day, can't remember starting on the job he works at, can't remember—anything back of three years before?"

Abruptly he struck the desk again with his fist, and then looked foolish about it. He said, "I'm sorry. I didn't mean to get wound up about it like that."

Candler said, "Sit down."

"The answer's still no."

"Sit down, anyway."

He sat down and fumbled a cigarette out of his pocket, got it lighted.

Candler said, "I didn't even mean to mention it, but I've got to now. Now that you talked that way. I didn't know you felt like that about your amnesia. I thought that was water under the bridge.

"Listen, when Dr. Randolph asked me what reporter we had that could best cover it, I told him about you. What your background was. He remembered meeting you, too, incidentally. But he hadn't known you had amnesia."

"Is that why you suggested me?"

"Skip that till I make my point. He said that while you were there, he'd be glad to try one of the newer, milder forms of shock treatment on you, and that it might restore your lost memories. He said it would be worth trying."

"He didn't say it would work."

"He said it might; that it wouldn't do any harm."

He stubbed out the cigarette from which he'd taken only three drags. He glared at Candler. He didn't have to say what was in his mind; the managing editor could read it.

Candler said, "Calm down, boy. Remember I didn't bring it up until you yourself started in on how much that memory-wall bothered you. I wasn't saving it for ammunition. I mentioned it only out of fairness to you, after the way you talked."

"Fairness!"

Candler shrugged. "You said no. I accepted it. Then you started raving at me and put me in a spot where I had to mention something I'd hardly thought of at the time. Forget it. How's that graft story coming? Any new leads?"

"You going to put someone else on the asylum story?"

"No. You're the logical one for it."

"What *is* the story? It must be pretty woolly if it makes you wonder if Dr. Randolph is sane. Does he think his patients ought to trade places with his doctors, or what?"

He laughed. "Sure, you can't tell me. That's really beautiful double bait. Curiosity—and hope of knocking down that wall. So what's the rest of it? If I say yes instead of no, how long will I be there, under what circumstances? What chance have I got of getting out again? How do I get in?"

Candler said slowly, "Vine, I'm not sure any more I want you to try it. Let's skip the whole thing."

"Let's not. Not until you answer my questions, anyway."

"All right. You'd go in anonymously, so there wouldn't be any stigma attached if the story wouldn't work out. If it does, you can tell the whole truth—including Dr. Randolph's collusion in getting you in and out again. The cat will be out of the bag, then.

"You might get what you want in a few days—and you wouldn't stay on it more than a couple of weeks in any case."

"How many at the asylum would know who I was and what I was there for, besides Randolph?"

"No one." Candler leaned forward and held up four fingers of his left hand. "Four people would have to be in on it. You." He pointed to one finger. "Me." A second. "Dr. Randolph." The third finger. "And one other reporter from here."

"Not that I'd object, but why the other reporter?"

"Intermediary. In two ways. First, he'll go with you to some psychiatrist; Randolph will recommend one you can fool comparatively easily. He'll be your brother and request that you be examined and certified. You convince the psychiatrist you're nuts and he'll certify you. Of course it takes two doctors to put you away, but Randolph will be the second. Your alleged brother will want Randolph for the second one."

"All this under an assumed name?"

"If you prefer. Of course there's no real reason why it should be."

"That's the way I feel about it. Keep it out of the papers, of course. Tell everybody around here—except my—hey, in that case we couldn't make up a brother. But Charlie Doerr, in Circulation, is my first cousin and my nearest living relative. He'd do, wouldn't he?"

"Sure. And he'd have to be intermediary the rest of the way, then. Visit you at the asylum and bring back anything you have to send back."

"And if, in a couple of weeks, I've found nothing, you'll spring me?"

Candler nodded. "I'll pass the word to Randolph; he'll interview you and pronounce you cured, and you're out. You come back here, and you've been on vacation. That's all."

"What kind of insanity should I pretend to have?"

He thought Candler squirmed a little in his chair. Candler said, "Well—wouldn't this Nappy business be a natural? I mean, paranoia is a form of insanity which Dr. Randolph told me, hasn't any physical symptoms. It's just a delusion supported by a systematic framework of rationalization. A paranoiac can be sane in every way except one."

He watched Candler and there was a faint twisted grin on his lips. "You mean I should think I'm Napoleon?"

Candler gestured slightly. "Choose your own delusion. But—isn't that one a natural? I mean, the boys around the office al-

ways kidding you and calling you Nappy. And—" He finished
weakly, "—and everything."

And then Candler looked at him squarely. "Want to do it?"

He stood up. "I think so. I'll let you know for sure tomorrow
morning after I've slept on it, but unofficially—yes. Is that good
enough?"

Candler nodded.

He said, "I'm taking the rest of the afternoon off; I'm going to
the library to read up on paranoia. Haven't anything else to do
anyway. And I'll talk to Charlie Doerr this evening. Okay?"

"Fine. Thanks."

He grinned at Candler. He leaned across the desk. He said,
"I'll let you in on a little secret, now that things have gone this
far. Don't tell anyone. I *am* Napoleon!"

It was a good exit line, so he went out.

II

He got his hat and coat and went outside, out of the air-condi-
tioning and into the hot sunlight. Out of the quiet madhouse of
a newspaper office after deadline, into the quieter madhouse of
the streets on a sultry July afternoon.

He tilted his panama back on his head and ran his handkerchief across his forehead. Where was he going? Not to the library to bone up on paranoia; that had been a gag to get off for
the rest of the afternoon. He'd read everything the library had
on paranoia—and on allied subjects—over two years ago. He was
an expert on it. He could fool any psychiatrist in the country
into thinking that he was sane—or that he wasn't.

He walked north to the park and sat down on one of the
benches in the shade. He put his hat on the bench beside him
and mopped his forehead again.

He stared out at the grass, bright green in the sunlight, at the
pigeons with their silly head-bobbing method of walking, at a
red squirrel that came down one side of a tree, looked about him
and scurried up the other side of the same tree.

And he thought back to the wall of amnesia of three years
ago.

The wall that hadn't been a wall at all. The phrase intrigued him: a wall at all. Pigeons on the grass, alas. A wall at all.

It wasn't a wall at all; it was a shift, an abrupt change. A line had been drawn between two lives. Twenty-seven years of a life before the accident. Three years of a life since the accident.

They were not the same life.

But no one knew. Until this afternoon he had never even hinted the truth—if it *was* the truth—to anyone. He'd used it as an exit line in leaving Candler's office, knowing Candler would take it as a gag. Even so, one had to be careful; use a gag-line like that often, and people begin to wonder.

The fact that his extensive injuries from that accident had included a broken jaw was probably responsible for the fact that today he was free and not in an insane asylum. That broken jaw —it had been in a cast when he'd retuned to consciousness forty-eight hours after his car had run head-on into a truck ten miles out of town—had prevented him from talking for three weeks.

And by the end of three weeks, despite the pain and the confusion that had filled him, he'd had a chance to think things over. He'd invented the wall. The amnesia, the convenient amnesia that was so much more believable than the truth as he knew it.

But *was* the truth as he knew it?

That was the haunting ghost that had ridden him for three years now, since the very hour when he had awakened to whiteness in a white room and a stranger, strangely dressed, had been sitting beside a bed the like of which had been in no field hospital he'd ever heard of or seen. A bed with an overhead framework. And when he looked from the stranger's face down at his own body, he saw that one of his legs and both of his arms were in casts and that the cast of the leg stuck upward at an angle, a rope running over a pulley holding it so.

He'd tried to open his mouth to ask where he was, what had happened to him, and that was when he discovered the cast on his jaw.

He'd stared at the stranger, hoping the latter would have sense enough to volunteer the information and the stranger had grinned at him and said, "Hi, George. Back with us, huh? You'll be all right."

And there was something strange about the language—until

he placed what it was. English. Was he in the hands of the English? And it was a language, too, which he knew little of, yet he understood the stranger perfectly. And why did the stranger call him George?

Maybe some of the doubt, some of the fierce bewilderment, showed in his eyes, for the stranger leaned closer to the bed. He said, "Maybe you're still confused, George. You were in a pretty bad smash-up. You ran that coupe of yours head-on into a gravel truck. That was two days ago, and you're just coming out of it for the first time. You're all right, but you'll be in the hospital for a while, till all the bones you busted knit. Nothing seriously wrong with you."

And then waves of pain had come and swept away the confusion, and he had closed his eyes.

Another voice in the room said, "We're going to give you a hypo, Mr. Vine," but he hadn't dared open his eyes again. It was easier to fight the pain without seeing.

There had been the prick of a needle in his upper arm. And pretty soon there'd been nothingness.

When he came back again—twelve hours later, he learned afterwards—it had been to the same white room, the same strange bed, but this time there was a woman in the room, a woman in a strange white costume standing at the foot of the bed studying a paper that was fastened to a piece of board.

She smiled at him when she saw that his eyes were open. She said, "Good morning, Mr. Vine. Hope you're feeling better. I'll tell Dr. Holt that you're back with us."

She went away and came back with a man who was also strangely dressed, in roughly the same fashion as had been the stranger who had called him George.

The doctor looked at him and chuckled. "Got a patient, for once, who can't talk back to me. Or even write notes." Then his face sobered. "Are you in pain, though? Blink once if you're not, twice if you are."

The pain wasn't really very bad this time, and he blinked once. The doctor nodded with satisfaction. "That cousin of yours," he said, "has kept calling up. He'll be glad to know you're going to be back in shape to—well, to listen if not to talk. Guess it won't hurt you to see him a while this evening."

The nurse rearranged his bedclothing and then, mercifully,

both she and the doctor had gone, leaving him alone to straighten out his chaotic thoughts.

Straighten them out? That had been three years ago, and he hadn't been able to straighten them out yet:

The startling fact that they'd spoken English and that he'd understood that barbaric tongue perfectly, despite his slight previous knowledge of it. How could an accident have made him suddenly fluent in a language which he had known but slightly?

The startling fact that they'd called him by a different name. "George" had been the name used by the man who'd been beside his bed last night. "Mr. Vine," the nurse had called him. George Vine, an English name, surely.

But there was one thing a thousand times more startling than either of those: It was what last night's stranger (Could he be the "cousin" of whom the doctor had spoken?) had told him about the accident. "You ran that coupe of yours head-on into a gravel truck."

The amazing thing, the contradictory thing, was that he *knew* what a *coupe* was and what a *truck* was. Not that he had any recollection of having driven either, of the accident itself, or of anything beyond that moment when he'd been sitting in the tent after Lodi—but—but how could a picture of a coupe, something driven by a gasoline engine arise to his mind when such a concept had never been *in* his mind before.

There was that mad mingling of two worlds—the one sharp and clear and definite. The world he'd lived his twenty-seven years of life in, the world into which he'd been born twenty-seven years ago, on August 15th, 1769, in Corsica. The world in which he'd gone to sleep—it seemed like last night—in his tent at Lodi, as General of the Army in Italy, after his first important victory in the field.

And then there was this disturbing world into which he had been awakened, this white world in which people spoke an English—now that he thought of it—which was different from the English he had heard spoken at Brienne, in Valence, at Toulon, and yet which he understood perfectly, which he knew instinctively that he could speak if his jaw were not in a cast. This world in which people called him George Vine, and in which, strangest of all, people used words that he did not know, could not conceivably know, and yet which brought pictures to his mind.

Coupe, truck. They were both forms of—the word came to his mind unbidden—automobiles. He concentrated on what an automobile was and how it worked, and the information was there. The cylinder block, the pistons driven by explosions of gasoline vapor, ignited by a spark of electricity from a generator—

Electricity. He opened his eyes and looked upward at the shaded light in the ceiling, and he knew, somehow, that it was an *electric* light, and in a general way he knew what electricity was.

The Italian Galvani—yes, he'd read of some experiments of Galvani, but they hadn't encompassed anything practical such as a light like that. And staring at the shaded light, he visualized behind it water power running dynamos, miles of wire, motors running generators. He caught his breath at the concept that came to him out of his own mind, or part of his own mind.

The faint, fumbling experiments of Galvani with their weak currents and kicking frogs' legs had scarcely foreshadowed the unmysterious mystery of that light up in the ceiling; and that was the strangest thing yet; part of his mind found it mysterious and another part took it for granted and understood in a general sort of way how it all worked.

Let's see, he thought, the electric light was invented by Thomas Alva Edison somewhere around—Ridiculous; he'd been going to say around 1900, and it was now only 1796!

And then the really horrible thing came to him and he tried— painfully, in vain—to sit up in bed. It *had* been 1900, his memory told him, and Edison had died in 1931—And a man named Napoleon Bonaparte had died a hundred and ten years before that, in 1821.

He'd nearly gone insane then.

And, sane or insane, only the fact that he could not speak had kept him out of a madhouse; it gave him time to think things out, time to realize that his only chance lay in pretending amnesia, in pretending that he remembered nothing of life prior to the accident. They don't put you in a madhouse for amnesia. They tell you who you are, let you go back to what they tell you your former life was. They let you pick up the threads and weave them, while you try to remember.

Three years ago he'd done that. Now, tomorrow, he was going to a psychiatrist and say that he was—Napoleon!

III

The slant of the sun was greater. Overhead a big bird of a plane droned by and he looked up at it and began laughing, quietly to himself—not the laughter of madness. True laughter because it sprang from the conception of Napoleon Bonaparte riding in a plane like that and from the overwhelming incongruity of that idea.

It came to him then that he'd never ridden in a plane that he remembered. Maybe George Vine had; at some time in the twenty-seven years of life George Vine had spent, he must have. But did that mean that *he* had ridden in one? That was a question that was part of the big question.

He got up and started to walk again. It was almost five o'clock; pretty soon Charlie Doerr would be leaving the paper and going home for dinner. Maybe he'd better phone Charlie and be sure he'd be home this evening.

He headed for the nearest bar and phoned; he got Charlie just in time. He said, "This is George. Going to be home this evening?"

"Sure, George. I was going to a poker game, but I called it off when I learned you'd be around."

"When you learned—Oh, Candler talked to you?"

"Yeah. Say, I didn't know you'd phone me or I'd have called Marge, but how about coming out for dinner? It'll be all right with her, I'll call her now if you can."

He said, "Thanks, no, Charlie. Got a dinner date. And say, about that card game; you can go. I can get there about seven and we won't have to talk all evening; an hour'll be enough. You wouldn't be leaving before eight anyway."

Charlie said, "Don't worry about it; I don't much want to go anyway, and you haven't been out for a while. So I'll see you at seven, then."

From the phone booth, he walked over to the bar and ordered a beer. He wondered why he'd turned down the invitation to dinner; probably because, subconsciously, he wanted another couple of hours by himself before he talked to anyone, even Charlie and Marge.

He sipped his beer slowly, because he wanted to make it last; he had to stay sober tonight, plenty sober. There was still time to change his mind; he'd left himself a loophole, however small. He could still go to Candler in the morning and say he'd decided not to do it.

Over the rim of his glass he stared at himself in the back-bar mirror. Small, sandy-haired, with freckles on his nose, stocky. The small and stocky part fitted all right; but the rest of it! Not the remotest resemblance.

He drank another beer slowly, and that made it half past five.

He wandered out again and walked, this time toward town. He walked past the *Blade* and looked up to the third floor and at the window he'd been looking out of when Candler had sent for him. He wondered if he'd ever sit by that window again and look out across a sunlit afternoon.

Maybe. Maybe not.

He thought about Clare. Did he want to see her tonight?

Well, no, to be honest about it, he didn't. But if he disappeared for two weeks or so without having even said good-bye to her, then he'd have to write her off his books.

He'd better.

He stopped in at a drug store and called her home. He said, "This is George, Clare. Listen, I'm being sent out of town tomorrow on an assignment; don't know how long I'll be gone. One of those things that might be a few days or a few weeks. But could I see you late this evening, to say so long?"

"Why sure, George. What time?"

"It might be after nine, but not much after. That be okay? I'm seeing Charlie first, on business; may not be able to get away before nine."

"Of course, George. Any time."

He stopped in at a hamburger stand, although he wasn't hungry, and managed to eat a sandwich and a piece of pie. That made it a quarter after six and, if he walked, he'd get to Charlie's at just about the right time. So he walked.

Charlie met him at the door. With fingers on his lips, he jerked his head backward toward the kitchen where Marge was wiping dishes. He whispered, "I didn't tell Marge, George. It'd worry her."

He wanted to ask Charlie why it would, or should, worry Marge, but he didn't. Maybe he was a little afraid of the answer.

It would have to mean that Marge was worrying about him already, and that was a bad sign. He thought he'd been carrying everything off pretty well for three years now.

Anyway, he couldn't ask because Charlie was leading him into the living room and the kitchen was within easy earshot, and Charlie was saying, "Glad you decided you'd like a game of chess, George. Marge is going out tonight; movie she wants to see down at the neighborhood show. I was going to that card game out of self-defense, but I didn't want to."

He got the chessboard and men out of the closet and started to set up a game on the coffee table.

Marge came in with a tray bearing tall cold glasses of beer and put it down beside the chessboard. She said, "Hi, George. Hear you're going away a couple of weeks."

He nodded. "But I don't know where. Candler—the managing editor—asked me if I'd be free for an out of town assignment and I said sure, and he said he'd tell me about it tomorrow."

Charlie was holding out clenched hands, a pawn in each, and he touched Charlie's left hand and got white. He moved pawn to king's fourth and, when Charlie did the same, advanced his queen's pawn.

Marge was fussing with her hat in front of the mirror. She said, "If you're not here when I get back, George, so long and good luck."

He said, "Thanks, Marge. 'Bye."

He made a few more moves before Marge came over, ready to go, kissed Charlie good-bye, and then kissed him lightly on the forehead. She said, "Take care of yourself, George."

For a moment his eyes met her pale blue ones and he thought, she *is* worrying about me. It scared him a little.

After the door had closed behind her, he said, "Let's not finish the game, Charlie. Let's get to the brass tacks, because I've got to see Clare about nine. Dunno how long I'll be gone, so I can't very well not say good-bye to her."

Charlie looked up at him. "You and Clare serious, George?"
"I don't know."

Charlie picked up his beer and took a sip. Suddenly his voice was brisk and businesslike. He said, "All right, let's sit on the brass tacks. We've got an appointment for eleven o'clock tomorrow morning with a guy named Irving, Dr. W. E. Irving, in the

Appleton Block. He's a psychiatrist; Dr. Randolph recommended him.

"I called him up this afternoon after Candler talked to me; Candler had already phoned Randolph. I gave my right name. My story was this: I've got a cousin who's been acting queer lately and whom I wanted him to talk to. I didn't give the cousin's name. I didn't tell him in what way you'd been acting queer; I ducked the question and said I'd rather have him judge for himself without prejudice. I said I'd talked you into talking to a psychiatrist and that the only one I knew of was Randolph; that I'd called Randolph, who said he didn't do much private practice and recommended Irving. I told him I was your nearest living relative.

"That leaves the way open to Randolph for the second name on the certificate. If you can talk Irving into thinking you're really insane and he wants to sign you up, I can insist on having Randolph, whom I wanted in the first place. And this time, of course, Randolph will agree."

"You didn't say a thing about what kind of insanity you suspected me of having?"

Charlie shook his head. He said, "So, anyway, neither of us goes to work at the *Blade* tomorrow. I'll leave home the usual time so Marge won't know anything, but I'll meet you downtown—say, in the lobby of the Christina—at a quarter of eleven. And if you can convince Irving that you're commitable—if that's the word—we'll get Randolph right away and get the whole thing settled tomorrow."

"And if I change my mind?"

"Then I'll call the appointment off. That's all. Look, isn't that all there is to talk over? Let's play this game of chess out; it's only twenty after seven."

He shook his head. "I'd rather talk, Charlie. One thing you forgot to cover, anyway. After tomorrow. How often you coming to see me to pick up bulletins for Candler?"

"Oh, sure, I forgot that. As often as visiting hours will permit —three times a week. Monday, Wednesday, Friday afternoons. Tomorrow's Friday, so if you get in, the first time I'll be able to see you is Monday."

"Okay. Say, Charlie, did Candler even hint to you at what the story is that I'm supposed to get in there?"

Charlie Doerr shook his head slowly. "Not a word. What is it? Or is it too secret for you to talk about?"

He stared at Charlie, wondering. And suddenly he felt that he couldn't tell the truth: that he didn't know either. It would make him look so silly. It hadn't sounded so foolish when Candler had given the reason—*a* reason, anyway—for not telling him, but it would sound foolish now.

He said, "If he didn't tell you, I guess I'd better not either, Charlie." And since that didn't sound too convincing, he added, "I promised Candler I wouldn't."

Both glasses of beer were empty by then, and Charlie took them into the kitchen for refilling.

He followed Charlie, somehow preferring the informality of the kitchen. He sat a-straddle of a kitchen chair, leaning his elbows on the back of it, and Charlie leaned against the refrigerator.

Charlie said, "Prosit!" and they drank, and then Charlie asked, "Have you got your story ready for Doc Irving?"

He nodded. "Did Candler tell you what I'm to tell him?"

"You mean, that you're Napoleon?" Charlie chuckled.

Did that chuckle ring true? He looked at Charlie, and he knew that what he was thinking was completely incredible. Charlie was square and honest as they came. Charlie and Marge were his best friends; they'd been his best friends for three years that he knew of. Longer than that, a hell of a lot longer, according to Charlie. But beyond those three years—that was something else again.

He cleared his throat because the words were going to stick a little. But he had to ask, he had to be sure. "Charlie, I'm going to ask you a hell of a question. Is this business on the up and up?"

"Huh?"

"It's a hell of a thing to ask. But—look, you and Candler don't think I'm crazy, do you? You didn't work this out between you to get me put away—or anyway examined—painlessly, without my knowing it was happening, till too late, did you?"

Charlie was staring at him. He said, "Jeez, George, you don't think I'd do a thing like that, do you?"

"No, I don't. But—you could think it was for my own good, and you might on that basis. Look, Charlie, if it *is* that, if you *think* that, let me point out that this isn't fair. I'm going up against a psychiatrist tomorrow to lie to him, to try to convince him that I have delusions. Not to be honest with him. And that would be unfair as hell, to me. You see that, don't you, Charlie?"

Charlie's face got a little white. He said slowly, "Before God, George, it's nothing like that. All I know about this is what Candler and you have told me."

"You think I'm sane, fully sane?"

Charlie licked his lips. He said, "You want it straight?"

"Yes."

"I never doubted it, until this moment. Unless—well, amnesia is a form of mental aberration, I suppose, and you've never got over that, but that isn't what you mean, is it?"

"No."

"Then, until right now—George, that sounds like a persecution complex, if you really meant what you asked me. A conspiracy to get you to— Surely you can see how ridiculous it is. What possible reason would either Candler or I have to get you to lie yourself into being committed?"

He said, "I'm sorry, Charlie. It was just a screwy momentary notion. No, I don't think that, of course." He glanced at his wristwatch. "Let's finish that chess game, huh?"

"Fine. Wait till I give us a refill to take along."

He played carelessly and managed to lose within fifteen minutes. He turned down Charlie's offer of a chance for revenge and leaned back in his chair.

He said, "Charlie, ever hear of chessmen coming in red and black?"

"N-no. Either black and white, or red and white, any I've ever seen. Why?"

"Well—" He grinned. "I suppose I oughtn't to tell you this after just making you wonder whether I'm really sane after all, but I've been having recurrent dreams recently. No crazier than ordinary dreams except that I've been dreaming the same things over and over. One of them is something about a game between the red and the black; I don't even know whether it's chess. You know how it is when you dream; things seem to make sense whether they do or not. In the dream I don't wonder whether the red-and-black business is chess or not; I know, I guess, or seem to know. But the knowledge doesn't carry over. You know what I mean?"

"Sure. Go on."

"Well, Charlie, I've been wondering if it just might have something to do with the other side of that wall of amnesia I've never able to cross. This is the first time in my—well, not in my life, maybe, but in the three years I remember of it, that I've had recurrent dreams. I wonder if—if my memory may not be trying to get through.

"Did I ever have a set of red and black chessmen, for instance? Or, in any school I went to, did they have intramural basketball or baseball between red teams and black teams, or—or anything like that?"

Charlie thought for a long moment before he shook his head. "No," he said, "nothing like that. Of course there's red and black in roulette—*rouge et noir*. And it's the two colors in a deck of playing cards."

"No, I'm pretty sure it doesn't tie in with cards or roulette. It's not—not like that. It's a game *between* the red and the black. They're the players, somehow. Think hard, Charlie; not about where you might have run into that idea, but where *I* might have."

He watched Charlie struggle and after a while he said, "Okay, don't sprain your brain, Charlie. Try this one. *The brightly shining.*"

"The brightly shining what?"

"Just that phrase, *the brightly shining*. Does it mean anything to you, at all?"

"No."

"Okay," he said. "Forget it."

IV

He was early and he walked past Clare's house, as far as the corner and stood under the big elm there, smoking the rest of his cigarette, thinking bleakly.

There wasn't anything to think about, really; all he had to do was say good-bye to her. Two easy syllables. And stall off her questions as to where he was going, exactly how long he'd be gone. Be quiet and casual and unemotional about it, just as though they didn't mean anything in particular to each other.

It *had* to be that way. He'd known Clare Wilson a year and a half now, and he'd kept her dangling that long; it wasn't fair. This had to be the end, for her sake. He had about as much business asking a woman to marry him as—as a madman who thinks he's Napoleon!

He dropped his cigarette and ground it viciously into the walk with his heel, then went back to the house, up on the porch, and rang the bell.

Clare herself came to the door. The light from the hallway behind her made her hair a circlet of spun gold around her shadowed face.

He wanted to take her into his arms so badly that he clenched his fists with the effort it took to keep his arms down.

Stupidly, he said, "Hi, Clare. How's everything?"

"I don't know, George. How *is* everything? Aren't you coming in?"

She'd stepped back from the doorway to let him past and the light was on her face now, sweetly grave. She knew something was up, he thought; her expression and the tone of her voice gave that away.

He didn't want to go in. He said, "It's such a beautiful night, Clare. Let's take a stroll."

"All right, George." She came out onto the porch. "It is a fine night, such beautiful stars." She turned and looked at him. "Is one of them yours?"

He started a little. Then he stepped forward and took her elbow, guiding her down the porch steps. He said lightly, "All of them are mine. Want to buy any?"

"You wouldn't *give* me one? Just a teeny little dwarf star, maybe? Even one that I'd have to use a telescope to see?"

They were out on the sidewalk then, out of hearing of the house, and abruptly her voice changed, the playful note dropped from it, and she asked another question, "What's wrong, George?"

He opened his mouth to say nothing was wrong, and then closed it again. There wasn't any lie that he could tell her, and he couldn't tell her the truth, either. Her asking of that question, in that way, should have made things easier; it made them more difficult.

She asked another, "You mean to say good-bye for—for good, don't you, George?"

He said, "Yes," and his mouth was very dry. He didn't know

whether it came out as an articulate monosyllable or not, and he wetted his lips and tried again. He said, "Yes, I'm afraid so, Clare."

"Why?"

He couldn't make himself turn to look at her, he stared blindly ahead. He said, "I—I can't tell you, Clare. But it's the only thing I can do. It's best for both of us."

"Tell me one thing, George. Are you really going away? Or was that just—an excuse?"

"It's true. I'm going away; I don't know for how long. But don't ask me where, please. I can't tell you that."

"Maybe I can tell you, George. Do you mind if I do?"

He minded all right; he minded terribly. But how could he say so? He didn't say anything, because he couldn't say yes, either.

They were beside the park now, the little neighborhood park that was only a block square and didn't offer much in the way of privacy, but which did have benches. And he steered her—or she steered him; he didn't know which—into the park and they sat down on a bench. There were other people in the park, but not too near. Still he hadn't answered her question.

She sat very close to him on the bench. She said, "You've been worried about your mind, haven't you, George?"

"Well—yes, in a way, yes, I have."

"And your going away has something to do with that, hasn't it? You're going somewhere for observation or treatment, or both?"

"Something like that. It's not as simple as that, Clare, and I—I just can't tell you about it."

She put her hand on his hand, lying on his knee. She said, "I knew it was something like that, George. And I don't ask you to tell me anything about it.

"Just—just don't say what you meant to say. Say so long instead of good-bye. Don't even write me, if you don't want to. But don't be noble and call everything off here and now, for my sake. At least wait until you've been wherever you're going. Will you?"

He gulped. She made it sound so simple when actually it was so complicated. Miserably he said, "All right, Clare. If you want it that way."

Abruptly she stood up. "Let's get back, George."

He stood beside her. "But it's early."

"I know, but sometimes— Well, there's a psychological moment to end a date, George. I know that sounds silly, but after what we've said, wouldn't it be—uh—anticlimactic—to—"

He laughed a little. He said, "I see what you mean."

They walked back to her home in silence. He didn't know whether it was happy or unhappy silence; he was too mixed up for that.

On the shadowed porch, in front of the door, she turned and faced him. "George," she said. Silence.

"Oh, damn you, George; quit being so *noble* or whatever you're being. Unless, of course, you *don't* love me. Unless this is just an elaborate form of—of runaround you're giving me. Is it?"

There were only two things he could do. One was run like hell. The other was what he did. He put his arms around her and kissed her. Hungrily.

When that was over, and it wasn't over too quickly, he was breathing a little hard and not thinking too clearly, for he was saying what he hadn't meant to say at all, "I love you, Clare. I love you; I love you so."

And she said, "I love you, too, dear. You'll come back to me, won't you?" And he said, "Yes. *Yes*."

It was four miles or so from her home to his rooming house, but he walked, and the walk seemed to take only seconds.

He sat at the window of his room, with the light out, thinking, but the thoughts went in the same old circles they'd gone in for three years.

No new factor had been added except that now he was going to stick his neck out, way out, miles out. Maybe, just maybe, this thing was going to be settled one way or the other.

Out there, out his window, the stars were bright diamonds in the sky. Was one of them his star of destiny? If so, he was going to follow it, follow it even into the madhouse if it led there. Inside him was a deeply rooted conviction that this wasn't accident, that it wasn't coincidence that had led to his being asked to tell the truth under guise of falsehood.

His star of destiny.

Brightly shining? No, the phrase from his dreams did not refer to that; it was not an adjective phrase, but a noun. *The brightly shining.* What was *the brightly shining?*

And the red and the black? He'd thought of everything Char-

lie had suggested, and other things, too. Checkers, for instance.
But it was not that.

The red and the black.

Well, whatever the answer was, he was running full-speed toward it now, not away from it.

After a while he went to bed, but it was a long time before he
went to sleep.

V

Charlie Doerr came out of the inner office marked Private and
put his hand out. He said, "Good luck, George. The doc's ready
to talk to you now."

He shook Charlie's hand and said, "You might as well run
along. I'll see you Monday, first visiting day."

"I'll wait here," Charlie said. "I took the day off work anyway, remember? Besides, maybe you won't have to go."

He dropped Charlie's hand, and stared into Charlie's face. He
said slowly, "What do you mean, Charlie—maybe I won't have
to go."

"Why—" Charlie looked puzzled. "Why, maybe he'll tell you
you're all right, or just suggest regular visits to see him until
you're straightened out, or—" Charlie finished weakly, "—or
something."

Unbelievingly, he stared at Charlie. He wanted to ask, am I
crazy or are you, but that sounded crazy under the circumstances. But he had to be sure, sure that Charlie just hadn't let
something slip from his mind; maybe he'd fallen into the role he
was supposed to be playing when he talked to the doctor just
now. He asked, "Charlie, don't you remember that—" And even
the rest of that question seemed insane for him to be asking,
with Charlie staring blankly at him. The answer was in Charlie's face; it didn't have to be brought to Charlie's lips.

Charlie said again, "I'll wait, of course. Good luck, George."

He looked into Charlie's eyes and nodded, then turned and
went through the door marked Private. He closed it behind him,
meanwhile studying the man who had been sitting behind the
desk and who had risen as he entered. A big man, broad shoul-
dered, iron gray hair.

"Dr. Irving?"

"Yes, Mr. Vine. Will you be seated, please?"

He slid into the comfortable, padded armchair across the desk from the doctor.

"Mr. Vine," said the doctor, "a first interview of this sort is always a bit difficult. For the patient, I mean. Until you know me better, it will be difficult for you to overcome a certain reticence in discussing yourself. Would you prefer to talk, to tell things your own way, or would you rather I asked questions?"

He thought that over. He'd had a story ready, but those few words with Charlie in the waiting room had changed everything.

He said, "Perhaps you'd better ask questions."

"Very well." There was a pencil in Dr. Irving's hand and paper on the desk before him. "Where and when were you born?"

He took a deep breath. "To the best of my knowledge, in Corsica on August 15th, 1769. I don't actually remember being born, of course. I do remember things from my boyhood on Corsica, though. We stayed there until I was ten, and after that I was sent to school at Brienne."

Instead of writing, the doctor was tapping the paper lightly with the tip of the pencil. He asked, "What month and year is this?"

"August, 1769. Yes, I know that should make me a hundred and seventy-some years old. You want to know how I account for that. I don't. Nor do I account for the fact that Napoleon Bonaparte died in 1821."

He leaned back in the chair and crossed his arms, staring up at the ceiling. "I don't attempt to account for the paradoxes or the discrepancies. I recognize them as such. But according to my own memory, and aside from logic pro or con, I was Napoleon for twenty-seven years. I won't recount what happened during that time; it's all down in the history books.

"But in 1796, after the battle of Lodi, while I was in charge of the armies in Italy, I went to sleep. As far as I knew, just as anyone goes to sleep anywhere, any time. But I woke up—with no sense whatever of duration by the way—in a hospital in town here, and I was informed that my name was George Vine, that the year was 1944, and that I was twenty-seven years old.

"The twenty-seven years old part checked, and that was all.

Absolutely all. I have no recollections of any parts of George Vine's life, prior to his—my—waking up in the hospital after the accident. I know quite a bit about his early life now, but only because I've been told.

"I know when and where he was born, where he went to school, and when he started work at the *Blade*. I know when he enlisted in the army and when he was discharged—late in 1943 —because he developed a trick knee after a leg injury. Not in combat, incidentally, and there wasn't any 'psycho-neurotic' on my—his—discharge."

The doctor quit doodling with the pencil. He asked, "You've felt this way for three years—and kept it a secret?"

"Yes. I had time to think things over after the accident, and yes, I decided then to accept what they told me about my identity. They'd have locked me up, of course. Incidentally, I've *tried* to figure out an answer. I've studied Dunne's theory of time—even Charles Fort!" He grinned suddenly. "Ever read about Casper Hauser?"

Dr. Irving nodded.

"Maybe he was playing smart the way I did. And I wonder how many other amnesiacs pretended they didn't know what happened prior to a certain date—rather than admit they had memories at obvious variance with the facts."

Dr. Irving said slowly, "Your cousin informs me that you were a bit—ah—'hepped' was his word—on the subject of Napoleon before your accident. How do you account for that?"

"I've told you I don't account for any of it. But I can verify that fact, aside from what Charlie Doerr says about it. Apparently I—the George Vine I, if I was ever George Vine—was quite interested in Napoleon, had read about him, made a hero of him, and had talked about him quite a bit. Enough so that the fellows he worked with at the *Blade* had nicknamed him 'Nappy.'"

"I notice you distinguish between yourself and George Vine. Are you or are you not he?"

"I have been for three years. Before that—I have no recollection of being George Vine. I don't think I was. I think—as nearly as I think anything—that *I*, three years ago, woke up in George Vine's body."

"Having done what for a hundred and seventy-some years?"

"I haven't the faintest idea. Incidentally, I don't doubt that this *is* George Vine's body, and with it I inherited his knowledge —except his personal memories. For example, I knew how to handle his job at the newspaper, although I didn't remember any of the people I worked with there. I have his knowledge of English, for instance, and his ability to write. I knew how to operate a typewriter. My handwriting is the same as his."

"If you think that you are not Vine, how do you account for that?"

He leaned forward. "I think part of me *is* George Vine, and part of me isn't. I think some transference has happened which is outside the run of ordinary human experience. That doesn't necessarily mean that it's supernatural—nor that I'm insane. *Does it?*"

Dr. Irving didn't answer. Instead, he asked, "You kept this secret for three years, for understandable reasons. Now, presumably for other reasons, you decide to tell. What are the other reasons? What has happened to change your attitude?"

It was the question that had been bothering him.

He said slowly, "Because I don't believe in coincidence. Because something in the situation itself has changed. Because I'm willing to risk imprisonment as a paranoiac to find out the truth."

"What in the situation has changed?"

"Yesterday it was suggested—by my employer—that I feign insanity for a practical reason. And the very kind of insanity which I have, if any. Surely, I will admit the possibility that I'm insane. But I can only operate on the theory that I'm not. You know that you're Dr. Willard E. Irving; you can only operate on that theory—but how do you *know* you are? Maybe you're insane, but you can only act as though you're not."

"You think your employer is part of a plot—ah—against you? You think there is a conspiracy to get you into a sanitarium?"

"I don't know. Here's what has happened since yesterday noon." He took a deep breath. Then he plunged. He told Dr. Irving the whole story of his interview with Candler, what Candler had said about Dr. Randolph, about his talk with Charlie Doerr last night and about Charlie's bewildering about-face in the waiting room.

When he was through he said, "That's all." He looked at Dr. Irving's expressionless face with more curiosity than concern, trying to read it. He added, quite casually, "You don't believe me, of course. You think I'm insane."

He met Irving's eyes squarely. He said, "You have no choice —unless you would choose to believe I'm telling you an elaborate set of lies to convince you I'm insane. I mean, as a scientist and as a psychiatrist, you cannot even admit the possibility that the things I believe—*know*—are objectively true. Am I not right?"

"I fear that you are. So?"

"So go ahead and sign your commitment. I'm going to follow this thing through. Even to the detail of having Dr. Ellsworth Joyce Randolph sign the second one."

"You make no objection?"

"Would it do any good if I did?"

"On one point, yes, Mr. Vine. If a patient has a prejudice against—or a delusion concerning—one psychiatrist, it is best not to have him under that particular psychiatrist's care. If you think Dr. Randolph is concerned in a plot against you, I would suggest that another one be named."

He said softly, "Even if I choose Randolph?"

Dr. Irving waved a deprecating hand, "Of course, if both you and Mr. Doerr prefer—"

"We prefer."

The iron gray head nodded gravely. "Of course you understand one thing; if Dr. Randolph and I decide you should go to the sanitarium, it will not be for custodial care. It will be for your recovery through treatment."

He nodded.

Dr. Irving stood. "You'll pardon me a moment? I'll phone Dr. Randolph."

He watched Dr. Irving go through a door to an inner room. He thought; there's a phone on his desk right there; but he doesn't want me to overhear the conversation.

He sat there very quietly until Irving came back and said, "Dr. Randolph is free. And I phoned for a cab to take us there. You'll pardon me again? I'd like to speak to your cousin, Mr. Doerr."

He sat there and didn't watch the doctor leave in the opposite direction for the waiting room. He could have gone to the door and tried to catch words in the low-voiced conversation, but he didn't. He just sat there until he heard the waiting room door open behind him and Charlie's voice said, "Come on, George. The cab will be waiting downstairs by now."

They went down in the elevator and the cab was there. Dr. Irving gave the address.

In the cab, about half way there, he said, "It's a beautiful day," and Charlie cleared his throat and said, "Yeah, it is." The rest of the way he didn't try it again and nobody said anything.

VI

He wore gray trousers and a gray shirt, open at the collar and with no necktie that he might decide to hang himself with. No belt, either, for the same reason, although the trousers buttoned so snugly around the waist that there was no danger of them falling off. Just as there was no danger of his falling out any of the windows; they were barred.

He was not in a cell, however; it was a large ward on the third floor. There were seven other men in the ward. His eyes ran over them. Two were playing checkers, sitting on the floor with a board on the floor between them. One sat in a chair, staring fixedly at nothing; two leaned against the bars of one of the open windows, looking out and talking casually and sanely. One read a magazine. One sat in a corner, playing smooth arpeggios on a piano that wasn't there at all.

He stood leaning against the wall, watching the other seven. He'd been here two hours now; it seemed like two years.

The interview with Dr. Ellsworth Joyce Randolph had gone smoothly; it had been practically a duplicate of his interview with Irving. And quite obviously, Dr. Randolph had never heard of him before.

He'd expected that, of course.

He felt very calm, now. For a while, he'd decided, he wasn't going to think, wasn't going to worry, wasn't even going to feel.

He strolled over and stood watching the checker game.

It was a sane checker game; the rules were being followed.

One of the men looked up and asked, "What's your name?" It was a perfectly sane question; the only thing wrong with it was that the same man had asked the same question four times now within the two hours he'd been here.

He said, "George Vine."

"Mine's Bassington, Ray Bassington. Call me Ray. Are you insane?"

"No."

"Some of us are and some of us aren't. He is." He looked at the man who was playing the imaginary piano. "Do you play checkers?"

"Not very well."

"Good. We eat pretty soon now. Anything you want to know, just ask me."

"How do you get out of here? Wait, I don't mean that for a gag, or anything. Seriously, what's the procedure?"

"You go in front of the board once a month. They ask you questions and decide if you go or stay. Sometimes they stick needles in you. What you down for?"

"Down for? What do you mean?"

"Feeble-minded, manic-depressive, dementia praecox, involutional melancholia—"

"Oh. Paranoia, I guess."

"That's bad. Then they stick needles in you."

A bell rang somewhere.

"That's dinner," said the other checker player. "Ever try to commit suicide? Or kill anyone?"

"No."

"They'll let you eat at an A table then, with knife and fork."

The door of the ward was being opened. It opened outward and a guard stood outside and said, "All right." They filed out, all except the man who was sitting in the chair staring into space.

"How about him?" he asked Ray Bassington.

"He'll miss a meal tonight. Manic-depressive, just going into the depressive stage. They let you miss one meal; if you're not able to go to the next they take you and feed you. You a manic-depressive?"

"No."

"You're lucky. It's hell when you're on the down-swing. Here, through this door."

It was a big room. Tables and benches were crowded with men in gray shirts and gray trousers, like his. A guard grabbed his arm as he went through the doorway and said, "There. That seat."

It was right beside the door. There was a tin plate, messy with food, and a spoon beside it. He asked, "Don't I get a knife and fork? I was told—"

The guard gave him a shove toward the seat. "Observation period, seven days. Nobody gets silverware till their observation period's over. Siddown."

He sat down. No one at his table had silverware. All the others were eating, several of them noisily and messily. He kept his eyes on his own plate, unappetizing as that was. He toyed with his spoon and managed to eat a few pieces of potato out of the stew and one or two of the chunks of meat that were mostly lean.

The coffee was in a tin cup and he wondered why until he realized how breakable an ordinary cup would be and how lethal could be one of the heavy mugs cheap restaurants use.

The coffee was weak and cool; he couldn't drink it.

He sat back and closed his eyes. When he opened them again there was an empty plate and an empty cup in front of him and the man at his left was eating very rapidly. It was the man who'd been playing the non-existent piano.

He thought, if I'm here long enough, I'll get hungry enough to eat that stuff. He didn't like the thought of being there that long.

After a while a bell rang and they got up, one table at a time on signals he didn't catch, and filed out. His group had come in last; it went out first.

Ray Bassington was behind him on the stairs. He said, "You'll get used to it. What'd you say your name is?"

"George Vine."

Bassington laughed. The door shut on them and a key turned.

He saw it was dark outside. He went over to one of the windows and stared out through the bars. There was a single bright star that showed just above the top of the elm tree in the yard. *His* star? Well, he'd followed it here. A cloud drifted across it.

Someone was standing beside him. He turned his head and saw it was the man who'd been playing piano. He had a dark, foreign-looking face with intense black eyes; just then he was smiling, as though at a secret joke.

"You're new here, aren't you? Or just get put in this ward, which?"

"New. George Vine's the name."

"Baroni. Musician. Used to be, anyway. Now—let it go. Anything you want to know about the place?"

"Sure. How to get out of it."

Baroni laughed, without particular amusement but not bitterly either. "First, convince them you're all right again. Mind telling what's wrong with you—or don't you want to talk about it? Some of us mind, others don't."

He looked at Baroni, wondering which way he felt. Finally he said, "I guess I don't mind. I—think I'm Napoleon."

"Are you?"

"Am I what?"

"*Are* you Napoleon? If you aren't, that's one thing. Then maybe you'll get out of here in six months or so. If you really *are* —that's bad. You'll probably die here."

"Why? I mean, if I *am*, then I'm sane and—"

"Not the point. Point's whether they think you're sane or not. Way they figure, if you think you're Napoleon you're not sane. Q. E. D. You stay here."

"Even if I tell them I'm convinced I'm George Vine?"

"They've worked with paranoia before. And that's what they've got you down for, count on it. And any time a paranoiac gets tired of a place, he'll try to lie his way out of it. They weren't born yesterday. They know that."

"In general, yes, but how—"

A sudden cold chill went down his spine. He didn't have to finish the question. *They stick needles in you*— It hadn't meant anything when Ray Bassington had said it.

The dark man nodded. "Truth serum," he said. "When a paranoiac reaches the stage where he's cured *if* he's telling the truth, they make sure he's telling it before they let him go."

He thought what a beautiful trap it had been that he'd walked into. He'd probably die here, now.

He leaned his head against the cool iron bars and closed his eyes. He heard footsteps walking away from him and knew he was alone.

He opened his eyes and looked out into blackness; now the clouds had drifted across the moon, too.

Clare, he thought; *Clare*.

A trap.

But—if there was a trap, there must be a trapper.

He was sane or he was insane. If he was sane, he'd walked into a trap, and *if there was a trap, there must be a trapper, or trappers*.

If he was insane—

God, let it be that he *was* insane. That way everything made such sweetly simple sense, and someday he might be out of here, he might go back to working for the *Blade*, possibly even with a memory of all the years he'd worked there. Or that George Vine had worked there.

That was the catch. *He* wasn't George Vine.

And there was another catch. He *wasn't* insane.

The cool iron of the bars against his forehead.

After a while he heard the door open and looked around. Two guards had come in. A wild hope, reasonless, surged up inside him. It didn't last.

"Bedtime, you guys," said one of the guards. He looked at the manic-depressive sitting motionless on the chair and said, "Nuts. Hey, Bassington, help me get this guy in."

The other guard, a heavy-set man with hair close-cropped like a wrestler's, came over to the window.

"You. You're the new one in here. Vine, ain't it?"

He nodded.

"Want trouble, or going to be good?" Fingers of the guard's right hand clenched, the fist went back.

"Don't want trouble. Got enough."

The guard relaxed a little. "Okay, stick to that and you'll get along. Vacant bunk's in there." He pointed. "One on the right. Make it up yourself in the morning. Stay in the bunk and mind your own business. If there's any noise or trouble here in the ward, we come in and take care of it. Our own way. You wouldn't like it."

He didn't trust himself to speak, so he just nodded. He turned and went through the door of the cubicle to which the guard had pointed. There were two bunks in there; the manic-depressive who'd been on the chair was lying flat on his back on the other, staring blindly up at the ceiling through wide-open eyes. They'd pulled his shoes off, leaving him otherwise dressed.

He turned to his own bunk, knowing there was nothing on earth he could do for the other man, no way he could reach him through the impenetrable shell of blank misery which is the manic-depressive's intermittent companion.

He turned down a gray sheet-blanket on his own bunk and found under it another gray sheet-blanket atop a hard but smooth pad. He slipped off his shirt and trousers and hung them on a hook on the wall at the foot of his bed. He looked around for a switch to turn off the light overhead and couldn't find one. But, even as he looked, the light went out.

A single light still burned somewhere in the ward room outside, and by it he could see to take his shoes and socks off and get into the bunk.

He lay very quiet for a while, hearing only two sounds, both faint and seeming far away. Somewhere in another cubicle off the ward someone was singing quietly to himself, a wordless monody; somewhere else someone else was sobbing. In his own cubicle, he couldn't hear even the sound of breathing from his roommate.

Then there was a shuffle of bare feet and someone in the open doorway said, "George Vine."

He said, "Yes?"

"Shhhh, not so loud. This is Bassington. Want to tell you about that guard; I should have warned you before. Don't ever tangle with him."

"I didn't."

"I heard; you were smart. He'll slug you to pieces if you give him half a chance. He's a sadist. A lot of guards are; that's why they're bughousers; that's what they call themselves, bughousers. If they get fired one place for being too brutal they get on at another one. He'll be in again in the morning; I thought I'd warn you."

The shadow in the doorway was gone.

He lay there in the dimness, the almost-darkness, feeling rather than thinking. Wondering. Did mad people ever know that they were mad? Could they tell? Was every one of them sure, as he was sure—?

That quiet, still thing lying in the bunk near his, inarticulately suffering, withdrawn from human reach into a profound misery beyond the understanding of the sane—

"Napoleon Bonaparte!"

A clear voice, but had it been within his mind, or from without? He sat up on the bunk. His eyes pierced the dimness, could discern no form, no shadow, in the doorway.

He said, "Yes?"

VII

Only then, sitting up on the bunk and having answered "Yes," did he realize the name by which the voice had called him.

"Get up. Dress."

He swung his legs out over the edge of the bunk, stood up. He reached for his shirt and was slipping his arms into it before he stopped and asked, "Why?"

"To learn the truth."

"Who are you?" he asked.

"Do not speak aloud. I can hear you. I am within you and without. I have no name."

"Then *what* are you?" He said it aloud, without thinking.

"An instrument of The Brightly Shining."

He dropped the trousers he'd been holding. He sat down carefully on the edge of the bunk, leaned over and groped around for them.

His mind groped, too. Groped for he knew not what. Finally he found a question—*the* question. He didn't ask it aloud this time; he thought it, concentrated on it as he straightened out his trousers and thrust his legs in them.

"*Am I mad?*"

The answer—*No*—came clear and sharp as a spoken word, but had it been spoken? Or was it a sound that was only in his mind?

He found his shoes and pulled them on his feet. As he fumbled the laces into some sort of knots, he thought, "Who—what—is The Brightly Shining?"

"The Brightly Shining is *that which is Earth*. It is the intelligence of our planet. It is one of three intelligences in the solar system, one of many in the universe. Earth is one; it is called The Brightly Shining."

"I do not understand," he thought.

"You will. Are you ready?"

He finished the second knot. He stood up. The voice said, "Come. Walk silently."

It was as though he was being led through the almost-darkness, although he felt no physical touch upon him; he saw no physical presence beside him. But he walked confidently, although quietly on tiptoe, knowing he would not walk into anything nor stumble. Through the big room that was the ward, and then his outstretched hand touched the knob of a door.

He turned it gently and the door opened inward. Light blinded him. The voice said, "Wait," and he stood immobile. He could hear sound—the rustle of paper, the turn of a page—outside the door, in the lighted corridor.

Then from across the hall came the sound of a shrill scream. A chair scraped and feet hit the floor of the corridor, walking away toward the sound of the scream. A door opened and closed.

The voice said, "Come," and he pulled the door open the rest of the way and went outside, past the desk and the empty chair that had been just outside the door of the ward.

Another door, another corridor. The voice said, "Wait," the voice said, "Come"; this time a guard slept. He tiptoed past. Down steps.

He thought the question, "Where am I going?"

"Mad," said the voice.

"But you said I wasn't—" He'd spoken aloud and the sound startled him almost more than had the answer to his last question. And in the silence that followed the words he'd spoken there came—from the bottom of the stairs and around the corner—the sound of a buzzing switchboard, and someone said, "Yes? . . . Okay, Doctor, I'll be right up." Footsteps and the closing of an elevator door.

He went down the remaining stairs and around the corner and he was in the front main hall. There was an empty desk with a switchboard beside it. He walked past it and to the front door. It was bolted and he threw the heavy bolt.

He went outside, into the night.

He walked quietly across cement, across gravel; then his shoes were on grass and he didn't have to tiptoe any more. It was as dark now as the inside of an elephant; he felt the presence of trees nearby and leaves brushed his face occasionally, but he walked rapidly, confidently, and his hand went forward just in time to touch a brick wall.

He reached up and he could touch the top of it; he pulled himself up and over it. There was broken glass on the flat top of the wall; he cut his clothes and his flesh badly, but he felt no pain, only the wetness of blood and the stickiness of blood.

He walked along a lighted road, he walked along dark and empty streets, he walked down a darker alley. He opened the back gate of a yard and walked to the back door of a house. He opened the door and went in. There was a lighted room at the front of the house; he could see the rectangle of light at the end of a corridor. He went along the corridor and into the lighted room.

Someone who had been seated at a desk stood up. Someone, a man, whose face he knew but whom he could not—

"Yes," said the man, smiling, "you know me, but you do not know me. Your mind is under partial control and your ability to recognize me is blocked out. Other than that and your analgesia —you are covered with blood from the glass on the wall, but you don't feel any pain—your mind is normal and you are sane."

"What's it all about?" he asked. "Why was I brought here?"

"Because you are sane. I'm sorry about that, because you can't be. It is not so much that you retained memory of your previous life, after you'd been moved. That happens. It is that you somehow know something of what you shouldn't—something of The Brightly Shining, and of the Game between the red and the black. For that reason—"

"For that reason, what?" he asked.

The man he knew and did not know smiled gently. "For that reason you must know the rest, so that you will know nothing at all. For everything will add to nothing. The truth will drive you mad."

"That I do not believe."

"Of course you don't. If the truth were conceivable to you, it would not drive you mad. But you cannot remotely conceive the truth."

A powerful anger surged up within him. He stared at the familiar face that he knew and did not know, and he stared down at himself; at the torn and bloody gray uniform, at his torn and bloody hands. The hands hooked like claws with the desire to kill—someone, the someone, whoever it was, who stood before him.

He asked, "What are you?"

"I am an instrument of The Brightly Shining."

"The same which led me here, or another?"

"One is all, all is one. Within the whole and its parts, there is no difference. One instrument is another and the red is the black and the black is the white and there is no difference. The Brightly Shining is the soul of the Earth. I use *soul* as the nearest word in your vocabulary."

Hatred was almost a bright light. It was almost something that he could lean into, lean his weight against.

He asked, "What is The Brightly Shining?" He made the words a curse in his mouth.

"Knowing will make you mad. You want to know?"

"Yes." He made a curse out of that simple, sibilant syllable.

The lights were dimming. Or was it his eyes? The room was becoming dimmer, and at the same time receding. It was becoming a tiny cube of dim light, seen from afar and outside, from somewhere in the distant dark, ever receding, turning into a pinpoint of light, and within that point of light ever the hated Thing, the man—or was it a man?—standing beside the desk.

Into darkness, into space, up and apart from the earth—a dim sphere in the night, a receding sphere outlined against the spangled blackness of eternal space, occulting the stars, a disk of black.

It stopped receding, and time stopped. It was as though the clock of the universe stood still. Beside him, out of the void, spoke the voice of the instrument of The Brightly Shining.

"Behold," it said. "The Being of Earth."

He beheld. Not as though an outward change was occurring, but an inward one, as though his senses were being changed to enable him to perceive something hitherto unseeable.

The ball that was Earth began to glow. Brightly to shine.

"You see the intelligence that rules Earth," said the voice. "The sum of the black and the white and the red, that are one, divided only as the lobes of a brain are divided, the trinity that is one."

The glowing ball and the stars behind it faded, and the darkness became deeper darkness and then there was dim light, growing brighter, and he was back in the room with the man standing at the desk.

"You saw," said the man whom he hated. "But you do not understand. You ask, *what* have you seen, *what* is The Brightly Shining? It is a group intelligence, the true intelligence of Earth, one intelligence among three in the Solar system, one among many in the universe.

"What, then, is man? Men are pawns, in games of—to you—unbelievable complexity, between the red and the black, the white and the black, for amusement. Played by one part of an organism against another part, to while away an instant of eternity. There are vaster games, played between galaxies. Not with man.

"Man is a parasite peculiar to Earth, which tolerates his presence for a little while. He exists nowhere else in the cosmos, and he does not exist here for long. A little while, a few chessboard wars, which he thinks he fights himself— You begin to understand."

The man at the desk smiled.

"You want to know of yourself. Nothing is less important. A move was made, before Lodi. The opportunity was there for a move of the red; a stronger, more ruthless personality was needed; it was a turning point in history—which means in the game. Do you understand now? A pinch hitter was put in to become Napoleon."

He managed two words. "And then?"

"The Brightly Shining does not kill. You had to be put somewhere, some time. Long later a man named George Vine was killed in an accident; his body was still usable. George Vine had not been insane, but he had had a Napoleonic complex. The transference was amusing."

"No doubt." Again it was impossible to reach the man at the desk. The hatred itself was a wall between them. "Then George Vine is dead?"

"Yes. And you, because you knew a little too much, must go mad so that you will know nothing. Knowing the truth will drive you mad."

"No!"

The instrument only smiled.

VIII

The room, the cube of light, dimmed; it seemed to tilt. Still standing, he was going over backward, his position becoming horizontal instead of vertical.

His weight was on his back and under him was the soft-hard smoothness of his bunk, the roughness of a gray sheet-blanket. And he could move; he sat up.

Had he been dreaming? Had he really been outside the asylum? He held up his hands, touched one to the other, and they were wet with something sticky. So was the front of his shirt and the thighs and knees of his trousers.

And his shoes were on.

The blood was there from climbing the wall. And now the analgesia was leaving, and pain was beginning to come into his hands, his chest, his stomach and his legs. Sharp biting pain.

He said aloud, *"I am not mad. I am not mad."* Was he screaming it?

A voice said, "No. Not yet." Was it the voice that had been here in the room before? Or was it the voice of the man who had stood in the lighted room? Or had both been the same voice?

It said, "Ask, 'What is man?' "

Mechanically, he asked it.

"Man is a blind alley in evolution, who came too late to compete, who has always been controlled and played with by The Brightly Shining, which was old and wise before man walked erect.

"Man is a parasite upon a planet populated before he came, populated by a Being that is one and many, a billion cells but a single mind, a single intelligence, a single will—as is true of every other populated planet in the universe.

"Man is a joke, a clown, a parasite. He is nothing; he will be less."

"Come and go mad."

He was getting out of bed again; he was walking. Through the doorway of the cubicle, along the ward. To the door that led to the corridor; a thin crack of light showed under it. But this time his hand did not reach out for the knob. Instead he stood there facing the door, and it began to glow; slowly it became light and visible.

As though from somewhere an invisible spotlight played upon it, the door became a visible rectangle in the surrounding blackness; as brightly visible as the crack under it.

The voice said, "You see before you a cell of your ruler, a cell unintelligent in itself, yet a tiny part of a unit which is intelligent, one of a trillion units which make up *the* intelligence which rules the earth—and you. And which earth-wide intelligence is one of a million intelligences which rule the universe."

"The *door?* I don't—"

The voice spoke no more; it had withdrawn, but somehow inside his mind was the echo of silent laughter.

He leaned closer and saw what he was meant to see. An ant was crawling up the door.

His eyes followed it, and numbing horror crawled apace, up his spine. A hundred things that had been told and shown him suddenly fitted into a pattern, a pattern of sheer horror. The black, the white, the red; the black ants, the white ants, the red ants; the players with men, separate lobes of a single group brain, the intelligence that was one. Man an accident, a parasite, a pawn; a million planets in the universe inhabited each by an insect race that was a single intelligence for the planet—and all the intelligences together were the single cosmic intelligence that was—*God!*

The one-syllable word wouldn't come.

He went mad, instead.

He beat upon the now-dark door which his bloody hands, with his knees, his face, with himself, although already he had forgotten why, had forgotten what he wanted to crush.

He was raving mad—dementia praecox, not paranoia—when they released his body by putting it into a strait jacket, released it from frenzy to quietude.

He was quietly mad—paranoia, not dementia praecox—when they released him as sane eleven months later.

Paranoia, you see, is a peculiar affliction; it has no physical symptoms, it is merely the presence of a fixed delusion. A series of metrazol shocks had cleared up the dementia praecox and left only the fixed delusion that he was George Vine, a reporter.

The asylum authorities thought he was, too, so the delusion

was not recognized as such and they released him and gave him a certificate to prove he was sane.

He married Clare; he still works at the *Blade*—for a man named Candler. He still plays chess with his cousin, Charlie Doerr. He still sees—for periodic checkups—both Dr. Irving and Dr. Randolph.

Which of them smiles inwardly? What good would it do you to know?

It doesn't matter. Don't you understand? Nothing matters!

The End

PROFESSOR JONES had been working on time theory for many years.

"And I have found the key equation," he told his daughter one day. "Time is a field. This machine I have made can manipulate, even reverse, that field."

Pushing a button as he spoke, he said, "This should make time run backward run time make should this," said he, spoke he as button a pushing.

"Field that, reverse even, manipulate can made have I machine this. Field a is time." Day one daughter his told he, "Equation key the found have I and."

Years many for theory time on working been had Jones Professor.